THE MERRO TREE

Katie Waitman

A Del Rey® Book
BALLANTINE BOOKS • NEW YORK

A Del Rey® Book
Published by Ballantine Books
Copyright © 1997 by Katharine L. Waitman

http://www.randomhouse.com

Library of Congress Catalog Number: 97-92171

ISBN 0-345-41436-5

Manufactured in the United States of America

First Edition: October 1997

10   9   8   7   6   5   4   3   2   1

Mikk's flying feet picked up tempo as he spun and leapt and danced over the dangerously frangible crystal and made it sing, a percussive chiming that filled the theater. One false move, one misplaced or overly sharp step, and the goblets would fall or break under Mikk's dancing weight, but he tore across the slick surfaces with the abandon of a man running on concrete. He defied gravity. Cries of anguish rose from the audience as Mikk became a spinning blur and the ringing from the goblets became continuous. People jumped to their feet, waving their arms, and the Belian next to Martin burst into tears.

On and on Mikk danced, opening invisible, half-understood wounds in Martin's memory, hallucinations of fiery fields and phantom corpses. Mikk was the Death Angel, master of the invisible, the ringing one sustained scream that throbbed on the ear like a siren . . .

For Laurie

"All the worlds are a stage."
—from the Belian edition of
As You Like It
by William Shakespeare

Opening Act: Kekoi Kaery: The Window

[Crown Year of Saar XII: 1075]

On every world, no matter how long the night or how deeply he slept, Mikk the performance master woke before dawn, his body eager for the elaborate dance he'd invented as an apprentice to keep his long limbs supple and his mind agile. However, Mikk had not slept well in over sixty days. His skin-clinging dance suit and loose, short, full-sleeved silk jacket with the hundreds of fancifully embroidered pockets— his "surprise tunic"—were inadequate to fend off the insidious chill of night on Kekoi Kaery, and his cold muscles complained as he bent and stretched and moved through the abbreviated distances: pallet to wash basin, stool to waste bowl, dank high wall to glowing blue energy grid. The air smelled like a wet animal and pressed its misery against his nostrils as it tried to gain access to his lungs. Mikk was surprised he hadn't caught a rheum during his days in the cell.

He flipped untrimmed crimson hair out of pale, nearly transparent, lavender eyes and looked at his hands. "How can you defend yourself without claws?" the Kekoi always asked, but the absence of nails of any kind was normal and not what made him frown. His skin's pure, alabaster white had lost some of its opacity, and, in spite of the predawn darkness, Mikk's acute vision picked out the minute pink threads of capillaries running between his fingers.

Blessed gods, he thought, I must look like a corpse.

He heard a soft snort and glanced at the night guard, a young Freen, dozing at his post in the corridor outside the energy gate.

1

The stocky outworlder's rough tunic, flat, bare feet, and mournful, thick gray features underlined his poverty.

Not that a Freen would be ashamed to admit he was poor, Mikk considered, a little bitterly. Most of them spent their lives in voluntary exile on whichever world they could find work. Bipti was lucky. None of the Kekoi wanted this shift, but, for the Freen, it meant a roof over his head for at least part of the night.

Bipti twitched, and his outer eyelids, followed at a tardy pace by his inner eyelids, parted. He yawned grandly.

"I'm sorry, Bipti. I didn't mean to wake you."

"That is no problem, Mikk-sir." The guard crossed his short, sturdy legs, pulled a bantroot out of his pocket, and, sticking its tip in his mouth at a rakish angle, began chewing lustily. His large square teeth displayed the yellow stains of a long habit.

"After all these nights at your side, my sleep has changed," he said. "And perhaps today will be different, yes? Perhaps today they will announce the names of the tribunes."

"Definitely something to look forward to," Mikk said with tainted enthusiasm. He slid smoothly to the floor in a horizontal split then pushed himself up with his fingers and brought his feet together in a handstand. The Freen, who had witnessed Mikk's morning ritual many times, nevertheless watched with interest.

"I don't understand, Mikk-sir. Why does it take them so long to choose?"

Mikk sprang off his hands into a tightly curled airborne somersault and landed on his toes.

"The Council has to preserve the appearance of fairness, Bipti. That complicates the job considerably."

"*Will* they be fair?"

Mikk laughed and gave the Freen a quick flash of his justifiably famous grin.

"I doubt it. The selection process wouldn't be secret if they intended to be fair."

"Then why did you insist on a tribunal at all?" Bipti uncrossed his legs and scooted along the floor closer to the grid. "You've already admitted guilt, Mikk-sir. Wouldn't they be more lenient if you just accepted your sentence?"

"I won't accept any sentence without a fight, my friend. The ban was absurd, and, promise or no promise, I should not have been required to submit to it in the first place." The cell gradually brightened as dawn poked a finger through the puny window high in the wall; Mikk's eyes caught some of the light.

The guard removed the bantroot from his teeth and his permanently sad features became authentically morose.

"The Council hates you, sir," he whispered. "This is a hopeless fight." Both sets of eyelids sagged. "The galaxy is going to lose its greatest performance master. No one knows more about theater and music than you."

Mikk smiled again, but his brow was tense and he looked away. Personal compliments made him uncomfortable.

"They used to say *I* was hopeless, Bipti. Did you know that?" He folded his arms and tucked his hands up inside the sleeves of his tunic. "When I was a child, my spirit was broken into so many pieces that I might as well have been blind, deaf, and dumb. No reasonable person ever would have thought I'd become a performance master."

"Is this true, Mikk-sir?"

"Of course, reason had little to do with it . . ." Mikk paused a moment, his thoughts briefly eddying in the brackish pool of his childhood, then he shrugged. "Still, I managed to salvage my dreams, and at least one man believed in them."

"I've forgotten my childhood, Mikk-sir."

"That could be a blessing, Bipti! Once we Vyzanians have something planted in our memories, it's virtually impossible to uproot it."

The Freen bit off the soggy, mashed piece of his bantroot and began working on the fresh end of the thin, black-brown twig.

"The past is past, Mikk-sir. I wish we could see the future."

"I don't. I already receive enough mangled glimpses to disturb my equilibrium."

He fished his salt pendant out from under his surprise tunic, flipped it open, and sprinkled its modest measure of crystals on his tongue.

"How is your supply, Mikk-sir?"

"That was the last of it." Mikk snapped the pendant closed and tapped it against his lip. "It's still early. Perhaps you could get some more before the others come to relieve you."

Bipti swung to his feet with a grunt.

"Ask them to crush it a little finer this time," Mikk said. "I don't mind relying on a veterinarian, but I would prefer not to lick a chunk as if I were a lab rodent."

Bipti sauntered down the corridor into the shadows.

When Mikk no longer heard the soft flap of the Freen's feet on the stone floor, he looked up at the window. It was too small to crawl through, but he still didn't want the guard to know that, remote as it was, nearly double his height, he could reach it. The Kekoi might put him in an inside cell to prevent him from calling out to passersby, and Mikk had even fabricated false errands for the genial Freen just so he could be alone with this precious little eye on the outside world.

Mikk stood directly under the square of light, quieted the nine valves of his heart, flexed his legs, and, after a quick calculation of the trajectory, leapt up to the window and caught hold with his fingertips. He pulled himself up until his chin cleared the ledge and he could see the courtyard below.

A handful of Kekoi street vendors, sellers of roasted meats, were already bickering over the best locations to set up their carts and awnings. The canine-faced bipeds snarled and snapped at each other's pointed ears and quilted doublets until one of them gave way with a short whine and trundled off to fight over another space.

I wish *I* had fur! Mikk sighed, envying the Kekoi's splendid pelages. Thissizz would know how to warm me, he thought, and the ache of despair welled up in his breast like blood from an internal wound. How often had the Droos wrapped his wonderful, long heavy body around him, tightened the hot coils until the tiny slick scales pressed into his skin, then breathed gently on his eyelashes?

"I am here, my friend, do not be afraid . . ."

We may never share our warmth again, Mikk thought. He swallowed and the masonry pressed painfully against his chin and throat. How, in the name of the gods, had it come to this?

He lifted his eyes as the gray dawn turned a virulent flame

orange over the bare granite teeth of the mountains. The color stirred the oldest, darkest depths of his memory.

However it had happened, *she* played a major role and she's never buried so deep I can't resurrect her yet one more time . . .

Part One: The First People

[C.Y.S. XII: 560–710]

Chapter One: Mother

Although it was also a stunning social coup that raised the cabaret zimrah player well above her former station, Mikk's mother had married for love. Therefore, when her tall, quiet husband announced he had been assigned to the new Vyzanian Consulate on Bar Omega Sept and would depart in the morning—alone—Ranya became anxious.

"Why can't I go with you?" She was fiddling with her coiffure and the entire edifice suddenly came undone and masses of thick, brilliant orange curls tumbled about her face.

"Our relations with the Septans are in their infancy and very tenuous," her husband said. "They have been known to kidnap diplomats' wives and hold them as bargaining chips—especially pregnant ones."

"But, how long will you be gone?" Ranya stroked his smooth, still face and wondered why, even this close, his large, light eyes did not appear to be looking at her.

"I don't know."

He went away . . . and stayed away, leaving her with nothing but a sprawling mansion deep in the parkland outside the capital city of Wynt, a host of servants, the estate's broad garden full of flowers, fruit trees, and fountains, and ten generations' worth of heavy, priceless jewelry.

Ranya, devastated, promptly fired all the servants, thought better of it and rehired them, then shut herself in her lonely bedchamber until she delivered a son whose hair was much redder than her own.

"Madam!" cried Henni, her tiny high-strung maid with the

overbite. "Such a pretty little boy! Surely he has been marked by the gods for great things."

Ranya touched his cheek but would not hold him. He looked a lot like his father and she was not sure she could bear to get close to the baby's all too familiar pale lavender eyes.

"Why does he keep crying?"

"He's hungry, madam. You must nurse him."

So she would have to touch him after all. Ranya opened her tunic and gingerly lifted the wiggling creature to her breast. Mikk immediately locked his mouth around her nipple—his desperation shocked her a little—and began to knead her flesh with his tiny white hands. Ranya had to admit the sensation was not unpleasant and relieved some of the uncomfortable pressure in her breast. Besides, as he nursed, Mikk closed his eyes. What a strange little thing! Even his eyelashes were a dazzling crimson.

Very well. She would do this. He was her son, after all, someone dependent on her. Someone she could be sure of.

Ranya smiled at him . . . and he promptly spit up on her tunic. She shrieked and instantly tossed him aside. Luckily, he dropped onto the bloody pile of cushions and bedclothes where she had given birth.

"Madam!"

"What's wrong with him? My tunic is ruined!"

The baby puckered up his face and began to howl up and down the scale like the city's fire alarm.

"Madam, he's just a baby!" Henni scooped Mikk up, wiped the sour-smelling birth blood and curdled breast milk from his face, and rocked him until he quieted. Ranya couldn't face her and tugged nervously on a wayward orange curl.

"I don't feel well, Henni. I think I'll lie down."

"Yes, madam. Of course."

"I mean, I didn't expect . . ." Ranya looked at the milky mess on her tunic, her distorted breasts, the sore sagging sack of her empty abdomen, and moaned.

"I am so ugly!"

"Madam, you're not . . ."

"Leave me alone, Henni, and keep the baby away from me!"

She rushed out of the room.

When she was finally slim again and felt more like herself, Ranya put on some dark green silk, frosted her eyes, came out of hiding, and gave a dinner party for the most influential society people she could convince to come. One of them, an eccentric dowager bound up so tightly in costly but filthy yellow gauze that she resembled a Rogoine mummy ready for interment, insisted on seeing the baby. She bent stiffly over Mikk's hammock and studied the carefully cocooned child a long time before she clicked her tongue and made her pronouncement.

"A truly out-ra-ge-ous color, my dear! Quite delicious!" She touched the boy's feathery wisps with her pointy finger. "What are you going to do with him?"

"I thought I'd raise him to be a performer," Ranya said softly. She had had plenty of time to think about it while holed up, guilty and humiliated, in the back guest chamber. It was the best possible future she could imagine for anyone, let alone her son, but she was worried. This old freak in rancid yellow was the wealthiest landowner in Wynt and intimate with the royal family. Her opinion carried a lot of weight.

The matron straightened as though forcing a rusty hinge.

"Don't be ridiculous, child! You've left that vulgar life behind. It's time to assert yourself in your new position." She smiled, displaying black, broken teeth, the familiar final stage of excessive bantroot use. Ranya tried not to show her disgust and must have succeeded because the woman rested her claw on her shoulder.

"How I envy you, dear! A rich, beautiful woman whose husband is away. Indulge yourself! Take a lover! But let's not hear another word about performing, either for you or this funny little progeny of yours. Artists are servants and you are no longer a servant." She patted the younger woman's cheek and lurched a little to kick her body into its fettered shuffle out of the room. "Hire a nanny, darling, and come to town. You're wasting your life cooped up in this house."

That night, Ranya tossed fitfully in the silken seine of her double hammock and listened to the warm rain echo down the open white corridors and patios of the house.

How dare that hag belittle her career! Performers were not servants and she had been good, even famous! She tore open the window tapestries so the night breezes, subtly sharpened by the alcoholic scent of the lakes, could cool her body. All those long years wishing for a way out of the endless cycle of tours, the roaming from town to town, cabaret to cabaret, the mean meals in mean lodgings, the advances of her viperous manager . . . But, the performance itself—to cradle the rare and delicate instrument and dance her fingertips over the invisible, vibrating strands of light, to feel the caress of the sister vibration in her throat and the warm, seductive communion with the audience—that had always been wonderful. Always! Ranya loved to perform and missed it terribly but had not been able to play since her husband's departure. Her fingers were too sad.

Bitterness oozed through her heart and mind like the black, muddy slurry that collected around the lips of the ponds during the Dormant Season, and she decided she would be avenged through her son.

"He will be a performer," she whispered to the darkness, "but not a mere cabaret artist living in closets with a shriveled-up lackey who can't hear his orders let alone follow them, oh no! He'll be a performer of distinction, a classical actor perhaps, maybe a concert singer, even," she sighed, "a performance master! No one would dare call a performance master a servant!"

She would take her new wealth and engage the best teachers—vocalists, instrumentalists, acting coaches—and Mikk would shame the world with his brilliance.

She resettled herself in the hammock and closed her eyes. Such a magnificent vision! It had to come true.

Unfortunately, her spindly spawn seemed bent on thwarting all of his mother's dreams. As he grew, Mikk turned out to be just as uncoordinated as any other toddler. He seemed congenitally incapable of paying attention to what he, or anyone else, was doing and had an absolute knack for dropping things. Ranya lost forty-three cups and dishes in one particularly awful month.

"Madam," Henni protested, "he's too small to use adult crockery."

"One more word out of you and you'll lose your position. I know how to raise my own son."

It was a lie, but Ranya was having enough trouble without

insubordinate servants. Mikk cried a great deal and begged shamelessly to be held, which she still could not bring herself to do. That sad, fawning little face looked more and more like her husband's every day except for a girlish delicacy around the mouth and that horrible hair. Ranya's own scarlet tresses dulled in comparison.

"Get away from me! I can't look at you when you're whining like that."

What had she done to deserve this aggravation? No husband in her bed, house guests who continued to ask her with coy condescension about her "quaint past," and now a weird child as ungainly as an orphaned marsh deer let loose in a glass dealer's, a child she had hoped would vindicate her.

On top of everything, early in his life Mikk contracted arranic throat fever, not an ordinary childhood disease but a serious adult malady usually suffered by poor fishermen who lived on the mud flats of the Grand West Lagoon. He was delirious for weeks and thrashed about in his hammock as he coughed up dark pink blood from his torn vocal cords. For many years after, Mikk could not speak above a raspy whisper and could not sing at all. Even when doctors pronounced his throat completely healed, the boy continued to whisper, which infuriated his mother past all patience.

"What did you say?" The glittering cascades of her long earrings clacked as Ranya snapped her head in his direction. "I cannot hear you. Speak up or say nothing! And don't stare at me like a fish, you little brat. No one wants to see your tongue."

Mikk decided discretion was the best way to deal with his mother's imperious tone and intimidatingly beautiful purple eyes. He closed his mouth and looked away, silent.

"Gods above!" his mother cried. "You're not a mute. Are you deaf?"

Mikk winced at the increase in volume and put his hands over his ears.

"Very nice!" Ranya grabbed his slender arms and yanked them down. "Very dramatic! What a marvelous actor you'll make not listening to your mother!" She shoved him away. "I guess you'll have to stay in your room during supper again. I won't dine with idiots."

"Please," Mikk whispered, "let me come. I'm sorry."

"Why should I?"

"I haven't had supper in four days."

"You'll live," said his mother. "When I was a singer, I often went without food for weeks at a time, but I was happy. I sang for nothing, do you hear me? Nothing! And you think you know something about privation . . ."

Sometimes Henni snuck the disgraced Mikk a morsel or two after supper and a quick hug, made all the more thrilling by its furtive heat against his skin—and sometimes she got away with it. When she didn't, Mikk's mother hit her with a slipper, which she bore in absolute silence. Since the boy's throat fever, the maid had become almost as insensible as a stone, as if she, too, had been damaged by it.

Ranya never beat Mikk. She didn't have to. She shrieked at him until he vomited. The first time this happened, she was horrified and screamed all the louder.

"Is there nothing right about you at all?" she wailed. "How can you get sick like that? I haven't touched you! Why are you doing this to me?"

Mikk could not explain to her that her voice cut straight through his ears into his brain with its shrill siren sound, that it made his heart skip it was so painful. Even Henni didn't find his mother's shrieks nearly as agonizing. At least, she didn't double up on the floor as he did.

There *must* be something wrong with me, just as Ranya says, he thought. Why else would I be so sensitive?

He tried everything to avoid this torture—pleading, tears, flight—but, unfortunately, he failed repeatedly.

Every music teacher, every dance instructor, every acting coach Mikk's mother engaged quit within days. All of them declared it impossible to teach the boy anything. He jumped at the slightest sound, was startled by every change in light, and, as a result, could not take in a word they said.

"The most skittish little boy I've ever seen," said one of the dance teachers to his assistant. "He's consumed with anxiety, as though he expects the roof to fall in at any moment if he treads the ground too heavily. I'm not going back to that house no matter what they pay me."

"I know why you can't learn, wretch!" Ranya screamed as Mikk hugged his shrunken stomach and prayed with all his might for her to stop. "You don't *want* to! You don't want to learn anything!"

She screamed it and screamed it until he almost began to believe it himself. However, there was nothing in the world Mikk wanted more than to be a performer. Whenever he could, he escaped into the large garden where the sighing merro trees with their clusters of swollen scarlet fruit and the whispering sprays of mauve night mallows, creamy moon flowers, and puffy yellow kits' paws were gentler to his ears and wonderful to his eyes, and there he pretended he was on stage. In his mind's eye, he was savvy, sensitive, learned, and bold—and wildly triumphant. The invisible rows of ladies and gentlemen in their brightly colored garments shot through with gold and emerald threads wept, laughed, and gasped at his command. He played them like an instrument, tuned to any great actor's key he chose: one minute, the sonorous tragedian Caarn Vir; the next, the pipe-voiced clown Zizzy Oopla. He even impersonated the grand opera heroine Shiltara. For the diva, he thrust out his narrow chest in imitation of her heavy bosom and stalked about the soft grasses waving his arms frantically as the singer usually did during her arias, regardless of tone or content.

In spite of his hoarse whisper, Mikk was pleased with his run in his imaginary theater and didn't care whether his mimicry was accurate or not. The flowers certainly couldn't tell the difference. Neither could the kitchen felines who sometimes expanded their predatory prowls for insects from the pantry into the dense leaves and petals outside.

And, sometimes, for the briefest of blissful moments, the phantom applause enfolded him with the illusion of affection and he felt whole.

The garden was safe. After particularly bad days full of terror, the confusion of sounds in Mikk's head would rise to a scream that rivaled Ranya's, only warped and twisted somehow around fragments of a dark, manic music. His own bedchamber felt close and oppressive no matter how many windows he opened so he would lie out on the cool damp soil instead, risking a chill, until the nausea and dizziness subsided. The night lifted him out of his unhappiness with its majestic indigo darkness, the pale twin moons, and the dense, brilliant dusting of stars, and he felt free to wonder about mysteries beyond his cramped little circle of suffering. For example, why was the constellation directly overhead called the Nine Dancers? Mikk counted at least fifteen stars and a couple of glowing blurs that were probably other galaxies or nebulae.

Also, why was a blue fly called a "blue" fly? The garden was full of them and they did have quite a bit of blue on them, but they also had fine streaks of green and yellow and red running down their long bodies and a coppery sheen to their wings. He once tried to describe what he saw to Henni, but she claimed all she saw was blue.

As the years passed, Mikk had greater and greater trouble pleasing Ranya, and although she never struck him, he always feared that someday she would. Dishes got broken, tunics soiled, words misspoken as though these catastrophes had lives of their own and could not be prevented or controlled no matter how vigilant and cautious Mikk was. It became too exhausting to guess his mother's mind before she herself knew what she was thinking.

Perhaps she should beat me for no reason at all, Mikk thought, just to get it over with. Everything is hers anyway. It won't be long before I damage something too valuable to mourn with a scream.

He sighed. He wished he could have something of his own, something more real than a theater in the air. Something he could keep. Something that wouldn't break.

The episode with the zimrah master was the last straw. It began with the usual expressions of frustration.

"Mikk does not seem willing to learn, madam," said the zimrah master, a delicately boned elderly man with a refined manner.

"What do you mean 'not willing'?" Ranya asked, warming up her ire for the expected tantrum and rising threateningly to her feet. The zimrah master eyed her disdainfully and tilted his head back. She could see down his nostrils—not at all a pleasant view.

"The sound agitates him, madam. He twitches most unattractively when I play and he says there are too many strings. He claims he doesn't know which light strands I mean when I say 'the mid-four.' "

"That's ridiculous! Those are the only four you can see. The obscure strings are invisible."

"I am quite aware of that, madam, but he swears the other strands confuse him. He even asked me if I could teach him to play by touch instead."

"No beginner learns the zimrah by touch!" Ranya cried. "Unless you master the mid-four by sight, you'll never get your bearings."

"Perhaps madam would like to teach the boy herself?" the zimrah master suggested with a faint, hard smile. "I understand you were once a professional."

Ranya picked up a bowl of half-eaten merro fruit and hurled it at him, but her aim was terrible and it sailed over the small man's head into the pantry, landing on a kitchen feline, who yowled and bolted under the bake oven.

The zimrah master calmly noted the feline's progress then returned his attention to Mikk's mother.

"I can see that the most crucial lesson the boy will have to learn in this house is survival."

"How dare you, you little . . . !"

"No need for madam to trouble herself." The zimrah master bowed. "I will show myself out."

Mikk knew long before his mother got to the music solarium that he was in desperate trouble. Even with his hands over his ears, he could hear her voice rise through the house. He heard the fruit bowl strike the feline and now he heard the quick small smack of his mother's silk-clad feet on the tiles as she hurried his way—the short stiff steps of a furious woman.

He could run. Duck out the window and lose himself in the garden as he had many times before. However, he had learned that this only postponed his punishment and he would be subjected to an extra-special dose of that horrendous, skull-shattering shriek as well as various deprivations of meals, even water. This time, even though his limbs quivered with the desperate impulse to flee, he would face it out. The zimrah had once been his mother's instrument, she'd said so many times, and his inability with it had to be the most personal of all his transgressions. He deserved her fury; he deserved her punishment.

His one hope was that she wouldn't kill him, but when his mother appeared in the solarium archway, panting vigorously, orange hair down and disheveled, her hand gripping the zimrah by the neck, that hope deserted him. Ranya's eyes had turned a horrible black.

Mikk was optic sensate and he knew by the faint, burning sting that the emotionally triggered pigment was darkening his irises again, betraying his guilt. However, his mother was optic obtuse. It took an enormous psychic upheaval to darken her eyes, and they were blacker than he'd ever seen them. She was definitely going to hurt him this time and not just with sound.

Sure enough, as Mikk cowered in the corner, scrambling over the floor cushions in an attempt to fold himself up so small she couldn't see him, Ranya stiffly raised the zimrah.

"How—many—strings—do—you—see?" Her voice sounded as if it were being pulled out of her throat a link at a time.

Too terrified to concern himself with the logic of this question, Mikk swallowed, squinted at the instrument, and counted as quickly and accurately as he could.

"Sixteen?"

"Don't give me another of your lies! 'I saw this, I heard that!' You counted them with your fingers, didn't you? You felt the vibrations!" His mother's arm began to shake.

"N-no."

"What—did—you—say?"

"No!" Mikk whimpered and nearly lost his whisper. "Master Tymm put the—the—clear pieces over them."

"But you took the guards *off* the obscure strings, didn't you?"

Mikk shook his head. His eyes were really throbbing now, and although he knew it would only make her angrier, he began to weep. He had nothing left inside to stop it.

When his mother took a step toward him, he uttered a small, uncharacteristically clean cry, an animal's cry, and pressed himself harder against the wall.

"You don't have to hit me! I'll be good!"

Then, something very strange, something Mikk never would have expected, happened to his mother. The murderous rage in her face quietly faded into blankness. She studied her terrified son as though not only couldn't she understand why he was quaking in the corner, but she could barely remember who he was. She looked at the zimrah in her hand, started violently, and dropped it. The fragile lightwave harp shattered on the floor.

"Oh, dear," she said softly, "now that's a mess." Ranya's face quivered and she burst into tears. Mikk watched in stunned silence as his mother stood all alone in the middle of the bright, airy music solarium with its silk floor cushions, racks of flutes and tabors, and amber-veined crystal cabinets full of musical notations, and sobbed until the pink frost around her eyes melted and ran down her cheeks.

Mikk had never seen his mother cry. It frightened him much more than her wrath. He knew what to expect when she was angry; he had no idea what she would do in grief. He hugged the red cushion, the one Henni had said was his father's and not to be touched, and waited.

In the end, Ranya just cried, cried as though she had lost everything in the world, cried until she was hoarse, exhausted, and hiccupping. She wiped her eyes and got the pink all over her white fingertips.

"I can't bear it anymore," she sighed. "I can't." She gazed mournfully at her thin young son with the deep crimson hair and, in the calmest tones she had used all day, withdrew from battle.

"I'm giving a very large, very important dinner party this evening, Mikk, so stay out from under foot." She turned her back on him and walked slowly out of the room.

"If you can't be talented, at least be inconspicuous and don't humiliate me in front of my guests."

When she was gone, Mikk slid down the wall and slumped into the cushions.

Perhaps he should have been relieved. After all, he doubted Ranya would ever speak to him again after this, let alone touch him in any way whatsoever. But her terrible words had given him a last little push into the wilderness where the wind screamed at him from all directions, forever.

His mother had beaten him after all, but the blow was much harder, and deeper, than he had expected.

Mikk usually enjoyed Ranya's dinner parties because everyone left him alone and, as long as he was careful, he could play with the felines, tumble in the garden, and act in his pretend theater unmolested for hours.

This evening, Mikk headed for the lower terrace where the vines curled around the balustrades like the exuberant scribblings of a child's first drawings. Since he was too distraught for tragedy, he hopped about the terrace in respectable imposture of Zizzy Oopla—although even his unseen audience sat on its hands—until Henni hurried down the stone steps from the main garden and took him by the arm.

"The lady wants you to come."

"Now?" Mikk asked without disguising his alarm at Henni's first words in weeks.

"I'm afraid so, Mikk."

Mikk didn't like how she put that. It hinted at terrible, even public, disasters, but he grasped the maid's hand and trotted back with her through the twilight to the golden glow of the house, his pulse pounding wildly in his throat.

To Mikk's surprise, Henni skirted around the parlor rooms full of laughing, bird-plumaged guests and led him along the exterior gallery to the garden-side door of his father's library.

The library was a dark, solemn space full of the dry, dead smell of abandonment. Even though Henni sometimes spirited out a colorful illustrated history to slip in with his unauthorized meals, Mikk avoided the library whenever possible. He was afraid of it.

Tonight, however, the room was brilliantly illuminated and temporarily blinded the boy so, at first, he could not tell whether he was alone. When his eyes recovered, the exquisite gold script on the bindings of the scrolls and texts dazzled them anew. Never had Mikk seen this many tapers in any of the rooms of the house, not even the parlors. The library had been transformed into an opulent, glowing treasure vault.

Then he saw his mother, glorious in a long cascade of complicated turquoise folds and tucks, her orange hair studded with crystals, her eyes, purple again, ringed with silver frost. She looked splendid, and Mikk couldn't understand why she was so subdued. She usually came to life in the finery of a dinner party and glided from parlor to parlor, a smiling, sparkling empress far too imposing and beautiful to share breath with ordinary mortals.

Perhaps the man at Ranya's side had something to do with it. In the glare of the tapers and the mystery of his mother's diminished glamour, Mikk had only just noticed him, and as he studied the tall, motionless fair-haired official in severe government maroon tunic and leggings, he felt a fluttery queasiness in his stomach. The man had very pale lavender eyes, exactly the same shade as Mikk's, and the boy suddenly realized this stranger might be his father, a father he had known only as a forbidden, and forbidding, rumor. Just in case, Mikk bowed and the man confirmed his suspicions with a short, decorous nod of entitlement.

"Your mother and I have been discussing your welfare," the diplomat said. Mikk shivered. The soft aristocratic accent was lovely but empty, like the surface of a pond at dusk. A voice designed not to betray a single nuance of personal feeling.

"We've decided it might be better for you to leave here and enter a boarding school."

Mikk did not answer. He stared at his father, unsure whether to trust any words dressed in such a sensuous, deceptive cadence.

"I spoke with some gentlemen I know and I can enroll you in the Academy of Languages and Arts in Wynt."

This strange man had to be lying to him. Mikk had had one of the worst days of his life. He had offended Master Tymm, come close to getting killed for his inadequacies, and witnessed the awful spectacle of his mother's tears. Why would he be offered the realization of one of his greatest dreams? He had no talent whatsoever, everybody said so. The only way he could get into the Academy would be if the diplomat asked the Dean to return a favor.

Mikk's father leaned forward and placed his long hands on his knees, a fairly awkward attempt to cut his height down to intimacy, and Mikk couldn't help shrinking back a little.

"Would you like that, Mikk?"

The diplomat's eyes were pale, just like his. Man and boy

shared the same natural slenderness. This was his father! That was supposed to be important and, therefore, wasn't this offer of escape important? Could it be true? Even if it wasn't, even if both parents were playing an obscure, cruel joke on him, how could he turn down the Academy?

"Yes. I would."

"Fine then. I will speak to the Dean."

Mikk's mother, who had said nothing during this exchange, said nothing now and rustled softly out of the library back to her guests.

When she was gone, Mikk allowed himself to rub the itch that tormented his ear.

"The Academy?"

The strange man smiled.

The Academy was the only gift Mikk's father ever gave him.

Chapter Two: The Academy

In one of his columns, the Lively Arts editor for the *Wynt Conversation* dismissed the Academy as "an actor factory, haven to the adequate, anathema to the gifted," but Mikk didn't care. Both Caarn Vir and Zizzy Oopla were Academy alumni and that was good enough for him.

When Mikk passed through the grillwork gates of this ancient seat of learning, nestled in the forested hills above Wynt, he felt all his sins had fallen off outside and he could start over. What a beautiful place! He loved the Academy's warm ivory walls, russet tiled roofs, its mosaic-encrusted fountains, courtyards, colonnades, and its celebrated acres of flowers and trees. So many kinds of birds and unusual butterflies found sanctuary in the gardens that a host of distracted naturalists and botanists wandered the lush foliage with their pocket teleopticons and notebooks, sharing the grounds with students who practiced their instruments or sang out of doors. Most wonderful of all, a fruit-eating night warbler had made her nest in the branches of a giant merro tree outside Mikk's tiny cell on the highest floor. He stayed up all that first night to listen to her elaborate, ever-evolving song, and vowed he would work very hard and somehow be worthy of this incredible stroke of good fortune.

Unfortunately, it wasn't long before Mikk's instructors started going to the Dean with odd stories about him, stories the humiliated boy heard through student gossip no matter how carefully the adults tried to hide them.

"He was late four times last week," said one. "He said the sound from that faulty water steamer in the basement made him lose his way."

"We misplaced him again in the garden. That makes six times this month. He wandered off in the middle of the lecture."

"An impossible boy. He can describe what he has to do very well, he just refuses to do it, and yet I can't tell you how many times I've seen him outside making up his own dances and tumbling about quite happily. Does he think I'm a fool?"

This last instructor, the dance teacher, also admitted he had, out of sheer exasperation, struck Mikk across the mouth and the boy hadn't come back to class for ten days.

"That ought to tell you something, don't you think?" asked the Dean, who was no advocate of corporal punishment.

"It certainly does," said the dance instructor. "The boy's soft. He has no backbone at all."

Dean Mooj sighed. He was a retired dancer himself and secretly believed he had no business running an educational institution full of touchy prima donnas, most of whom had never succeeded as performers. Nevertheless, here he was, spending his days hitching his bad hip up and down the halls, smiling benignly at student and teacher alike, and hoping with every mote of his being that no irksome problem ever darkened his office door. The diplomat's mixed-up son was one such problem, and Mooj might have considered doing something for him if the boy hadn't also been, of all things, a gifted linguist, probably the most incredible student of languages they had ever had.

"Astonishing!" the overwhelmed instructors said. "He picks up a language and speaks it almost fluently within a couple of days and reads it inside of a week. The accent is down in a matter of minutes! You should tell his father. The diplomatic corps could use such a marvel in their ranks."

What was Mooj to make of all this? A boy who couldn't memorize even the shortest piece of music and yet learned a language as complicated as H'n N'kae overnight and wrote graffiti in it on the walls of his cell. It seemed a shame to make him scrub it off; the script was beautiful. The Dean decided to wait and see.

Finally, Madam Kaari, the teacher of instrumental music, a thoughtful older woman who had been a celebrated kai-shan player in her youth, confronted the Dean with the strangest story of all, and Mooj began to worry he might actually have to act.

"Mikk is not capable of concentration," she said. "I think he should be sent home before he hurts himself."

The Dean, who had gotten some hints about Mikk's home life from the boy's father, disagreed.

"I don't think that would be very helpful. There must be some other solution."

"I don't know what it would be. It's not that he doesn't try. He's just not capable."

"You think he has a problem with his memory?"

"I didn't say that." The teacher paced restlessly with her deeply veined hands clutching and unclutching behind her back. "I said he couldn't concentrate. He can't focus at all. I'm sure he absorbs everything, absolutely everything, if you know what I mean. Completely indiscriminately. I asked him to play something all the way through and it sounded like a terrible jumble until my assistant, who has an incredible ear, pointed out that not only was the melody from one piece and the harmony from another, but Mikk had played both of them backwards and worked in the chirpings of a bird that was singing in the garden." Madam Kaari stopped pacing and spread her hands, helplessly.

"He's a bright boy," she said, "very friendly and terribly eager to please. I'd say painfully eager—he cries when I tell him it's wrong—but he says he's happy here. He laughs all the time when he's alone and he'll imitate anything: trees in the wind, animals, the older students kissing in the garden, me, other teachers . . . I even caught him impersonating you. I told him you might not like it and he stopped immediately and apologized." The teacher sat on the narrow bench near the open garden doors.

"Whatever is in the boy has been seriously fragmented and he'll need someone much more familiar with this kind of problem than I am to reconstruct it. In the meantime, I'm afraid he'll lose himself or have an accident or otherwise do himself injury."

Dean Mooj slowly pinched his fingertips, one at a time in succession, his habit when forced to study a puzzle that seemed unsolvable.

"I'll give the matter some thought."

"Do more than think, Mooj. Be decisive for once." Madam Kaari stood and crossed her arms with an air of impatience that made the Dean feel he was one of her students.

"Mikk's a sweet child, but he doesn't have many friends. The others think he's odd. He prefers the company of the toddlers."

"He's an excellent nanny, Madam Kaari."

"That's not why he's here," the teacher said, lips pressed together in a hard line. Mooj almost expected her to assign him extra scales.

"All right," he said with conciliatory mildness. "We'll see."

Late one afternoon toward the end of the Blossom Season, Mikk once again got turned around in the Academy corridors and wandered into the wing where the older students studied voice.

He hadn't exactly lost his way; he'd misplaced it. Mikk had been loitering outside a room full of younger children who were practicing floor acrobatics when the chime for the end of the session rang and he was instantly overrun by a screaming, laughing, rushing torrent of arms and legs and bumping bodies. It was delightful—several of the little ones called him by name—but disorienting and he took a wrong turn. Once he realized he wasn't where he was supposed to be, he didn't panic or try to retrace his steps. Mikk had originally been heading for that horrible man's dance class and wasn't eager to get yelled at or called an imbecile again. He decided to explore. He had never been in this part of the Academy.

He became a captive to enchantment. Doors opened and closed in the cool, airy halls, briefly releasing snatches of delicious music, young women doing scales, young men practicing arias, the whispers and lectures of a dozen different classes. The students themselves were lovely with their soft, dancing hairstyles and clinging tunics of shimmering, semitransparent reds and blues and golds, nothing like the simple, stiff, childish tunics he and his classmates wore. Many of the girls wore eye frost and gaily colored jewelry that dangled from their ears or draped about their shoulders. He wanted to touch these baubles and find out if the ones that sparkled brightest also felt different from the stones that, although of similar shape, had tiny dark spots inside and didn't flash as cleanly. His mother always made a great fuss over "real" gems, claiming she would have nothing to do with "inferior" stones, but she still wore many pieces with those tiny spots.

Mikk shadowed one of the girls, a girl with copper-flecked beads braided into her lustrous black hair, and passed the choristry just as the men's choir broke into an a cappella hymn for the dead. The sound knocked him down and pinned him to the floor where he writhed and wept and beat his hands against his ears, but could not shut out the tragic sweetness of the voices. The harmonics overwhelmed the shriek and music of his inner static, raced up his nerves, and shivered in his muscles, and the bass vibrations throbbed in his stomach and lungs without mercy. The music poured into Mikk's body, filling him with gorgeous bits of ground up crystal that tore him open and left him bleeding.

"Please . . . p-please . . . more . . ."

The girl with the braids witnessed the entire violent display. Shocked, she backed away from the boy and ran for the Dean's office.

In spite of the chorus of teacher complaints, the Dean had not seen Mikk since the day the diplomat's distracted son came through the gates and stumbled over his own toes. Mooj was surprised by the spare red-haired boy who rubbed one foot against the opposite ankle while keeping his nervous, pale lavender eyes on the Dean. Mikk was at least a hand taller and showed all the gawky, misbalanced signs of an early puberty. His legs were ridiculously long for his height, as were his hands and feet. Very narrow feet—his slippers gaped.

"I understand you were overcome by the excellence of our men's choir."

The pigment rushed into Mikk's eyes and he quickly covered them with his hand in embarrassment. "I'm so sorry!"

"Never mind, Mikk. I know you're sensitive. Colors and music in particular, am I right?"

Mikk lowered his hand. His eyes were black-purple with agitation. "I try not to, but it's so . . . Oh, I wish I could sort it all out!"

"Why are you speaking so softly? Do you always whisper?" Mikk nodded and the Dean smiled and held out his hand. "Well, come here, Mikk. Don't be afraid. I want to try something."

Baffled, eyes still dark, Mikk crept up to the Dean, who picked up a small tuning bell and rod. He put his hand on the boy's shoulder and drew him close. "Just relax and let me know when you can no longer hear the bell." He struck the tiny hollow globe and it rang a high soft note.

Mikk cringed. Remarkable, the Dean thought, the highest audible tuning bell and I barely touched it. He tapped it again, this time even more lightly. Mikk blinked at the sound. Finally, the Dean held the tuning bell behind Mikk's head and merely stroked it with his finger. Mikk squinted, but apparently he had heard that as well. The Dean certainly hadn't.

"H'm." He set down the tuning bell and picked up a zimrah balancer, a circle of glowing metal whose clear blue light was used to adjust the different "strings" on the instrument.

"All right, Mikk, let your eyes drain. Good. Now watch the light."

The blue glow refracted in Mikk's lavender eyes, and as the Dean altered the frequency, he noticed that the boy's retinas continued to react long after the normally visible range on the zimrah balancer was passed. The frequencies he now played over Mikk's eyes were used for the most delicate sounds, the invisible "obscure" strings, light bands that had to be played by touch. Nevertheless, Mikk could see them.

The Dean set down the balancer and Mikk hugged himself tightly, apprehensively pinching the scant flesh on his arms.

"Do you know the story of the merro tree?" the Dean asked. Mikk's eyes widened.

"Um, yes, sir. Of course."

"The first merro tree was a latecomer to our world," said the Dean, "and not immune to the Intoxication. As a result, its branches grew every which way, its leaves curled in fantastic shapes, and it bore no fruit. The First People believed that, latecomer that it was, even if it did adapt it was unlikely to produce anything of value. Do you remember that part?"

"Yes, sir."

"What happened?"

Mikk took a deep breath and dutifully recited the conclusion of the myth. "One Blossom Season, after years on the edge of extinction, the merro tree suddenly produced a display of beautiful dark green leaves. It had finally adapted to the Intoxication. To the First People's amazement, it also produced fruit, fruit of such rare and wonderful scent and flavor that the First People were ashamed. They declared the merro tree sacred and its fruit a gift from Heaven, to be served with reverence and eaten in silence."

"As we still eat it today." The Dean moved away from Mikk and looked out at the garden where several merro trees were dropping the last of their large, sweet-smelling white flowers.

"Do you understand the story, Mikk?" The boy didn't answer, and when the Dean turned around he saw Mikk staring at the floor.

"I want you to do something for me, Mikk." The boy looked up, a sober expression on his face. "You don't have to do it when others are around, but I want you to stop whispering. Practice those languages you love so much, but speak boldly. There's nothing wrong with your voice."

"Yes, sir."

"And, I don't care if you never go to that asinine Rellin Orbin's class again. Dance and tumble on your own and mimic the animals as you always do, but be careful about imitating the people here. They might not get the joke."

Mikk smiled a little, very shyly. He is a pleasant-looking boy, the Dean thought, even pretty.

"Be yourself, Mikk." The Dean picked up the tuning bell again and tapped it. "Don't think about it, just sing the note."

Mikk complied with a fragile, breathy vowel.

"Fine. Now off with you and don't worry so much about pleasing others."

What the Dean didn't tell Mikk was that his soft, sad little note had been absolutely true, in perfect pitch.

The next time Mikk ventured into Rellin Orbin's class, a peculiar thing happened—nothing. The dance instructor glowered at him a moment, then ignored him. Mikk hung back behind everyone else and watched without joining in, and Rellin Orbin made no comment whatsoever. When the class broke up and all the students except Mikk filed out, the instructor dabbed his hot face with a small towel and frowned at the boy with a combination of resentment and weary bewilderment.

"Well? What is it?"

"I didn't dance."

"No, you didn't."

"But you didn't say anything."

"I'm through saying anything," Rellin Orbin growled. "You obviously don't want to learn."

"But I do. It's just that . . . well . . ."

"Well, what?"

"I get confused. There are so many here and you . . . you don't like me."

"That's irrelevant." The dance instructor worked the towel with his hands as though trying to knead it into another substance. The tendons in his sinewy arms shifted angrily. "Whether I like you or not is meaningless when it comes to learning how to dance."

"It means something to me."

"I'm not here to hand out affection. What I do is teach. You seem to prefer playing at dance. So, why are you here?"

"Could you show me the fountain leap again?"

"Why?"

"Please?"

The instructor sighed, threw down the towel, and performed the leap, fairly perfunctorily.

"Satisfied?"

"Yes, sir."

"Fine." Rellin Orbin headed for the wardrobe cabinets. "I have to change."

The dance instructor muttered and cursed as he peeled off his dancewear and pulled on his tunic. This new "laissez-faire" strategy the Dean wanted to try with Mikk was the most ridiculous idea he had ever heard. Let Mikk learn at his own pace? Hah! The scrawny scatterskit had trouble telling his left from his right. He would never learn a thing on his own.

However, on his way out, Rellin Orbin went back into the studio to collect his notes and found Mikk still there, leaping about from one side of the room to the other. The boy was ungainly, his leaps far from expert, but he made up for it with enthusiasm and a reckless speed.

"Oh, no, no!" The instructor clapped his hand to his forehead. "Knees straighter at the peak, bent when you land! What are you? A galloping wahr-calf? Keep it light like the arc of a spray of water! That's it! Better!" He picked up his notes and continued on his way out of the studio. "Honestly! Such a basic step . . ."

Mikk continued to practice and included other interesting pieces he had been able to sift out of the confusion of the class. He began to hum and, for a few moments, the hard floor was more forgiving and the air smelled sweet. Without realizing it, he had learned something, and he bounded about the studio with an unfamiliarly light heart.

It became a pattern. Soon Mikk could be seen hovering in the back of all of his classes—except the language classes where he was revamping the textbooks—jittery and glancing about and seemingly not paying attention until, at some point, he stiffened, attention arrested by a dance step, passage of music, or snippet of dramatic dialogue. This sudden, intense interest didn't last very long, but at the end of the class he often cornered the instructor and asked him or her very specific questions about that particular bit of performance.

"What can I do?" the acting coach sighed. "Of course I tell him as much as I can. I admire his persistence, but he bothers me."

"Why is that?" asked the Dean.

"It's that stare of his. It's very disturbing."

"Oh, come now. " Mooj shifted sharply in his seat to take the pressure off his complaining hip. "All children go into occasional stare states when they're learning something new. It's normal. I even know some adults, very creative people, who freeze. Besides, Mikk is trying to catch up."

"This isn't just a stare state, this is the most intense glare I've ever seen. It's so *active*. He frightens the other students."

"Tell them to get over it. That poor boy isn't going to hurt anyone."

Every day Mikk focussed his starving eyes on something different, picking up information in bits and snatches, but although many students reported seeing Mikk practice these fragments over and over for hours in the gardens, or hearing the musical phrases issue from his room at all times of the day, no one saw or heard him perform for others or in class.

"Give him time," the Dean said. "He has a lot to overcome."

One day Mikk crept up on the instrumental music teacher while she was alone on a small terrace overlooking the wooded hillside.

"Madam Kaari?"

The teacher jumped and one of her copper hairpins popped out. A kink of feathery white promptly stood straight up.

"Oh! I didn't see you! Are you here to enjoy the view, too?"

Mikk cleared his throat and with what seemed a great act of will said, "I've come to play for you." He produced the kai-shan he had hidden behind his back and its merro wood backing flashed a deep russet brown. The boy must have polished it for the occasion.

"Indeed!" Madam Kaari arched her brows. "What are you going to play?"

" 'Plaachaya Verdu,' " Mikk said, the piece he had scrambled so tellingly weeks before.

"I see," she nodded. "Go ahead."

Mikk sat at the very end of the bench, tested the valved instrument's action, then started to play. Madam Kaari leaned her chin on her hand. This was not the same mangled jumble at all. The familiar piece flowed out of the kai-shan a bit too quietly, but it wasn't tinny and Mikk didn't hit a single false note. He even caught the tricky double trill at the end.

"Very good, Mikk," she said when he was done. "Very nicely played."

The boy's face lit up like a candle and the teacher almost wept. The child was desperate for a positive word!

"I wanted to be sure I had it perfect before I played for you," he whispered. "I was terrified I was going to mess up somewhere."

"Mikk, contrary to what other instructors here believe, mistakes while you're learning *are* allowed." She touched his arm. "I understand you're very good with languages. Well, did anyone ever tell you that different kinds of music are actually different languages? They all use a certain vocabulary in endless combinations to communicate something. They have grammar, diction, accents, even slang." She patted her wayward wire of hair and tried to feed it back under her coil of braids but gave up when a second pin sprang away and shot across the terrace.

"Why don't you try to think of music as a new foreign language you want to learn, and not some esoteric science you can grasp only in broken pieces?"

Instrumental music was the first class in which Mikk resumed his place with the others. Acrobatics was the second. The burly instructor said, "He's gangly and hardly graceful, but he's brave and surprisingly strong for a boy his age and size. He'll survive spills that would tear another's knee apart and run off to try something new. I don't think he'll ever be very good, but it won't be for lack of effort."

Dean Mooj was reassured. Mikk was going to be all right, not one of his star students, but not a disgrace either. The boy would graduate with some modest expertise in performing arts and undoubtedly head straight into diplomacy where he, and his linguistic gifts, belonged. Case closed.

Or so the Dean thought, but as the seasons passed, new and stranger stories about the diplomat's son began to circulate.

"He did it again, Mooj!" the Vice-Dean complained. "I don't like being made fun of. His impersonations are getting out of hand. They're almost subversive."

"Subversive?"

"Yes! They're too—too . . ."

"Accurate?" the Dean smiled.

"Make him stop, Mooj!" the Vice-Dean stamped loudly out of the Dean's office.

Why don't you? Mooj wondered. Why is it always my job?

Mikk's impersonations were not the only thing that caught people's attention. He had started singing in the halls, something the instructors uniformly condemned as disruptive but which the students, the older ones at least, didn't seem to mind.

"His voice is breathy, but nice," said one girl in the advanced speech class. "He does sound lonely. Maybe that's what upsets everyone."

The acrobatics instructor added to the chorus of bewilderment by reporting very reluctantly, as though he feared discussing it would rob the phenomenon of its magic, that, on occasion, one of Mikk's flips or turns would surprise everyone with its flawless beauty.

"Although if you blink, you miss it."

Mikk even perplexed Madam Kaari. She was startled to discover that, when the boy was alone in his room, he improvised little melodics based on pieces her class had just learned.

Rellin Orbin was the only one with nothing to say.

"He comes to my classes and subjects everyone to that awful stare state of his," he sniffed, "but I haven't seen him dance in months."

Mooj thought all of these tales were very interesting, but he didn't have time to investigate. Huud Maroc, the famous performance master, was paying an unprecedented visit to the Academy and everything had to be made ready.

Chapter Three: Huud Maroc

Huud Maroc had just celebrated his nine hundredth birthday and for years had been threatening to retire.

"I'm getting too old for this," he rumbled in his rich, theatrical bass voice, tossing his long silver locks with an air of extreme irritation. "I'm tired of being an icon." But the performance master always managed to find an excuse for one more "farewell tour" followed by yet another "comeback." It got so that booking agents around the galaxy merely nodded indulgently at the elderly performance master's irascibility and scheduled his usual dates in their respective time coordinates without even consulting him.

"When Master Huud dies," they quipped, "maybe then he'll go on his last farewell tour."

In any case, Huud Maroc made it quite clear he would not take on any more apprentices. Over his long career, he had had only a dozen of them, whereas most performance masters trained up at least twenty in a much shorter time. However, most of these did not remain masters long. After facing the difficulties of being every performer to every occasion, most decided to specialize. In contrast, all of Huud Maroc's former apprentices had stayed masters and were among the most lionized and cherished performers of all time. Master Huud was no ordinary teacher and he knew it.

"I'm a perfectionist and a bastard," he said, "but I'm the best performance master in the galaxy. No point denying reality."

Even so, Huud Maroc had had enough of "young fry."

"Too much trouble at any time. Out of the question now. I haven't got the patience."

Dean Mooj had no idea why the performance master had finally decided to visit the Academy at Wynt. No performance master had ever visited the Academy, the haven for decent, but, Mooj had to admit, unremarkable talent. The invitation had been a formality, a courtesy shown to a cultural treasure. No one expected it to be accepted, but, since it had been, the Dean ordered the staff to scrub down the grand banquet hall and fill it with long rows of tables decorated with narrow glass troughs holding live incandescent poppy fish. Fluted vases spilled over at each place with tender curls of edible pond vines, scarlet and silver silk ribbons twisted around the hall's pillars, and the Academy's best utensils, usually reserved for Commencement, marched across the tabletops in the "high court guest" style. To accompany dinner, the instructors put together a special program showcasing the work of the Academy's top students, and many of the other pupils, including Mikk, were recruited to serve sliced fruit, peppra eggs, and other delicacies.

That afternoon the students, ranked according to age and, if they had one, specialization, lined up on the front terraces of the Academy to greet the performance master before the Dean gave him a tour of the campus. Mikk, who had no specialization, volunteered to corral the smallest members of the Academy and make sure all of them showed up in their little matching pale blue tunics.

Mikk had helped out with the children before and liked it. They said what was on their minds and now, more than ever, Mikk craved their candor. Although he was making steady, if uneven, progress as a "free student," Madam Kaari's pleasant euphemism for his new status, it was not comfortable. He heard the whispers, saw the puzzled stares, and felt the tense disapproval as he wandered the Academy's halls "heedless of direction," "in open mockery of the schedule," and "absent all decorum due an institute of learning." No one said anything to his face, which rekindled some of the anxiety he'd once felt waiting for Ranya to lose control—and a prickly exasperation.

Do they know how awful it makes me feel? he wondered. It's so . . .

But he couldn't bring himself to name their cowardice. He hadn't the right.

The children were different. As Mikk walked down the line,

they shared whatever popped into their heads without caring one bit who or what he was.

"Who is Mr. Huud? Is he rich?"

"Prann knocked me down yesterday. Want to see my knee?"

"Do you paint your hair?"

"I think I have to go again."

Mikk was still fluttering about his charges like a mother red fowl, catching would-be escapees, wiping noses, and reassuring the smallest who had never before been involved in such a large gathering and were a bit frightened by all the people, when Huud Maroc strode through the gate and laughed at the end of the Dean's joke.

Master Huud had grown a touch stouter with age but was still a striking figure, barrel-chested with an upright posture worthy of a more warlike world's military, dressed in saffron from tunic to legging to slipper; a simple gold ring hung from his left ear. The students broke into applause and the great performance master nodded, a gracious bending of his body reminiscent of the Crown's courtly bearing.

At the sharp sound of the students' acclaim, Mikk, who had been kneeling before a toddler and asking him to blow into an enormous silk kerchief, jumped up too quickly, lost his footing on the step, and pitched over the terrace wall. A spectacular mishap. However, not only did he not end up in an ignominious heap in the bushes below, he flew clear of the landscaping entirely, twisted about in the air like a falling kitchen feline, and landed upright, if a bit shaken, not an arm's length from the master, who guffawed like the boom of a cannon.

"Not bad!" he cried. "Nice timing!" and he led the way into the Academy. The flabbergasted Mooj trotted behind.

Mikk was stunned. Tunic askew, red hair on end, pigeon-toed, he gawked after Huud Maroc, absolutely unable to believe what he had heard.

"N-nice t-timing?"

He heard giggling behind him, then chuckling, and when he peeked over his shoulder his classmates began to clap.

"Bravo, Mikk!" one of them cried and everyone laughed.

But—it didn't hurt. All those eyes on him, all that mirth at his expense, and he didn't feel humiliated. Somehow, instinctively, Mikk had performed a marvelous comic flip and people had enjoyed it. This was an entirely new experience and his body filled with shivery heat.

The acrobatics instructor slapped him on the back with his wide, tough palm before following the Dean inside.

"Very eccentric, Mikk. Highly entertaining."

"But, I wasn't even trying."

"All the better."

The quivering warmth in Mikk's limbs intensified. Breaking out in brief, involuntary smiles that he tried to hide, he hurried off to the kitchen to help ready the dishes for the banquet.

Huud Maroc listened politely, craggy features composed into an image of genuine interest, as the Dean bobbed ahead of him down endless corridors of classrooms, recital halls, and dormitory facilities, and told him about enrollment, instructor recruitment, prizes, and scholarships. However, the performance master's mind was elsewhere.

Master Huud had not wanted to come to the Academy this year any more than any other. He had been ready to send off his usual polite regrets when, at the last minute, he composed an acceptance instead. Why? He'd had a premonition, one of the occasional discharges of repressed clairvoyance common to the race. Most people believed that if full, uninhibited second sight crowded its way into the teeming Vyzanian mnemonic cortex, it would disrupt the psyche, causing cerebral crisis, schizophrenia, even psychosis. Premonitions acted as a mental safety valve by relieving some of the pressure. However, their insights were not trustworthy. Master Huud had once had a premonition that a friend was coming to visit and it turned into the unpleasant reality of government authorities arriving to audit him for back taxes.

Perhaps he had given in to his premonition about the Academy because instead of attacking his knuckles like a suggestive form of arthritis, it had come in the rare guise of a dream, a dream of a glowing child with red hair. Unfortunately, when the skinny boy with the fright-wig hair sailed through the air and landed before him, the master suspected the prophecy had been fulfilled and the rest of his visit would be a tedious waste of time.

Maybe I can make excuses and leave early in the morning, he thought, rather than stay a second night.

The banquet was pleasant enough: peppra eggs and spiced greens served in the golden glow of hundreds of long thin tapers whose flames danced in the soft early dusk. The gardens' complex perfume came in with the gathering shadows and added a sensory charm Huud Maroc deeply appreciated considering the quality of the evening's opening act. An earnest cluster of young men recited old seven-part poetry that, instead of invoking a heroic past, droned in the master's ears, and his eyes wandered over the faces lining the tables, faces as blank as those of the ornamental fish swimming back and forth in the troughs.

As the students began to set out the merro fruit, which meant there would be a moment of silence for the first bite, the master's traveling attention came to rest on a boy serving two tables away.

"Isn't that the lad who did the flip in the courtyard?" he whispered to the Dean.

Mooj squinted. "Yes," he sighed. "His name is Mikk. I doubt he intended it."

"Nevertheless, a good recovery." Huud Maroc watched the boy more closely. "Moves quite well under normal circumstances."

"Does he?" Now the Dean studied Mikk. "Interesting. I don't remember such ease in his . . ."

"One of your dance students?"

"Not exactly," Mooj said uncomfortably. "Mikk is . . . special."

"Special? How?"

"He's scattered. Interested in everything, but unfocussed. We've had to let him go his own way. The regular classroom setting doesn't work for him." Mooj shrugged. "I hope he'll eventually settle down, pull himself together, and go into diplomacy like his father. He's good with languages, but I doubt he'll be much of a performer, much as he wants to be."

"Why? Desire is most of the battle."

"He has a sensory defect. Unusually acute sight and hearing. I'm sure it explains much of his distraction. That and, well, his mother was hardly what one could hope for. An excessive woman."

"I see." The performance master tapped his lip and narrowed his blue-purple eyes. "He could still learn to focus."

"I'm not sure of that. He could be scattered the rest of his life."

"But you saw him in the courtyard. Look at the way he walks! Something is centering that boy or, if what you say is true, he'd have gotten himself killed long before now."

The Dean regretted not checking out those recent rumors about Mikk. The slender boy went through the simple ritual of serving merro fruit with a dreamy elegance that seemed new and completely natural and Mooj's bad hip tingled, the familiar sign of one of his own premonitions.

"Master Huud, I must profess a great deal of ignorance as far as Mikk is concerned. He's a bright boy, but odd."

A queer spark of interest lit up the old performance master's eyes.

The catastrophe happened during the performance by the girls' choir. Mikk leaned against a pillar in the back, momentarily unemployed, eyes glazed with pleasure. The girls, unlike the young men who recited ancient poetry, were world class, and Mikk's mind floated on the sound and his limbs relaxed. Earlier that year he had had a terrible unspoken crush on one of the soloists and his eyes lingered happily on her round, unblemished cheek.

Across the room, Huud Maroc observed his distraction. There was something about this lad. The music wove its soothing web and Mikk's thin body rubbed against the pillar, absently swaying with the rhythm. The boy was unconsciously seductive. Unconscious. That was it. Mikk was not aware of his abilities. What were those abilities? the master wondered. With proper training instead of Academy pedantry, what could he become? A dancer? Singer? Actor? Huud Maroc's speculations took a long leap: *all* of them? A performance master?

A girl in the choir, a curly-haired adolescent with round cheeks, hit a flat note. It was quiet, hardly noticeable, but Mikk's body snapped like a whip and his pale lavender eyes went dark.

"No!" he cried and the poppy fish darted to the far corners of their troughs. The choir fell silent and the entire room turned to him in horror.

The boy swallowed, raised a shaky hand to his deep red hair, and fled the hall.

"Good Lord of the Sky!" the Dean said. "I've never heard Mikk speak like that!" Mikk's protest at the false note had been loud, clear, clean—a command. In a moment of sudden passion, his voice had shed its whisper and become an actor's.

Huud Maroc rose from his seat.

"Bring that boy to me," he growled tersely.

"Master Huud, please! Mikk meant no harm."

"Don't be a fool, Mooj! Didn't you hear? That 'no' was right on key. He took that wretched girl's botched note and corrected it—perfectly!"

They're going to kill me, Mikk thought. Not literally, of course; that was just how the students characterized severe punishment for major transgressions and Mikk had committed a very serious crime. He had interrupted a performance. This was the ultimate breach of theatrical etiquette and the meat of his very first lesson at the Academy: no performer ever interrupted another's performance, even an atrocious one, unless it was a matter of life and death.

If I've offended Master Huud, the greatest performer in the world, Mikk thought gloomily, my life will be worth less than the beetles in the kitchen. Food for felines.

He shivered in the evening shadows of the corridor outside the Dean's office and waited to be summoned inside. It was no comfort that the long windows here as well were open to let in the moist, sweet aroma of the flowers. He was "dead."

So, when the Dean's doors finally swung inward, Mikk was surprised to see the master and Mooj comfortably seated on large cushions and chewing bantroots as though relaxing after a fine evening of dining and conversation. They looked up when he entered and began to discuss him as though he weren't there.

"A thin lad," Huud Maroc said, "but his skin tone is very even. Good texture. What they used to call 'milk pale' back before the war killed off all the cattle."

"He's not been sick a day since he came here, Master Huud, and he's grown a great deal. Sometimes he needs extra salt."

"Low serum salinity?"

"Nothing serious, but it's something to keep in mind on other worlds so he doesn't get dehydrated . . ."

Other worlds? Mikk's mouth went dry.

". . . he can tell when he needs it."

"Come here, boy," the master said. There was no mistaking the authority in that deep, rolling voice, but the undercurrent of softness, even warmth, puzzled him. He crept carefully up to the master.

"There," Huud Maroc said to the Dean as Mikk approached, "see what I mean? There's an integrity that can't be hidden."

The Dean shook his head. "I have no idea how that came about. He's always been a daring tumbler, but graceful? No."

"How old are you, boy?" the master asked.

"One hundred fifty years, sir," Mikk whispered. He began to feel very hot and wondered if either adult could see it in his face.

The performance master grunted as though Mikk's answer confirmed his suspicions.

"I've heard of this. Never actually encountered it, though. Puberty acts as a catalyst or drawstring, pulling the pieces together. Quite rare and not usually so obvious."

To Mikk's alarm, the performance master grabbed him by the chin and opened his mouth. He peered into Mikk's throat.

"What's this scarring on the vocal cords?"

"Infantile arranic throat fever," Mooj said.

"Interesting," Huud Maroc mused. Then he added, apparently to himself, "In every beautiful thing there's something very strange." He released Mikk's jaw and glared at the boy.

"On Terra," he said, "there's a nearly extinct wild predator called a wolf, something like the ancient Kekoi four footer. It's known for its song, which the Terrans mistakenly call a howl. Are you following me, boy?"

"Yes, sir," Mikk said and, in his confusion, forgot to whisper.

"Good. This song often appears very suddenly, and when a wolf pup first hears it come out of himself, it can surprise him as much as anyone else. Still following me?"

Mikk nodded. He was too frightened not to follow.

"Fine. I'm not going to kill you for your little display this evening."

"Yes, sir. Thank you, sir."

"Now, listen carefully, young Mikk." The performance master's silver eyebrows bunched down over his eyes. "True natural talent, as opposed to mere ability, is difficult to develop. It must be ridden very hard to give it the discipline it needs but, at the same time, care must be taken not to break its spirit or damage its desire for creation. Do you understand?"

"Yes, sir." Mikk started to tremble again.

Huud Maroc clasped Mikk's slender arms and squeezed them, studying them the way a Terran might appraise the legs of a horse.

"Look at me." The master spoke in the low thunder of a god in a classic tragedy. "Tell me. Do you trust me?"

Mikk's troubled eyes, strained and sore, gazed deeply into the great performance master's dark blue-purple ones and searched for a clue as to how the man really felt about him. He didn't know whether he trusted *himself* under the circumstances, but somewhere in those piercing depths he thought he saw a sparkle of gentle amusement.

"Yes." The amazing word was out before he could stop it.

The rugged angles and lines of the old performer's face softened into a quiet smile that even the gruffness of his subsequent words could not erase.

"I'm not yet sure I want an apprentice. I probably don't, but I intend to take you along on my, what is it now? ninth? comeback tour to Droos. I promise nothing, but you'll get a chance to experience some *real* song and dance."

Mikk did become Huud Maroc's thirteenth, and last, apprentice. Two days later he clambered aboard the performance master's bright green hoverboat with a small bundle of possessions tied up in heavy canvas.

"Undoubtedly you've heard stories about me," the master said as he gave the boy a hand up. "Stories that I'm a tough man to please, an arrogant taskmaster."

"Yes, sir."

Huud Maroc chuckled. "I like your honesty, boy. Shows courage. Well, those stories are true. I *work* my apprentices. I want them to excel, but you have to understand something else, Mikk." He put his arm around the boy's shoulders. "I am never cruel and I encourage experimentation. Never be afraid to share an idea with me, no matter how far-fetched."

"Yes, sir."

"And the proper etiquette is to call me 'Master Huud.' 'Sir' is for ordinary teachers."

"Yes, s—Master Huud."

"Good lad." The master pulled a bright gold ball out of his pocket and placed it in Mikk's palm. The ball felt very strange. It shifted its weight about with the smallest motion of Mikk's fingers and even reacted to his pulse.

"What is it?" he asked, suddenly excited. "Is it alive?"

"Hardly. It's a bolba juggling ball. The Bolbans make them out of a substance that alters its center of gravity in response to how it's manipulated. A tricky thing at first, but once mastered, a performer can do some wonderful stunts with it. I've given you only one, to start with, and whenever you have a free moment, I want you to play with it. Take it with you when you wander off."

Mikk lowered his eyes. The Dean must have told the master about his fondness for getting lost in gardens.

"Your particular problem, Mikk, is that your mind and your body are going their own separate journeys, quite unaware of each other. This will help correct that. When you're comfortable with one ball, I'll give you another, and when you've worked your way up to three, I'll teach you the basic patterns."

"What is the highest number of balls someone can use?" Mikk asked.

"The most I've seen anyone juggle is thirty."

"How many do you use, Master Huud?"

"Thirty."

Entr'acte: Kekoi Kaery: The List

In spite of the frigid damp, Mikk removed his slippers, the surprise tunic, and peeled off his dance suit to do some rudimentary cleaning up at the wash basin, pumping the lever until he heard an unhappy gargling groan from deep inside the wall and the spigot spat out a ragged stream of red-brown ice water. Once the flow was steady and clear, Mikk splashed his body, which, still warm from his exercise, shuddered at the shock. He washed his face then stood gasping and shivering until the drops evaporated.

I wonder what's happened to Bipti? he thought as he hurriedly wrestled back into his dance suit. He's been gone for hours. The Kekoi guards will be here soon. He leapt back up to the window.

It was full morning, a market day, and hundreds of people, both outworld and native, crowded the flags of the courtyard to haggle over roots and seeds and cured game. Some of the vendors still sold campaign souvenirs but, as a result of Mikk's arrest, the Kekoi jesters refused to perform and the Election Games had been suspended. It would have been impossible to continue the rounds anyway because of the arrival of hordes of outworld media personnel to cover the case. The journalists taxed the resources of the already voter-swollen capital and overwhelmed the inns and taverns with their incompatible equipment and volatile opinions. Brownouts and brawls were common. In fact, it looked as though a skirmish was brewing in the courtyard that very minute. Mikk kicked the air to boost himself a little higher.

One of the carts, a heavy farm dray stacked with cages of picnic feepits, had slipped off its block and tipped its entire chittering pyramid into the crowd. The tiny red and yellow fowl escaped and fluttered in a panicked cloud around people's heads. Most of the

Kekoi tried to beat them out of their fur, but some of the younger, cockier males, as well as a few adventurous outworlders, caught the birds in their sharp teeth and swallowed them whole.

"What are you doing!" the owner of the dray howled. "I haven't been paid for those!"

He shoved one of the outworlders, a sullen, gold-skinned Lambdan, and that's when the real trouble began. The Lambdan pulled a heat knife and the female vendors, with cries of "You bastards! There are small pups here!" hitched their skirts up over their hairy legs for better mobility and began to pummel the delinquent youths with fists, roots, and joints of stag meat.

Just when Mikk felt they'd have to summon the security "dog" officers to clear the street, the flow of the crowd shifted from the dray and, with a low roar, rushed across the courtyard to Mikk's far right, in the direction of the heavy keranium courthouse doors.

No matter how extreme Mikk's contortions, he could not get a clear view around the thick wall of the cell so he could not see what had attracted the crowd. However, he did see Bipti pushing his way back toward the jail—empty-handed.

Damn him! Mikk thought. What has he been doing all this time?

The performance master dropped lightly to the floor and brushed off his hands.

"He's going to have a lot of explaining to do," Mikk growled to himself. "I need that salt soon or I'll be flopping on the ground like a fish."

However, his determination to grill the guard about his protracted absence evaporated when he heard the Freen's excited words.

"Mikk-sir! Good news!" Bipti's bare feet slapped rapidly along the corridor. "They've posted the names of the tribunes!"

Mikk closed his eyes and murmured his gratitude. "Gods be thanked! It's about time."

The guard trotted up to the cell and slumped against the opposite wall to catch his breath. "I ran as fast as I could, Mikk-sir. I did not want to forget who they were."

"You memorized the names? Why didn't you just copy the list? You're not Vyzanian, Bipti."

"I can't read, Mikk-sir. Someone repeated the names for me."

Mikk stared blankly at the Freen, then cupped his hand over his cheek, mortified. "I'm sorry, Bipti! How rude of me!"

"I am not offended, Mikk-sir," Bipti said with a yellow grin. "I am flattered you would assume such a thing of a Freen, but now the list, yes?"

"Yes, please." Mikk withdrew to his pallet and lowered himself gingerly onto its mildewed ticking. He hugged his knees.

"The High Tribune will be Pairip, the Garplen banquet master."

"Conservative, but honest," Mikk said thoughtfully. "The Council probably chose him to prevent things from getting completely out of hand."

"What is a banquet master, Mikk-sir?"

"He sings the Sacred Texts of Plenty over a Garplen feast." Mikk trapped a tiny black hay flea in his fingers and crushed it. "In exchange for his services, the guests save the best and largest portions for him. Who's next?"

"Twee the Borovfian."

Mikk rolled his eyes and groaned.

"Bad choice, Mikk-sir?"

"Mutt shit masquerading as pedigree," Mikk sighed. "Exactly the kind of tribune I expected. Go on."

As the guard continued to recite the names, Mikk became very quiet and his expression became more grim until the Freen mentioned Amda ar'k, the tribune from Bar Omega Sept. The performance master suddenly laughed.

"What is it, Mikk-sir?"

"Nothing, Bipti. Never mind. It still helps to know who the tribunes are. I can tailor a more informed defense." Mikk chuckled again, humorlessly. "I certainly have time to do it, don't I! These tribunes are from all over the sector. It'll take them weeks to get to Kekoi Kaery."

"Oh, no, Mikk-sir! They're already here."

Mikk stiffened. "What?"

"They're already here." Bipti glanced anxiously down the corridor and lowered his voice. "The Council has been bringing them in one at a time for many days. They're hidden in the diplomatic suites above the courthouse."

"I don't believe you . . ."

"It must be true, Mikk-sir. The tribunal begins today. When the Kekoi guards come, they will take you to the court."

Mikk's pale eyes slowly darkened as though a shadow was passing over the panes of a stained crystal window. He lowered his head and hid his face in his knees.

"Mikk-sir?"

"Just hurry up with the rest of the list before your memory fails!" Mikk hissed. Bipti quickly complied.

"There's Féqé-ad the Rogoine, Bythr the Nyan Sewpan, that Lambdan fellow . . . you know the one. The actor who makes all those rut films. Oh, and Counsel 6 of Spaira."

The performance master remained immobile and Bipti chewed a hangnail.

"Counsel 6?" he asked. "Isn't that a lawyer, Mikk-sir? I thought this was to be a tribunal of your peers."

No reply.

"Well, then, Mikk-sir, perhaps I should find out what's keeping the Kekoi guards . . ."

"Stay right where you are, Bipti."

The Freen froze mid-step. "Sir?"

Mikk raised his head and, in spite of the energy gate, Bipti drew back. The performance master's expression was cold and terrible.

"That was only ten," he said in a flat whisper. "Who is the eleventh?"

The Freen's inner eyelids fluttered. "Ah, well, it looks like I forgot one after all! I'll go back and find out . . ."

"Beast, Bipti!" Mikk sprang to his feet, his body vibrating with fury. "What's the matter with you? My *life* is at stake! What are you hiding from me?"

The Freen wrung his thick gray hands. "Please don't yell at me, Mikk-sir! I meant no harm."

"Tell me!"

"Thissizz!" the Freen cried. "The tribune who will speak before the lawyer is Thissizz."

The roar of blood in Mikk's ears staggered him and he almost fainted. Tears quickly melted the clarity of his vision and the cell rocked and jiggled like an aquarian mirage, but he pressed his hands against the rough wall and was able to reorient himself.

Heart of my heart! he grieved. How can you sit in judgment over me?

Chapter Four: Thissizz

From lush, temperate Vyzania, with its lakes, ponds, lagoons, rolling woodlands, and gardens, Mikk traveled to a world of massive mountains, deep ravines, thundering waterfalls, and wide fluctuations of temperature. Long, steamy, almost tropical days gave way to equally long, bitterly frigid nights. The enormous tree flowers, their stalks as thick as columns and as tall as the towers on the Crown's palace in Wynt, their broad, colorfully patterned petals, draping from high above like banners and canopies, drew in on themselves at the approach of darkness, curling their leaves and petals up tight or swallowing them into their stalks entirely. The green and violet vines and grasses of the undergrowth underwent a marked change in texture, from smooth and soft to rough and bumpy, to preserve heat.

According to Master Huud, the Droos could elevate their body temperature at will, warming the fluids in their veins and organs merely by thinking about it.

"You and I, however, will have to change into nighttime boots and parkas," he had said.

Mikk had never been so far away from home, and a deep sense of dislocation vied with his eagerness to see this wonderful place and meet its remarkable inhabitants. Still, Droos' unfamiliarity renewed his hope, bitterly dashed at the Academy, that he could start his life over.

They're strangers, he thought. They don't know about my faults and accidents.

So he was very disappointed when, once on the surface, there was no one to greet them. He and Huud Maroc stood alone outside the vast round opening to a stone cavern that resembled a great temple of polished concentric circles. Mikk's eyes got lost in the pattern of ridges that displayed the natural whorls of color in the dense rock, and he sighed involuntarily.

"Yes, splendid, isn't it?" the master said. "The stonemasons who did this work were some of the finest artists in Droosian history."

"But, where is everyone, Master Huud?"

"Down inside the burrows, of course. Dawn was only about an hour ago. Stay here and I'll see if Oosmoosis is up. Amuse yourself if you like, but be careful. If I have to send a search party after you I will not be in a good mood when I see you again."

"Yes, Master Huud." Mikk's mentor marched into the echoey cavern and disappeared.

Mikk fidgeted as the giant flowers did their last bit of unfurling, then got out his bolba ball and began to play with it to distract his restlessness. He tried to keep the ball in the air with his feet as well as his hands and his mistakes and retrievals drew him into the wood of bright colors. The tree flowers' petals were beyond Mikk's powers of description, their patterns as delicate and intricate as the finest glass mosaics, and when he found a fallen petal, he realized that its moist fragrant silkiness could have served as a coverlet for himself and his master, with room for a dozen kitchen felines to cozy up underneath as well. Sunlight filtered through the flowers and dappled the undergrowth with bright shards of rose, canary, turquoise, and emerald.

"I wonder what the Droos people are like to live in such a beautiful world. . . ."

As he chased down his willful gold sphere, Mikk tripped over what he at first thought was an unusual vine—until it moved and coiled in on itself. He had stumbled on the tail of a Droos, and when they saw each other, Mikk's irises turned black and the Droos reared her shimmering, off-purple, smooth-scaled body until she towered over the boy. She spread the fanlike hood folded along her spine and hissed. When Mikk merely blinked at her, too stunned to run, the Droos compressed the sleek, supple features of her large wedge-shaped head into a ferocious frown and began to speak rapidly in a lilting, lisping singsong the apprentice had never heard before—had never heard anything comparable. For all he knew, the Droos was cursing him with the worst obscenities imaginable, but he melted in bewitched delight and grinned at her helplessly, unable to move. He had entered a woozy stare state.

The Droos scowled dubiously at the boy, as if trying to decide whether he was uncommonly brave or a complete idiot, then smacked him across the face with her long heavy blue tongue and sent him sprawling into the underbrush. Mikk sat up quickly and the great serpentlike creature snarled at him, but her eyes did not seem to harbor any real malice. In fact, she looked very uncomfortable and a bit frightened. Mikk then noticed that the Droos' abdomen undulated with irregular ripplings and he finally realized what was going on.

Mikk had seen his mother's fisher stork lay its black eggs, and one of the kitchen felines at the Academy had recently dropped a clutch of kits, but he did not know what to expect from this enormous reptile with the elegant language. She was beginning to suffer in earnest and she clenched her teeth and started to writhe, thrashing the end of her long body back and forth. Mikk had to leap about smartly to keep out of the way. Finally, she let out a long wavering wail so full of psychic torment that Mikk burst into tears. The Droos cut her cry short and stared at the sentimental boy with an expression of weary bemusement. Apparently, she didn't think her moans and groans were anything special, but another spasm brought tears to her own huge black eyes and Mikk couldn't bear it. He felt an overwhelming desire to soothe this strange and noble being and, at a loss for what else to do, he began to sing an old ballad Huud Maroc had taught him on the trip, a fairly ordinary piece but one with a wide range in the melody; the master had said it would loosen Mikk's "unique" vocal cords.

The Droos rolled her eyes, made a small barking noise Mikk could not interpret, then leaned her face toward his and cried out sharply, "Zmap! Zmap!" in time with the music. She pounded her tail for emphasis. Mikk was not sure what she wanted but continued to sing and accentuated the beat by clapping his hands. His efforts seemed to help. The Droos closed her eyes and rocked her head, humming a little, and Mikk reached out to caress her body. The nearly invisible slit in the Droos' lower abdomen suddenly popped open and, with a heavy shudder, she expelled a large quantity of milky jelly—all over Mikk. It was slimy, but warm, and smelled not unpleasantly of sweetened roast fowl.

"Um, well . . ." Mikk inspected his beslimed hair and tunic and heard a quiet staccato hissing. The Droos was snickering at him in spite of her pain. No need to translate. Mikk smiled at her then saw her amusement dissolve into wonder. Her livid coloring shifted dramatically to a bright turquoise and the slick pastel green nose of the first of her twelve babies issued from the birth canal.

"Oh! Aren't they pretty!" Mikk cried.

Already covered with birth slime, he gave in to his urge to pet the shiny, wiggling Droos babies and they responded by licking him with their soft blue tongues. The mother did not interfere. She alternately smiled tenderly at her brood and gazed with curious respect at the red-haired outworlder. The pups' tongues tickled and Mikk, almost faint with ecstasy, giggled uncontrollably, a sound the mother understood. She cooed some especially liquid vowels and playfully shoved his arm with her nose. However, when she happened to look over and past him, she quickly ducked her head into her coils and grinned bashfully, exposing all of her four hundred teeth. Mikk followed her glance and scrambled to his feet. At the edge of the clearing stood Huud Maroc and a larger, gold-colored Droos.

The master's jaw muscles tensed as though he was trying to suppress some kind of outburst and he passed his hands over his eyes.

"Oosmoosis, meet Mikk, my new apprentice," he sighed, indicating the slime-covered crimson-haired boy.

"My daughter, Nessiri," the elder Droos said with a heavy accent and a nod to the new mother.

Thissizz, the youngest of Oosmoosis' 216 children, a coral-pink adolescent, had been too excited to sleep. He was the only one in his enormous family who wanted to travel to other worlds and sing for distant peoples and he hoped the newly returned Master Huud would convince Oosmoosis he was ready to tour. Thissizz was so excited, in fact, that he barely noticed his sister's predawn departure for the flower wood, but as he hurried to the Great Cavern, he remembered.

"I'm going to be an uncle again! All the wonderful things happen at once!"

Sure enough, when he arrived at the Great Cavern, Thissizz not only found the silver-haired performance master discussing galactic politics with Oosmoosis, he also found a beaming Nessiri proudly leading a parade of shiny bright pups to the nursery burrows.

Thissizz's heart overflowed at these joyous sights, but it nearly stopped, mid-beat, when he saw the thin, quiet boy rinsing his fiery hair in one of the numerous side cavern springs. The boy flipped his wet locks from his eyes and smiled shyly at him, and the fascinated young Droos almost didn't hear Master Huud's offhand introduction of him as "Mikk, my newly apprenticed disaster."

An apprentice! Thissizz circled the silent, wide-eyed Mikk and looked at him from every angle.

He's nothing at all like the master! the Droos mused. He's slender and smooth and his hair is redder than prickle berries.

Utterly enchanted, Thissizz forgot the boy didn't know any of his language and he began to chatter happily about everything young males found interesting.

The Droos' voice seduced Mikk's sensitive ears until the apprentice didn't know where or who he was. He couldn't believe this amazing creature was speaking and not singing, and the way Thissizz moved as he circled him intoxicated him even more. The Droos carried the front part of his body erect to about the height of a man while the rest of his length, his coils, rippled and swayed behind him. In spite of his febrile enthusiasm, Thissizz had an unusually refined swing to his gait, and Mikk followed him blindly when he abruptly broke his circling and led the way into the Great Cavern. Mikk's mind raced after the Droos' words, absorbing the language, sorting out patterns, looking for structure. The effort allowed little room for contemplating the beauty of the cavern, but when Thissizz finally paused to catch his breath and swayed before the boy, panting and flushed a deep salmon, Mikk laughed with unrestrained pleasure. Thissizz's color deepened.

"Oh, I sorry am!" he said in halting Vyzanian. "Forgot I did! Not you understand at all what I say." But, to his astonishment, Mikk responded in broken Droos.

"It fine is," he said. "Talk more. Quick will learn me."

Thissizz immediately insisted Mikk climb onto his back and, with the boy clinging to his coils, took him on a swift rollicking gallop back to the private burrow where Huud Maroc and Oosmoosis were sharing a dual-spouted beaker of reegsh, a sweet fruit drink, Huud Maroc using a reed, Oosmoosis his tongue.

"Papa! Papa, listen! This is a wonderful pup! He already knows our speech!"

The master cut Oosmoosis off before the elder could respond. "What? Is this true?"

Mikk bit his lower lip but smiled, then spoke in Droos. "I good am at tongues. Be better will I when more I hear."

"Gods flying, boy!" Huud Maroc swore softly, face serious but eyes dancing. "If you're as quick with everything else as you are in this, I'm going to be hard pressed to keep my irascible reputation."

"Well," Mikk said, returning to his own language, "I *am* a clumsy dancer."

The master grabbed Mikk's jaw so quickly, and in such a tight grip, the boy squeaked. He was genuinely furious. "Don't *ever* express such a negative thing again! Be realistic about your abilities, know where you need to improve, but *never* denigrate your talent. You will begin to believe it and I will not tolerate an apprentice who defeats himself before he's given himself a chance. Do you hear me, Mikk?"

Mikk nodded as best he could, and the storm clouds gathered under Huud Maroc's silver brows suddenly dispersed. He released Mikk's jaw, then embraced him roughly with his hard arm. "Droos is a good thing to learn. Follow Thissizz about if you like him. He'll keep you out of trouble, but be sure you're back in time this evening."

"Yes, Master Huud."

However, before the young friends went anywhere, Oosmoosis

drew Thissizz aside. "I don't want you to carry Mikk on your back anymore."

"But, why, papa? I was only . . ."

"No. Now listen to me, Thissizz," Oosmoosis said sternly. "Biped pups are not as strong as Droos and this one looks especially fragile. He could fall and be seriously injured."

"Papa, I didn't mean to . . ."

"I know you weren't trying to hurt him, but you must be very careful. The last thing I want is for you to damage the master's new apprentice. The boy is special or Master Huud would not be interested in him."

"I know that, papa!" Thissizz snapped, adolescent temper flaring. "How many outworlders can speak Droos in only an hour? I'll bet even the master couldn't do that."

"Watch your tongue, pup, or I won't let you play with Mikk at all."

Thissizz pouted and hung his head. His father did not understand. True, the boy's fingers had dug into him a little desperately on that ride, but he had giggled. It had been fun! Maybe when you get old, Thissizz thought, you forget how to have fun.

"Be gentle with your friend, Thissizz."

"Yes, papa."

When Thissizz rejoined Mikk, the boy's partially darkened eyes darted over him anxiously, a tense interest the Droos could almost feel as though the boy had touched him.

"Did I trouble you give? Sorry am I!"

"Oh, no! It's just that my papa, well . . ." Thissizz shrugged, a short kinking of the upper vertebrae followed by a release. "He's so *old* sometimes."

"Ah! Hm . . ." Mikk wondered just how old "old" was on Droos, but felt too shy to ask.

The young Droos led Mikk again through the Great Cavern, explaining afresh, and more slowly so the boy could catch and decipher the words, that it was the most ancient, important, and largest gathering place in the city.

"Thousands will come tonight even though the master performs alone this time. Are you to be part of a new troupe?"

"I know not—do not know." Mikk gazed up at the elaborate

patterns of the cavern's vault and the softly glowing orbs set into the designs like stars in a nebula. "Are those lightings?"

"Those? Those are very old-fashioned. Phosphor resin from before the Belians! Most caverns and burrows have touch-keyed light boxes. Come on! I want to show you everything."

They left the Great Cavern and headed into the main tunnel, the central artery of the city, a labyrinth hewn out of the living rock of a collection of mountain spurs and outcroppings. Natural vaults with inherently attractive whorls of colored stone or complex groupings of stalactites had been left unfinished, but most of the caverns were carved with repetitive swirls.

Mikk wanted to ask Thissizz, if he could think of a polite way of phrasing it, how limbless creatures sculpted stone, but he got his answer when they came upon a group of masons, exceptionally broad and heavy males and females, dressing the entrance to a new burrow. The masons did the rough work with Belian-made stone cutters, which they held in the dexterous tips of their coils as the bright blue beams sliced off chunks of quartz. They did the fine work "by hand" in teams of two. One mason steadied a chisel while another swung a mallet, and in this way the team moved along the wall in a rhythm resembling a dance: a turn of the chisel, a swing of the mallet, another position, another swing. The quartz flaked away with a small chink and the masons hummed in time to their work. Mikk stopped to listen to this happy, percussive music. Everything about the Droos flowed rhythmically: their language, their bodies, and, now, their art.

"Here is beautiful!" he said. "A beautiful world."

Thissizz grinned—about 250 teeth—and curled and uncurled the tip of his coils. He had always enjoyed watching the masons and was delighted his friend enjoyed them too.

"If you like the tunnels, wait until you see what's up ahead. It's one of my most favorite places." He nudged the distracted boy's shoulder. "Come on, Mikk, I'm over here."

They headed to one of the natural caverns near the surface. Its open vault allowed the sunlight to pour in through a skylight. Directly below the skylight was a large dark pool fed by subterranean hot springs and a grove of mutated tree flowers, pale, slender counterparts of their outdoor cousins, reached up through the filtered light to the distant patch of blue. Hundreds of Droos of all ages gathered around the pool to drink the steaming mineral water, splash and roll in it, or bask amiably in the broad carpet of morning sun.

"I love it here. See the purple moss hanging from the skylight? We call it 'cavern hair.' I meet all my friends here and we swim." Thissizz studied Mikk's somewhat gangly proportions. "Do you swim?"

Mikk, staring at a Droos couple who were wrestling near the water's edge, did not answer. He was amazed how casually physical the Droos were, lounging together with their coils draped over each other as they chatted, laughed, or dozed. He saw the occasional spat, short outbursts of hissing and rearing and displaying of hoods but, on the whole, the Droos were exceptionally affectionate and peaceful. They nuzzled and kissed everyone and Mikk could not tell which were mates and which were just friends—except this couple, a deep blue male and a turquoise female, young adults according to the brief color-phase rundown Thissizz had given him earlier. The two Droos were engaged in some kind of courtship ritual, if not outright coupling, and whipped their coils around and around each other, tangling themselves together and rolling on the ground completely oblivious to anyone or anything else. Their bright eyes were half-closed and they hissed softly through subtle, knowing smiles. Mikk thought they were beautiful, vaguely dangerous, and disturbingly public.

He rubbed his foot against his ankle. Standing in Thissizz's shadow, transfixed by the spectacle of the amorous couple, he felt very small and very young indeed.

"Mikk? Is something the matter?"

The boy's anguished glance cut into Thissizz's heart, and the Droos felt something break open, similar to the splitting of the skin during molt, but buried deep below the surface. "Of course!" he whispered fiercely. "How stupid of me! It *hurts*, doesn't it? Me, too, sometimes. I am sorry! I thought you were too young."

Mikk shakily ran his fingers through his hair, and his eyes, which had turned a shadowy violet, lightened. "You must think I am very strange," he said. Thissizz started. The boy had uttered a perfectly constructed Droosian sentence in a good clear voice.

"No!" Thissizz replied, feverishly scrambling his own grammar, "I thinking you *we* thought strange were . . . oh, dear . . ."

"What?" Mikk giggled and both friends broke into laughter. "Does this happen often?"

"With me, all the time." Thissizz laughed again before settling into a wistful contemplation of the slight but appealing creature at his side.

"*Are* we strange?"

"No," Mikk said. "I mean, it is different here and I am very new, but . . ."

"I like how new you are!"

"You do?"

Thissizz flipped out his long blue tongue and cautiously, using just the tip, toyed with the boy's crimson hair.

"That makes the skin shiver," Mikk said.

"Tickles." Thissizz withdrew his tongue.

"Yes."

"Are you hungry?"

"I don't know." Mikk touched his hair to see if it was slimy again. He discovered, to his surprise, that it was not.

"I'm always hungry," said the Droos. "It's a curse. Papa says it's the 'young crazies.' Eat everything, want everything, love everything, cry over everything—you know, crazies."

Mikk grinned, the first full one Thissizz had seen. The warm splitting inside his heart spread open even further.

"Do you like flowers?" the Droos asked.

"Yes. They're lovely."

"Oh, no!" Thissizz snickered. "I mean to eat!"

"You eat flowers? I thought the bowls of petals in the burrows were for prettiness."

"Food *is* pretty."

They went down a coil ramp, a tight switchback Droos used instead of stairs, to another large tunnel packed with limbless, including a marauding cluster of juveniles who raced for an opening that led outside to the flower forest. They skittered around a bend and bore down on the friends with the rustling, pounding roar of a small flash flood and, for a moment, Mikk was back at the Academy, lost in the older students' hallways. He would have headed down the wrong side tunnel if Thissizz hadn't called to him and pulled back the pieces of his scattered attention.

"Mikk? Mikk!"

"Yes?" he replied meekly, retreating into the security of his whisper.

"You see and hear everything, don't you?"

"All at once," Mikk sighed.

"It's all right," the Droos said kindly. "You don't have to worry. I am not about to lose you."

Chapter Five: Night on Droos

Huud Maroc expected Mikk to be space-lagged and exhausted after a full day roaming the city with an adolescent Droos, but when Thissizz brought the boy back to the Great Cavern—late, of course—Mikk seemed none the worse for wear. In fact, the apprentice looked in better shape than the master who had been snapping and growling at the Droos musicians all day. The impractical artists were supposed to have rehearsed on their own for several weeks but had unsealed the music scrolls for the first time only a couple days before the master's arrival. It wasn't exactly a disaster—the musicians were adept and corrected their blunders rapidly—but it had been a chaotic day.

That's Droos for you, the master mused. It was true what they said about the limbless: without hands, possessions and time-keeping lose importance. Even so, it was difficult to stay angry with them. Droos might be extraordinarily careless with the few things they had, but they cared deeply for each other, and no matter how exasperated he got, Huud Maroc had to admit he loved them. If reincarnation really happened, as these romantic beings fervently believed, he would not mind at all if he had to come back as a Droos.

Mikk obviously liked them, too. He called his unusually clear farewells in an admirable rendering of Thissizz's convoluted language and waved as the Droos rippled away down the tunnel to his father's burrows. Beast! The boy was every bit as quick with foreign tongues as the Dean had said.

"So, Mikk, did the day go well? Did that young lunatic get you anything to eat?"

"Yes. They grow marvelous squash here, blue with orange stripes."

"Fine, but you don't have to speak Droos to me."

"Was I? Oh, dear . . ."

"Don't give it another thought, lad. That is something outside my purview. I would never presume to advise someone on their own kind of mastery."

"I've never thought of myself as a master of anything." Mikk sounded subdued by the idea. "Languages are easy."

"Life doesn't have to be difficult, Mikk. I could take you back to Wynt right now, present you to the Diplomatic Council, and, with your special gift, they would take you on the spot, I'm sure of it. The Crown is still engaged in negotiations with the Septans. They're an easily threatened people, but I doubt they'd be afraid of a child." He hooked his thumbs in his belt. "You'd be set for life."

Mikk frowned—no, scowled. Huud Maroc's implication had angered him, an emotion the master had not yet seen.

"I do not want to perform because of the money," he said. Much of the renewed roughness of his voice disappeared with the partial surfacing of his considerable fury. Huud Maroc took note of the change and moved on.

"No, Mikk, that would be the worst reason. You're right not to think much of it. However, you have chosen a very hard road. I want you to be sure of your choice because it is not the only one."

"Yes, it is."

The master clicked his tongue. It was pointless to pursue the issue further. He led Mikk to the raked platform stage the crew had put up that morning. A couple of Droos were still rigging light boxes or hauling away empty shipping cartons, dragging them along the ground by rope harnesses.

"Tonight, Mikk, all I want you to do is watch and listen, but that doesn't mean I want you to drift off in the easy pleasure of an evening's entertainment." Huud Maroc toyed with his earring and nodded with satisfaction at the work going on around them. "Absorb everything you see. Make it part of yourself. The more you practice this, the better you'll do when it comes time for you to perform."

"I'll try." Mikk stepped aside to let by a tiny outworlder he could not identify, a crab scuttling on a hundred legs and balancing a stack of cosmetic boxes on its flat pink shell. He had to run to catch up with the master, who hadn't slackened his pace.

"I know everything is new, Mikk, and I wouldn't be surprised if your senses are seriously overloaded, but put your heart into it. The greatest performers are those who reach into themselves and find sources of strength they did not think they had." A faraway gleam glinted in the master's blue-purple eyes. "In the course of your career, you may have to take on roles you don't want to play because they're poorly written, badly directed, or not appropriate for you. We do not always have the luxury of choice, but . . ."

The boy was looking out so intently for other diminutive outworlders that he almost walked right into one of the Droos. Mikk jumped away, mouthed an apology, and the massive dark brown male grunted and moved on.

"Are you all right, boy?"

"Yes, Master Huud."

"Trust your feet, lad," Huud Maroc smiled. "They're not going anywhere without you."

"Yes, Master Huud."

"Papa, I am not a child anymore! I know better than to pounce on someone smaller than me." The young Droos switched his tail back and forth in agitation, eager to end this interminable lect-hiss in his father's drafty burrow.

"Do you indeed? I know that look in your eye, Thissizz, and I'm warning you . . ."

"But, why? I've never hurt any of my friends before and I'm

not going to start now. Why are you so worried? I know he's not a Droos. Neither is the master and you and he have been friends forever! What are you afraid of?"

Oosmoosis frowned, but did not answer. His son took advantage of the silence and swished off, on his way to the evening's performance.

The elder Droos sighed. Was he overreacting? In spite of the "young crazies," Thissizz had always been a thoughtful, careful pup. What was it about his son's budding friendship with Mikk that made his vertebrae ache with anxiety?

Perhaps the master knows, he thought, and he took a shortcut, a slippery, nearly vertical tunnel that asked a lot of those overtaxed vertebrae, to the backstage burrows of the Great Cavern.

"This isn't like you, Oosmoosis," the master said as he painted pale blue frost on his eyelids and darkened his silver eyebrows with ash powder. He smiled archly. "It isn't the first time a Droos and a biped have been close. As I recall, we did much worse than wrestle when we were young."

"This boy is not you." Oosmoosis rippled up and down the burrow in tight, nervous zigzags.

"No, he's not." The master wiped his fingers with a spice-scented sponge and inspected his face in the glare of the wall glass. "I don't yet know who he is, but it's not good to hover over a child's every move. He'll never grow in that kind of shade." He watched his friend's exercise for a moment then shook his head. "You'll wear a track in the floor, Oosmoosis."

Oosmoosis stopped pacing and, with an air of resignation, wound his coils into a stack and rested his head on top.

"I must be getting old," he groaned. "Do you realize I have great-grandchildren older than my daughter's new brood?"

The master chuckled warmly. "I'm older, too. I don't sleep through the night anymore. It's very annoying. However," he got up and stood over the coiled Droos, "it usually means I'm all alone for my morning bath."

Oosmoosis' large black eyes became larger and the edge of his hood rustled a little, a flash of gold in the artificial day of the cosmetic mirrors.

"Perhaps, if you're insomniac as well," the master continued, "we can find something to do that will beat back the passage of time."

Oosmoosis hissed softly.

Thissizz tried to sulk during Huud Maroc's opening song, but he was too happy seated in front next to Mikk to maintain a cloudy mood.

"At intermission," he whispered into the boy's ear, "would you like to meet my other friends? We can have something sweet."

"Master Huud wants me to join him backstage," Mikk sighed, and the disappointed Droos was reassured by the dismay in the boy's voice. "But I do want to meet your friends."

"Maybe tomorrow."

"Yes."

The Droos edged closer to the boy. Be good, Thissizz, be good! Oh, it was not easy! Tussling with friends was as natural as breathing and he wished he could just wrap himself around this pretty pup and be done with it. It certainly would warm the boy better than his ridiculous white quilted parka, at least two sizes too big, and heavy boots. They were so ugly! Besides, Thissizz did not believe Mikk was as fragile as his father claimed. The very first thing the boy had done on Droos was help Nessiri during labor. Not even Oosmoosis was brave enough to do that!

Papa doesn't know anything, Thissizz decided, and scooted even closer to Mikk. Without turning his attention from the stage, the boy put his white hand on Thissizz's flank and gently ran his fingertips down along the Droos' coils, then rested his hand in his own lap.

Thissizz quickly swallowed some tears. Being good was awful.

Although he had seen the master's famous optitube sagas and heard his recorded music at the Academy, Mikk had never seen Huud Maroc perform live. He did not know what to expect and was caught off guard because the master strode out alone, without any props or fanfare, stood downstage—and conjured a world out of thin air. Instead of a lone silver-haired man in saffron silk, Mikk saw a fortress of dark gray granite atop a mountain made entirely of crystallized salt on a world where the sun did not rise or set and the people never aged, had no children, and never died. The fortress imprisoned the Song of Time.

"We must never let it out," the people said. "If we do, everything will come to an end."

Only the mottled serpent, who could meet her own tail when she passed around the world, knew this was not true.

"Every end is a beginning," she said. In spite of the people's terrified protests, she wrapped her body around the salt mountain and shook it until the door to the fortress shivered off its fixtures and the Song rushed out over the world. The sun rose and set and the people began to age and die. However, they could now bear children, and they began to create things for them, new songs and new stories, that would outlast their mortality.

"The serpent was right," they said. "Life continues and has become more precious."

As for the serpent, when she heard the Song of Time, her great mottled back cracked open and a new serpent with golden skin emerged.

Mikk heard the amazing song, too, and could smell the serpent's blood as she shed her flesh as well as her skin and was reborn. It shocked him deeply when the tail thumpings and cries of the Droos broke the spell and he realized that none of what he had witnessed had actually happened. Everything, down to the sighs and groans of the salt crystal mountain as the serpent shook it, had been seduced from the audience's imagination by Huud Maroc's words and gestures—and nothing more. The master stood alone on stage as he had at the beginning and spread his arms to accept the Droos' praise.

Mikk tried to lose himself inside his oversized parka. What could this wonderful actor possibly see in a skinny, skittish, scrambled-up misfit?

A young female Droos now joined the master for a duet, and the richness and power of Huud Maroc's deep bass voice made it difficult for Mikk to believe he was not listening to a much younger man. The soprano Droos blushed a darker turquoise every time Huud Maroc rumbled his love lyrics into her ear hole.

I trust you, but I'm frightened! Mikk wanted to cry. Thank the gods Thissizz was there and he didn't have to be all alone with his fears. Thissizz wasn't like the boys back at the Academy. They would have made fun of his anxieties, especially his earlier distress before the mating Droos. Misfits weren't supposed to have feelings about such things. Many times, late at night, Mikk had wakened terrified that someone would see his vividly explicit dreams unreeling from his mind like gaudy, glittering ribbons and expose him before the entire school. Thissizz was different. He stood by Mikk and admitted he felt the pain, too.

Maybe it was because Thissizz was a Droos. Mikk didn't care. When the dark pink limbless eased up to him, Mikk stroked the coils in a much more expressive manner than the half-panicked, half-ecstatic clutching he had given Thissizz when he'd raced with him across the Great Cavern that morning. Mikk had liked the feel of the smooth, warm scales as the Droos moved and was far from satisfied after one short ride, but, for some reason, Thissizz had barely touched him since and the boy didn't dare initiate more than this small caress.

At intermission, Mikk reluctantly excused himself to go behind the heavy dark blue screens that sheltered "backstage." The master was in high humor.

"A fine evening, lad! What do you think so far?"

"The soprano was lovely. Who was she?"

"Gods, boy!" the master roared and cuffed him cheerfully on the arm, "what kind of roguish alter ego are you hiding in that skinny frame of yours?"

"You were good, too."

"You'll pay for this, boy," the master grinned and wagged his finger at him. "Now, let's work the chill out of those long legs."

They strolled into the relaxing crowd where the master greeted many of the Droos by name and introduced Mikk as his new apprentice. Mikk bowed respectfully but said little. He did not think it was his place, and his efforts to absorb the first part of the program had tired him. He was having trouble keeping names and faces straight, and rather than embarrass the master with a public mistake, he kept quiet. The Droos made up for it with their own chatter.

"A new apprentice?" said one large green male with pleasant crinkles around his round black eyes. "Why, Master Huud! We'd almost given up hope what with all this retirement talk, but an apprentice! This must mean a renaissance of some kind. Next thing you know, you'll be putting together a new troupe."

"Time could even run backwards," the master said.

The Droos laughed and cocked his head at Mikk.

"Study hard, young man," he said in excellent Vyzanian, "and trust the master. He's the best there is, but don't tell him I said so."

"I like him," Mikk said when the Droos had sashayed airily into the crowd. "Is he someone important?"

"He just thinks he is," the master chuckled. "But Sassnooriss is a good-hearted fellow all the same and a damned fine poet. When the Droos chorus sings after intermission, you'll get a taste of his work. Most of his pieces have been set to music."

Mikk tugged nervously on one of his untamed locks.

"Thissizz wants to sing for you," he whispered.

"I know."

"Is he good? I asked him to sing for me but he said he was saving up for you."

"Thissizz *saving up* something?" The master raised his thick eyebrows. "Now that's a new one. . . ."

Other Droos came up to visit the master, and Mikk's question went unanswered. Many of the limbless had children who swayed by their sides and stared curiously at the strange pup with the crimson hair.

"Are you a boy?" asked one, apparently confused by Mikk's clothing.

"Yes."

"May I see?"

"No! I mean, well . . . I'll catch cold."

"Ah! That would be unpleasant."

"Yes, it would."

"Couldn't you just warm up your blood?"

"No."

"I'm very sorry. I hope you get well soon."

All this attention made Mikk very anxious. He looked out over the crowd, hoping to find Thissizz, and noticed a knot of out-worlders at the end of the cavern. All of them wore camspecs strapped around their eyes so they resembled insectoids. One was having trouble with his reception and kept shaking his head, causing the antennae to bob wildly.

"Who are those people?" Mikk pointed.

"Press, boy," the master said. "Critics."

"Why aren't any of them Droos?"

"Droos don't believe in reviews, Mikk. They believe in word of mouth."

Mikk watched the outworld critics chat among themselves. The one with the faulty camspecs finally tore them off with a cry of disgust and banged them on the floor. Since he was a Kekoi, such a display was hardly unusual and, in this case, not particularly dangerous. The other critics laughed at him.

"Have you ever gotten a bad review, Master Huud?"

"Hundreds of them."

"Did they hurt?"

"Of course. But you get over it. Critics are just people, lad. They're entitled to their opinions. They're not the enemy."

"Who is the enemy?"

"Censors." Huud Maroc narrowed his eyes and lowered his voice. "Speak of the Beast . . ." He stepped away from Mikk and nodded in greeting to an outworld biped who waddled their way. Mikk had never seen such an enormously fat creature and assumed it was a hallucination of his overtaxed senses.

"Councilor Oplup," the master said politely, "it's good of you to come." He gently grasped Oplup's fleshy shoulder, as much to keep the Councilor at a distance, it seemed, as to welcome him, but the fat rocked and bobbed throughout Oplup's body as though he'd slapped it. Mikk gulped. The thing was real.

"Please. Join me for some refreshment," the master said.

"No, thank you," the lipoid Councilor said in gargly Vyzanian. "The Droos have invited me to a banquet this evening. Six courses. I must leave room for dessert."

Huud Maroc laughed softly but Mikk wanted to run away and take cover. It was the laughter of a canny predator deliberately withholding its claws.

"I understand," the master said coolly. "You always were Garpa's most devout gourmand."

Oplup did not seem aware of the malice in the master's words.

He gave him an oily, self-satisfied smile, and his tiny eyes all but disappeared in the fatty folds of his cheeks.

"Spare me the gratuitous compliments," he gurgled. "I want your opinion on this matter of the H'n N'kae tragedy cycles."

"The cycles are a wonderful contribution to galactic literature, Councilor. One of my apprentices was from H'n N'k."

"You don't find these works unseemly? I could never endure hour after hour of screaming, weeping insectoids." Oplup pressed his features together as though he'd bitten into something bitter. "Mother was right," he sniffed. "Never trust anyone who eats only sugars."

"But, don't the Banquet Texts advise something quite different?" Huud Maroc asked. " 'Be generous, oh feasters. Show mercy to those who consume but one food.' "

"Hm." Oplup thoughtfully stroked what would have been his chin if he'd had a neck. "Yes. Yes, indeed. Poor things. Well, I'll recommend we let them tour with their tragedies. It'd be a benevolent gesture, don't you think?"

"Very magnanimous," the master nodded. "I'm sure the H'n N'kae will appreciate it."

"Yes." The adiposal Councilor reeled back into the crowd. "They'll have to."

Once Oplup was safely out of sight, Huud Maroc's strained civility evaporated.

"Pond bilge!" he snarled. "That man wouldn't know good tragedy if it was enrobed in brown sauce and served with wheyapples."

"Who was he?" Mikk asked cautiously, unsure how angry the master really was. "He wasn't very pleasant."

"He's a Council Member and no, he isn't very pleasant. In fact, he's dangerous. It's just as well he ignored you, Mikk. You have to be very careful around Council Members."

"Why?"

The master glanced about and his wariness made Mikk nervous.

"Let's go backstage, lad. I need to change."

Since the local performers had gone out during the long intermission to mingle with friends, the backstage caverns were deserted except for a handful of technicians. The soundproofing panels sealed off the noise of the crowd, and, in the near silence, Mikk heard the muffled buzz from the glaring cosmetic mirrors.

Huud Maroc took Mikk to his inner dressing room, which, in spite of its high vault, nearly as lofty as the Great Cavern's, was difficult to maneuver in. It was so crammed with battered trunks and boxes that Mikk, thin as he was, wished he were even smaller.

"Back when the Galactic Association of Performing Artists was young," the master said, "it made a terrible mistake." He shoved aside a crate that was blocking an enormous rectangular closet: his travel wardrobe. "They relinquished the guild's administrative duties to a group of entrepreneurs, believing such people knew more about business than artists did, but these pirates promptly seized control of all the galactic performance charters."

The master slid open the panel of his wardrobe, briefly wrestling with it to force the much abused plank of blond merro wood past a sticky point, then stood before its tightly massed contents with his arms crossed. Mikk didn't know whether it was proper to stand or sit while the master meditated so he backed up against a vertical crate and tucked his hands inside the sleeves of his parka. The dressing room was very cold.

The master finally made his choice, grabbed the sleeve of a dark blue tunic, and wiggled it out of the overstuffed wardrobe and tossed it to Mikk. The boy fumbled a little, but caught it.

"It didn't take long for the Council, as they call themselves, to start dictating what performers can and cannot do." The master tugged impatiently on his knotted belt, swore under his breath, then worked it apart, wadded the silken strip into a ball, and pushed it into a corner of the wardrobe. "If you don't like what they say, you can quit the Association, but then you're stuck on your own world performing only for your own people."

The master removed his yellow tunic and Mikk crushed the blue one in his hands against his mouth. The master's broad back and chest were striped with long narrow scars as though he'd been whipped with wires, a dense, terrible cross-hatching of tiny ridges. The scars were old and as white as the rest of Huud Maroc's flesh, but Mikk's imagination filled them with blood and pain. Tears collected on his red lashes.

"I'm going to wear that tunic, Mikk. Please don't chew it."

"Master Huud!" Mikk breathed. "Did Councilor Oplup . . . ?"

The master gently pried the tunic from Mikk's fingers and shook it out. "Ev-Mobiks, Mikk," he said as he drew the tunic over his arms and belted it with a black cord he'd fished from one of the wide, loose sleeves. "Oplup is far too circumspect to do his own dirty work and, to this day, I can't swear he was the one who hired them. Still, I did catch him helping himself to a Belian cooperative's profits and then lampooned the situation on my tour. The Belians opened an investigation, after which they banished him to a penal colony for 150 years." The master shrugged. "Oplup's not a forgiving man, Mikk. He's been watching me closely ever since."

The master noticed Mikk's intense, but mute, consternation.

"Don't worry, lad," he smiled. "I'm too savvy to get caught and the Ev-Mobiks, well, they have their pride. They don't accept contracts to assault old men."

He took up a sponge from a basin sitting on a cluttered cosmetic table and offered it to Mikk. It smelled like fresh marsh lilies.

"Dab your eyes, boy. It's time to find your friend."

They went back into the great Cavern and Huud Maroc saw Thissizz at the same time Thissizz saw Mikk. The Droos grinned and hurried in and out of the piles of limbless to join them.

"Here he comes, Mikk, but before he gets here, I want to ask you something."

Mikk's already shadowy eyes turned black.

"Oh, no, lad! What did you think I was going to say?"

"I thought maybe you didn't want me to sit with him," the boy whispered.

"I don't care who you sit with, Mikk. It's certainly nothing to go dark over. How very odd! I wanted to find out if everything is still going well between you, but I guess it is."

"Oh, yes! Why wouldn't it?"

"I have no idea, but Oosmoosis seemed concerned. You know how fathers are."

"No, I don't," Mikk said simply. The master pursed his lips, but the boy had stated what, for him, was a plain fact. No bitterness clouded those slowly clearing lavender eyes.

"My mistake, lad. We'll talk about it later."

"Did the master scold you for something?" Thissizz asked when Mikk sat down with him for the second half. "You look unhappy."

"No," Mikk sighed, "it's nothing." He smiled at Thissizz. "Actually, it's nice to have someone worry about you, don't you think?" He leaned against his friend and the Droos reddened with pleasure.

"This has been such a long day." Mikk yawned. "My mind is swimming."

"Let it go," Thissizz said. The light globes dimmed. "I'll watch over you."

Mikk heard spirits singing from the waters in the There Beyond, calling to him as they swayed in the reeds, but it was only the Droos chorus and dancers moving before him on the platform stage, lulling him with their sinuous, rhythmic beauty.

"Please," he murmured.

"Mikk?"

"Please let me out. . . ."

"I don't understand. Let you out of what?"

But Mikk was asleep. Not even the pounding applause woke him. Thissizz stayed at his side until everyone else had gone to their burrows and the master came out and hefted the boy in his arms. The loss of the apprentice's weight against his coils triggered a startling pang of real grief, but he kept it to himself.

"You wanted to sing for me, Thissizz?"

"Yes, sir! Please!" The Droos was trembling.

"Shh! Calm yourself, you crazy pup!" the master chuckled. "Come out with Mikk tomorrow to the woods."

"Yes! Yes, thank you, Master Huud!"

"Good lad." The master hitched Mikk up more securely. "Huh! He's heavier than he looks. Go on home, Thissizz. Get some sleep."

"Good night, Master Huud!" The Droos slipped quickly away into the darkness and the master studied the sleeping boy.

"Tell me. What is going on in Oosmoosis' mind? The pup is crazy about you. He would have watched you all night."

Mikk, as expected, did not reply and the master carried him to a specially prepared burrow full of thistle floss. He pulled off the boy's boots and parka, scooped the fluff around him, and packed it in close.

"Sleep well, Mikk. We've barely begun."

Mikk was swimming in a dark pool full of invisible but friendly sea creatures who slithered in and out between his legs when a far-away voice called to him.

"Mikk! Wake up, boy."

It was completely black in the burrow except for a ball of gold light around a single chunk of phosphor-algae floating in a small bowl, a Droosian night light, but Mikk shook off the thick pile of floss and easily made out his master's form hunkered low at the burrow's entrance.

"Master Huud? Is something wrong?"

"Not at all, lad. Just keep your voice down and come with me. I want you to see something."

Mikk brushed off a few straggling bits of floss, dressed quickly, and crawled out of the burrow. The master tossed him some gloves.

"It's *freezing*!"

"That's Droos at night," said Huud Maroc. "But there's more to it. Follow me."

The master led Mikk along unfamiliar tunnels, up steep coil ramps, past scores of burrows full of warm, sleeping Droos piled on top of each other in casual promiscuity, to an opening that led to the frigid Droosian night.

"There," the master said as he stopped at the lip. "I know you've heard about this, but I doubt you've seen it except in still shots."

Outside, a few Belian night tapers on pikes illuminated the clearing between the burrows and the flower woods, but Huud Maroc and Mikk were the only ones there to watch the billions of tiny white flakes fall into the light and collect on the ground. The clearing was already thickly blanketed.

Mikk stared at the flakes, felt the chill in their passing, and gasped softly.

"It's snowing!" he breathed, overcome by the silent loveliness of the storm.

"It'll melt at dawn," the master said. "The Droos pups like to roll in it, but they must be too tired after the evening's excitement."

Mikk removed his glove, gathered up a handful of the cold, powdery crystals, and watched them dissolve and drop away.

"It's wonderful!" He put some in his mouth. "It tastes like metal . . . oh, it's wonderful!"

He couldn't resist and jumped into the unblemished carpet, where he ran about, slipping a little, made patterns with his footprints, and caught up more handfuls of the stuff and tossed them in the air. Huud Maroc, smiling cryptically to himself, followed at a more leisurely stroll as his young apprentice tore up the pristine powder.

"Of course," the master said slowly, "there's more you can do with snow than hop in it."

Mikk stopped and turned around in time for a soft lump of white to plop apart against his chest. Startled, he looked up at Huud Maroc. His master couldn't actually have thrown snow at him, could he?

"Expect the unexpected, Mikk," Huud Maroc grinned as he prepared another frosty missile. "Besides, I told you you'd pay, didn't I?"

Mikk rolled out of the way when the new ball zipped toward him and he got much more snow on himself than if he had let it hit him.

"As you can see, lad," the master laughed, "evasive action isn't always the best choice. Sometimes you have to confront a problem directly."

The master's laughter was no longer the dark, veiled thunder it had been for Oplup, and, emboldened by its mischievous music, Mikk quickly packed together his own snowball and fired it—but where was the master? He'd been standing right in front of him only a second ago.

"Then again," came a voice from behind, "some puzzles confound every attempt at resolution."

Mikk felt an icy splat on the back of his neck and he whirled about and flung another fistful of snow at the master, but it broke apart before it reached its target.

The master's mirth rang in the darkness and he skipped a high, quick jig, boots flying from drift to drift. Then he whistled and turned his back, daring the apprentice to try again. Mikk obliged, but this silver-haired theatrical veteran, a man old enough to be Mikk's grandfather, leaped over or dodged every salvo while all of the master's snowballs, most of which he snatched up in mid-flight, hit home. Mikk was soon covered in frost from crimson hair to outsized boots and Huud Maroc didn't have a single patch of broken ice anywhere on him.

However, Mikk found himself incapable of being upset by his defeat. He was transfixed by the master's impossible athleticism as he capered nimbly over the snow without leaving the faintest trace of a footprint.

"How do you do that?" Mikk whispered then, unexpectedly, broke into giggles. Huud Maroc stopped dancing.

"What is it, boy?" he asked, blue-purple eyes glittering. "Give up yet?"

Mikk laughed even harder.

"You're a mess, Mikk, and you're shivering. We'd better go in."

He turned and started up the slope to the dark mouth in the carved rock.

"Master Huud?"

The master looked over his shoulder and a clump of icy bits smacked into his ear. As the crystals slowly dropped away, leaving a plug of frost in his earring, the master stared steadily at the silent, deadpan boy—then grinned.

"I underestimated you, lad." He held out his gloved hand and Mikk clasped it. "I definitely need to rethink this. . . ."

However, once they had changed out of their wet things, Huud Maroc's amused admiration faded.

"You're still shivering, boy."

"I'll be all right, I think." Mikk rubbed his numb, ice-cold nose. "I just have to get back in the floss."

"I will not tolerate your getting ill," the master growled. "I intend to start teaching you how to sing, *really* sing, tomorrow."

"Yes, Master Huud."

The master considered a moment then took Mikk by the shoulders and propelled him down the tunnel. "Forget the floss, Mikk, I want you warm *now*." He steered the boy into a large burrow full of sleeping juvenile Droos of all ages. "Here. Scramble up inside their coils. You'll be fine."

"But won't I wake them?" Mikk asked, suddenly awkward before the great hot mass of Droos flesh slumbering in the shadows. His heart began to beat rapidly.

"No. Droos pups can sleep through anything. Go on."

"But I'm not a Droos."

"Do you think they care? You're making me impatient. Get in there and warm up or I'll warm you myself, if you know what I mean."

Mikk immediately dived into the living mound of coils, arranged them about himself until he thought he would suffocate from the heat, and peeked out at Huud Maroc.

"Good," the master said. "Warm now?"

"Yes."

"Fine. Go to sleep. I asked Thissizz to join us tomorrow. You can learn something from him."

Mikk grinned through the gap in his coil cocoon.

"Yes, Master Huud."

When the master was gone, Mikk wriggled down deeper into the mass of coils. He couldn't believe how marvelous this heavy, slick, but soft mountain felt against his cold body. Although there was little air, Mikk felt cozier and safer than he ever had in his life. His heart quieted and he fell asleep almost instantly.

Chapter Six: The Singing Lesson

The muffled giggling woke Mikk not long after the sudden bright dawn melted the night snow. He opened his eyes and saw he was surrounded by a swaying circle of Droos pups who nudged each other teasingly. However, when Mikk tried to get up, he couldn't. He was bound in the coils of the last Droos of the stack, Thissizz, and the pup was snoring.

When did Thissizz come? Mikk wondered in a flash of embarrassed heat. Was he here all along? Did the master know?

Mikk gently poked the Droos. There was no response and the giggling grew louder.

"Thissizz," he whispered, "wake up, please."

The pup mumbled something, but otherwise didn't stir, and it dawned on Mikk he didn't really want to escape Thissizz's embrace.

Why don't the others go away and leave us alone? he thought.

"*Please* get up, Thissizz. They're looking at us."

"He hear not you if so speak soft," one of the older pink adolescents said in broken Vyzanian. "Shout you must. Kick give."

Mikk tried to kick, but Thissizz's coils were too tight. The boy dropped his head back, panting, and he heard that sweet snicker he had first encountered from the lips of Thissizz's sister. He closed his eyes, took a deep breath, and, hoping to find the actor's projection that had shocked everyone back in the Academy's banquet hall, shouted:

"Thissizz, get up!"

The pup bolted straight into the air and all his coils unwound at once so that Mikk spun across the floor and crashed into the circle of juvenile Droos who toppled over on top of him. Thissizz, in a crumpled heap on the other side of the burrow, looked dazedly about with his enormous black eyes and saw Mikk's foot sticking out of the pile of fallen pups.

"Oh! There you are. Is it morning already?"

A searching hand popped out of the coils, felt about for something to grip, caught hold of the folds of one of the pups' hoods, and pulled. Mikk's disheveled red mop appeared above the tangled bodies.

"Yes!" he gasped.

"Wonderful how happy! We today are to sing!"

Mikk groaned and sank back under the coils.

In the shadow of a massive tree flower that mottled the ground with cool blues and muted scarlet, Huud Maroc began the serious instruction of Mikk's voice by asking Thissizz to sing first. "Consider this your audition, lad. Don't hold back."

The Droos flushed hotly, but straightened up, licked his long lips, and began an aria from a much-performed tragic opera.

The piece was a bit ponderous for the young Droos' voice, but he sang it with feeling and Mikk's eyes darkened in dismay. His friend's voice was lovely, sweet and warm with excellent control and a marvelous half-echoing quality. It reached into the most intimate corners of Mikk's sensitive hearing and caressed those places once scraped and hammered by Ranya's shrieks.

The apprentice shuffled his feet, clenched his hands in his pockets, and kept his gaze on the steamy purple depths of the flower forest. He wanted to melt into the ground and disappear.

When Thissizz ended his song, Mikk glanced anxiously at the master, who seemed to be pondering a puzzle of deep significance.

"Hum," Huud Maroc rumbled low in his chest, almost a song itself. "Well sung, Thissizz, but I will be candid. There are many singers who, at their peak, sing no better than you do now, but *you* have only started."

Thissizz's face fell. "Master Huud? I don't understand."

"If I took you on tour now, you would do quite well, but it would shortchange your potential. You're not destined to be a *good* singer, lad. With more training, and patience, you will be a *great* singer." The master gave the Droos a friendly stroke on the nose. "You would prefer that, wouldn't you? Wait and be wonderful rather than go and be average?"

Thissizz looked sadly at Mikk and sighed. "I guess so." He aimlessly flipped the tip of his coils.

"Take heart, Thissizz. Time just seems slow because you're young." The master turned to Mikk and his expression toughened into gruffness. "What's the matter, boy? You look gray."

"I, well . . ."

"Out with it, lad." The master put his fists on his hips.

"I liked Thissizz's song very much. It was pretty and, um . . ."

"Yes?"

"I don't sing as well."

"No. You're not trained. That's what we're starting today. Do you have a problem with that?"

"Oh, no, Master Huud! I *want* to sing, but . . ." His lip trembled.

"I see." The master rocked on his heels and contemplated the canopy before continuing in a very deliberate tone. "Listen, Mikk, your voice will never be like Thissizz's because it is *your* voice. Few things anger me more than this kind of needless, destructive comparison." His eyes leveled on the quaking boy. "I will tell you only once. Sing for me now or abandon the idea for good. I will not wait."

This isn't fair! Mikk thought. The master already knew what he sounded like, but Thissizz didn't. This was not the same as singing for an unknown creature in the woods. If Thissizz heard how weak and rough his voice was, he might be ashamed of him and not want to see him anymore. Their friendship, less than a day old, might crumble.

Mikk was about to stall by rubbing his ankle with his toe when he felt something smooth slide over his foot—the sensation raised gooseflesh. He glanced down. Thissizz had curled the tip of his coils around his ankle. The master did not seem to have noticed; he was still rocking on his heels, waiting.

No one had ever touched Mikk with such extraordinary tenderness, and the glistening, liquid swoon of his dream, the slick warmth of the phantom Droos gliding along his skin, flooded his senses. Mikk hadn't had an ordinary dream at all. He'd had a premonition—his first—and he trembled. The older boys at the Academy used to whisper in secret corners about their first premonitions, the thrill and fear, the proud grief to know they had left their childhoods and entered the "between time," but none of them ever boasted of the elusive dream premonition and none of their visions had been vaguely accurate. Not like this. Something amazing lived in Thissizz's touch, as if it weren't a physical thing at all but the light of an idea, something the senses were too gross to contemplate.

Mikk teetered on the brink of ecstasy, but the master was present and watching him closely, so, rather than throw his arms around Thissizz and kiss him, he sang.

Thissizz tightened his grip on Mikk's ankle. Papa could eat grass. This pup with the vulnerable, but true, voice was his friend and he would touch him and he would play with him and he would be the boy's hero if Mikk could not defend himself. However, the longer he held Mikk's ankle, the more convinced he became of the sturdiness of those slender bones, and the longer he listened to Mikk sing, the more clearly he heard the strange, underlying vibration in the boy's voice, like a bell muffled behind a wall. It hinted at considerable untapped vocal power.

This is better than I hoped, Thissizz thought. Much better!

"You survived after all, didn't you, lad?" the master smiled when Mikk concluded his song. "Now we know what we need to work on. Ideas, Thissizz?"

The Droos, who was still basking in the attractive qualities of his friend, jumped and reddened, then, surprisingly, answered in Vyzanian.

"I, perhaps, think, Mikk needs bring his voice up the bottom from?"

"Not bad," the master chuckled. " 'Bring his voice up the bottom from.' All that complex nonsense from so-called 'masters' and here we have the truth in the broken grammar of an adolescent Droos. Very good, Thissizz."

Thissizz quickly looked at the ground, his face and half his body almost purple with embarrassment.

"Why don't you sing with Mikk this time? Show him what you mean."

Mikk had no more trouble that day bringing himself to sing. In fact, the master had to remind him repeatedly not to force his voice.

"Coax it slowly," he said. "We don't want to strain it."

The friends tried several duets and kept breaking into giggle fits that Huud Maroc pretended not to find very funny at all, but he had accomplished all he intended that day. He had forced a small wedge into his apprentice's fear of performing for others.

However, the coil around the ankle, which the master *hud* noticed, concerned him. It was a remarkably elegant gesture considering the Droos pup was in the throes of a severe and unsubtle adolescence. At one point, Thissizz even burst into tears for no other reason, apparently, than that his nerves were overstimulated. Remarkably, one pass of Mikk's hands over the pup's semi-feverish body calmed Thissizz instantly.

Also, for the balance of the lesson, Mikk spoke Droos and Thissizz spoke Vyzanian. It seemed an unconscious decision on the part of the young friends, and neither of them seemed to care that Mikk's Droos was already vastly superior to Thissizz's Vyzanian. They chattered away with happy, even exuberant, animation.

The master's fingers began to ache and, in spite of the heat of the Droosian day, he shivered. All along he had assumed the gods were amusing themselves by repeating history, and encouraging this friendship had warmed his nostalgia. Besides, Mikk certainly needed affection and Thissizz was more than eager to provide it. However, the master began to wonder if he had misread this closeness. It had a more obscure, more penetrating side he could not readily identify. He didn't recall anything similar between himself and Oosmoosis.

Something is happening to them, he thought, something serious.

He observed the boy and the Droos from the corner of his eye as they whispered together and tried to hide their snickering from his stern attention.

Oosmoosis senses it too, I'm sure of it. That's why he came to me.

The master sighed and massaged his hands. He would have to monitor this relationship more closely after all.

"When you lads are quite finished," he said, "we'll try those harmonic scales again."

Chapter Seven: The Abandoned Burrows

Mikk had been on Droos one hundred days when Thissizz took him into the flower forest to show him yet another of his "most favorite places in all the world."

"You have a great many favorite places," Mikk teased. His Droos was fluent now and well modulated. He did not whisper when he was alone with Thissizz. "Where are we going this time?"

"The Rainbow Ravine. It's very beautiful. You can see all kinds of colors in the stone."

"Like the Great Cavern?"

"Even nicer. Sunlight breaks up better in the quartz than inside light does."

The deeper the friends ventured into the wood, the thicker and more tangled the undergrowth became. The air was heavy with the hiss and chitter of insects. Mikk jumped down from a vine five times thicker than he was himself.

"Did the master say how long it would take to train you?" Thissizz asked.

"No. 'It'll take as long as it takes,' he says, but I'm not sure he'll be able to train me at all." Mikk pretended to study a gold and green striped multipede rippling along the trunk of a fallen flower.

"I'm a little afraid of him, Thissizz," he said softly. "He's . . . he's like a mountain."

"Don't be silly, Mikk!" Thissizz nosed his way through a thicket full of tiny orange blossoms and his face got covered with pollen. Mikk brushed it off for him. "The master can do anything he wants and he's not that scary. Everybody talks about how strict and impatient he is, but papa says he's the most kind-hearted man he's ever met. You just have to look deeper."

"I hope that's true. I want to please him. It worries me very much." He pulled down a branch and peered ahead.

"Oh! Look at that!"

"Is it the ravine?"

"No. They look like burrows."

Thissizz stuck his head through the hole in the foliage. "It must be part of the old city. Those burrows haven't been used in thousands of years."

"Are they like the burrows you live in now?"

"I don't know."

They pushed out of the brush into the sunny, weedy clearing before the row of rounded caverns. The dark mouths gaped stark and lonely in the bleached stone of the outer walls.

"They look small but deep," Thissizz said. "Come on. Let's explore one."

"Is it safe?"

Thissizz nudged the stone and slapped it with the tip of his coils.

"It seems to be."

Mikk followed Thissizz into the first cavern.

Although both friends could see in the dark, Mikk because of his sensory anomaly, Thissizz because he was a Droos, there wasn't much to see. The caverns were empty, no discarded personal belongings at all, and tiny white spiders had choked up the spaces with ragged, dusty webs that clung to Mikk's hands as he cleared the way.

"What a mess!" He shook the matted spider silk from his fingers. "It smells like dead birds in here."

"The carvings aren't very interesting either."

"Maybe it's better over here." Mikk headed for an inconspicuous side burrow and, after blowing away some webbing, ducked inside.

"I doubt it," Thissizz said, not following. He was trying to remove some of the silk from his brow with his tongue. "That looks like a squat hole."

"A what?"

"A burrow for squatting. You know, a latrine."

He heard Mikk laughing.

"Is that what you call them? How do you squat when you don't have any legs?"

The unusual vibration under Mikk's voice was also present in his laugh, and suddenly a chunk of the wall above the ancient little burrow collapsed and fell in front of the entrance, blocking it completely.

"Mikk!" Thissizz scrambled over the debris. "Mikk!"

No response. Either the rubble was too thick or Mikk couldn't answer, and Thissizz panicked. He tore at the pile of rocks with his nose, flinging them aside with the frenzy of a burrowing Spairan dryax trying to escape a raptor. The flesh above his lips ripped and bled but he flailed away until he broke through.

"Oh, dear . . . oh, dear!"

Mikk had curled up into a ball and was shuddering violently, eyes staring blindly at the walls. When Thissizz touched him, he cringed and pulled in tighter.

"Mikk . . . Mikk, it's me."

Mikk looked up, eyes black with terror, but did not seem to recognize his friend.

"Come on!" Thissizz nudged Mikk again with his bloody nostrils. "We have to get out. The walls are brittle."

Mikk still didn't seem to know who was talking to him so Thissizz wrapped his coils tightly around the boy's waist and carried him out. Mikk never said a word.

However, once he was back in the sunlight, the apprentice came to himself and broke into such heartrending sobs that the Droos kissed the boy over and over in an effort to console him and left behind smears of rust-colored blood.

"It's all right. We're safe now. Oh, Mikk! I'm so sorry."

"It's something I can't *remember*!" the boy cried. "Something about a basket . . ."

"Please don't be upset, Mikk. If it was bad, maybe it's lucky you forgot."

"You don't understand!" Mikk twisted and convulsed in his friend's coils as his distress escalated into hysteria. "*Vyza-nians don't forget things!* Why can't I see it? What's the matter with me?"

"But we're *safe*, Mikk." Thissizz kissed the struggling boy again. "We're outside, see? And there's the ravine. I knew it was over here somewhere." He carried Mikk to a grassy ledge where they could look at the rich geologic layers of the quartz and ore Rainbow Ravine. The bands of green, red, yellow, and blue undulated brightly in the morning sun and some diving kites skreed and circled in the updrafts that rose from the tear in the world's crust.

"Isn't it beautiful?" Thissizz asked. "Look how the sunlight sparkles on the yellow."

After a few more feeble kicks, Mikk finally calmed down and wiped his eyes.

"Your poor nose," he said and moved his fingers around the wounds on Thissizz's lips and nostrils.

"I'll heal. Here. Let me lick some of that mess off your face."

Mikk held still while the Droos' soft blue tongue sponged away the dust and blood.

"I don't understand," he said. "Why can't I be like everyone else?"

"I don't want you to be like everyone else. I want you to be the way you are."

Mikk soberly studied the large wedge-shaped reptilian head hovering solicitously over him.

"I've never had a friend like you, Thissizz," he murmured. "I want to stay here forever." He embraced the young Droos and rubbed his cheek against his scales.

"I want you to stay, too," Thissizz whispered. "You're a wonderful pup."

When they tried to sneak into the bathing springs without being seen, they failed.

"Don't move, you two," Huud Maroc growled slowly. The friends froze. Thissizz feigned nonchalance, very poorly considering he had blood all over his nose. Mikk was wide-eyed with alarm but did not flinch when Huud Maroc grabbed his chin and burned him with his angry eyes. Strangely, the moment the master touched him, all of his anxiety drained away and Mikk felt calm, as though watching his teacher from a great distance. It wasn't important anymore. The master could ask his questions—what happened? why didn't you tell me where you were going?—and they would barely ripple on his ears. All that mattered was shielding Thissizz from the master's wrath.

But the expected questions did not come. Huud Maroc gently turned Mikk's head with his hand and inspected the boy's face closely before letting him go. He glanced at the waiting Droos.

"Go clean up, Thissizz. I need to speak with Mikk alone."

Thissizz hesitated, opened and closed his mouth a few times, fidgeted, hissed a little, but, in the end, turned abruptly away and rushed down the dark tunnel, his hood pinched in tightly along his spine.

In the stillness of the cavernous shadows, a single drip, drip echoed faintly somewhere deep in the fissures of the wall, grating the nerves of the already anxious master as he pondered his silent apprentice. The boy was looking directly at him, but he doubted it was a show of bravery. More likely Mikk had slipped into stoic fatalism, but that was the least of Huud Maroc's worries. He clasped his hands behind his back, the better to hide their spasms as the premonitory shocks beat through them in waves.

"Are you still sleeping with the Droos pups?" he asked mildly. "You realize that will come to an end when we leave for Belia."

The pigment in Mikk's eyes fluttered but stabilized quickly. An act of will. Huud Maroc nearly had to crush his knuckles to keep his hands still.

"Why can't we stay on Droos?" Mikk whispered. "You could train me here."

"All my apprentices begin with private study on Belia, lad. I told you that."

Actually, he'd told him the chalet was the best place *for* private study, which he knew Mikk needed, but if the boy thought all apprentices required a period of isolated tutelage on Belia, the hard gleam settling into his pale stare might dissolve.

It didn't.

"I want to stay here."

"I understand, lad. I like Droos, too." Gods' fire! Any more of this pain and I'll howl, the master thought. "But I don't think it's up to you to—"

"I can't leave."

Mikk had never interrupted the master before and Huud Maroc briefly lost his preoccupation with his unhappy fingers. "Oh? Why not?"

Mikk licked his lips nervously as he sometimes did when he needed salt and his eyes at last inked over. "Because . . . because . . . Master Huud, please! My heart hurts!" He grabbed the master's sleeve and twisted it. "Please don't take me away from Thissizz!"

Huud Maroc blessed the centuries of dramatic training that enabled him to conceal his reaction to the nightmarish psychic vision that overtook him at these words: the desperate young apprentice cutting off his own limbs to be "more like a Droos." Thissizz attempting to swallow the mutilated boy so he could "have Mikk with him forever." Both friends dying in hideous agony.

Impossible! Huud Maroc thought. This kind of relationship occurs once a generation if at all! There isn't even a Vyzanian word for it.

Infatuation he had expected, even love, but how sweet and simple those long ago nights with Oosmoosis seemed in comparison! Nothing in any language, on any world . . .

They're too young. They aren't strong enough to control what's happening and it will devour their personalities before they even know who they are.

The relationship was fated—he couldn't change that—but he could postpone its force until they were ready. Unfortunately, that meant betraying the boy's trust. He'd sworn he wasn't cruel.

The master placed his sore hands on Mikk's narrow shoulders and steeled himself.

"I am going to make you a performance master because, in your deepest soul, that is what you want." He drew a heavy breath. "We cannot wait, Mikk. We're leaving."

Councilor Oplup, who had lingered on Droos, ostensibly to "take in the scenery and the local cuisine," wanted an explanation.

"This is an unusually abbreviated tour for you, isn't it?" He frowned at the glowing Belian shuttle waiting at the edge of the clearing outside the Great Cavern. Evening was creeping across the grass and the flower forest had already begun to sigh and snap as the petals folded up their banners of bright, broken colors.

"I'm not sure I understand you, Councilor," Huud Maroc replied. "Two hundred performances in one hundred days is hardly an abbreviated run."

"But why Belia?" Oplup pressed. "I contacted the Association. You have no bookings there."

"And you have no visa there. Now, if you'll excuse me . . ."

Oosmoosis deserved an explanation, but declined to hear it.

"You don't need to justify your decision to me. You fulfilled your contract."

"Not the unspoken one. I usually extend my stay."

"I know." Oosmoosis pulled one of Nessiri's curious pups back from the shuttle ramp with his coils. "You will return."

"Your son . . . He's very upset."

"Yes," Oosmoosis nodded, "but he will live. We're a resilient people."

The master ran his thumb along Oosmoosis' golden hood. "This isn't easy for me, my friend. I may be gone a long time."

"It doesn't matter. You will return."

Mikk, in a state of shock since the master's decision, slowly sagged into despair as the final box of personal belongings was lifted into the shuttle. He looked forlornly at the dark pink Droos at his side and Thissizz whipped the tip of his coils around the boy's ankle.

"No! Go don't! You miss!" The Droos dissolved into tears.

Mikk embraced his friend and carefully worked his ankle free.

"I'll miss you, too." His hoarse whisper was barely audible.

Thissizz rested his head on Mikk's shoulder and shook. Huud Maroc was embarrassed. He'd seen plenty of violent mood swings from adolescent Droos, but he'd never seen a young male weep this piteously.

"Now, lad, it's not the end of everything. We'll come back."

Thissizz's flooded eyes turned to Mikk for confirmation.

"I promise," the apprentice said. "I'll telewave you, too. I like to write."

He embraced Thissizz again and gently, with shy stealth, placed a kiss on the Droos' throat skin just at the crease below the jaw. Thissizz's already flushed body heated dramatically.

"Good-bye," Mikk murmured. When he let go, the sudden chill made him shiver. "G-good-b-bye!"

The apprentice could not control his grief any longer. He ran up the ramp into the shuttle, folded himself under a pod in the back, and sobbed.

"Thissizz," Huud Maroc said, "you have a fine voice and will do well, but I have to help Mikk now. Everything he has has been shut away in the wrong burrows. Do you understand?"

Thissizz nodded and his tongue flicked up around his eyes to mop away some of his tears.

"Take care of your sister. The first brood is always the most difficult."

Huud Maroc ascended into the belly of the small vessel, the ramp withdrew, and with a high whistle the shuttle eased out over the clearing before lifting itself into the purple clouds of early evening. Thissizz watched until the oval ring of green and yellow lights disappeared, then curled his body around and undulated back to the burrows to find Nessiri. She'd taken the babies inside and he wanted to play with them. It would soothe the pain.

Mikk didn't have any Droos infants to dandle. He stared out the diamond-shaped window as the broad curve of the large world gradually took shape. Then, just as he could see the entire globe through the polyglass, the Belian wave reactor kicked in and Droos vanished, replaced by ionic streak flashes, the unexplained by-product of "outrunning" light.

"Mikk?"

The apprentice looked up, and the master tossed him a new gold ball.

"Try two."

Entr'acte: Kekoi Kaery: The Coney

Mikk knew two of the approaching Kekoi guards. One was Raf the bailiff, a rangy gray penal veteran with tufted ears who wore a battered tan tunic and loose blue trousers stuffed into muddy black boots. Raf was bow-legged and off-kilter, one shoulder noticeably higher than the other, but his black eyes were keen and intelligent, his sharp nose always aquiver, and the other guards bowed to his authority. Mikk liked him.

The second was Korl, Raf's sandy-furred sergeant, a soft-bellied middle-aged male who didn't say much but laughed with little adenoidal snorts at all of his superior's witticisms even if he often had to ask afterward what they meant. Mikk didn't think Korl was stupid, since Raf trusted him with the bulk of the day's watch. "Uncomplicated" was a better word.

The third Kekoi, a huge black male, Mikk did not recognize. He had to be one of the security dogs since he exhibited the familiar swaggering gait and arrogant grin, but he looked unusually young. In spite of his more than adult muscular bulk, the fur around his neck and shoulders was still short, not the full ruff of the mature male, and his boots were new. He was picking his immaculate canines with a sliver of antelope bone.

"Quit gawking about, Fod," Raf said to the newcomer, "we're late already." Raf scowled at the damp walls of the corridor and his mobile nose pad twitched faster.

"It's colder than the Beast's prick in here," he said and Korl snorted softly. "I don't know what that Belian thinks he's doing, but he isn't fixing the heat unit. First thing after your shift, Korl, track that little blue shit down and bring him to me so I can chew on his toes. See if that doesn't motivate him."

They reached the energy gate and Fod flicked his toothpick into the grid. The bone chip incinerated with a small fizzle, and Bipti, who hovered deferentially in the shadows, winced.

"For the love of—! Beast, Fod!" Raf cried.

"What!?" The big youth's shoulders lifted massively.

"This isn't your mama's kitchen char-wave! Stop playing around." Raf looked at Bipti. "Get lost, Freen."

The night guard scooted around the Kekoi and pattered off. Raf gave the performance master a crooked smile and flipped open the wall panel next to the energy gate.

"I'll bet you've been looking forward to this," he said.

"I see you brought reinforcements."

"Hey!" Fod cried. "He speaks Kekoi!"

"Of course he does, puppy. He's Master Mikk, not some two-copper street jester."

The silent pattern of blue radiation vanished and Fod marched up to Mikk to frisk him, but the performance master, in no mood to be pawed over, snarled darkly. Fod, unused to resistance, balked.

"Do you think I would carry anything dangerous in pockets intended for *children*?" Mikk snapped. "This is my surprise tunic!"

Korl chortled and his loose gut danced about over his belt. Raf, less amused, covered his eyes with his furry hand.

"Well, Beast," Fod pouted, "he could have *made* a weapon, you know."

"I have other ways of defending myself," Mikk said quietly, and Fod, still stinging from the other guards' amusement, bared his fangs.

"Like what? Are you going to dance on my face?"

Mikk put his own face close to the Kekoi's and treated him to a fully inked forced startle. Fod recoiled, ears flattened.

"Whelp," Mikk said frostily.

"Give it up, Fod," Raf said. "Hand me the cuffs."

The young guard pulled an ordinary set of wrist shackles out of the leather purse slung over his shoulder. Korl went down the corridor to give his renewed and noisy mirth more room.

"*Now* what's wrong?" the flustered Fod whined.

Raf quietly took the manacles from Fod and snapped them

securely around Mikk's wrists. The performance master arched a crimson eyebrow.

"Go ahead," Raf sighed, and with a short twist and a sudden tug Mikk sprung the handcuffs. They clattered to the floor.

"He's a magician, too," Raf explained to the wide-eyed Fod. "We can't use conventional cuffs. Fetch a loop."

Fod loped heavily into the shadows and Raf shook his head.

"What can I say? Fod's a rookie."

"I understand."

"I'm sorry about the cold. If it were up to me, I'd move you to the detention hostel, it's much drier and warmer, but the Council thinks security is better here." Raf's eyes locked onto Mikk's lavender ones. "You would try to escape, wouldn't you?"

Mikk looked away without answering.

"I was shocked when I found out. They must have threatened him somehow. Thissizz would never willingly be a tribune." Raf grasped Mikk's sleeve and gently tightened his claws. "It's a travesty start to finish," he continued in a heated whisper. "Such a thing on Kekoi Kaery, the freest world in the galaxy! Do you realize you're the first 'guest' in this jail for 165 years? It's reserved for state criminals, but we don't have any. Not one! You shouldn't be here either." His claws pierced the silk.

Mikk moaned softly and licked his lips.

"I need salt."

Raf quickly dropped something into one of the surprise tunic's pockets.

"What's that?"

"Caviar."

"*Terran* caviar? On Kekoi Kaery?"

"Shh! Fod's coming back."

So was Korl. He seemed fascinated by the elegant figure eight of keranium twirling on the younger Kekoi's finger and the tiny luminescent key hanging from a cord around Fod's thick neck.

"It's very simple," Raf said, supposedly for Fod's benefit, as the rookie handed him both the loop and the key, but Korl watched, too, mouth slack, the tip of his tongue sticking out.

"There's an antiwave pellet embedded in the crossing of the

loop. You take the key—it's the light that does it—and pass it over the crossing to uncouple the pellet's magnetic field."

The loop broke into two pieces.

"Feed the halves around like this . . ."

He sandwiched Mikk's white wrists between the keranium.

". . . pass the key back over the other way, and, there, it's locked." Raf hung the key about his own gray ruff. "Now it's as solid as a single piece of keranium and we all know nothing can break keranium."

Two pieces into one, Mikk thought as he gazed sadly at his pinioned hands. It was never supposed to mean confinement.

The guards led him along the corridor to the spiral stair that wormed down through the wall to the windowless passage under the jail, under the courthouse—under the world. The tunnels on Droos were always full of movement, life, and light, no matter how deep they went. Not like this slate-colored intestine.

Mikk looked up. They had stopped at the point the tunnel tipped up and met a stairway to a side door in the courtroom.

"Wait here," Raf said. "I'll find out if the High Tribune is ready." He sprinted up the steps. Fod got out a new toothpick and Korl began to play with his collar laces.

Where Mikk stood, there actually was a "window" in the tunnel: a small grate at eye level set flush with the flagstones outside. Through the grate, Mikk saw one last vendor barely an arm's length away, an especially scrawny, dun female Kekoi of indeterminate age hunkered over a small, rough wooden box. Something inside the box scratched frantically.

"Painted coney!" the Kekoi cried. Mikk's sensitive ears detected the wet flutter of consumption in her lungs. "Painted coney! Last one! Best for mixed grill or stewed in gon!"

Painted coney? Mikk thought. That box isn't big enough for a painted coney.

A young Kekoi dressed in a tight yellow jerkin and full quilted breeches, and sporting a clipped ruff and curled chin fur, strolled up to the vendor and eyed her skeptically. His quivering nostrils and slightly ruffled lip made clear that the gypsy offended his senses.

"Coney? Really?"

The vendor thrust her hand under the lid and pulled out the

black, white, and russet striped rodent by its ears. It kicked feebly with its long hind feet and its wall-eyes rolled back into its head.

It's only a kit! Mikk was horrified. How can she get away with selling an undersized baby?

The vendor shook the animal and it squeaked.

"Full of life, ain't it?" she asked.

"Pretty small, though."

"It'll be very tender, sir."

The young male tapped a finger against his canines, shrugged, pulled a coin from his hip pouch, and held it out to her. Consumptive or not, the gypsy snatched at the coin with remarkable alacrity, but her customer was faster and whisked it out of reach.

"Kill it for me first, will you?" he said with a leer. "I don't want to spoil my gloves."

The vendor promptly wrung the kit's head off and let it drop. It bounced twice and rolled gruesomely to the grate, where it bumped to a stop. She held the carcass up to the young male, who recoiled.

"You horrid bitch!" he cried. "Why didn't you just break its neck? Get that bloody mess away from me!"

The vendor flung the body aside.

"My! We're picky, aren't we?" she sneered. "Took me three hours to dig that coney out of its burrow and now Mr. Won't-Dirty-His-Claws doesn't want it! Well!"

The gypsy suddenly cocked her head. Mikk had heard it, too. More scratching from inside the box.

"What the—?" The vendor lifted the lid and her rheumy eyes widened in astonishment. She pulled a second coney out of the box, a kit so like the first it could have been its twin, even a clone.

"Isn't that the queerest thing? I was sure that was my last one." She scratched her matted cheek fur. "Ah, Beast. You want this one instead?"

Mikk decided he'd had enough killing for one morning. Throwing the sound so the vendor's ears, and no one else's, would hear it, he pressed his tongue against his teeth and released a series of clipped hisses, the final warning of a Kekoi pit viper. The vendor shrieked, jumped up, and, coughing desperately, batted her broadcloth skirts with her fists and stamped her feet. The coney plopped onto the flags where, momentarily disoriented, it froze, legs splayed in all directions.

"You're crazy, you know that?" Her young customer quickly retreated. "Crazy!"

The vendor's pounding boot heels edged wildly close to the stunned coney and Mikk closed his eyes. Any second and the creature's tender body would be mashed to a furry pink mulch.

Merciful divinity, please! I've already enough to atone for.

The stamping suddenly ceased. All the performance master could hear was the consumptive Kekoi vendor's labored wheezing. He opened his eyes. The coney was gone.

Mikk checked the guards. Fod had wandered into the shadows to piss and Korl was deeply absorbed in untangling the snarl he'd made of his collar laces.

No guarantees, are there? Mikk thought. *The coney got away today, but a raptor could find him tomorrow.*

He lifted the tin of caviar from his surprise tunic and smiled. Beluga. He opened it and with a deft swipe of the tongue a dollop of the salty black roe slid down his throat.

Every cell in his body cheered.

Part Two: Apprentice

[C.Y.S. XII: 710–810]

Chapter Eight: Maya

Mikk was ill the entire trip from Droos. Unable to eat, barely able to sleep, the boy was still shaky when the shuttle lifted off the hill and left him and Master Huud ankle deep in blue-green moss before the carved wooden beams and bevelled oval windows of the four-story chalet in the mountainous eastern continent of Belia. Below the hill, mist enshrouded all but the tallest conifers of the steep valley and obscured the village completely.

"My home away from home," the master smiled. He handed Mikk a salt stick, which the apprentice sucked on nervously. "What do you think?"

Mikk shrugged. In spite of the genial, bright afternoon, his teeth chattered.

"Come on, lad. Let's see if Mapa has fired up the oven. Don't worry about her daughter Maya. She's rude to everyone, even me, but she's a hard worker and gods forbid I send Mapa's littlest baby packing!"

When they stepped into the front hall, a highly polished wooden room with a huge Ti-tokan maze rug on the floor and glass mosaics in half of the long elliptical windows that lined the far wall, Mikk heard a quick slapping patter and suddenly Mapa, Huud Maroc's housekeeper, charged into the room. With a shrill, delighted squeal, she flung herself at the master and wrapped her tentacles around his chest.

"Beast in a burnoose, woman!" Huud Maroc roared, his laughter rattling the windows. "Show a little decorum!"

Mapa was a Werevan cephalopod, a petite eight-legged, six-eyed creature with slick gray-green skin and a small, flexible, beak-shaped mouth. Behind her, just entering the room, came her darker, less enthusiastic daughter, Maya. While her mother shrieked excitedly in Huud Maroc's arms and fussed with his tunic collar, Maya glared balefully at the uncertain young boy with the deep red locks.

"All right now," the master said as he finally extricated himself from Mapa's tenacious grip. "Why don't you put together something for us in the kitchen, my dear? We're very hungry."

Mapa cheerfully trotted off, twittering to herself, and the master turned to Maya, who had crossed four of her legs in front of her and was looking highly displeased.

"Maya," he said and, taking Mikk's hand, he pulled the reluctant boy forward, "this is Mikk, my new apprentice."

Maya's six round jelly-filled organs scrutinized Mikk with unmistakable distaste.

"Hunh," she squeaked. "Too thin." She uncrossed her tentacles and shimmied haughtily after her mother.

"Well, well, Mikk," the master smiled at his depressed apprentice, "I think she likes you."

Huud Maroc put Mikk in a small but cozy room on the first floor at the foot of the stairway that led to his own chamber on the second, at the opposite end of the chalet from Mapa and Maya's rooms. Mapa was no problem, but "tact" was not part of her daughter's vocabulary and the master wanted to spare the boy's fragile ego some of the younger cephalopod's assaults.

Nevertheless, Mikk got battered his first evening at the chalet.

"Where from?" Maya asked after setting the boy's plate, a little roughly, before him.

"Wynt," Mikk whispered.

"Red thing Academy brat," she sniffed. "Not real performer."

"Maya," the master warned, "that's for me to decide, not you."

"Maybe," said the cephalopod, not conceding anything, "but red thing too old, too thin. How make performer?"

"He's not a 'red thing,' Maya. His name is Mikk."

"Funny name. Like door shut."

"It's a perfectly fine name, Maya," the master said. "It belonged to an ancient Crown."

"Not have two name?"

The boy shook his head. He poked his food with his pronged skewer, but did not eat it.

"Why?"

"Vyzanians don't always use two names, Maya, you know that." The master threw a short concerned glance at Mikk. Come on, lad, he almost said aloud, Speak up! Defend yourself.

"Much odd," the cephalopod sighed. "Maya not understand. Master almost retire, now new apprentice. You do rich man favor for son?"

This, finally, was too much for the boy, but he did not fight back. He simply got up from the table and left.

"Maya," the master rumbled, "that was very unkind."

"Maya not kind." Her six eyes flashed. "Maya true."

"You were not true. I don't take on apprentices as a favor to anyone, not even myself. That boy will be performing long after I've become ashes."

"Maya wonder." She picked up Mikk's untouched dinner. "Boy weak."

"Maya blind."

Mikk never returned to the table, and when the master retired for the evening several hours later, he heard the boy crying. A stiff draft gusted from under the door. Mikk must have opened the window, but why? He chilled easily.

The master gently rested his hand on the door and the crying stopped. That incredible hearing! Chagrined, Huud Maroc decided not to disturb the boy further and withdrew.

The sooner we get to work, he thought, the better.

Teaching Mikk wouldn't have been nearly as frustrating if the boy had been fully, and consistently, incompetent. Unfortunately, Mikk occasionally displayed flashes of genuine brilliance, and Huud Maroc had to suffer the terrible ache of watching the apprentice capture a gesture, a step, a phrase of music, render it with exquisite, heart-stopping beauty, then fumble everything else so his entire performance fell apart. Mikk could not take in anything new without extreme concentration, which he could not hold very long in spite of the most chilling stare state the master had ever seen. It transformed the boy into a wax image with molten glass eyes. The worst of it never lasted more than a second or two, but Mikk jumped in and out of the state as if it were a form of mental hiccups.

To make matters worse, Maya had declared war on the boy. Rudeness was one thing, but the cephalopod behaved as though she had a personal vendetta against Mikk. She watched him dance and laughed when he tripped. She hooted when he sang and mocked his acting with a nasty form of mimicry that rendered everything an obscene gesture in Werevan parlance. The master regretted having told her Mikk knew many languages, including hers. The cephalopod also enjoyed "accidentally" spilling buckets of soap or tubs of vegetable peelings on the outraged, but consistently silent, apprentice.

As much as he could, Huud Maroc refrained from interfering. The boy had to stand up for himself sometime, and, even if it was painful to observe, the master let the cephalopod continue her attacks. However, as on the first night, Mikk never expressed any anger toward Maya.

I don't think he knows how to protest, the master thought as, for the fifth time that month, Maya anointed Mikk with garbage and the apprentice quietly picked the slimy bits from his tunic without even looking at her. Huud Maroc remembered what Dean Mooj had said about the boy's mother.

How "extreme" was she? he wondered. Did she torment him, too? Did she punish him if he complained? The boy's a blocked stream.

Finally, Maya buried Mikk's kai-shan and earned a beating with a spatula.

"Bad thing!" Mapa cried as she chased her daughter around the kitchen. "Cruel thing! So mean I spit!"

Mikk was afraid to go to Mapa with his accusation—the master had to push him into the kitchen—and at the sight of the cephalopod thumping her daughter with the cooking utensil, the boy's eyes went black. He shrank into the corner then escaped out the back door, a badly hung wooden plank that banged loudly no matter how gently it was released. Mikk flung it shut as though trying to shatter it and vomited into the moss.

"Dear gods, boy," murmured the master, standing only a few feet away. "Why?"

Mikk glanced at him with mute, feral terror, ran around the corner of the chalet, dashed through the front hall, and shut himself in his room. The master followed and pounded his palm on the door.

"Mikk! Open up, boy!"

Mikk didn't answer.

"Beast, lad! I can't help you if you won't talk to me."

Mikk still didn't answer.

"Look, Mikk," the master said, more softly, "Maya had no right to do what she did. You had to tell her mother."

"Mapa beat her," came the faint response.

"That's not your concern. Maya has always been mean—and very tough."

"It still hurts to be beaten."

"Well, yes, I have no answer for that." The master pressed his ear against the door, the better to catch the boy's low whisper.

"Mikk? Did your mother beat you?"

"No," Mikk answered without hesitation.

"Did your father?"

"I don't even know my father," the boy said, but with an edge. The master pursed his lips.

"When you're ready, Mikk, come back outside. We'll go to the lake."

"Why?"

Huud Maroc's eyebrows shot up. No mistake about it. There was a vein of genuine defiance in Mikk's voice. The glint of a knife in the shadows.

Not a stream, he thought—a cataract.

"You're a Vyzanian, Mikk. You know what a lake is for."

"Swimming?"

"Make up your mind soon, lad. It's a long walk."

The master encouraged Mikk to swim lap after lap until the boy was so spent he could hardly stand up. When they returned, it was late and dark in the chalet. Before he let his apprentice go, Huud Maroc once again grasped the boy's chin and looked him in the eyes. Mikk didn't react much at all. He was becoming accustomed to the master's way of getting his attention.

"Do you still trust me, boy?"

Mikk merely blinked sleepily, but his sullen tension seemed to have been worked out of him.

"Maya will back off eventually," Huud Maroc said. "She has to. Nothing that extreme can last forever."

Mikk listened dutifully, but the expression in his pale eyes said he knew differently, firsthand.

"I'm sorry, Mikk. This hasn't been a very good day."

"I liked the lake."

"Ah! Then it wasn't a total loss." The master mussed up Mikk's crimson hair. "Good night, boy."

"Good night, Master Huud."

The master went up the stairs to his quarters. When Mikk opened his own door, Maya was waiting inside. She jumped him and knocked him down, then spat in his face.

"Maya lame!" she hissed. "Blame you!"

Too exhausted to consider the consequences of his actions, Mikk threw himself across the polished floor at Maya, grabbed her eight slick feet in his hands, and yanked her down.

"Let go!" Maya squeaked.

"Why are you so mean to me?" Mikk cried. "What have I done to you?"

"Let go! Maya bite!"

"Why do you hate me!"

Maya stopped struggling and leveled her six eyes on Mikk. In the darkness, their fury smoldered caustic green.

"You extra trouble! Take Maya from real work."

"*Real* work? What real work?"

"Maya bite."

Mikk let go of her feet, and the cephalopod scrambled out of the room and pattered into the darkness.

A few days later, on an afternoon when Mapa and Maya had gone down the hill to collect fungi and the master had released him from a long morning of scene study, Mikk headed for the kitchen to look for a bolha ball the chalet's semiferal mountain shepherd had run off with. When he passed Maya's room, he stopped. Maya always kept her door closed; not even Mapa was allowed to enter. Mikk knew it would be wicked of him, but the cephalopod's comment about her "real work" had been bothering him. Perhaps if he found out what it was, he could discover a way to make her leave him alone. He pushed open the door and peeked inside.

The tiny closet was chaotic, a jumbled nest of loose pillow stuffing, boxes, and knickknacks that, for all Mikk knew, was perfectly normal, even fastidious by Werevan cephalopod standards. He tiptoed into the room and dared to violate Maya's privacy even further: he opened one of the boxes.

It was full of the strangest collection of rubbish Mikk had ever seen: still shots of outworlders of every description and age dressed in every conceivable style; woefully outdated and dog-eared history pamphlets; snippets and strips of cloth of all textures and colors; bits of braid, bone, and glass; packets of hooks and frogs and other fastenings; dismantled slippers; tiny jars of dried-out pigments and cosmetics. Mikk put everything back and opened another box. This one held ratty, moth-eaten fur pieces, many from animals he could not identify, and rotting crushed Vyzanian felt. He wrinkled his nose, set the box aside, and chewed his thumb, perplexed. Why did a Werevan cephalopod need such flotsam? He picked up a third box, a wide, flat paperboard carton, opened it, and found the answer.

Inside were dozens of drawings in cheap vegetable oil crayons on old Belian dailies. The drawings depicted ancient and modern outworld costume, hairstyles, and makeup patterns—and they were wonderful. Even using rough, unresponsive pigments, Maya had an extraordinary sense of pattern and design. The colors were richly blended and subtle, and it gradually became apparent that Maya's favorite color, by far, was red.

In a corner of the box, Mikk found the most eloquent creations of all: tiny paper figures dressed in clothing cut from the same poor pulp stock, carefully colored with the same miserable crayons, and glued together with homemade root starch paste. Mikk cradled the delicate figures in his slender fingers and turned them over to see that Maya had also duplicated, in paper, the elaborate braids and crimpings of outworld hairstyles. He carefully set them back in the box with the drawings and replaced the lid. Then, after rearranging the boxes as he had found them, he stepped cautiously into the hall and closed the door.

In the evening, the master gave Mikk another kai-shan and together they sat on the Ti-tokan maze rug to tackle a north country duet.

"Not bad," the master said, pleasantly surprised by Mikk's playing. "A little soft, but you have a feel for it."

"The teacher at the Academy was very patient."

"Remind me to put him in my will."

"Her."

"All right."

They continued a bit longer, then the master, seeing Mikk suppress a grimace, chuckled softly.

"You're right, boy," he said, "the valves are loose. Take mine and I'll retune yours."

Mikk watched the master pry open the valves and pick at the guts of the instrument with a long narrow hook. He decided this would be a good time to ask.

"Master Huud? I'd like to send for something in town."

"Oh?" The master interrupted his tuning.

"Nothing expensive. Just . . . something."

The master's blue-purple eyes squinted curiously and Mikk was afraid he'd have to elaborate, but the master apparently decided not to pursue the issue.

"Well, don't make a habit of this, boy." He resumed his tuning. Mikk absently fingered the master's considerably larger, and heavier, kai-shan. The maker had carved elaborate scrolls in the russet belly of the wooden instrument.

"And I don't want Maya cleaning my room or laundering my clothes anymore. I can do it myself."

The master looked up.

"You think that might help?"

Mikk kept his eyes on the intertwining pattern in the rug.

"You really want to do this?" the master persisted. "You don't have to. Your studies are more than enough work."

"I'm not some rich man's spoiled son," Mikk whispered.

When Maya next shut herself in her room to indulge in her "real work," she opened the flat box and found several folio books of fine Belian art paper and a box of pigment styli.

Out behind the kitchen, the master, perched like a meditating eagle on the stump of a conifer that had been blown apart by one of Belia's rare "hundred century" electromagnetic tornadoes, studied his apprentice's gymnastic attempts and tried to divine the source of their perplexing inconsistency. Roughly one out of seven tries, Mikk actually accomplished the walk-over quite easily, and he could perform almost any flip or tumble quickly. Unfortunately, when asked to do the same movements slowly, deliberately, he lost control and grace became gangly disaster. His leggings were covered with deep blue-green stains.

Still, Huud Maroc was fascinated by the way Mikk used his back. He had rarely seen anyone, of any race, who was that supple.

"Try again, Mikk. Picture yourself doing it."

The boy's arms wobbled—he was tiring.

Please, lad, the master thought. One more good one. I have to see what makes them different.

Maya suddenly slammed through the kitchen door with a large bucket of dirty water. She had been scrubbing the floor. She stopped when she saw Mikk and her eyes narrowed to shiny slits.

Here it comes, the master thought. If Mikk doesn't say something this time, I'll forbid Maya to do it again. I can't bear this game anymore.

But Maya quietly poured the water into the moss near the steps and set the bucket down just as Mikk, without warning, performed a splendidly realized, elegant walk-over.

"Hunh," she said and banged back into the kitchen. The master hopped down from his perch.

"Mikk," he said as the boy tried another walk-over and failed, "Maya came to see me last night."

"Oh?" Mikk brushed himself off.

"I've never seen her so nervous. She was actually trembling. She had a box of sketches with her. It seems she's been drawing costumes and hairstyles for a long time. They were quite good."

"Really?" Mikk seemed deeply interested in the way the morning breeze bent the tops of the conifers clustered below the hill.

"She wanted to know if I had any texts on costume and makeup she could borrow."

"Do you?"

"Of course I do, lad, I'm a performance master, but these arts are all Maya has ever wanted to practice. She never told me until last night." The master scratched his chin. "What do you know about this, Mikk?"

Mikk ran his fingers through his hair.

"I like colors. I guess I'm sensitive to them."

"That's not what I mean. Half of Maya's drawings were on scraps of old journals, but the other half were brand new, on Belian art stock."

"Did Maya go into town? I thought she hated flying in the ultralight."

"You're playacting before a professional, boy."

Mikk glanced guiltily at the master and curled in his shoulders as if he expected some kind of blow. "I'm sorry," he mouthed.

"Did I say you'd done anything wrong?" the master asked gently. "Why didn't you tell me?"

The boy's shoulders relaxed, but he still would not look at the master. "I was afraid to. I thought you would say no."

"I might have said yes."

Mikk's pulse doubled. The master might have said yes! He had to take advantage of this compliant mood before it evaporated. "Master Huud, wh-why did we leave Droos?"

There was a long pause before the master responded, unexpectedly, with a question of his own. "Why do you think we left, Mikk?"

Mikk's heart sank. How could he answer without stirring the master's wrath? He considered pleading ignorance but, under the circumstances, and the peculiar sadness of the master's eyes, decided he had no choice but honesty. Anything less would be ungrateful.

"We left because I wanted to stay," he murmured.

The master shifted his weight to the opposite hip but never wavered in scrutinizing the apprentice with the same intimate, yet abstract, melancholy.

"That wouldn't be fair, would it? Denying something merely because you wanted it? No reason at all?"

He's offended, Mikk thought. He's calm now, but he'll explode any minute. Why couldn't I keep quiet?

But the master did not raise his voice.

"I'd like to tell you why we left, lad, but I mustn't," he said slowly. "You probably think I enjoy being mysterious, that it enhances my sense of power, but, believe me, in this case, that is not so."

He tugged on his earring. Mikk was never sure which nerve the master pinched when he played with this gold hoop, but he always said his most exasperatingly obscure things when he did.

"If the years turn as they should, Mikk, you won't need me to explain why we left. You'll know." He smiled. "You've put in a long, hard morning, lad. Are you sore?"

Mikk shook his head. It wasn't his body that hurt.

"Even so, you shouldn't overdo it. Why don't you finish Ahraan Bey's text on Terran theater? We'll discuss it tonight after supper."

Mikk returned to his tiny room, climbed into his hammock with the old-fashioned, top-bound, hand-scripted book, and flipped over the pages until he reached the section on Brecht and German experimental theater. However, after a few columns, he set the volume aside. The scramble of sounds in his head, both shrill and lyrical, had become especially loud and he couldn't concentrate. He made himself small in the seines of the hammock and closed his eyes against the pain.

He fell asleep with the window open. As usual.

Chapter Nine: The Basket

.

"Why does everything on Belia have blue in it, Master Huud? Even the people are blue."

It was a hot afternoon, too hot, in the master's opinion, to go gallivanting all over the countryside, but he'd let Mikk talk him into leading the way down the hill and into the woods to teach him about Belia's plants and animals. Mikk got very excited on these exploratory hikes and showered Huud Maroc with questions that came from all directions, more like the queries of a young child than those of an adolescent. However, the master strongly suspected there was an underlying order, or theme, to these questions that belied their innocence.

"The blue comes from certain chemicals in the soil and water. Oh, Beast boils! What did I step in this time?"

"If I stayed here long enough, would I turn blue, too?"

"What? No! I mean, you have to be part of the world's chemistry to begin with, lad. 'Blue feeds blue'—that's what the Belians say."

"Too bad." Mikk picked up a small cobalt striped stone. "It's pretty. I think it would be fun to change color."

"You have some curious ideas, boy," the master said, skirting what he sensed was a veiled reference to the Droos. Not today, boy, please, he thought. It's too hot and I'm not in the mood for that game.

"Oh!" Mikk cried and dropped the stone, his attention drawn toward a dense thicket. "What is that wonderful smell?"

Huud Maroc locked his fingers around Mikk's arm and the boy's eyes darkened slightly.

"No, Mikk. Don't go over there."

"What? Why not?"

"That scent is a warning. Follow me and I'll show you."

He led Mikk around the thicket and across the brow of the sunlit hill until they were behind the massed foliage and could see, in the shade, a clump of brilliant blue-white flowers.

"How beautiful!" Mikk said, but the master's hand once again tightened around his arm. "Ow! Master Huud, if you don't want me to pick them . . ."

"I don't want you anywhere near them, Mikk. They're death lilies."

"Death lilies?"

"Very beautiful, very sweet, but extremely poisonous. To touch one is fatal."

"But they're lovely." Mikk seemed strangely, even inappropriately, distressed.

"Not everything lovely is safe, Mikk." The master pointed to the ground next to the flowers. "Look."

A small purplish blue snake, about as wide as a finger, eased its way through the weeds toward the flowers and, as it passed through the shadows, brushed its back against one of the drooping blossoms—and immediately went into a short, violent fit of convulsions, became rigid, and died.

Mikk was shocked almost into the stare state, a look of paralyzed horror on his face.

"A penetrating neurotoxin," the master said. "It prevents any creatures but insects from touching them."

"No!" Mikk cried and, to the master's complete surprise, burst into tears.

"Gods, boy! Get hold of yourself. These things happen."

"No, it mustn't!" Mikk crumpled to the ground, buried his face in the weeds, and wailed.

"For the love of . . . What odd fancy has overtaken you this time? I knew we should have stayed back at the chalet! The heat seems to have staggered your reason."

Mikk's sobs intensified and the master threw up his hands in exasperation. This hypersensitive child was incapable of reacting to anything halfway.

"What do you want me to do, Mikk? What would make things easier for you? Shall I cover your eyes every time life throws one of its little tragedies your way? Well, I can't and you want to know why? Because that's *life*, boy. No one has the power to erase all the unpleasantness in the world and you've got to learn to face it. Now, stop bawling and get up. I'm tired of it."

But Mikk curled in his body like a frightened vole and continued to water the weeds. The master lost control.

"It's dead, boy!" he cried. "Dead! You can't bring it back with all this noise and it wasn't worth it anyway! It wasn't a person, Mikk! It was just a lousy little Beast-turd of a—"

The master bit his tongue. Furious at his own stupidity, he stamped away from the anguished boy to collect himself.

"You're really getting old, Huud Maroc," he growled to himself. "Just a snake indeed!" He kicked the weeds and the dusty pollen flew up in pale blue clouds, then he smoothed back his long silver hair.

"All right," he said, still angry with himself, "clear up the confusion. Be firm about it."

He strode back to the hysterical apprentice.

"Get up, boy. We're going home. You should telewave Thissizz."

Mikk lifted his face, bleary-eyed and incredulous, to the master. "B-but it's a day early."

To curb Mikk's tendency to telewave Droos every free moment he got, the master restricted him to one letter every Tenth Day, the holiday that belonged to the Vyzanian Crown no matter which world they were on. Curiously, Thissizz seemed to be under the same restriction and sent only one response per letter.

"Doesn't matter, lad. You want to, don't you?"

Mikk's tears had carved bright white lines in the pollen on his face but, at these words, his grin outshone them. "Yes!"

Thissizz's response came later that evening, and watching Mikk read it was like watching a crumpled piece of stiff cloth ease open, straighten, and fall smooth.

See, lad? thought the master, your friend is fine. No sympathetic sorcery.

Mikk folded the thin sheet of cellulose with its blue-inked transmission, prefatory to stashing it in the box in his room, and smiled bashfully at Huud Maroc. "I'm sorry I made a spectacle of myself today," he whispered.

"Actually, that's a good description of our job, boy, but we usually do it by design."

Mikk rubbed his cheek against his shoulder. His gaze was inward, but happy, and his scene work that night, comic patter from Zizzy Oopla's only written farce, was especially natural.

Unfortunately, the following week, the telewave, like all pieces of essential machinery in Huud Maroc's experience, turned evil at the worst possible moment and went down. To make matters even more unpleasant, the lone technician in the village was swamped with orders and couldn't fit in the chalet's telewave for at least four days.

"Beast," the master muttered, "the most technologically advanced people in the galaxy and I can't get anyone to repair a simple frozen wave repeater."

Mikk said nothing, but the master felt his agitation, a mantle of emotional radioactivity, and the boy's already unreliable concentration was severely impaired.

Huud Maroc wasn't just frustrated this time, he was angry. He was tired of the terrible scattering that undermined all of Mikk's, and his, very hard work. It sabotaged and humiliated the apprentice entirely against his will, choking the beautiful song as it struggled from his throat and hobbling the exquisite dance as it fought out of his body. Mikk hid his tears in his bed, but the master was aware of them and became even more infuriated.

"I detest war with invisible enemies!" he snarled in private.

Three days after the telewave crashed, Huud Maroc ran out of patience.

"*Flex* your foot, Mikk!" he cried to the quaking boy who balanced on one leg in the moss. "This is Ichtian temple dance, not Terran ballet."

Mikk flexed his foot.

"Now, turn. Carefully. Concentrate, boy! Hold on! Ah, no . . ."

Mikk stumbled—again.

"It's very difficult," he mumbled.

"Of course it is! If what we did were easy we'd be out of a job. Now try again."

Mikk did, and failed.

"This is getting us nowhere! You have got to pay attention to what you're doing."

"I'm sorry, Master Huud . . ."

"Oh, that's very nice!" The master's huge voice rose sharply. "I'm glad of that at least. Sorry! Well, that's not enough, boy! You'll practice this until you get it right, understand?"

"Yes, Master Huud." One narrow slippered foot rubbed the opposite ankle.

Huud Maroc turned his back on his apprentice and left him alone. He was too irritated with him, with the world, to handle another minute of lessons. Mikk would have to puzzle it out on his own. He, the master, was done for the day. He retreated to his room, locked himself in, and did not come out until the next morning when, having splashed his face and eaten a bowl of mixed grains and cultured deer milk, he felt ready to resume the task of training this sincere but exasperating boy. He went downstairs to Mikk's tiny bedroom and discovered the apprentice was not there. The hammock was up but had not been slept in. The silk covering was smooth, its knotted corners fluttering softly in the breeze from the open window.

For a moment, Huud Maroc feared the boy had run off. In spite of their hikes, Mikk was not yet familiar with Belia. Toxic plants besides death lilies grew in this rural sector, and it was home to several kinds of unpredictable wild creatures. Then the master glanced outside. Mikk was still on the hill. Huud Maroc left the bedchamber, went out the kitchen plank, and stood staring at the slender red-haired boy who danced in the dew-drenched moss. Stared with something close to terror. He did not understand what he was seeing.

Mikk waved to him.

"Look, Master Huud!" he cried happily. "I think I've got it!"

Sure enough, the apprentice executed a perfect Ichtian slow turn without a single wobble. Then he ran to him, clothing and hair sopping with evening moisture, eyes glassy and hollow from lack of sleep, face shining with triumph.

Huud Maroc slapped him. Mikk yelped but before he could bolt the master crushed him in a heavy embrace, immobilizing him.

"I'm sorry, Mikk," he whispered into the boy's hair, "I don't handle guilt well." He hugged Mikk harder, smothering the boy's eyes and ears in his broad chest and thick arms. "Gods' breath, boy! Are you trying to catch your death? When I told you to practice, I didn't mean all night! That would have been absurdly unreasonable, even for me. Did you really think I expected you to do that? Why didn't you say something?"

The apprentice began to struggle in Huud Maroc's arms. In spite of the firmness of his embrace, the master knew he wasn't hurting him and Mikk's desperation puzzled him. He loosened his grasp to look into the boy's face. Mikk was unrecognizable with grief, a sobbing scream, eyes wrinkled shut and running over with tears, mouth open, body shaking violently—but without a sound. Not even a gasp.

"Ah, Mikk! What did that pathetic woman do to you?"

The cry erupted from Mikk's throat. Too full-bodied for a scream, too piercing for a howl, it blew back the master's hair with its pure, wordless anguish and raced out of control in sonic waves for several seconds before abruptly cutting off. The ensuing silence was almost as shocking as the cry itself, and the master, who had let go of the boy to cover his ears, hesitated before uncovering them.

Mikk lay unconscious at his feet, a thin line of dark pink blood running from the corner of his mouth. Huud Maroc quickly bent over him, pinched open his lips, and looked into his throat. The tear, a small one, was in the soft palate. Incredibly, Mikk's vocal cords were undamaged. The old scars had not ruptured.

The master carried the apprentice inside, laid him in the hammock, and stayed at his side until, at midday, Mikk finally opened his eyes.

"Master Huud?" he whispered, no more hoarse than usual.

"Relax, Mikk. There won't be any lessons today."

He put his hand on the apprentice's forehead and was relieved to find it had cooled.

"You've an impressive set of lungs, boy. In my prime, I could produce a sound like that, but I avoided doing so. It frightened the actresses."

Mikk stared at the master as though he hadn't the slightest idea what he was talking about.

"Do you remember what happened, lad?"

Mikk absently touched his cheek.

"Yes. I guess you do."

"It's all right, Master Huud. You didn't hurt me."

"I certainly did, Mikk, and it's not all right at all. I lost control, something a master must never do." His brow furrowed. "You have to be honest with me. Absolutely true, understand?"

Mikk nodded.

"I'm going to ask you again. Did your mother ever strike you?"

"No. She almost did, once, but no. She didn't."

"Fine, but I want you to concentrate. Don't worry if you've blocked the memory, I won't be angry. What happened when your mother got angry with you?"

"She shrieked at me. Sometimes she sent me to my room without supper."

"Given your hearing and metabolism, that would be enough, but I'm sure there's more. Think carefully, lad."

Mikk gazed disconsolately at his master and slowly, very slowly, his eyes filled. His lip began to tremble.

"*Tell* me, Mikk."

"I spilled berries on the cushion . . ." His voice sounded smaller, younger. "They stained the silks."

"What happened?"

"She wrapped her scarf around my eyes, tied my hands and feet behind my back, and shut me in a basket."

"In the dark?"

"She said she'd come back when I was sorry, but she forgot."

"*Forgot?* How long were you in the basket, Mikk?"

The boy's expression became dull. He was retreating from the memory.

"Mikk!"

The pain cracked through Mikk in a spasm. He clutched the master's sleeve and began to worry it between his fingers, scowling intensely as though it was vitally important to wear a hole through the silk as quickly as possible.

"Henni visited her family during the Dormant Season," he said with a weak shrug, but the master understood exactly what he meant and his blood turned to ice.

It was a statistic from the past, from the Black and Red War, one of those truths proved through siege and catastrophe: No Vyzanian lived more than sixty days without food. Less than twenty if deprived of water as well.

The Dormant Season was ninety days long.

The master wanted to tear his hair. How, in the name of all holiness, had Mikk survived? No wonder the boy's blood salts, and perceptions, were out of balance!

"I couldn't see anything," Mikk whispered, "but I heard *everything*. The paint on the walls sighed to me. I couldn't stop it. Everything had a voice and . . . and there was music."

"Music? What kind of music?"

"I don't know. Maybe it *wasn't* music. I never heard it again, but it keeps coming back, like the scream and the pain. Oh, Master Huud! I couldn't tell *anything* apart anymore!"

"Did you cry out, Mikk? Did you call for help?"

"I tried, but my throat hurt too much."

The master gripped one of the support seines of the hammock to avoid breaking something. "You had arranic throat fever while you were in the basket?" he hissed.

"It started there. I was lying in my own shit."

Huud Maroc took a deep breath and released it slowly. The Ev-Mobiks had a cruel saying he heard over and over the day they whipped him: If you want to break a Vyzanian, give him something terrible to remember.

Mikk should be dead, or at least insane, the master thought, but, again, I've underestimated him. This gaunt, lonely child is the strongest person I've ever met.

Mikk began to weep softly.

"I *tried* to please her, Master Huud! She told Henni she'd kill both of us if anyone found out."

The master pulled away from Mikk, went to the window, and leaned his shoulder on the oval sill. He didn't want to see the boy's eyes. Not now.

What do I do? he wondered. I'm a teacher, not a parent. It's impossible for me to make up what he's lost.

He faced the reclining boy. In the midday light filtering through the colored panes, Mikk resembled a corpse wrapped in a netted shroud, but his eyes were alive. Just. The master was not sure what he had expected. An accusation from the gods, perhaps. Certainly not these harmless bits of lavender glass.

"Is the dark hard on you, Mikk?"

"Sometimes. Not if I can move around."

"Not if you can get out."

"I wasn't afraid to sleep with the Droos pups," Mikk murmured.

"That's very different, lad. I don't need to tell you why." The master considered a moment. "There's a classic Terran magic trick involving a cabinet. It might help to teach it to you."

"I like magic tricks."

"Good! I know lots of them." The master searched the boy's face again, the bruise-colored hollows around the eyes, the sharp edges of the jaw and cheekbones, and felt a surge of distress more outraged and tender than guilt. He gently scooped Mikk up and cushioned that wasted countenance against his chest, careful this time to leave his eyes and ears free.

"She bound and gagged more than your body, Mikk, but I swear on my reputation as a master, you will come through this or the gods themselves will be shamed."

Chapter Ten: Hom

"Polite boy, but odd," the Belian telewave technician said a week later as he wiped the moisture from his slick blue scalp with spidery five-jointed fingers. "He crouched on top of that chest next to the receiver and just stared at me the entire time I was working."

"He's been exceedingly anxious about the telewave," Huud Maroc said, "and you were very late."

"The sunspots are affecting everyone. Anyway, I told him what I was doing. He seemed to like that." He lowered his voice. "What are those markings on his face?"

The master glanced over the small naked blue man's shoulder at the slight young boy in the next room who was intently tapping away at the telewave's oval keyboard panel.

"Ichtian ceremonial patterns. Blue and yellow are worn by the dancer portraying the sky demon. Maya must have been practicing again."

"Sky demon?" The technician's long, slanting, gem-faceted eyes widened. "I'm not surprised. He unnerves me." He shouldered his tool pack.

"He's just a boy," said the master.

"I know, but something's wrong. His eyes are empty. Now, I'm not one to give advice, but . . ."

"Then don't. I'm glad you repaired the wave repeater, but I will deal with my apprentice my way."

Once the Belian was gone, the master walked up behind Mikk and watched him compose his letter to Thissizz. The boy's thin fingers danced unerringly over the codes twice as quickly as they had before the instrument crashed.

How would he deal with his apprentice? he wondered. Physically, Mikk had recovered rapidly from the revelation about the basket, but his soul had gone into mourning. He didn't seem interested in anything anymore except his letters to Thissizz. This was in spite of a noticeable improvement in his work. His concentration had sharpened, but it was cold and the master could not rejoice. Mikk's new expertise lacked life.

"Mikk?"

The boy stopped composing and looked at the master. As the Belian had said, his eyes were attentive, but empty—the eyes of a shell-shocked soldier.

"I've invited a colleague to visit us. A former apprentice of mine named Hom. He'll arrive in five days and I want you to be at your best while he's here."

"Yes, Master Huud."

No questions, no surprise, no curiosity. The master stroked the apprentice's hair and smiled gently at that serious blue and yellow face.

"Take the makeup off as soon as you can, lad. It's not good for your skin to wear it all day."

"Yes, Master Huud."

The ordeal of the slow turn convinced Mikk he had to work on his balance and he was up in the third floor hall, a space used as a dance studio and storage room, standing on one foot, eyes closed, his hands on his head, when he heard a light patter behind him. He assumed it was Maya and ignored it. Mapa was preparing a special supper for Hom's arrival and Maya was probably retrieving linens from the heavy trunks that lined the walls—an ordinary thing. Nothing short of the delightful rasp of scales on stone deserved his attention.

At least, that's what he thought. However, as he listened, Mikk picked up this other person's breathing, a soft small brushing over delicate vocal cords. It did not sound like Maya's breathing at all and it was right behind him.

"Who—?"

The unseen visitor didn't bother to identify himself before striking. With a cry of victory, he threw his arms around the apprentice's waist and Mikk tipped over, nearly spraining an ankle. He caught himself in time and tried to unlock the embrace of his short assailant.

"Hi-hee!" cried the unknown attacker, a child apparently. "What other games do you know?"

He was hard to shake off, but Mikk finally pried the little hands apart and jumped back.

"You are so funny!" the child laughed, pointing a finger. "Standing there like a tree! Are you ticklish?" Again he charged Mikk, who caught him by the shoulders.

"Hey, now! Wait! Who are you?"

He would have asked "what are you?" but that would have been unforgivably rude. The boy seemed much younger than Mikk and was considerably smaller, but had the long white hair of age. He skipped about with the agility of a whir cricket and his soft brown skin looked sleek and healthy, but his eyes were couched in deep lines and folds as though he had been squinting into the sun for many years. His teeth, although straight and unpitted, were dark and worn along the cusps. All in all, the child resembled a young Mrkusi—one with an exotic aging disease.

"I'm not telling!" he giggled. "But I know who *you* are. You're Master Huud's new apprentice."

"Where did you come from?"

The odd child ignored the question and instead began to poke into the chests and hang on the oval windowsills. Mikk tried to keep him from spoiling the linens, but the boy was too quick.

"Out of that! Mind the taper! Oh, no, not the cutlery!"

"It's all the same!" the child cried. "I've played here hundreds of times! Come on, Mikk, let's go to the basement and look for ground owls."

"I can't. I have to practice."

"Now?"

"It takes a lot of work to become a performer."

"Work?!" the child cried, flabbergasted. "Performing isn't work! It's fun! You're very silly!"

"*I'm* silly?" Mikk chuckled. In spite of himself, he found this weird aged boy highly entertaining.

"No," the child said thoughtfully, "I guess not. Too bad! I'll go to the basement by myself." He hopped out of the room.

A moment later, Huud Maroc appeared with an elderly Belian woman. Her hairless blue nudity's comfortable sag suggested a placid, eternally patient nature.

"Ah, Mikk!" the master said. "Have you seen Hom?"

"No, but the oddest little boy was just here and . . ."

"Where did he go?"

"The basement. Looking for ground owls."

The Belian woman smiled benignly and patted Huud Maroc's arm. "I'll find him," she said. "Hom gets so excited around animals."

When she was gone, Huud Maroc approached his stunned apprentice. "It's not polite to stare, boy."

"That . . . that was Hom the performance master?"

"Yes," the master sighed. "I hope Vira cleans him up in time or Mapa's wonderful supper is going to be burnt."

"But he's a child!"

"He's twice as old as I am. He was one of my first apprentices." He sat in the windowsill and smiled at Mikk's incredulity. "Hom isn't an ordinary little boy, Mikk, he's a Longchild, one of nature's flights of fancy."

"A Longchild?"

"A mutation. Every now and then Hom's people produce a child who lives a vastly extended lifespan, sometimes ten times as long as normal, but these children never mature. They remain little boys and girls forever. The eye wrinkling and white hair are glitches, genetic markers that announce their true antiquity."

"If Hom will always be a child," Mikk asked, "how can he be a performance master?" He perched on the trunk nearest the master and, self-conscious about his legs' gangly proportions, drew them up.

"He's also a child prodigy—an *eternal* child prodigy. I couldn't resist taking him on. He'll always need a guardian like Vira to keep him out of trouble, but he's a marvelous performer. He thinks everything is a game and would perform for nothing if Vira didn't see to his affairs." Huud Maroc's eyes softened. "You've been awfully quiet, lad, and it's having a gloomy effect on the entire household. It can't hurt to have Hom crashing around raising the Beast." He got up. "This supper is for you, too, Mikk. Mapa's afraid she'll go through her whole repertoire before you eat anything. Give it a good try, lad. For her sake."

At supper, Hom chattered through every course, hung his spoon on his nose, slipped some of his stew under the table to the appreciative mountain herder, and climbed about in his seat. Mikk was very distracted and watched the Longchild with a mixture of alarm and confused delight. When Hom flipped a spoonful of jelled fruit at the apprentice, hitting him full in the face, Mikk jumped to his feet.

"You're in for it now!" He bounded over Hom's chair to chase the nimble Longchild out of the chalet and into the cool evening moss of the hillside.

The master smiled at Vira.

"Thank you for bringing Hom. I know it wasn't easy, cancelling three engagements like that."

"They weren't important. Besides, if the young can't be young when they *are* young, they will never become adults."

"Quite a thing coming from the guardian of a Longchild!"

"Hom is a touchstone. You can tell a great deal about another child's soul by how he relates to the Longchild."

The master looked outside. The boys were wrestling in the moss. Hom pulled Mikk to the ground and climbed on top of him, but when the protesting apprentice carefully lifted the Longchild up a bit to get more comfortable, Huud Maroc realized Mikk was indulging him, letting someone smaller win. For the first time in many days, Mikk laughed.

The seeds are there, the master thought. Anyone who is generous to the weak can learn to be generous to himself.

*   *   *

Hom certainly did raise the Beast, and often Mikk did not know how to deal with him. The Longchild could coax the purest, most angelic wonder out of whatever performance art he put his hand to, and he could be the most exasperating little brat in the galaxy. He played the kai-shan so beautifully one morning that Mikk slipped into complete stare state paralysis and was unable to recover in time to stop the mountain herder from chewing up the instrument after Hom, suddenly bored, carelessly dropped it on the floor. Hom also routinely left food all over the chalet, which Maya had to clean up before it attracted vermin.

"Small master big problem," she grumbled, but she did not chastise him directly.

Neither did Master Huud. Although Hom was inordinately curious about Mikk's training and couldn't resist making suggestions—excellent ones, to Huud Maroc's evident displeasure—the master limited himself to verbal threats he never carried out.

"Please, Hom!" the master protested during a Terran jazz dance lesson in the third floor hall. "This is *my* job."

"But if he bent his knees more it'd be simple," Hom said.

"Fine, but let me be the one to tell him."

"You have been telling him, but you make him nervous."

"If I were you," the master snarled, "I'd be more concerned about making *me* nervous. If you want to teach Mikk something, do it when he's free and not before. Do I make myself clear?"

Hom shrugged, but when the master's back was turned he pulled a face and Mikk bit his lip so he wouldn't giggle. He was beginning to think of Hom as an amusing younger brother and could not help admiring the Longchild's naive daring in spite of his troublesome gift for distraction. One minute Hom would barge in on the apprentice while he was studying and insist he follow him to the ground owl nests, the next he wanted to teach him a new skill, perhaps a fancy way to spin a platter on his fingertips, or an illusion with a wader's egg and a vial of green dye. But before Mikk had a chance to practice the new trick, Hom would change his mind again and demand to be carried piggyback down the hill.

"Hi-hee! Hi-hee!" he'd call as he bounced on the apprentice's sorely tried shoulders. "Faster! Can't you go faster?"

Mikk put up with his chaos not only because Hom was a child, but for the same reason Maya and Master Huud put up with it: Hom was not an apprentice.

"You don't have any siblings, Mikk," Huud Maroc said during one of their afternoon hikes. "And I understand your peers at the Academy were not particularly friendly. Why is it you can tolerate Hom when he is often completely intolerable?"

"I've always fit in better with younger children. Maybe it's because I'm so slow."

"Give that up, boy. You're doing fine."

"Am I? Hom doesn't think so."

"Did he say that?"

"No. He laughs at me." Mikk climbed over a pale gray-blue boulder after the master. In the weeks since Hom's arrival, the apprentice's endurance had grown and they had been taking longer, steeper trails.

"He's a child, Mikk."

"He's a master, too. He knows."

"And I don't?" Huud Maroc slapped the blue dust from his leggings. "Mikk, you've improved remarkably in the past few weeks. Doesn't that mean anything to you? You look better, too. You've lost that hollowness around your eyes. Maybe Hom laughs because he enjoys your company, have you considered that?"

"Well, I . . ."

"It took Hom over three hundred years to become a master, in spite of his genius. You're not lagging behind, lad, no matter what you might think."

Mikk was unsure how to take this. The master never said anything he didn't mean, but Mikk knew he was far from an adept, or even adequate, apprentice. He lay awake in his hammock that night mulling it over, a thick quilt covering his legs to ward off the chill coming through the window, when he heard an animal scrabbling about outside. Before he could investigate, Hom's head popped into view.

"Hi-hee!"

"Hom!" Mikk whispered. "What are you doing out there?"

"Nothing."

Mikk frowned. "You were trying to break into the kitchen again, weren't you?"

After Hom had put a large two-headed mud worm in one of Mapa's cookpots, the cephalopod had banned him from the kitchen and locked it up whenever she was out. Naturally, anything denied the Longchild instantly became overwhelmingly appealing, and, thinking it the most likely weak spot in Mapa's defense, Hom had been trying to find a way through the warped plank of the kitchen's back door, so far without success.

Hom scrambled over the windowsill and dropped into Mikk's bedchamber. Bits of moss and twigs were tangled in his white hair. "I don't care about Mapa's smelly old kitchen," he pouted. "I've been in the basement. There are *six* eggs, now, Mikk!"

"Hom, it's the middle of the night."

"So? Night's the best time for discovering things." He looked around the chamber and sighed. "No wonder you sleep with the window open! It's like being in a bottle." He grabbed Mikk's hand. "Come on! Now that I have you to myself, I'll show you my puppets."

Mikk's desire for solitude vanished. He'd been hoping for days that Hom would show him his puppets, but the Longchild was very possessive about them. He kept them in a heavy trunk similar to the ones that held the chalet's linens, but bound with bands of keranium and secured with triple-tumbler Belian combination locks. Whatever had prompted Hom to share his treasures could not be considered a mere whim, and Mikk crept silently after the Longchild's taper up to the attic, deeply aware of the solemnity of the occasion. The chalet muttered in its sleep, full of restless rustlings and secret crackles. Although Mikk knew these sounds were normal and most people couldn't hear them at all, an odd rippling stirred the sinews deep between his shoulders.

"How old are these puppets?" he asked after Hom ceremoniously unlocked the trunk and heaved back the lid.

"Some of them are *very* old," Hom whispered. "Like these two. They're from England on Terra." He handed out two soft-bodied hand puppets with large, grotesque papier-mâché heads. "This one with the hook nose is Punch. The other is Judy. They beat each other with sticks."

"I thought the Terran English were a mild people." Mikk felt uncomfortable holding the puppets. Their garish faces leered at him in the dark as though they were alive, or would be the minute he wasn't paying attention.

"Don't be fooled. The English are as tricky as any Terrans. Here. Put them on. Let Punch bash Judy or the other way around."

"Perhaps something less violent." Mikk put the unpleasant couple aside, turning their faces so he wouldn't have to look at them.

"All right." Hom shuffled through the trunk, half his body hanging down into its jumbled depths. "These are Ichtian shadow puppets," he said when he emerged. "Gods and goddesses. You hold them up to the light and they make colored patterns on the wall."

"What's that one in the corner? The one dressed in blue?"

"Oh! He's special." Hom set down the shadow puppets and eased the porcelain and silk figure out from under a pile of Bolban streamer dancers. "He's from Terra, too. A rod puppet. You can make him do some very lifelike things." He fingered the rods delicately and the fine, serious little man bowed with haughty grace. "He's a Nipponese prince. These are traditional robes and I love the funny black hat. It looks like it's going to fly away."

"He's beautiful," Mikk said, fascinated by the figure's sober expression. "May I handle him?"

"Of course, but be careful. He's fragile."

Mikk took the puppet and experimented with the rods, making the prince fold his arms and glide along the ground, nodding to invisible retainers. He raised the tiny arms, lowered the head, and let the hands fall slowly, sadly, until the prince was in an attitude of acute despair. After a moment, the prince lifted his head, straightened his shoulders, and walked on, brave again. Mikk's eyes, bright and focussed, never left the little man.

"That's pretty good," Hom said. "He's not an easy one."

"You're wrong about him," Mikk said softly. "He's not fragile at all."

"Mikk, are you all right? You have pink spots on your cheeks."

"What?" Mikk was still concentrating on the prince.

"Oh, but here's the most difficult puppet in the galaxy!" Hom held up a large square of soft cloth.

"That's just a scarf." Mikk gently laid the rod puppet back in the trunk.

"Is it? Who does this look like?" Creasing and pulling the scarf around his fingers, Hom duplicated the crags and prominences of a certain Vyzanian performance master's face. Mikk covered his mouth.

"Oh, dear! That's wonderful!"

"Watch it, boy!" Hom growled, wiggling the cloth caricature in the light from the taper. "This is art, not a freak show."

Mikk spluttered into giggles. "No, no!" he cried. "More like this." He stood up, thrust out his chest, and scowled. Hom whooped and pretended to cower.

"Concentrate, boy!" Mikk boomed. "Focus, but don't try so hard! You'll practice until you get it right, but go easy! This is work, lad, enjoy it!"

Hom held his sides and rolled on the floor cackling like a Mrku macaw, but then stopped suddenly, his brown complexion turning olive. Mikk spun around and there, silhouetted in the doorframe, stood Huud Maroc himself, eyeing them with granite severity. Mikk gulped.

"M-master H-huud?"

The master raised an eyebrow.

"Bigger, lad," he said evenly. "Play it bigger. Mine is not a small personality."

The master turned on his heel and departed with an air of imperial grandness, leaving his childlike colleague and half-baked apprentice gaping at each other in complete stupefaction.

"Do you think he's angry?" Mikk whispered.

"I don't know," Hom whispered back.

Mikk ran to the door and peered down the attic stair, but in the second or two it had taken to recover from the encounter, the master had vanished.

"We'd better go back to bed, Hom."

The boys sneaked down the stairs, passed the master's bedchamber where a faint light shone under the door, and parted company outside Mikk's room.

Before he got into his hammock, Mikk took out a hand glass from his modest wardrobe and inspected his face. He didn't see any pink spots, but Master Huud was right. He wasn't dark under his eyes anymore.

He set the glass down and tried to rub between his shoulder blades. The strange rippling was stronger and made him feel a bit queasy.

Then he froze. Moss and twigs in Hom's hair? There wasn't any moss in the basement.

Mikk leapt out the window and ran around the side of the chalet in the moonlight. Hopefully, he could get to the kitchen before Hom made too much of a mess.

As he suspected, Hom had managed to pry open the small grate near the back door that let the water and soap run out of the kitchen when Maya washed down the floors. The moss around the grate was torn out, but the opening was still too narrow for Mikk to follow. He put his ear to the opening and heard the soft shuffle of Hom's feet on the kitchen flags. He also heard the scratch of the Longchild's clothing as it briefly caught against the edge of something.

"Hom! What are you doing? Get out of there before they hear you!"

Hom didn't answer.

"Hey, let me in! Mapa stashed some root sweets in the pantry and I know the combination."

That tactic didn't work either. Mikk stood up and scowled at the warped plank. Although it still didn't fit into the jamb properly, Mapa had double dead-bolted it inside and only a moss vole could get through the gaps near the steps.

He heard a small squeak, then something metallic crashed to the floor. The Longchild let out a short cry, quickly muffled.

"Hom!"

Mikk kicked the plank. Kicked it again and tripped. Jumped up and kicked it a third time; the wood splintered apart at the dead bolts and swung open.

Hom was hopping up and down, screaming into the bleeding hand he'd crammed into his mouth to stifle the sound. Judging by the muddy fingerprints around the pantry security panel, the Longchild had first tried to figure out the combination. Then he must have scaled the stove to get one of Mapa's boning knives to pry the lock open but had knocked down the entire rack of cooking weapons, one of which had sliced open his palm. There was dark brown blood everywhere.

Mikk snatched Hom up in his arms, plopped him on the table, and yanked open the cabinet where Mapa kept her first aid supplies. He grabbed a wad of spider floss, crushed it into Hom's wound, then uncorked a bottle of antiseptic with his teeth and emptied it all over the bloody floss. Hom gasped at the sting—even in pain he was not about to wake up any vengeful adults—and tried to get away, but Mikk held him fast, his eyes steady and pale until he had wrapped up his hasty, but effective, work and embraced the Longchild. At that point, he wondered why no one had come running to find out what was wrong. Hadn't they heard him kick the door?

Oh, gods . . . had he actually kicked the door *in*?

Gradually, Hom stopped his heaving strangled sobs to gaze curiously into Mikk's eyes. The apprentice could imagine how strange it looked: the agitated irises shifting rapidly from purple to black and back before returning to their customary pale lavender. The Longchild sighed.

"You're going to grow up, aren't you?"

Mikk straightened the dressing on Hom's hand. In spite of the spray of blood on the walls, the wound was superficial. "Yes," he said quietly.

"It won't hurt, will it?"

"It already does."

"But you won't be like the other grown ones, will you?"

Mikk released Hom's hand and listened again. Still no stir from the rest of the chalet. The Longchild scooted to the edge of the table and pressed his nose against Mikk's.

"Are you afraid?"

"Yes."

To Mikk's astonishment, Hom laughed. "You are so funny!" he cried. "Master Huud is afraid, too!"

"What do you mean? Afraid of what?"

"Afraid of *you*, silly!"

Mikk grabbed Hom's shoulders and forced him to look at him. "What are you talking about, afraid of me?"

"Well, not as though he thinks you're going to hurt him." The Longchild worked his finger in and out of his small brown ear. "But he is afraid."

"Why?"

"I don't know. He gets a strange look when he watches you dance. I think he wants to say something but can't."

"He says all sorts of things when I dance," Mikk sighed.

"Not everything. It's in his face, but it doesn't come out." Hom grinned. "*I'm* not afraid of you. You're not like the old apprentices. You're nice to me."

"Why shouldn't I be?" Mikk squeezed the Longchild again to keep him from seeing the tears in his eyes. "You make me smile."

Mikk tapped lightly on the master's door.

"Come in, lad."

The apprentice hesitated, surprised the master knew who it was. Although Huud Maroc had made it clear his door was always open, Mikk had never been to his chamber.

"Mikk? Are you still there?"

The boy entered and stood silently a long moment, temporarily sidetracked from his mission by the amazing décor of the chamber. Huud Maroc had papered the walls with playbills of shows he had been in from all over the galaxy, making the room a silent explosion of words, pictures, and holograms in many colors, most of them images of the master himself at various ages. The master smiled sheepishly.

"Pretty indulgent, isn't it? I don't do this back in Wynt. People think it's vulgar. But the Belians, bless their little blue hearts, get quite a kick out of it."

Mikk was intimidated by the sheer number and range of productions and grimaced.

"I've been around for some time, boy. Comedies, tragedies, farces, song cycles, trilogies, parodies, epics, morality plays, fabulae, verse tales, ballets, echo threnodies, subaquarian tone dramas . . . keep at it long enough and you'll do them all."

The apprentice looked at his feet.

"You've had a little adventure, haven't you, Mikk? You have Longchild blood on your tunic."

"It's my fault. I should have—"

"It's not your fault," the master interrupted. "I know what happened. I heard you break in."

"Hom's all right, Master Huud."

"Yes. I knew you could handle it and I told the others to let you do so."

Mikk's face twitched. He was having trouble controlling his anguish.

"This is about something else, isn't it?"

"I think you should take me back to the Academy," Mikk whispered. The master sat up in his hammock.

"Why?"

"This is not going to work." Mikk raised his black, glistening eyes. "You've been very kind, but I don't, I can't . . ." His voice broke.

"Don't you want to be a performance master?"

The boy took a ragged breath, started to shake his head, then looked down again. "I don't know."

"I think you do, lad," the master said gently, "but it isn't clear why you . . ."

"Master Huud!" Mikk sobbed. "You can't teach someone you're afraid of!"

"*Afraid* of?!" the master cried. "I'm not afraid of you! Where in the world . . . what did that little miscreant say to you this time?"

"Hom said that . . . that w-when you watch me dance . . ."

"Oh, no, no, no, no! What did I tell you, Mikk? There are things Hom cannot understand. How I feel when you dance, or do anything for that matter, is one of them."

"But you're always pointing out what's wrong." Mikk wiped his nose with the backs of his knuckles.

"That's because there's fear, and there's *fear*," the master smiled. "I'm tough on you Mikk, but not because I'm afraid of you. Rather, it's because there's a lot about the way you perform that does frighten me."

"I'm that bad?"

"Dear, no! You'll be that *good*, eventually. It's a terrifying vision."

"I don't want to terrify people."

"Oh, yes you do, boy," the master said fervently. "Oh, yes you do! You want to make them tremble all the way to the depths of their souls. You want to shake them! Move them so they feel it, feel it intensely. Look at these playbills, Mikk." The master swept his arm grandly. "Each one represents an attempt to reach people emotionally, communicate with their hearts. Not all of them worked, but most of them did and there's nothing that compares to the feeling of making true contact with an audience, even if it's just one man in camspecs. *Nothing*."

Mikk sniffled unhappily and shifted his shoulders as though they itched. Huud Maroc would have given anything to know what was going on inside that starving young spirit.

"My . . . my shoulders feel funny, Master Huud."

"Easy, Mikk. You know how devious premonitions can be. Any images?"

The boy shook his head and rubbed his eyes.

"Mikk, I've been meaning to ask you. You said you heard music while you were in the basket. Do you remember . . . ?"

"I'm tired, Master Huud."

The master abandoned the question, his compassion stirred by the anxious exhaustion in the apprentice's soft voice. "I know, lad. I'm sorry. Would you care to stay here tonight?"

Huud Maroc was not in the habit of sharing his bed with apprentices, but, just this once, he let the boy take comfort by lying back to back with him in the dark. Unfortunately, the apprentice talked in his sleep in a broken scramble of a dozen different languages and it wasn't until dawn, when Mikk finally became silent, that the master could nod off. When he did, he saw Ranya, her hair a pillar of flames, blood running down her face like melted eye frost. He heard her scream the way Mikk heard it and was about to flee its unbearably piercing torture when he became aware of another, different kind of voice singing softly under the shriek. A voice his more experienced ears instantly recognized.

The master jolted awake. At some point, he'd rolled over and rested his premonition-prone hands on Mikk's sensitive shoulders—and tapped into his nightmare.

Huud Maroc sat up and stared into the darkness a long time

before he leaned over the sleeping apprentice and kissed his hair. Then he climbed from the hammock and slipped silently out of the bedchamber.

When Mikk woke up, he tangled his foot in the seines of the master's hammock and nearly fell out on his head. He felt unrested and groggy and considered blundering his way down to his own bedchamber for some extra sleep when he heard something that made the blood throb through his entire body.

Dancing up the stairs, distant and small, was the voice of the instrument Mikk had been unable to learn because the strands of light confused him and the sound terrified him—but Master Tymm had not played this piece and hadn't played anything with such dark, exulting madness. Even so, the melody was intensely familiar. The scrambled song in Mikk's head had somehow reassembled itself and materialized *outside* as a real sound.

Mikk flew down the stairs, his feet barely making contact, and raced through the chalet after the music. His keen hearing led him unerringly, as if he were on a leash, to the back parlor where the master sat on the floor next to the telewave. Black-eyed, Mikk glared at the master's fingers as they skipped over the zimrah's bright white strands. The boy's trembling hands folded into fists.

"Stop!" he said, his voice strangled by rage to a low scratch. The master didn't seem to hear it.

"Mikk, I don't like the way your mother attacked this piece," he said casually. "Too violent. No matter how quick the tempo, you should always carefully control your fingering or you'll lose the 'girl's sigh' that's at the heart of the zimrah's magic. It's not easy, which is why few people play the instrument these days." He altered his playing and the brutal edges of the sound were transformed into a lighter, more joyous skipping.

Mikk shuddered. His ears were torn between the horror of the past and the beauty of the present, and the perpetual scream, Ranya's scream, got louder. Sparks began to spin about the periphery of his vision.

"S-stop!"

"It's a marvelous piece, really," the master said, picking up the tempo. "A real water gypsy skirl. I think I'll teach it to you."

"No!" Mikk's voice jumped into the audible range.

"What? Why not, lad? Don't you like the zimrah?"

No—he loved it. Its music was exquisite—but polluted beyond redemption, hopelessly mixed up with the pain in his joints and throat, the stench of his shit, and the unbroken roar of noise from every direction, from his unhappy bowels to the footsteps of the spiders on the wall. It had kindled his fury, a fury so great it had forced the blood through the nine valves of his heart, keeping him alive long after his body had wanted to die.

"She played that while I was in the basket!" he cried. "She was *celebrating*!"

The master kept on playing and Mikk could not look away. Faster and faster the gypsy danced until the sparks in his vision leapt out and clung to the master's skin. Every note, every slur ripped into Mikk's senses.

"Make her stop, Master Huud! I . . . *hate* her!" Finally admitting it broke open the dike of his anger and he fairly roared at the master.

"I hate her! I hate her! *I HATE HER!*"

Huud Maroc stopped playing and held the zimrah out to him.

"Here, lad, do what you want. Smash it if you like. It's only a box." The master's blue-purple eyes, although optic obtuse, deepened a shade toward indigo. "No one has ever been able to force anything out of you, lad, not your mother, not the Academy, not even me. All of your best moments have been *gifts*, spontaneous expressions of your will, a sword that even ninety days in a basket could not corrupt." He grinned and, for a moment, Mikk thought he could see what the master had looked like as a young man: a burly, black-haired firebrand with a thunderous voice.

"It's up to you," he said. "I can take you back to Wynt, if that's what you want. I can even take you back to Droos, although I think that would be dangerous for you right now. You have the right—and the power—to make your own choices." The master's voice dropped to a quiet intensity. "You have no idea how powerful you are."

Mikk put his shaky hand on the zimrah and the sparks drew together at his fingertips and burst with a single, brilliant flash. In the clear colors they left behind burned the memory of the entire piece, exactly as the master had played it, without a single gap or scramble—and Mikk understood.

I can play this box. *I* can be its master. *I* can be the one in control.

Very slowly, Mikk sat down with the zimrah, amazed at how light it was in his hands, then touched the strings of light, a quiet thrum in his ears and through his fingers. He started to play.

The master slumped with relief. In spite of his cavalier words, he'd been alarmed by the boy's agitation when he entered the room. It reached far beyond rage into a blazing euphoria, but, when Mikk touched the zimrah, he blushed. A Vyzanian blush was a very rare thing, but, in that flash of pink, all of Mikk's anguish steamed away. The apprentice began to manipulate both the visible and obscure strings, and Huud Maroc knew Ranya had stopped screaming.

Mikk played the entire dance, slowly at first, his fingers cautious on the unfamiliar instrument, but he settled into the rhythm and gradually picked up speed until, near the end, the notes flew nearly as quick and agile as the master's and did, remarkably often, sigh as they sang.

It's mine! he thought. *My* song! *I'm* the player!

He sat in silence when he was finished, his eyes for the moment content to rest on the box with the pulsing geode inside, but when he raised them to Huud Maroc, they were bright and steady. "I want you to teach me everything you know," he said simply, and then, as if surprised by a visit from a long misplaced friend, his tight, lean cheeks spread into an enormous unrestrained grin.

"Master Huud! Everything . . . everything is shining!"

"Yes, lad. It is indeed."

Hom caught up with Mikk as he sat cross-legged on the Titokan maze carpet experimenting with the elaborate scales unique to the zimrah. The apprentice's slim fingers were already at home on the insubstantial strands of light, and he smiled softly when the Longchild's brow crinkled in confusion.

"How long have you played the zimrah?" Hom asked. He leaned up against Mikk's back and blew onto his neck. His breath smelled of stolen root sweets.

"Since this morning."

"But you're playing the obscure strings. How do you know where they are?"

"I can see them."

"No! You can't! . . . Really?"

"Yes."

The Longchild put his hands over Mikk's eyes. The bandage on his palm felt rough against the apprentice's cheek.

"Can you now?"

Mikk reached around behind him, tickled Hom's ribs, and the Longchild skipped away.

"You're not lying?" he asked. "You can see them?"

"Yes."

"What else can you see?"

"I can see Maya's going to have a tough job getting all the moss and blood stains out of your tunic."

"No, no!" Hom scowled. "Something special! Something I can't see."

Mikk set down the zimrah and squinted.

"Your hair isn't really white," he said. "It's silvery with a lot of blue and gray in it, and the gray isn't really gray. It's fawn. Was your hair dark brown once?"

"A long time ago!" Hom cried, incredulous. "You can see that?"

"Yes. Oh! One of the ground owl eggs just hatched."

"You can't see that," Hom said, but uncertainly. "They're in the basement."

"Of course not." Mikk got to his feet. "I heard the peep. Come on!"

The Longchild, never willing to follow, dashed out of the room with Mikk in close pursuit. They slid down the banister into the cavernous basement, ran past empty casks that had once held Belian wood liquor, and found the messy nest of feathers, dead leaves, and lint in the dingy corner behind the softly humming cistern. Half-buried in the rubbish, a tiny chick wriggled, large pieces of dark blue shell still clinging to its wet blue-black down.

"Mikk!" Hom breathed. "You were right!" He bent close to the chick, but didn't touch it. "Look how small he is. . . ." The Longchild beamed at the apprentice and the creases around his eyes puckered up and almost buried them.

"You are wonderful!" The child master leapt onto the apprentice and clung to him.

"Would you like to know a secret?" he whispered. "I want an apprentice. I've always wanted one. Will you come with me?"

"I can't. I'm Master Huud's apprentice. He's taking Maya and me back to Wynt in a few months to put together a new troupe."

Hom was silent a long time, his fingers clutching Mikk's tunic, his legs wrapped tightly around Mikk's narrow waist.

"Can I have a piece of you?"

"A piece of me?"

The Longchild dropped down.

"Something that is yours."

Mikk searched his pocket, but all he had was an extra bolba ball. He handed it to Hom.

"I know you will remember me," the Longchild said. "That's what Vyzanians do, but now *I* have something to remember you by." He clasped Mikk's hands and became very serious. "I'll tell you all I know." He cleared his throat. "When you sing, think of birds. When you dance, think of fish."

"Fish?"

"Or snakes. Doesn't matter. When you play music, think of water, and when you act, think of god." He released Mikk's hands.

"That's about it."

"Yes, Master Hom." Mikk smiled.

Chapter Eleven: The Audition

Huud Maroc held auditions over several days in the Crown's Theater in Wynt, the oldest, largest, most venerable theater on Vyzania. Mikk's status as an apprentice meant that, regardless of ability, he automatically had a place in the new troupe. Nevertheless, the master put him through the particular agony of every single audition, whether for dance, acrobatics, or music, and the boy acquitted himself very respectably.

"Not bad," said one of the Belian musicians who had traveled with the master before. "Did you really find this one at the Academy? That's hard to believe. I should think that would be the last place you'd find such a promising talent."

"Hey, Maroc!" a Kekoi comedian cried from the catwalk over the stage. "That skinny pup's all right. Are you going to feed him now or does he have to roll over and beg, too?"

However, no one, not even the master, expected the shock at the actors' audition.

The master's auditions, although open only to the very best performers, were public affairs and the populace of Wynt turned out in force, filling the thousands of tight, uncomfortable seats in the echoey vault of the Crown's Theater for a free, and free-form, show of some of the finest talent in their galactic sector. Huud Maroc had been criticized many times for this practice—Vyzanians of every class and level of sophistication, or lack thereof, came to the auditions, sometimes with food, which they threw in the aisles or at the actors—but the master defended his actions, claiming it was good medicine for the performers.

"They can look forward to much worse elsewhere," he said.

In any case, the crowd that afternoon was in a merry mood and

136

chattered incessantly through the actors' monologues. Someone's baby screamed in an upper gallery and a pack of barge sailors, burly men in rough leggings and the distinctive quilted tunics of water folk, loudly baited a clutch of icy-eyed silk-clad ladies from the suburban estates.

"Riff raff, bitch rich," Maya quipped as she pattered past with pots of cosmetics and boxes of wig crimpers. "Some choice!"

Veern Illist, a classic tragedian from Ur-shai, a city in the northern continent known for its dense fogs, refused to perform under such conditions. "This is absurd, Master Huud." He rapidly fanned his long, lugubrious face with a broad merro leaf. "No artist should have to subject himself to this kind of disrespect. I will not go on unless they behave themselves."

"I'm surprised, Veern. I thought you had more backbone than that."

"It's not a question of backbone," the actor sniffed, "it's a question of common decency. I will not be fed to wolverines."

"Wolves. If you're going to use an outworld phrase, you should first be sure you know what it is." Huud Maroc sighed. "I guess it's my apprentice's turn then."

"Not the boy! He's far too green."

"It's his turn."

"Spare him this once, Master Huud. They're throwing melon rinds."

"It's up to him." The master motioned the boy to come forward. Mikk had been peeking out from behind the massive tapestries that separated backstage from onstage to watch the antics of the audience and gaze at the white ornamental buttressing of the ceiling—ribs of an enormous stone animal. His eyes expressed a strange, detached fascination, crystalline and piercing, but not a true stare state because it kept moving, pinning down one group of hecklers then another.

"If you don't want to deal with it," Huud Maroc said to him, "I'll understand. 'Greater lights than yours have paled before the mob.' " The master glared at Veern Illist.

"Bakak D'lu," the actor sneered. "Act six, scene twelve, line forty-two. Far too elementary, Huud Maroc. You're getting soft."

"I want to try," Mikk said.

"That's my lad." The master squeezed the apprentice's shoulder. "Always your best. Remember."

"Yes, Master Huud."

The apprentice walked resolutely out onto the semicircular stage, avoiding the debris and heedless of the whistles, and stood down center.

"What is he going to give us?" Veern Illist asked.

"I have no idea. He gets up before dawn to practice."

The actor groaned.

"I hope it's not that lover's speech from *Ryd à Laya*! Every damned apprentice in the galaxy does that one."

Mikk stood quietly as though waiting for everyone's attention, which he did not get, but the master was pleased by the attempt. Veern Illist could fume all he wanted about the audience's lack of manners, but a good performer had to have them regardless, as well as a lot of patience. The boy was virtually naked out there, but did not charge on ahead to shorten his ordeal; he gave the crowd the opportunity to go with him and thereby risked greater exposure to derision. Since no one in the crowd knew who this gracile adolescent with the startling hair was, most of them ignored him and carried on with their picnics and increasingly profane verbal exchanges. One sailor did heave an overripe merro fruit, which splattered on the stage near Mikk's toes, a supreme insult since the fruit represented, among other things, sexual potency. The sailor had just symbolically castrated the young apprentice.

Undaunted, Mikk launched into his monologue.

> "I will be my own boatman in the There Beyond
> And the waters of forgetfulness
> Will swallow my regret . . ."

Huud Maroc's skin crawled. This wasn't the expected swooning love poetry from *Ryd à Laya* or a light comic piece from a chamber play, but a dramatic recitation of Brock-ell's "Last Poem," the one the bard's aide-de-camp found on his corpse the morning after the Battle of the All Night Fire, the culminating conflagration of the Black and Red War.

The antique verses were laden with premonitions of death and hallucinations of the afterlife and as chillingly, intensely rendered by such a young performer, one the age of many of the soldiers who had died by the millions in the Black and Red War, deeply disturbing. The restive crowd fell quiet and fixed their eyes on the slight, unknown boy who dared to darken the air with bitter memories. Huud Maroc couldn't believe it. A collective stare state! He hadn't seen one in 150 years. Even the baby in the balcony was hushed, whether voluntarily or with a wadded-up napkin, the master could not tell.

The poem was not the longest piece Brock-ell ever wrote, but the audience hovered a long time in silent paralysis after Mikk finished. It wasn't until one of the barge sailors began to beat his hands on his knees, breaking the tension, that Mikk received his first heartfelt applause from an audience of strangers. Even from the far end of the stage, Huud Maroc saw the flame leap up in Mikk's eyes as the boy experienced the rush of the most addictive drug in the galaxy.

Veern Illist gnawed his finger nervously.

"Beast," he said. "This one has teeth."

"Fangs. The Kekoi say 'fangs.' "

"Whatever. The boy's dangerous. Teach him glass dancing. He already knows how to tap into our common guilt." Veern Illist frowned at his finger. He'd drawn blood. "Mikk's good," he said with a touch of jealous iron tightening his voice. "Someone special. Take care of him or I'll track you down and beat the bones out of your body."

Someone special. For the first time in his life, the master felt old, but it didn't distress him as much as he'd thought it would. Finally, after a dozen apprentices, he was witnessing the birth of his successor and, somehow, it was immensely reassuring. Still, common wisdom throughout the galaxy dictated that the special ones were not only the most treasured, but the most likely to get hurt, and that did distress him. All he could do to protect Mikk was give him as many tools as possible to contend with the vicissitudes of life, and a generous helping of affection. Huud Maroc had begun to think of himself as more than the boy's master. As far as he was concerned, Mikk's so-called parents had forfeited their rights to this red-haired wonder years ago. Mikk was his.

"Bravo, lad," he whispered as the apprentice bowed to acknowledge the applause.

Mikk's head lifted and he grinned. He'd heard him.

Entr'acte: Kekoi Kaery: Pairip and Twee

When Mikk entered the courtroom, the outworld journalists who crammed into the corners and up the side aisles pressed forward, still and motion camspecs whirring and clicking, to get the best angles. They almost tumbled into the crowd. The racks of optitube remote receiver cones set high in the gold-plated dome swivelled into position, and the packed masses of the gallery, nearly as many outworlders as Kekoi, murmured and shifted in their seats. A few called out Mikk's name and some even applauded.

The performance master ignored the commotion. His eyes searched down the row of tribunes seated on the long, narrow curve of the dais until near the end, next to the rigidly erect and alert Spairan Counsel 6, they found Thissizz. The brilliant green Droos was coiled in a tight stack, his wedge-shaped head resting on top, eyes closed as if he were asleep. He wasn't, but Thissizz had drawn in his energies and Mikk's heart felt like a bird battering itself bloody against a glass wall. For the first time in centuries, the performance master could not sense his friend's emotions and it frightened him.

Thissizz, I know you're in pain because I am. *Please,* let me in! It's so cold here.

Raf and Fod led him down center to the defendant's circle, a pattern of gold buttons set in the stone floor between the dais and the guardrail, behind which the crowd banked up in semicircular tiers and balconies almost to the dome itself. It seemed a naked, exposed spot, but the buttons marked the limits of Mikk's physical freedom within the courtroom because, once he stepped into the circle, a pressure-sensitive mechanism in the floor would trigger an energy gate similar in composition to the one in his cell, enclosing the performance master in a column of translucent blue current.

However, when Mikk entered the circle, nothing happened. He glanced questioningly at Raf, who jerked his clawed thumb toward the dais and shrugged. Mikk made a small, formal bow to Pairip, the High Tribune. With Raf and Fod present, the performance master could not realistically hope to escape, but Pairip's foregoing of the energy gate was an unexpectedly benevolent gesture.

Pairip remained regally impassive and did not acknowledge Mikk's bow. The High Tribune was small for a Garplen if still three times the girth of the average biped and, compared to Mikk, a veritable mountain of soft, rounded flesh. Thankfully, in marked contrast to Councilor Oplup, every inch of Pairip's ponderous body was immaculately groomed. The light glinted off his perfectly round, bald head and lost itself in his carefully trimmed, glossy black beard. He wore a deep green robe of a sumptuous material, similar to Vyzanian coronation velvet, trimmed with soft brown fur and his short, thick, meticulously manicured fingers sported several simple, highly polished silver bands. When Pairip spoke, his rolling, bottomless bass voice was as rich, as fat, as the rest of him and made Mikk vaguely drowsy, as though he had eaten a heavy meal.

"Hear now, all who are present," he intoned in Belian and rang a spherical bell dangling from a chain around his fleshy wrist. "This Tribunal Investigation of the Galactic Council of Performing Arts into the matter of Mikk of Vyzania, performance master, is now in session."

The galleries became quieter if not quite silent and the optitube remotes extended their lenses, doubling the length of the cones. Tiny electronic eyes on stalks, Mikk thought, or, perhaps, something more profane. Beast! At least open your eyes, This-sizz! Reassure me that this is comedy, not tragedy. . . .

Pairip launched into the charges.

"Mikk of Vyzania, you have pleaded guilty to the charge that on the fifth day of the seventh round of the 642nd Kekoi Election Games you did, in violation of a Galactic Council ban on behalf of the now celestial Somalites, willfully and publicly perform a Somalite ballad. Furthermore, you have agreed that inasmuch as the ban adhered to you personally and you alone, and your performance was not the result of coercion or conspiracy, you are entirely responsible for this transgression and are solely answerable thereto." The High Tribune paused and his small, dark eyes scrutinized the performance master.

"You have also claimed," he said slowly and with special emphasis, "as a member of the Galactic Association of Performing Artists, and in accordance with Section 1014 of the Council Rules and Regulations Governing Galactic Performance, the right to challenge this ban before a tribunal of your peers who will weigh the merits of your position so that the appropriate response may be decided in public."

He rested his elbows on his wide knees and steepled his fingers under his chins. Was the Garplen amused? Mikk found Pairip's puffy features difficult to read.

"You realize, Master Mikk, if you hadn't been a Vyzanian, the Council would have dismissed your claim as fraudulent. No one had ever heard of Section 1014. It took a three-day search to find it in the oldest Council Rules texts. It had never been entered into the Data Ledger. However," he gently scratched his long earlobe, "it also had never been purged."

That had to be the phantom of a smile on Pairip's lips, but Mikk could not tell whether the High Tribune was glad of the oversight or merely found the situation ironic.

"Do you have all the Rules memorized?" Pairip asked.

"Only the most useful sections, High Tribune," Mikk said and the already teetering journalists leaned in closer. "A much shorter task, I assure you."

The crowd in the gallery laughed and Pairip rang his bell again. "The galleries will please compose themselves," he said and rocked back in his seat so he could see up to the back of the court-room. "There has never been a Council Tribunal on Kekoi Kaery or you would know this is a serious undertaking. I will outline the procedures and perhaps you will conduct yourselves with greater dignity in the future."

"Not likely!" a heckler cried, apparently from the back gallery. Pairip deigned not to reply but squinted suspiciously at the shackled prisoner standing silently below him.

"Each tribune," he explained, "in the order in which he, she, or et was chosen, will examine Master Mikk. Unlike at a trial, the tribunes are not required to restrict their questions to the breaking of the ban itself if they feel that other information is pertinent to the issues underlying this tribunal. Just what constitutes an issue is left to individual discretion. . . ."

"Why not sentence Master Mikk right now and get it over with?" the heckler called again. "You've given the tribunes permission to butcher his reputation on live feed to four hundred worlds."

". . . Once the tribunes have finished their examination, the tribunal adjourns and each tribune returns to his quarters to meditate before casting his ballot. A simple majority is required to vindicate or condemn. If Mikk of Vyzania is condemned, the High Tribune levies the sentence."

"As I said!" the heckler roared, and this time the crowd became vocal in its confusion.

"Who is that? Can you see him?"

"What nerve!"

"I'm on his side! Why are we putting up with this Council nonsense anyway?"

"As I said," the unseen critic continued, "if this is how you people conduct business, Mikk is already condemned! Tell them what the penalties are for performing a ballad. Go on! Put tongue to the words!"

During this tirade, the High Tribune never took his eyes from Mikk and his expression remained calm. However, his complexion underwent a dramatic color change from creamy pink to deep scarlet.

"The Council is a galactic governmental body," he said in a

chilly basso. "To break a Council ban is to commit a galactic crime. Galactic treaty requires such crimes be punished by permanent exile or death."

The courtroom fell into mortified silence.

"I hope you are quite satisfied," Pairip murmured to the taciturn performance master.

Mikk blinked slowly.

"If you do that again, the tribunal is over. Understand?"

The performance master raised his manacled hands and spread his long fingers in an elegant, if somewhat sarcastic, gesture of acquiescence.

"Vyzanians," the High Tribune groaned. "An impossible people." He lifted his chins and recovered his official hauteur. "The ban was imposed on you verbally, was it not?"

"Yes, High Tribune."

"Hm . . ." Pairip fingered his beautiful beard with tender loving strokes. "I will defer to the tribune from Borovfia." Disbelief rustled through the crowd. The outworld press briefly shifted focus from Mikk to the Garplen.

"What is he doing?"

"Perhaps he wants to remain aloof from the actual examinations as a demonstration of impartiality."

"Or perhaps he has already made up his mind."

Mikk had considered that last possibility himself, and his ability to hear virtually every comment in the gallery, positive or negative, did little to bolster his confidence. His act of ventriloquism had had its desired shocking effect but had probably changed nothing. The gallery could not vote.

With a resigned sigh, Mikk turned to Twee, the Borovfian actor. Twee smiled blandly at the performance master and gave him a small salaam but whereas Pairip's refinement was genuine, Twee's was awkward, obvious, and as authentic as the crystaloid diamonds Maya used to make jewelry for miracle plays. The Borovfian's strong resemblance to a Terran frog smoking a hookah did not help. True, all Borovfians looked like that and the hookah was merely the mouthpiece to the tribune's portable tank of methane, but Mikk detested affectation. When Twee removed the mouthpiece and fussily balanced it on the tips of his three gray-green fingers, Mikk felt an intense urge to slap him.

"What with several thousand witnesses," the Borovfian drawled, "it would have been ridiculous to plead innocent, don't you think?"

Mikk did not reply.

"Instead you bring up some dusty little Section 1024 . . ."

"1014," Mikk corrected.

". . . 1014 in a desperate bid to negate the ban itself and save your hide. Isn't that true?"

"No."

"Then why are we here, Mikk?" Twee asked with an exaggerated lift of his slick, sloping shoulders and a pained glance at the gallery. "It's a long way to come for no reason."

"I have two reasons, tribune," Mikk said, his voice taking on quiet but noticeable force. "The Council claims the ban was made in accordance with the wishes of the Somalites, but I believe, in practice, the ban does not reflect those wishes."

"And?"

"Something not even the Somalites could expect me to abandon: freedom of expression."

The Kekoi in the galleries stomped appreciatively and barked, but Twee pursed his long lips and rolled his yellow eyes sardonically to one side.

"Mikk, Mikk, Mikk," he chided softly as though addressing a child, "you're a member of the Association, subject to Council authority."

"I do not acknowledge their authority when it comes to this ban."

"In what *do* you acknowledge their authority? There has to be authority and agreement somewhere." He scratched his throat and blinked rapidly at the bright dome of the courtroom.

"This is Kekoi Kaery," Twee continued. "Your so-called freedom of speech is sacrosanct here but only because the Kekoi are a forthright people whose anger is sudden and short-lived. They do not hold grudges. On Vyzania, however, things are different, aren't they? If a journal in Wynt accused you of murder, your career would be ruined before you had a chance to prove otherwise. The Council exists to curb such abuses."

"Maybe so. But, as you said, Kekoi Kaery and Vyzania are

very different. Perhaps on Vyzania one needs protection against libel, but how can the Council justify regulating Kekoi Kaery—or Droos or Ti-tok or any other charter holder, for that matter—the same way? Each world, each problem, is unique."

"How can there be government at all without standards?" The Borovfian sucked noisily on his mouthpiece and the tank gurgled. He'd made what he considered the great, unarguable point and it had used up a healthy chestful of gas.

"A valid question," Mikk said, "but standards that are rigid lead to ignorance, fear, and tyranny."

"Fear?"

"Of others, tribune. Anyone not like himself. I'm a performance master, a cultural diplomat. I take different art forms from world to world so people can enjoy them and learn about other ways of experiencing reality."

"What you learn on one world might be considered offensive on another."

"Sometimes. People distrust the unfamiliar, but it's my life's work to challenge people and expose them to new things. If I had wanted to keep to the safe and well known, I would have stayed on Vyzania."

The Borovfian tapped his mouthpiece against his wide jaw.

"Very noble," he yawned with theatrical boredom. "But isn't there a line you should not cross?"

"That depends on the particular world."

"Oh?" Twee's yellow eyes widened and he leaned forward. "*Somal* was a particular world. You crossed *their* line. Why shouldn't you suffer the consequences?"

"Excuse me, tribune." Mikk's irises turned a deep violet. "The Council drew this line, not the Somalites."

"The ban was made at the Somalites' request! You know that as well as I do. Don't think you can wheedle out of this one over a technicality, Mikk of Vyzania!"

Mikk pursed his lips and slowly shook his head.

"Whees-aru based his request on conditions he thought existed at the time. Those conditions have changed."

Twee folded his six fingers together in sarcastic imitation of a good pupil awaiting enlightenment.

"Explain," he smiled.

"Whees-aru believed songdance would die out if I did not perform it because he thought people would not find any value in poorer imitations and would lose interest. He wanted no songdance at all rather than false songdance. However, when Aro—"

"Aro is of no concern to this tribunal! He is not the one who violated the ban! Laws aren't to be broken merely because you've changed your mind."

"I had to demonstrate there is more to songdance than what people had seen!" Mikk cried, eyes going full black. "I had to give them a glimpse of the truth so they could be more discriminating. The Somalites would have wanted that."

"Spare me!" Twee sneered. "That's extremely presumptuous. How can you possibly know the continuing wishes of the Somalites? They are celestial."

"Your euphemism bores me. They are *dead*, tribune, and if I can't claim to know their continuing wishes, how can you?"

"I don't, but I do know how to respect the law. You seem to believe mere opinion holds greater weight than legal consensus, a dangerously cavalier and amoral attitude." Twee took a short toot of methane. "I can't imagine why that makes you think you're qualified to champion another people's sacred art."

"Who better?" Mikk said, pouncing on the tribune's words with a broad, flashing grin. " 'Rejoice in the marriage of opposites for in their union is the completion of god.' "

The mouthpiece fell from Twee's lips and clattered on the dais.

"You Beast piss!" he shrieked, all artificial aristocracy leaching out of his accent. "How dare you quote the Borovfian Book of Mysteries!"

"How dare you be such a hypocrite, tribune?" Mikk asked calmly. "What do you know about the Book of Mysteries? You haven't been inside the Sacred Precincts for years, and you can't read."

"What?!" The Borovfian broke protocol and leapt to his feet only to lose the last of the methane in his lungs with the sudden exertion. He began to cough violently and dropped like a loose, heavy sack of meal back into his seat. He felt about desperately for the mouthpiece until Pairip reached down and handed it to him.

Twee drew on it thirstily, glaring with open hatred at the performance master.

Mikk appealed to the Garplen. "High Tribune, if the Borovfian tribune is going to question my qualifications, he should do so properly. I'm not accustomed to working with amateurs."

"Especially illiterate ones!" a Kekoi journalist cried from his precarious perch on the upper steps and the courtroom again broke into laughter, including Mikk, who tried to contain it by covering his mouth with his fingers. When the crowd, grateful for this intermission, started to clap, Pairip rang his bell.

"There will be order or we will not continue! Council law is in effect here, not Kekoi license."

The crowd's applause shifted to jeers and whistles as Raf and Fod quickly moved forward to keep the crowd from pushing over the rail. A small Kekoi pup, taking advantage of the guards' momentary distraction, squeezed between the bars and began to rummage unheeded through the pockets of Mikk's surprise tunic. He found a tiny kaleidoscope, sat on the floor next to the performance master, and looked through the toy, shaking it and nodding with small grunts of pleasure. When Pairip saw the pup, he signalled angrily to Raf.

"Get that child out of here! This is a courtroom, not a circus."

Sardonic whoops rang down the gallery from the striking Kekoi jesters ensconced in the back balcony, and a slow smile curled Mikk's lips. Sixty days without employment had not shaken the clowns' loyalty to a fellow performer.

"Why are you wearing that wretched jacket anyway?" the High Tribune asked. "It's inappropriate for these proceedings."

"I was arrested in it," Mikk said simply.

Pairip stared at him, then snorted softly in dismay. "I see." He glanced at Twee, who turned away, methane tank gurgling with a low dyspeptic growl. Pairip addressed the courtroom. "I believe the tribune from Borovfia has concluded his examination. We will adjourn for one hour then continue with the Egagee-motar tribune."

Mikk looked down the line one more time, hoping against hope to catch Thissizz's eye but the Droos had not moved, had barely breathed, during the proceedings. However, the Spairan was watching the performance master closely, blinking her dark eyes with the crisp mechanical action of a clockwork doll.

This must be very uncomfortable for you, Mikk thought. Would you feel better knowing I am uncomfortable too? I wonder. I doubt you'd understand that one of the few things I'm glad of in all this madness is my poor silly surprise tunic.

Chapter Twelve: Spaira

Huud Maroc and Mikk toured many strange and wonderful worlds, but Spaira was unique. It had the most treacherous terrain Mikk had ever seen, including barren, flinty peaks whose slick, precipitous sides reached completely clear of the atmosphere then dropped without interruption straight to the bottom of the sea. Fresh water was scarce and the mountain passes hid packs of wily Mandan bush predators. The beasts, native to another world entirely, had been introduced by an outworld visitor early in the Spairans' history and were now as dangerously at home as the bald raptors that circled in the tremendous updrafts from the canyons. Nevertheless, out of these unlikely conditions, the Spairans had carved their utterly immaculate little shelf cities that had no crime, no pollution, no poverty, no delinquency, and no illiteracy. However, they also had no art galleries, no competitive sports, no fiction, no poetry, no comedy, no parks, no recreational facilities of any kind, practically no music, and no theaters. Huud Maroc's troupe performed its shows in a lecture hall, shows consisting of electronic tone poems, acrobatics, juggling—and nothing else.

After the first performance, the Spairans, placid and clean in their geometric haircuts and simple gray unisex jackets and trousers, nodded and clapped politely for a few moments, as though it was expected of them, then abruptly departed. Mikk, having worked especially hard to give his acrobatics and bolba juggling an extra purity and refinement he thought the Spairans would enjoy, was crestfallen until Huud Maroc bounded up and gave him an exuberant hug, lifting the young man off his feet.

"We're a hit, boy! I've never seen such a display from the Spairans my entire life! This calls for a celebration."

That night he introduced the bewildered apprentice to his first glass of corthane, and Mikk discovered this virtually universal poison, although not toxic to Vyzanians, was exceedingly intoxicating. He got violently sick on it and vowed this first glass would be his last.

The Spairans were not invited to the outworlders' party and, according to Huud Maroc, would not have understood it anyway.

"They're a conservative people, Mikk—here, lad, swallow this; it'll help settle your stomach—minimalists who believe in logic and discipline. It may seem extreme, but this is how they chose to survive on their world."

"But, Master Huud . . . oh, ooh!"

"See what happens when you sit up? Lie there and listen to me for a moment. We're guests on this world, Mikk. Try to see things from their point of view."

Mikk wasn't sure he could, although he did try. The troupe's abbreviated performances required minimal rehearsal, and the apprentice had plenty of time to stroll the spotless Spairan streets. It didn't take long for him to decipher the Spairan routine. At daybreak, all Spairans of every age came out of their undecorated, squarish apartment blocks and performed slow, rhythmic calisthenics. Mikk joined them a couple of mornings but dropped the practice when he discovered how flat and dull-witted the monotonous movements left him, quite the opposite effect from that of the elaborate workout he'd been perfecting on his own in the predawn hours.

When the sun cleared the point on the low roof of the Hall of Truth, the Spairans ended their exercise and began the day's work. Most of the men and women headed for the electronics factories where they made telewave components. The older citizens rounded up the children and led them into the school compounds, buildings identical to the apartments except that they lacked the tidy kitchen gardens and well-scrubbed animal pens. There were no ornamental plants or pets on Spaira. Everything they raised they consumed.

In the late afternoon, when the sun touched the horizon, the Spairans went home and stayed there. Every sixth day was a holiday from the factories, but not a day free of work. Sixth days were devoted to horticulture, animal husbandry, and discussions of the Book of Laws, the Spairan Civil Code. The Spairans worshipped no gods, but they revered their simple, plainly worded legal text as much as other people coveted their scriptures.

If it hadn't been for the Mrkusi acrobats' dice game, during which everyone's money changed hands so many times they ended up with exactly the amounts they had started with, Mikk would have gone out of his mind with boredom. He appreciated the discipline of the Spairan way, but did not understand how a race could exist without play, recreation, or even squabbling, of any kind whatsoever. The contrast with the Droos couldn't have been more stark, and Mikk, who had continued his telewave exchange with religious regularity, felt an especially keen pang.

One cloudless morning when the thin bright air was still enough to unveil peaks halfway across the continent, making them appear close enough to touch, Mikk leaned his shoulder against the windowsill in Maya's room while she repaired a seam he had split in one of his light tunics during gymnastic practice.

Maya kept one discreet eye on the apprentice. Vyzanian adolescence was a long-drawn-out affair compared to the feverish period of changes the cephalopod had had to endure but Mikk looked nearly over it. He had attained his full height and lost his gangly look. Maya would have died a horrible protracted death rather than admit it, but she thought Mikk was handsome—for a biped.

"Mikk quiet today. Moody."

Mikk shifted his weight and sighed in assent, then asked, "Is that a school below us?"

"No, that apartments."

"There are some children in a courtyard. Not an adult in sight and they're walking in lines. They're very young."

"Spaira children always in lines."

"Why? The space is safely fenced; they can do what they like. Hom would be tearing about like a wild animal. Why march in a straight line?"

"Maya not know. Maya circular."

Mikk was silent again and Maya went back to her sewing.

"Hunh," she muttered, "seam no good. Mikk need jacket wider shoulder."

Mikk's eyes narrowed on the cephalopod who had become his all-purpose dresser, costumer, and whatnot. She was using three needles at once, flicking them rapidly in and out of the damaged seam, repairing it in seconds.

"Maya, I'd like to ask you a very big favor. . . ."

"Lords of the wind!" Huud Maroc cried when he saw Mikk, a rather exotic oath for him. "What is that curious getup you're wearing?"

"I call it a surprise tunic," Mikk said, examining it self-consciously. "Maya helped me make it."

The new softly structured, full-sleeved, belted black jacket looked much like any other Vyzanian tunic except that it was literally covered with pockets of various sizes outlined in curlicues of colored thread.

"The embroidery was her idea," he said.

"Very nice, but what exactly is a surprise tunic?"

"I was watching some children outside and, well, I've been collecting all those small toys and games wherever we go—some of them are very clever. I thought I'd put them in the pockets and let the children choose a surprise. Even let them sneak up and pull one out themselves, if they like. Make it a game. The children here are so . . . serious. They seem afraid to play."

Huud Maroc smiled gently. "That's a very kind thought, but the Spairans don't understand the concept of play."

"Perhaps it's because no one has ever shown them."

"I hardly think that's the case. The Spairans have lived like this for hundreds of millennia and the people who visit this world have little effect on them. Why do you think all we present here is acrobatics and electronic music?"

"Because they're abstract?"

"Because they demonstrate mathematical and physical laws. It's in their genes, lad, you're bucking evolution."

Mikk's eyes narrowed and Huud Maroc was struck by their steely conviction.

"I still want to try."

"Suit yourself, but I advise against it."

Mikk could not find the gate to the fence so he hoisted himself up and vaulted over the metal structure, then raked his fingers through his hair to straighten it and sauntered over to the dozen or so children who were already watching him uneasily after his extraordinary use of something meant to keep animals out and them in.

"Hello," Mikk said. "It's a beautiful day, isn't it?"

The children looked at each other before one, operating as a spokesman, answered. "It is dry and warm," he said. "Very healthful."

"Um, yes. Very. I've come from the building next door. I was watching you . . . take the air."

"Why?"

"You're Brother Mikk the Vyzanian," a girl chimed in. "My father saw you toss gold balls."

"Yes! I've come to perform for *you* today. Would you like that?"

"We have no money," the boy said. "You perform for money."

"Not always. Sometimes I do it just because I want to."

"Why?"

"Do you want to toss the balls here?" the girl asked.

"I can," Mikk said, "but I had something else in mind. Something you can do."

"What?" asked a third child so crisp and translucently pure in appearance that Mikk couldn't tell what sex it was. The child resembled a lovely, featureless ceramic puppet.

"Ask for a pocket!" Mikk threw open his arms.

"We already have pockets," said the first boy.

"I have surprises in mine," Mikk smiled. "Ask for a pocket and whatever I pull out is yours to keep. Or, if you like, you can reach inside yourself. You can even take something when I'm not looking if that's better."

"You want us to steal from you?"

"Yes! Isn't that wicked of me?" Mikk winked. "It'll be fun."

The children looked at each other, perplexed.

"Fun?"

"Yes. Something for the sheer pleasure of it."

The children stared blankly.

"It's like the feeling you get when all your calculations come out right."

"Ah!" said the girl. "Peace."

"Um, no, not exactly . . ."

"How can breaking the law give us peace?" the androgynous child asked.

Mikk's shoulders sagged. He studied the small, nearly clone-perfect faces who waited patiently for a reasonable answer to their completely rational, and innocently heartless, question—and realized he had lost. There wasn't even much point in giving the playthings outright to these children.

My mother probably would have preferred a child like these, he thought, *although she'd have been denied the pleasure of hurting them. Gods! What a farce. I feel miserable enough to make up the difference.*

"I suppose it can't," he said and managed to smile in spite of his humiliation. "Thank you for letting me talk to you."

"You're welcome."

Huud Maroc knew what had happened the minute Mikk returned. The apprentice sat down heavily on the bench beside him and fished out a salt stick from an inner pocket of the surprise tunic.

"I'm sorry, lad. I really am."

Mikk sucked slowly on the salt stick and traced a finger around the embroidery of one of the pockets, red eyebrows knit in concentration, each at a slightly different angle.

"It's a good idea," he said quietly, "but this is the wrong place for it." He straightened his back. "I'm going to try the tunic on other worlds."

Setting the salt stick between his teeth the way another man might a bantroot, Mikk got up and strode out of the room.

I'm not dealing with a child anymore, Huud Maroc thought.

The ever inopportune Councilor Oplup made one of his periodic unannounced visits that evening. The apprentice pretended to busy himself about the lecture hall, checking the sound system, going over the details for the next performance, but Huud Maroc knew what the young man was really doing: keeping close in case his mentor needed rescue. The master did not know when Mikk had developed this protective streak, but he appreciated it. Oplup was not to be underestimated in spite of his hampered mobility.

"I thought the Spairans revoked his entrance visa," Mikk whispered to the master as the rotund Councilor maneuvered his way around the clusters of dark green desk pods in the lecture hall.

"I thought so, too," Huud Maroc whispered back. "The Council must have threatened the Spairan government, and the only weapons these people have are hunting bows."

"Too bad." Mikk whisked off to adjust the portable light panel, but remained nearby.

"Spaira, Master Huud?" Oplup asked as he rolled himself up the short side ramp. "Isn't this world a complete waste of time?"

"We have a standing invitation. Besides, the Spairans are very generous."

"Are they?"

"Does 400 rek a night sound like a waste of time?"

Oplup's forehead flab drew up like an awning.

"Really? That much?"

"Money is such a venal topic, but you and I go way back . . ."

"We certainly do."

". . . and there are no secrets between us, are there, Councilor?"

Oplup's already horizontal features became even more compressed and placid in expression. "I took the liberty of inspecting your living quarters. Plain, but adequate. My report will state that you are being well treated."

It won't, however, mention that you undoubtedly rummaged through our personal effects, the master mused.

"It's nice to know the Council is looking after our welfare," he smiled.

Oplup waddled about the stage, a raised strip of flooring the Spairan electronics professors used to display statistical charts and models of new telewave micro-fluctuo cylinders, their main export. He sidled over to Mikk. The apprentice was kneeling, apparently absorbed in replacing some faulty recording chips in a module sunk into the floor, but he rose when the Councilor approached and his height momentarily startled Oplup. Nevertheless, the Garplen nodded politely to the silent young man.

"Managing the sound system, are we?" Oplup's wet little eyes traveled with unpleasant keenness over Mikk's body.

"Yes, sir."

"And what have we here?" The Councilor reached out and fingered a corner of Mikk's surprise tunic. The apprentice glanced dubiously at Huud Maroc.

"Show the Councilor, Mikk," the master said, his eyes warning the young man to be very cautious.

Mikk retrieved a gyrotop from one of the pockets and set it spinning on the Councilor's lumpy shoulder. Then he pulled a scent fan from another pocket and fluttered it deftly in his hand like a moth, filling the small stage with its floral perfume.

"I see." Oplup turned to Huud Maroc. "What is the point of these cheap little amusements, Master Huud?"

"They're for the children," Mikk cut in. The Councilor slowly looked back at him, a nasty, syrupy smile distorting his lips.

"Cute," the Councilor said and flicked the gyrotop from his shoulder. The toy broke apart on the floor. "It'll never catch on." He lumbered past the master and headed down the ramp. "The boy's a dreamer," he said.

"Yes," Huud Maroc replied, "he is that."

"Well, everything seems in order here, Master Huud. I'll bid you good-bye, until next time, of course."

"Of course. Have a nice flight."

When the Councilor was safely out of the room, the master gave Mikk a reassuring squeeze. "You keep right on dreaming, Mikk. That tunic of yours is an excellent idea. It's going to be very popular when the time comes."

"Yes, Master Huud."

The master looked curiously at his dejected apprentice and gave his shoulders another squeeze.

"You're hard, lad. The H'n N'kae are good trainers."

"They almost killed me," Mikk mumbled and the master laughed.

"Whatever they did, you're much stronger. I'll have to think about giving you some real roles to play. Maybe the prince in *Bakak D'lu*."

"The *prince*?"

"Now, don't get your hopes up, Mikk. I said 'maybe.' We'll see how things go."

Even if it wasn't a sure thing, Mikk floated through the day in a private rapture. For Huud Maroc even to entertain the idea of Mikk's learning the role of the prince meant the gruff old performance master thought very highly of him indeed.

Chapter Thirteen: On the Border

Due to delays caused by heavy prominence activity on the Rogoine sun, fifteen vessels arrived at the sector border station at the same time and overwhelmed the station's staff. When the announcement came that there would be at least a quarter cycle wait for inspection and processing, the crowd began to hunt for ways to pass the time. A couple of Kekoi got into a fistfight that was diverting for a while, until they were split up by security officials, but soon people had to resort to gossip, dice games, hogging the telewave machines, and snoozing in the uncomfortable scoop-shaped pods scattered throughout the station.

A small Belian boy squirmed in one of the pods, climbing on the arms, sliding down, crawling underneath, and tangling up as best he could. His long, deep blue, multifaceted eyes darted from person to person as he tried to guess where they were from, where they were going, and whom they would meet when they got there, but he had no one with whom to share his game. His parents had gone off with another Belian couple who had been to Terra and had acquired an antique mah-jongg set, something they had never seen before. They instantly asked to be taught how to play it and left their small son behind to amuse himself.

He scratched his hairless scalp with twiglike fingers. That Kekoi scrap had been fun, lots of snarling and shoving and nips at the ears, but, like most Kekoi fights, bloodless. Plenty of threat, little follow-through. The boy thought the security people had overreacted, but maybe they were bored, too. He was beginning to wonder if he should track down his parents and demand to be shown the Terran game too, when he saw a tall young Vyzanian with very red hair and the oddest looking jacket he had ever seen on a biped. It was black with wild squiggles of color outlining what seemed to be pockets, dozens of them, pockets within pockets, pockets inside narrow pleats, pockets tucked into seams, pockets everywhere. What could this pale stranger possibly need with so many places to hide things? Belians did quite well without any clothing at all.

The boy could not stand the mystery. He slid out of his seat and cautiously crept up to the Vyzanian. Since the waiting room was noisy and the Vyzanian stood in a long, impatient line for the tele-wave, the boy did not think his bare feet would be heard. He jumped when the young man suddenly turned around and grinned right at him.

"Hello," the Vyzanian said in perfect Belian, "did you want to make a call?"

Caught out, but too curious to retreat, the boy coughed gently and picked inside his belly button.

"That's a very funny jacket."

"Oh?" The Vyzanian kept smiling.

"There are so many pockets. Why?"

The tall outworlder bent down to the boy's ear.

"Shh! I keep surprises in my pockets," he whispered.

"What kind of surprises?" the boy whispered back.

"Why don't you see?" The Vyzanian stepped out of line. "You point to a pocket, and I'll show you what's in it." The boy pointed to a pocket low on the jacket near the Vyzanian's right hip and, with a quick snatch of his long white fingers, the stranger retrieved a small, flat, metallic ring.

"What's that?" the boy asked.

"Watch." When the odd young man in the outlandish jacket lightly flipped the ring it hung just over the boy's head making tiny, soft sounds like dance bells. The boy stuffed his fingers in his mouth to stifle a delighted scream.

"Do you like it?"

The boy nodded.

"Well, then," the Vyzanian said, easily catching the hovering circle, "it's yours." He handed the ring to the boy, who ran off to practice tossing it.

Mikk realized he had lost his place forever, but it didn't seem to matter anymore—surely, by now, the Somalites knew the performers were late—so he strolled around the waiting room and wondered how much success Huud Maroc was having with the authorities over the delay. When three new children ran up, another Belian and two Kekoi pups, he was secretly ecstatic, but pretended to be annoyed and frowned at them with his hands on his hips.

"What's all this about?" he growled, but his eyes gave him away. The children twittered and giggled and hid behind one another, tugging on each other's hands and arms and making faces. Mikk couldn't suppress a giggle of his own; they were charming.

"What else do you have in your pockets?" the Belian, a girl, asked.

"I have no idea! Let's take a look . . ."

Soon Mikk had a small parade of children, all with surprises, following him about as, at their request, he walked backward and juggled the miniature bolba balls from his pockets, a feat they had thought impossible. Adults looked up from their own pursuits to see what was going on and smiled, or stared, or whispered to each other, and Mikk's retinue gradually collected much taller individuals. He added more elaborate patterns to his performance and his grin broadened.

When Huud Maroc returned, he found Mikk the center of attention in a sizable crowd that oohed! and aahed! and applauded his special flourishes. A number of hovering circles floated in the air, and children of all races sat on the floor playing with puzzle boxes, Mrku folding squares, hand puppets, and wayward little bolba balls of their own.

"Well, well . . ."

He crooked his finger at the apprentice. The master had been successful, but they had to leave immediately before the supervisor found out.

Mikk tossed the balls into the crowd and made a short bow to bright applause.

"I have to go now," he said, and one Kekoi pup threw herself around his thigh and got spice aspic on his legging. He gently removed her sticky hands and kissed her soft furry cheek. "Really, I do, but I had a wonderful time. Thank you."

When Mikk caught up with Huud Maroc, the master hugged him roughly around the neck.

"I can't leave you alone for a minute, can I?" he rumbled fondly. "What did I tell you, lad? The tunic's a winner."

Mikk bit his lip, suddenly self-conscious, but the master thought he looked exceptionally attractive in his happy embarrassment, cheekbones and the bridge of his nose quite pink.

"It answers something in you, doesn't it, Mikk?"

"Yes," the young man said, "it does."

Chapter Fourteen: Somal

The transit station on Somal was twice as crowded as the sector border station. In the press of people, Mikk saw Belians, Freens, Kekoi, Ichtians, Mrkusis, and Rogoines, even a Venwatt or two, but none of the rangy, green-skinned natives. He was disappointed, eager to meet these dignified, spiritual people.

On the other hand, he understood why the Somalites preferred to stay out of the transit station. Hawkers from outworld-run ashrams had turned the place into a chaotic bazaar. With their wares spread in rows on plaited mats, they cried out in Belian to newly arrived pilgrims or ambushed them before they had a chance to descend the ramps. Huud Maroc's troupe was quickly swallowed up in the cacophony of languages, the swirling snares and webs of braid, hair, cloth, fur, tentacles, and feelers, and the weeping, screaming dartings about of the pilgrims' children. The entire living mass of frustration reeked with a sticky clash of outworld perfumes, incense, and the natural, acrid odors of harried flesh.

"Get your Amulets of Serenity here, guaranteed to block all nagging doubts and help you achieve the Peace. Only five scrip."

"Lost, brother? Seeking the true path? Join our Meditation Center. Learn the different forms of authentic Somalite contemplation."

"Repent! Only through mortification of the flesh can you become pure enough to receive the Peace. Come to the Ashram for Abstemious Revelation and find the true meaning of . . ."

"At long last available to the outworld layman: *How I Received the Peace and Gave Away All Other Intoxicants.* Ten scrip a copy. Two for sixteen."

This last offer stopped Mikk in his swim through the mob. He looked down at the hawker, a Mrkusi, and the wiry brown biped gave him a gap-toothed grin.

"Interested, young man?" the hawker asked in Belian.

"I don't understand, sir," Mikk said in Mrku, "how . . ."

"My mother tongue! And you speak it so well! What a highly educated lad you are!"

Mikk smiled coolly. He knew not to trust the flattery of a salesman.

"I'm confused," he said. "I didn't think any outworlder had achieved the Somalite Peace. Everyone knows the Somalites refuse to explain it. They say it's an individual path."

The Mrkusi's grin hardened.

"Education has its limitations, my young friend. Do you believe everything you read?"

"Of course not." Mikk took the pamphlet from the hawker's hand and waved it delicately before the man's face. "Do you?"

"I believe the book, if that's what you mean."

"Have you read it?"

The Mrkusi's smile faded as he crossed his arms haughtily. "I wouldn't sell it if I hadn't."

"If you had, and it had worked, you wouldn't need to sell anything," Mikk said. "People would treat you like a Chosen, the first outworld Peaceful One." He dropped the pamphlet back on the mat. "Forgive me, but you don't look all that peaceful to me."

"He's got you there, Ahn-wing!" the hawker's competitors guffawed.

"This Vyzanian is not as innocent as he looks, is he?"

"Innocent?" The grating whisper at Mikk's elbow hooked his attention and he found himself face to face with the sorriest Kekoi he had ever seen. Large tufts of the ragged and malnourished old male's matted brown fur had fallen out and the bald patches were covered with weeping sores. His broken claws dug into Mikk's sleeve as he searched the apprentice's face with cataract-clouded eyes.

"Innocent?" he asked again. "Are any of us innocent?"

A rhetorical question, but Mikk could not have answered regardless. The mangy Kekoi's neediness overwhelmed him more than his stink.

"I will tell you the story of the penitent Vonchoi," the Kekoi wheezed. "Then you will tell me who you think is innocent."

Mikk nodded hesitantly and the Kekoi pressed himself tightly against the apprentice's body. His scraggly chin almost rested on Mikk's breastbone.

"A Vonchoi pirate came to Somal to prove the Peace a fraud. 'They are not divine!' he said. 'They are mortal people and have no special protection.' He crept up behind a Peaceful One, a Peaceful One reading quietly in his own home, solitary and unsuspecting. Do you understand? The Vonchoi wanted to kill him! Stab a Peaceful One in the back! Oh! Such a crime . . . !"

For a moment, the Kekoi was unable to continue. He wiped his streaming eyes on Mikk's chest and the apprentice looked away to avoid retching.

"But what happened?" the Kekoi continued. "A miracle! Just as the pirate raised his blade—a terrible weapon, curved and jagged—he became paralyzed! He couldn't move! He dropped the dagger and the Peaceful One turned to him and asked, 'Will you stay for supper?' A killer to supper! The Vonchoi fell to his knees and wept! Right then he gave up his violent ways and became a monk. It's all true, I swear it! Now! Can you tell me who is innocent? Who has power? Certainly it's none of us, is it?"

He began to quiver and Mikk feared he was on the verge of a seizure.

"The Somalites never build ashrams or sell trinkets," the Kekoi said, "and they never leave their world. Why? They could, they have the knowledge, but they don't. They find the Peace right here at home and they laugh at us. They know they don't have to go anywhere. But we do, don't we? The wicked must wander."

Mikk pulled some folded scrip from an inner pocket of his surprise tunic and, after forcing the Kekoi's claws loose, pressed them into his scaly palm.

"For your story," he said softly. The Kekoi bared his canines.

"I don't need money! I'm a free soul!"

"You're a body, too. Please. Buy a new cloak and get something to eat."

The Kekoi stepped back, his meager hackles raised in fury. He tore the scrip to pieces and threw them at the apprentice before stumbling away into the heaving throng.

"You should heed the mad one," a new voice hissed. "Money is the Beast's nectar. Perhaps you'd care to divest yourself of the rest of its evil and save your life as well as your soul?"

Mikk did not bother to look at the would-be holdup man. He could hear where the man stood, and, reaching back with one hand, he grabbed the unseen Lambdan by his heavy collar and flipped him over the heads of the startled hawkers into a pen of quarantined upland goats. The wet manure sprayed all over the outworlder's golden skin and hair as he skidded through it into the wall.

Mikk straightened his surprise tunic. "I need some air."

No one said a word as he passed completely unchallenged through customs and exited into the brilliant Somalite afternoon.

The low-slung oval station sat on a promontory that sloped gently down to a wide, slow, silty river. Some of the hundreds of thousands of marsh birds who lived on Somal stalked the shallows on stiltlike legs, jabbing their rapier bills into the mud to skewer crustaceans. In the distance, the flood plain ruffled up into grasslands and rolled away into the hazy, wooded horizon.

Mikk relaxed and sucked on a salt stick. He could not believe how quiet it was after the confusion of the transit station. Still, with only seven million Somalites on this modest-sized world, there was room enough to absorb the noisy desires of those miserable pilgrims once they got outside. A few of them headed to the river to hire one of the flat, open water taxis to take them downstream to the settlements and ashrams. Most of the taxi pilots were Freens, and Mikk watched them closely. He could tell a lot about a world's temperament by studying these resident exiles. On Ev-Mobix 'Gar, the mobster-run galactic free port, the Freens hoarded food and were suspicious to the point of hysteria, whereas Freens on Vyzania saved up their earnings and speculated in real estate or silk farms, often becoming insufferably bourgeois. Here, the rough-hewn, stocky outworlders looked unhurried and well fed. The pilots joked with each other and played arkabi, a game using numbered tiles. Mikk did not see a single bantroot. Not one.

Farther down the shore, in the shade of a tree whose branches wept into the water like a cascade of fine green ropes, eight naked Somalite children played in the mud, making lumpy towers and smearing the soft brown glop all over their bodies. They chattered animatedly, bright eyes glowing from the shadows, and Mikk smiled. Unlike Spairan children, these beautiful little creatures, with their sleek, dark green skin, gold eyes, and dense, tight black curls, obviously knew how to enjoy themselves, and were getting absolutely filthy.

Mikk heard another, older voice call to the children and saw a woman, the mother probably, walk down the hill toward them. She wore a long loose robe of lightweight cloth dyed an intricate zigzag pattern of tans, browns, black, and yellow. Mikk had not yet seen her face, but there was something unusual in the way she moved, as though walking were a concession to gravity and her true mode of transportation was levitation. At the shore, she removed her sandals and beckoned in turn to each child, who obediently came to her and let her wash the mud off with cupped palmsful of river water. Mikk suddenly remembered a similar scene many years before at the water stairs leading into the Grand West Lagoon and, to his surprise, felt tears run down his cheeks. He'd been a very young boy then, waiting alone in his mother's hovercraft while she went into the city to visit friends. He'd sat there for hours, hot and sticky in his best silks, and would have given anything to be the waterfolk child getting bathed at the steps by an older sister.

The Somalite turned her head, and as her eyes fell on Mikk a sharp jolt shot up his back into his shoulders and his ears filled with strange, distant half whispers. She was a young woman, not particularly attractive; her coarse black hair hung limp and uneven about her shoulders, but she had an amazing purity of expression. The calm of a saint shone in her yellow eyes and Mikk, locked into a stare state, could not move.

The children, following the woman's gaze, pointed to the lone Vyzanian then skipped out of the river and ran up the hill to him. Mikk managed to wrench his attention away from the mother in order to deal with the little ones, but he felt her supernatural eyes riveted on him and heard her slowly, deliberately glide along the grass after her brood.

The children did not know who Mikk was and had never seen his surprise tunic before, but after he snatched a scent fan out of a back pocket, fluttered it in front of his face while miming a case of the vapors, and handed it to the smallest boy, the one who tittered the loudest, they understood. They poked about in the pockets for their own surprises and, once satisfied, touched their foreheads in thanks and trotted back to the water. Mikk knew their mother had watched the entire game and he finally dared to look at her again.

Her luminous regard moved serenely over his hair, his face, and down his long body to his slippers. He shivered as though she had actually touched him, and, when she came close, she did, passing her fingertips slowly through his hair. He was not upset by this sudden intimacy—many races found his hair fascinating—but he was alarmed by the incessant rippling tingle between his shoulder blades and the bodiless, indecipherable voices. His premonitions tended to be tactile and visual, not auditory, so he knew meeting this woman was vitally important, although it was foolish to speculate how.

The woman stopped handling Mikk's hair and turned her scrutiny to his hands. She took one up and studied the nail-less fingers.

"I'm Vyzanian," he said, thinking she might be trying to identify his race.

"How appropriate." Her wonderful, terrible golden eyes looked deeply into his lavender ones.

"You are not a pilgrim."

"No. I'm a performer."

"Even better." This time she touched him in a way that was highly unusual: she ran her hand down his leg, from hip to thigh to calf. She paused when she reached his ankle and momentarily encircled it with her fingers. Mikk's stomach tightened. The gesture reminded him unnervingly of Thissizz. When she straightened, the woman smiled, scorching him with beneficence.

"Remember everything, Vyzanian," she said, and drifted away.

Only then did Mikk realize the woman had not spoken in popular Belian but in the rocking rhythms and half whistles of Somalite, which he had never heard before. However, not only had he understood every word, he had responded in the same language, flawlessly.

Just then, one of the other actors in Huud Maroc's troupe, another young Vyzanian, ran up to him, panting.

"Mikk! Thank the gods! The master has been roaring for you and none of us . . . oh, my . . . Mikk? Have you been speaking to that woman?"

"Yes."

"Beast!" The actor kicked a divot out of the hillside. "You have all the luck! Barely out of the station and you've already met a Peaceful One!"

"She made me feel decidedly unpeaceful."

"A premonition?"

"The strongest I've had in years."

"Maybe you should tell the master." The actor glanced furtively over his shoulder.

"I don't know. You know how uncomfortable he is with that sort of thing. . . ."

"Understatement of the season . . ."

"Besides, she spent more time touching me than talking to me."

The actor elbowed Mikk in the ribs and stuck out his long pink tongue.

"You animal! Where did that premonition hit you, eh? Between the legs?"

"No," Mikk said with a wicked smile, "but I can give you one there if you want, pipgip!"

Mikk's colleague crossed his eyes at him and bolted. Mikk pursued him as he headed for the cluster of performers waiting on the promontory but, at the last moment, held back and didn't catch him.

"Ha, ha!" the actor cried. "I won this time!"

"You had a head start!"

"Eat Beast!"

Huud Maroc promptly collared Mikk. "Why did you let him win? You're twice as fast as he is."

"Why not? It made him happy."

"Gods flying!" the master chuckled. "If I didn't know what a terror you are glass dancing, I'd swear there isn't a single drop of good old-fashioned killer instinct in your entire body."

"Oh! I'd better get some practice in. We arrived later than I thought we would."

"Not on your life, lad. No rehearsing tonight." The master whistled to the others. "That's enough of that! Sooren! Try to corral the Mrkusis before they get themselves arrested. Those Rogoine pilgrims won't put up with much teasing."

"But, Master Huud, I need to rehearse," Mikk said. "Our first performance is only days away!"

"We've been invited to see some songdance tonight. Something you must not miss."

"But . . ."

"Beast, Mikk! One evening won't ruin you. Give it a rest, boy!"

Mikk pouted and the master draped his arm over the apprentice's shoulder. Huud Maroc had been indulging in this old habit more and more recently, even if it was not as easy for him as it had once been. Mikk was a head taller than he was.

"This visit to Somal will do you good, lad. The Somalites know how to do nothing, and with greater grace and purpose, than any other race in the galaxy and you haven't taken any kind of break in months."

"I don't need a break."

"No? You directed and starred in our last tragedy cycle, arranged the dates for the Ichtian tour, and even got us through that grueling run in the Werevan Cluster. Four performances a day and you still found time to practice that H'n N'kae martial art and glass dancing. I ask you: What would the Somalites think of all that? Does that sound like a man 'at Peace'?"

"I don't trust the Peace. It sounds unnatural. Life is too various for perfection." A small green swamp moth dipped and fluttered around the apprentice's face and landed on the long red curl that fell over his forehead. He brushed the insect away. "When I work, that's when I'm peaceful, Master Huud. I get restless with nothing to do."

"I know all about that, Mikk, but there's such a thing as over-rehearsal and it can damage a performance as much as slacking off."

The master led the way to the waiting water taxis. Sixteen of them bobbed low in the river, laden with the troupe's "light" traveling equipment: basic scenery, costumes, props, personal effects, and other odds and ends, including Mikk's trunk of surprises to replenish his tunic. Mikk hopped into the front taxi and offered Huud Maroc his hand. The master scowled but grasped Mikk's fingers and let himself be assisted on board.

"You irritate me, boy," he grunted.

"You're welcome."

The master joined Mikk on a packing crate and watched him toy with three of the bolba balls from his tunic.

"What are you up to, lad?"

"Twenty-four."

The master snorted.

"You're lying, but I won't press it."

"Do you think I'm exaggerating?"

"Not at all. That's not your style, but you're lying just the same." The master grinned. "You'll make an excellent master, Mikk, if you don't spontaneously combust first."

"I'd better not," Mikk said shyly. "I'd never get to see Thissizz again."

"Don't worry about Thissizz, lad. We're returning to Droos very soon." The master's craggy features softened. "It has been a long time, hasn't it?"

The young man put the balls back in his surprise tunic and pulled nervously at a loose thread. The ailing Kekoi had torn one of the pockets.

"Master Huud," he said without looking at him, "the Belians solved the problem of distortion years ago. Why won't the Droos get new telewaves with voice decoders and image screens? I don't know what Thissizz looks like now."

"Blue, I imagine. He's the age for blue."

"I like blue."

Mikk was still using blue as a visual mantra later that evening when Master Huud herded his motley troupe under the giant white tent where the Somalites would present songdance. Hundreds of small hanging lamps filled with nut oils illuminated the tent, the pungent smoke curling over the heads of the audience and escaping through a round hole into the ebony night.

Mikk crossed his legs as he sat on the hard ground and handed Huud Maroc, who was grumbling, his own pillow in addition to the one the master had brought. The master accepted both of them with a little extra throat burr, but said nothing.

"What is songdance?" Mikk asked.

"Song and dance. The Somalites always perform the two together, usually solo ballads and movement, but sometimes choral work. We'll see both tonight."

"Do you know Somalite songdance, Master Huud?"

"No, lad. It's not in many people's repertoires. You'll learn why in a minute."

"Is it sacred?"

"All Somalite art is sacred, Mikk, even their jokes, but song-dance is special."

"Is there a songdance ashram?"

"Please, Mikk!" the master said, but his exasperation was unusually gentle. "Drop the questions for now and let the Somalites perform."

In the center of the broad smoky space under the canopy, a round empty patch of ground had been carefully swept clean and sprinkled with white and yellow sand. Short fat tapers sat in the sand at the edges of the circle, a ring of tiny bright flames. The Somalites did not extinguish any of the hanging lamps or tapers to lower the already dim light. Neither did they ring a bell, send out a clown, clap, or signal in any way that it was time for the performance to begin, but the crowd became silent and Mikk felt another tingling shiver. Whatever had told the audience to be quiet had been nonverbal, possibly telepathic, and, being Vyzanian, Mikk had picked up the static.

Five Somalites who had been sitting down front next to the ring of tapers, three women and two men, stood up and stepped into the empty sand-strewn dance ground. Mikk glanced over the crowd but saw no musicians. When he looked back at the dancers, he recognized, with some queasiness, the woman from the riverbank, though she was no longer in her loose, camouflaging robe. She and her partners wore nothing but very wide, patterned baggy trousers; their torsos, arms, and feet were bare. Mikk couldn't take his eyes from the woman. Her seminude body displayed an almost impossible marriage of fragility and power. She had the loveliest arms he had ever seen, sleek and sinuous as a pair of eels. All of her flesh was firm and seemed to glow from within like the green gems that twinkled in the riverbeds on Ichta. She also had remarkably high small breasts for a mother of eight.

At an invisible cue, the dancers took the meditation stance, a loose posture with eyes closed, knees slightly bent, head erect, and hands clasped before them. After a long moment of utter silence, they swayed in unison to the left and began to sing a choral ballad about a family searching down the river for a place to make their home.

Mikk shuddered and dug his fingers into the dirt. How could something this purely, coldly sublime, a perfect blend of sound and movement, be so painfully erotic? The young man had to squeeze his knees together and pinch himself to stay under control and yet the dancers did not touch themselves, let alone each other. They moved with a boneless fluidity effortlessly mated to the liquid music pouring from their throats. Song and dance were one thing, completely indivisible.

In spite of his discomfort, Mikk sensed songdance's true essence was not physical at all. In fact, it did not have the same effect on everyone. Some people in the audience did appear to be suffering the familiar intimate agony, a couple even worked their fingers into their groins in time with the music, but others rested their hands on their throats or blinked rapidly or wept. All of their faces, no matter their distress, shone with an ecstasy Mikk could not call merely sensual.

Songdance must strike people where they are most vulnerable, Mikk thought, then reveal itself as a purer experience, beyond the limits of the body. It's tearing me apart.

The apprentice's sensitive eyes and ears began to overload and he reached for Huud Maroc's arm. Could someone develop a tolerance for this miraculous art? he wondered. How did the Somalites manage it? Only the woman from the riverbank seemed to be a Peaceful One. Her radiance was unique. How could the others bear it, let alone contribute to the harmony? He tightened his grip and, in a blissful hallucination, saw the song and dance as colored smoke twining together like serpents, like Droos, like Thissizz running his coils around and around in his mind.

Of course! he thought. At the heart of this beauty, there you are! Please stay with me. Let me touch you. . . .

But the ballad finally concluded, and Mikk, surprised to discover he clutched silk and not scales, released his master's arm. Huud Maroc pushed back his sleeve. A row of deep pink bruises marred his white wrist.

"Come on, Mikk," he said, rising. "Let's go outside."

"But, Master Huud, there will be more."

"Of course, lad, they'll perform all night, but you need an intermission."

"No! Really, I don't. Please!"

"*Now,* Mikk."

There was no arguing with that imperious tone. Mikk followed his master out of the tent into the warm soft darkness. The moon cluster was up and the mud babies croaked with comfortable regularity in the marshes, their backs covered with fluorescent spawn froth waiting to hatch. The two strolled down to the water's edge and sat on an overturned crayfish scull whose bottom had been scraped for recaulking.

For a long time, master and apprentice sat quietly, listening to the vocal amphibians, and watched the moons slowly change places, as their dissimilar orbits dictated, in a stately cosmic pavane.

"What are you thinking, Mikk?"

"I'm thinking about the death lily."

"Songdance is not 'death lily,' Mikk."

"Then why did you bring me outside?"

The master rubbed his wrist and Mikk winced. He wished he could bury the master in apologies, but now was not the time.

"Because I saw what was happening, lad. I wanted you to step back and discuss it rationally before things went any further."

Mikk lowered his eyes. "Yes, you're right. I want to learn Somalite songdance."

"Do you know why?"

The young man hesitated. He did, but how could he put it in words? It was more a belief than a reason.

"Master Huud," he began tentatively, "our memory keeps pain fresh, but we still adapt. I think I've learned to hold the basket at a distance," he raised his arms, "so it doesn't blind me, but Thissizz . . ."

No, that wouldn't do. He lacked the invention. He lowered his arms and shook his head.

"Master Huud, it's like trying to describe a special shade of blue when everyone around you has been color-blind from birth. I'm not even sure I can define it to myself, but when the Somalites performed . . . it seemed clearer. What I'm feeling, I mean. I want to understand it. Maybe songdance can help."

The master scratched his chin thoughtfully. "I couldn't say, lad. Still, if it's that important to you . . ."

"It is, and I'd like to find someone to teach me, but . . ." Mikk pinched his ear in embarrassment before whispering, "You are the only teacher I've had since the Academy."

"That's not exactly true, lad. You can't leave out Hom, the H'n N'kae, the Belians, or, well, anyone. But it doesn't matter. Song-dance cannot be taught."

"Then how does one learn it?"

"By watching the Somalites, memorizing the movements and verses, and trying to divine the secrets on your own." Huud Maroc yawned. Although it had been a long day, Mikk was concerned. The master didn't usually begin to fade until well after everyone else in the troupe had collapsed, exhausted, in their beds.

"These pilgrims with their ashrams miss the point entirely although it's the one thing the Somalites are quite clear about," the master said. "Enlightenment is an individual goal. Studying with others is fine, doing charitable service is more than admirable, but the search is interior and unique to each person. There is no one way to the Peace. I'm sure you know what I mean even though the dancers moved and sang in unison."

"They were one voice, one dance, and yet completely different from one another. They were more closely attuned to their own individual work than to anyone else's, but everything fit together."

"A simple lesson, isn't it, lad? Perfect your own harmonies and the harmony of the whole will improve."

Mikk shifted uncomfortably on the rough hull. The gulf of differences separating Vyzanian from Droos yawned wide in his imagination. At least on Somal, the blending of disparates was achieved between people of a common race and common culture.

"That's the most difficult thing anyone can do," he said.

"Naturally. It scares people to death. My first apprentice studied songdance for years. Never even got close to unraveling its intricacies and he's a fine, brilliant performance master, one of the best. He abandoned the practice after deciding his fumblings were an insult to the race who created the art."

"Did you ever try to learn songdance?"

"I was intrigued, but, no, I never did."

"Why? You, of all performers—"

"Please, Mikk," the master interrupted, "spare me the flattery. I was never that limber even in my prime."

Mikk cocked his head, deeply puzzled. "Master Huud, you're as flexible as a contortionist now."

"I wasn't referring to my body, lad."

Mikk looked away and drew a circle in the mud with his toe.

"I still want to learn," he said. The master nodded as though he'd expected this.

"I'll introduce you to Whees-aru. If he thinks you have potential, he might give you some advice, or he might not. Every out-worlder who has tried songdance has had to wing it on his own. Still, the elder is an old acquaintance of mine. He might enjoy meeting my last apprentice."

Mikk's startled eyes caught the multiple moonlight and turned pink before darkening to an upset berry color.

"I'm your last?"

"Of course, lad. I'm old, remember? Why else do you keep helping me whether I want it or not?"

"I've never thought of you as old, Master Huud."

"Oh? You thought maybe I was a Longchild? Like Hom?"

"I never noticed your age at all," Mikk said and drew a square this time. "I just thought of you as my father."

In the silence that followed this admission, Mikk continued to doodle in the sand with his toe and did not look up. He knew Huud Maroc was still there, he heard his breathing, but he did not hear anything that would reveal how the master had taken his words.

Finally, Huud Maroc sighed. "Do you think you're up to more songdance?"

"Now that I know what to expect, yes. Definitely."

"All right." The master eased himself off the splintery wood. "Let's head back."

Mikk glanced up and his heart nearly stopped. Although Huud Maroc seemed calm, his eyes were deep black and shiny.

"But, remember," the master said, "if after we see Whees-aru you still want to learn songdance, it will be a sacred undertaking. All of our work at least flirts with the mysteries, Mikk, but this art confronts them head on."

Mikk had more to do than wait for an audience with Whees-aru, elder and spiritual father to the Somalites. Huud Maroc's troupe had little time before opening its series of performances, and Mikk not only had to rehearse his own material, he was assistant director and had to oversee the rehearsals of others. He also had to supervise the construction of the temporary stage. The Somalites performed everything outdoors and Huud Maroc's troupe would do the same, but the actors needed a slightly more elaborate space for their productions than a sandy circle.

Still, somewhere between the daily clashes of brittle egos, the catastrophes of paint and cable and canvas, Mikk found time to visit the ashrams and pick up what he could about songdance. The outworld literature did not tell him much, although the pilgrims themselves were excessively eager to help, to the point of obnoxiousness. All he could glean from their convoluted attempts to define songdance was what the master had already told him: It could not be taught, few outworlders had tried it, and those who had had given up on it as far too difficult, frequently after injuring themselves. However, most of the would-be songdancers had not been trained professional performers. Therefore, Mikk hoped he had a bit of an advantage. Besides, he doubted these predominantly bipedal outworlders were driven by a private vision of reptilian grace. Even the Somalites might find that odd.

Nevertheless, the entire business smacked strongly of that oppressive and annoying search for the Peace since the best songdancers invariably were of the enlightened elite. It unsettled Mikk because songdance was a performance art, an entertainment, and he wondered if the gods had invented this knot just to torment him personally. The Somalites claimed the Peace was perfect and, once you achieved it, you would never prefer another psychic condition again, but Mikk couldn't buy that. He was a Vyzanian, one with peculiar sensory powers and an insatiable curiosity to boot. A "single, perfect state"? There had to be something wrong with the description of the Peace itself—Mikk, the linguist, well understood this kind of failure. After all, the Somalites "at Peace" were hardly identical to one another. One especially famous individual was not even peaceful. He sang and raved in a grove of trees a few miles downriver and could be heard all over the valley, but he threatened to attack anyone who came near him. Mikk tried to see him because the pilgrims said the old lunatic knew more about songdance than anyone, but the apprentice had to beat a hasty retreat when the Peaceful One threw sticks at him.

Mikk didn't know what to do. If he didn't want the Peace, would his lack of "quest" make learning songdance even more impossible?

"My head hurts," he told Huud Maroc. "I'm going for a walk along the river."

He was so lost in thought he almost didn't notice her, but her unmistakable aura at last pierced his brooding and he saw the songdancer a short distance ahead of him. Seven of her children were splashing each other and imitating the fisher drakes by ducking into the brown water and kicking up their legs. The eighth squatted in the mud playing with the Belian puzzle box he had "stolen" from Mikk's surprise tunic. The mother herself, stripped to a small blue loincloth, was scrubbing her robe on a wide, flat stone.

Mikk stopped. Performed by the songdancer, even this most prosaic of activities was beautiful beyond description. His initial assessment of her narrow face, weak chin, and ragged hair as homely now seemed barbaric. How could he possibly have considered her anything but a miracle appearing before his unworthy, hypersensitive vision?

She looked over her shoulder at him.

"What is your name?" he wanted to ask, but couldn't move his tongue.

The woman smiled ironically, as though she knew all about his tongue-tied frustration, then rose to her feet, and turned her back on him—but not in rejection. Mikk knew he was supposed to watch her, but he didn't know why until the woman slowly raised her arms, swayed to the left, then rippled her upper body to the right as though it had turned into emerald oil. Mikk's own arms and shoulders trembled as he watched. The woman paused and soundlessly repeated the movement.

Mikk's memory clicked. This was the opening step of the choral ballad he'd seen his first night on Somal, but without the words, and his sharp senses quickly took it apart, reassembled it, slowed it down, sped it up—and he snarled in dismay. He'd registered every bit of the movement, every shift and slide of flesh and bone, but the whole remained much greater than its parts even without the song. How could she move every muscle—no, every fiber of muscle, even her skin, completely independently and yet in harmony?

She looked over her shoulder again and Mikk ground his teeth together.

It can't be as impossible as it looks, he thought, or you couldn't do it.

He spread his arms and attempted the step . . . and instantly knew it was wrong. The woman smiled again, a narrow band of crooked teeth.

Damn you! Mikk thought and he tried the step again, and again it was wrong. He stamped his foot and the woman actually giggled.

Oh? Try this!

Mikk performed a quick flash of Rogoine bell steps, some of the most intricate and rapid dance movements in the galaxy, a skittering blur of twisting feet and ankles.

I'll bet you've never seen that before! he thought triumphantly as he threw in a final flurry that raised the dust.

The woman, barefoot, immediately duplicated the dance, perfectly, then, with a soft shrug, knelt back to her laundry.

"No! Wait!" Mikk cried in Somalite. "Please! Show me more."

The woman rocked back and forth as she worked the robe over the stone, but didn't look at him. The lesson was over. Mikk clenched his fists.

"I'm coming back," he said and she stopped rocking. "I don't give up."

The woman sighed, then, inexplicably, shaded her eyes with her hand and lifted them to the sun as though searching its blazing glare for an answer.

"I *will* come back," Mikk said.

The woman lowered her head and resumed rocking.

As Mikk turned to go, the boy with the puzzle box ran up and offered it to the apprentice, holding it out very formally at arm's length.

"I figured out how it works. You can have it back now."

Mikk crouched on his heels to be eye to eye with the somber green child.

"You don't have to return it. It's a gift."

"I know." The boy still held the box like a ritual bowl of sweet-meal for the gods. "I like it, but now you can give it to someone who doesn't have one."

"Then you wouldn't have one."

"But I did and time is precious. Let another have a chance."

Overcome, Mikk impulsively embraced the boy.

"You break my heart," he whispered into the closely cropped whorls of black hair. "Please keep the box. I have more."

Down at the water's edge, the boy's mother had stopped rocking and was staring at her son with a sadness Mikk thought strange under the circumstances, but before he could speculate what in his exchange with the child could have brought on such grief, the woman had turned back to her laundry.

Chapter Fifteen: Whees-aru

Considering Whees-aru's position in Somalite society, the elder's house was shockingly modest: a plain but spotless stone hut in the dry hills above some flooded grain fields, reachable only by scaling a narrow rocky trail barely suitable for goats. Huud Maroc was not about to ride a goat so, with Mikk's patient assistance, he stumbled and grumbled up the hill and got pebbles and sharp seeds in his Vyzanian slippers.

"Why is it I can get through an all-day performance of the Bolban *Raka* but can't make it up this wretched hill without tripping and panting like an overheated canine?"

"Because you don't want to. If we'd brought along an audience you would be bounding up these rocks like an ibex." Mikk pulled the master to the crest of the hill and Huud Maroc mopped his forehead.

"Grace of all divinity," he said as he looked out over the valley, "I forgot how beautiful it was from up here."

"You *forgot?*"

"A figure of speech, lad. Other races use it for emphasis."

"You're making fun of me," Mikk said, pretending to be hurt, but his eyes were bright as he took in the view. It was not as dramatic as the blue distances on Belia, but it had a quiet serenity that appealed to him.

"No, Mikk. Just look. No wonder the Somalites are dedicated to peace. This valley is like the First Island. The land before strife."

Mikk smiled. " 'And the First People stepped out onto the land,' " he quoted. " 'The animals and birds came close and were not shy for they had never seen such creatures before and the First People spoke to them and the animals answered.' "

"Yes." the Master nodded. "I wouldn't be the least bit surprised if the Somalites could speak with the animals. Mind you," he gave his apprentice a fond grin, "pretty soon that might be the only language left for you to learn." He looked at the valley again. "One thing is certain, though," he said, "I do not remember it being this hot."

The hut squatted by itself in a grove of gnarled shade trees that had split the rock with their roots, insisting on their place in the most inhospitable soil imaginable. The garden next to the hut flourished in transplanted river mud fortified with goat droppings and was choked with the yellow flowers that, dried and mixed with grain, made up the bulk of the Somalite diet.

The shadowy dwelling held a minimum of objects: a reed sleeping mat, some gardening picks, a small moss-burning cookstove, a couple of dented pots, and a stack of rough paper. Whees-aru wrote poetry. In his researches, Mikk had read reams of it, and some of the elegant, lyrical verses had made their way into the songdance ballads. Whees-aru was as close to famous as any Somalite in the world, and few people other than fellow elders had ever seen him.

Mikk shivered. The elder, a stately individual sitting crosslegged with a very straight back as he read, was at Peace. The vibration filled the hut. Whees-aru lifted his head when the two

Vyzanians entered, took one look at the young apprentice, and said in that whispering Somalite melody of half whistles, "Now this one comes. Is it already so late?"

"Whees-aru?" Huud Maroc asked. "I'm sorry. I don't understand."

But the elder's bright gold eyes were dancing gaily over Huud Maroc's tall, red-haired apprentice, and he set aside his scroll.

"You would like to learn our songdance."

"Oh, yes, sir!" Mikk said as he sat before Whees-aru. "It's beautiful! I . . . I'm sorry. I can't find the words. There was so much I was going to say, but . . . yes. I very much want to perform songdance. I'm good at learning new things."

"Hush, my young friend," the Somalite said, raising his long green hand. "Songdance is not something you learn. It is something you *un*learn, and outworlders are not very good at that. Ah! I see I've hurt your feelings."

"Please," the apprentice said, subdued. "I watch your people perform and I can't keep my body from trying to follow."

"It's true," Huud Maroc said. "That happens only when something shakes this young man to the bone."

"Songdance has nothing to do with shaking, although it does have something to do with bones," said Whees-aru. "The barest bones, the bones of emptiness." His eyes narrowed on Mikk. "You are a young man filled with many things. Is there room in you for emptiness?"

Mikk's eye pigment fluttered and he looked away. "I don't know."

"An honest answer. A frightened answer, which is good. If you're not afraid of the emptiness, then you're not ready to take it on. You would be underestimating its power." The Somalite smiled. "Your master had another apprentice years ago. We had the same conversation. He, too, was frightened, but he lacked something you have."

Mikk looked up.

"Anger. You have a very great anger."

Mikk glanced nervously at Huud Maroc then looked back at the Somalite. "Anger?" he asked. "What does anger have to do with emptiness? With peace? Doesn't anger destroy peace?"

"If it does," the elder said, "then the peace was not a true and lasting one. Don't confuse peace with calm, my young friend, and don't label all anger destructive. I know you've seen plenty of that kind. She will answer for it in her own time."

Mikk started, but said nothing.

"And you will see more, but I want you to think about another anger, the kind that puts speed in your feet and strength in your voice. It isn't merely for love that you learn from your master, it's for anger, too."

Whees-aru dipped his fingers into a small bowl of perfumed nut oil and rubbed it on his arms.

"As for songdance," he said, "you will try whether I give my blessing or not." He worked the oil into his elbows. "The sun has been very hot these last summers. I need twice as much oil as I used to."

Mikk, sensing the elder was through with his discomfiting lecture, stood up, brushed the dust from his tunic, and prepared to leave. He sighed and gave the Somalite a short bow before joining Huud Maroc.

"Mikk," Whees-aru said just as they reached the door.

Mikk had never actually been introduced by name. He stopped.

"How long is death?"

"Forever," Mikk said.

"Is it?" Whees-aru grinned. "Oh, and concentrate on the knees. That's the trickiest part."

Mikk bowed again, very low, and headed down the hill with the master.

"The Somalites don't believe in reincarnation. Do you think Whees-aru was referring to cosmic recycling?"

They were in a cooperative café run by the sweet but tiresome pilgrims of the Daily Ritual Ashram, a mixed assortment of outworlders devoted to finding the Peace by emulating Somalite domestic life.

"Whees-aru would never ask anything with such a simple answer," Huud Maroc replied as he wrestled with a boiled flatland crustacean. "These monsters are very tough to crack."

"The crustacean as well, apparently."

"Very funny!" The master handed over his platter. "If you think

you can do better, be my guest. I have no patience with food that
fights back."

Mikk lifted the scarlet tank-bodied, sixteen-legged delicacy,
studied it a moment, then, grasping the main shell at both ends,
gave it a sharp twist. The shellfish broke in two and he dropped it
onto the plate.

"Physics," he said.

"Physique," said Huud Maroc. Mikk blushed and the master
changed the subject. "What were you studying so diligently yesterday? That Peaceful One with her children down by the river
certainly has captured your attention."

"I don't even speak to her, but sometimes she sees me and right
there, in the middle of her chores, she'll perform pieces of songdance. No explanations, nothing. I have to find the ballads in the
literature myself." Mikk wiped the fish juice from his fingers with
the scented towel that the ever solicitous pilgrims set out for that
purpose. "Yesterday, she did something wonderful with her
hands," he continued, "something like this." He held the heels of
his palms together and undulated his fingers slowly back and forth
with the lazy, buttery suppleness of an underwater plant. "The literature calls it 'the ear.' Isn't that interesting? Maybe it's because
of my own freakish hearing, but I find that very profound. What
do you listen to with your hands? Vibration? Maybe it's a
metaphor. See with your nose, hear with your hands, touch with
your eyes—a scrambling of the expected so your mind will let go
of preconceived ways of interpreting reality."

"Or maybe it's just a lovely way to move your hands," the
master smiled.

"Perhaps." Mikk pursed his lips thoughtfully. "It's not like
glass dancing, Master Huud, but I think the fury of the one helps
the, well, ineffableness of the other."

The master balanced his seafood skewer on his finger.

"They say the man who can dance on glass has the key to
dancing on water," he said.

"What does that mean?"

"I'm not sure," Huud Maroc stabbed a piece of the broken crustacean and swallowed it, "but it sounds Somalite, doesn't it?"

Mikk rested his forehead on his hand. "This definitely is not easy," he said. He caught the glint in the master's eye and grinned before they roared out in unison:

"If what we did was easy, we'd be out of a job!"

Then master and apprentice frightened the curl from the pilgrim's braids by shaking the roof with laughter.

The performances on Somal went well. The green people enjoyed the vulgarest farces as much as the loftiest epics, which never ceased to amuse and amaze Huud Maroc, but, as Whees-aru had once told him, "Everything is part of everything. Pass the soup." Even so, late one night, the master woke up and was too agitated to fall back asleep. He had no idea why insomnia would hit him near the end of a successful run, but it was useless to fight it. He had had sleepless nights before and all he could do was wait them out and hope he eventually got drowsy. He stretched and went to the glassless window of his cabin.

Although night had cooled the air considerably, it was still much warmer than Huud Maroc remembered from his last visit some years before he took Mikk on as an apprentice. It was not uncomfortable and probably due to a rare drought cycle. Still, the heat was a little disquieting.

Of course, Mikk, with his almost complete lack of body fat, adored the heat. When not working or hunting down children with his surprise tunic or tying his concentration in knots over the vagaries of songdance, he changed out of his dancewear and put on the light, casual silks Vyzanians favored for the hottest months of the Season of Fruit. It did not surprise the master that when the young man wore these bright, semitransparent colors the actresses and dancers in the troupe teased him and flirted mercilessly. It also didn't surprise him that Mikk quietly made a point of being seen in them as often as possible.

Mikk did "experiment." Huud Maroc had been a notorious rake in his youth, and the signs could not escape his practiced eye in spite of the apprentice's almost unheard-of discretion. Until Mikk, the master had never known a young Vyzanian male who did not boast ad nauseam of his liaisons. Mikk claimed he didn't think of them as conquests and had no problem whatsoever playing pursued to someone else's pursuer.

"I'm too shy," he said. "If people waited for me to act first, nothing would happen."

"I don't believe you, lad. You just prefer to let your looks do the talking."

Mikk laughed at this. "Oh, Master Huud! That's the last reason anyone would approach me."

"Then why do they?"

"I don't know," Mikk said with a tiny embarrassed pass of a finger through the hair over his ear. "Maybe it's because I'm nice to them."

Mikk's "niceness" differed from his contemporaries' in other ways as well. In the first place, not all of the wishful interested who loitered backstage or received a secret caress on the cheek were female. The master had little to say about this. He'd experimented in this fashion himself.

What was more unusual, and much more dangerous, was that not all of Mikk's partners were Vyzanian. Interspecies relations enjoyed considerably less tolerance in the galaxy than same-sex ones and carried widely varying degrees of physical and psychological risk. Still, Mikk's experiments in this direction had been limited and the master, no tyrant on this score either, felt no immediate cause for alarm.

Nevertheless, Huud Maroc was surprised this hot, dry night to see Oo-aika, the Ti-tokan dancer, speaking with Mikk in the slice of yellow light that issued from the open door of the apprentice's cabin. Mikk's expression suggested he was puzzled by her appearance at such a late hour and that what she said easily could have waited until morning. However, the master knew why she was there by the openly confrontational way she stood: feet apart, weight on one hip, arms crossed.

This would be very interesting if it wasn't so potentially explosive, the master thought. On Ti-tok, women were the dominant sex, much larger, stronger, and more aggressive than the males. Huud Maroc had had a Ti-tokan apprentice, and his main difficulty with her had been getting her to accept his authority.

Oo-aika was every bit as tall as Mikk and considerably heavier. She had enormous shoulders and her saffron-colored, military queue ran down the entire length of a thick, meaty back that resembled a wall of reddish brown boulders. She had once said Mikk was a pretty good dancer, for a "baby prick," which was about as genuine a declaration of admiration as any male could expect from a Ti-tokan female, but it offended the master and he had said so.

"Don't be so sensitive, Master Huud," she had cooed as though she thought he was being adorable. "I like Mikk. He's got a cute, tight ass."

"Keep your hands off it," the master had growled. "He's not a harem boy."

Now Oo-aika, willfully ignoring the master's proscription, chatted up his apprentice in the middle of the night and stirred suspicion in the young man's pale lavender eyes. When Oo-aika finally made herself clear by cupping Mikk's jaw in her huge palm, the apprentice frowned and pushed her hand away. However, Oo-aika was not easily dissuaded. She grabbed Mikk's arms and lifted him against her breast.

Calling for help would have been the appropriate response; anything else was too dangerous. Ti-tokan men who resisted rape were often torn apart, literally. Mikk must not have known this; he called on his underlying stubborn streak instead. He forced his arms up, broke Oo-aika's grip, and gave her a good hard kick that put some distance between them.

Huud Maroc was about to leap out the window to save his foolish apprentice but checked himself because, incredibly, Oo-aika did not renew her assault. She stared at Mikk, clearly baffled. The apprentice stood rigidly in the doorway, eyes dark, more than willing to continue his resistance in spite of his supposed disadvantage in size, and Oo-aika did not know what to make of it. Perhaps she had expected Mikk to yelp or run, it wasn't clear, but she did not approach the young man again. Instead, she got up, gave Mikk a stiff bow, as though he was another woman, and walked away.

After this encounter, Mikk did not go back inside his cabin. He leaned against the rough plaster wall and gazed out at the night, momentarily lost in thought as the pigment slowly eased from his eyes.

Then he did a very curious thing. As the master watched, Mikk took the meditation stance and, without singing a word, began to practice the steps of the songdance ballad the river woman had performed their first night on Somal.

Huud Maroc felt the hairs rise on his neck. Perhaps Mikk's eccentric execution had something to do with it, but the master had never before noticed how similar songdance movements were to the swaying of an amorous Droos. No wonder the young man insisted on learning this impossible art!

Now the master understood why he couldn't sleep. After Somal and a short visit to Mrk, the troupe was going to that great forested world of the sentient serpents. He had put it off as long as he could, but Mikk's training was nearly over and he could no longer justify keeping the friends apart. The young man was getting too restless.

I hope your heart is ready to accept its destiny, lad, he thought. It's well out of my hands.

Entr'acte: The Magna

At the end of a stunted arm of the galaxy on an obscure, highly fortified asteroid, the Great Magna of the Galactic Council of Performing Arts drummed his digits on his medicine table and scowled until the corners of his yellow mouth touched his prominent collarbone. He removed his infrashades and squinted away from the optitube screen where S!v't, the Egagee-motar tribune, a spidery-limbed biped with skin the texture of deep fried tofu, droned on in flat, uninflected Belian about the history of galactic performance treaties.

"Damned Egagee-motars never get to the point," the Magna muttered then winced. He had arthritis in his lower back, common for a Hrako his age, but still immensely annoying. He reached for his massage belt, buckled it on, set it to high heat, and carefully lowered himself into his settee.

The door panel slid open and his assistant, a Punhalian coelenterate almost two heads taller than the Magna, hop-sucked into the bedchamber.

"Ah! You've returned," the Magna said. "What news?"

The assistant bowed his pale polyps then straightened the stalk of his body to its full height.

"We finally managed to stop his supply of salt and our agent continues to sabotage the heat to the cell."

"Are you sure?" the Magna asked with a nod to the optitube. "Mikk looks too healthy for a man who's been sixty days in cold storage. His hands are steady. They'd be shaking like dead leaves if he hadn't had any salt today. Kekoi Kaery's air is too dry."

The invertebrate underling drooped, polyps flopping softly to one side. "I swear, sir, we did everything you asked. His endurance is notorious."

"Endurance is not the issue here!" the Magna snapped. "Guile is! We must be vigilant!"

"Yes, sir," the assistant murmured.

"I knew something like this would happen, but I'd hoped it wouldn't occur during my administration. Do you realize how dangerous this situation is?"

The assistant waved his polyps a little, the way a biped might shift anxiously from foot to foot.

"But he's guilty, sir. One lone performer against the entire Council. What harm can he do?"

The Magna spat out an expletive so vile that his assistant drew in all of his polyps and would not come out until the Magna threatened to have him salted for his queasiness.

"Plenty, fool!" the Magna cried. "This tribunal threatens our very existence. Mikk is questioning the basis of our power. Can't you see that?"

The assistant quivered, his translucent body with its visible dark blue and red organs rippling like a soft fruit-studded aspic.

"Never mind!" the Magna snarled and turned painfully back to the optitube. "I should know better than to expect intellectual acuity from the spineless."

S!v't had reached the current century, but the journalists had long ago lost interest and were panning their camspecs up and down the dais and running subliminal advertising slogans in Belian along the bottom of the remote transmission. They paused when they reached Thissizz, impassive as ever, eyes still closed, features neutral, coils slack and heavy in their stack.

"What did the Droos say when you told him he'd been drafted as a tribune?" the Magna asked in a calmer tone.

"Nothing, sir."

"Nothing?"

"Well, he did offer me something to drink. He said I looked thirsty."

"He didn't protest the choice? Was he glad of it?"

"No, sir. He seemed completely indifferent."

The Magna turned off his belt and picked his teeth with his fingernail as he brooded over his assistant's words. He'd done a lot of brooding lately; his nails were torn short and ragged.

"Why do you suppose Mikk cares so much?" he asked. "The Somalites themselves never cared a Beast's turd about anyone else. All they did was inspire normally sane people to abandon their livelihoods and become chanting fanatics. It doesn't make sense."

"Sir . . . the tribunal. Master Mikk is speaking."

The Magna quickly snapped on his infrashades and pumped up the volume using the optitube remote disc.

"Maybe there *should* be some galactic incidents to kick the Council out of its complacency!" Mikk said, his voice sharp. Then he added, more mildly, "Tribune, I appreciate the protective function of the Council, but the body was also established to further cultural exchange. One function shouldn't interfere with the other."

"And you know which function is the more important?" S!v't asked. The wattles dangling from his chin and throat wiggled anxiously.

"I'm just pointing out that there's room for debate on the issue and that the debate should be allowed."

"You are very naive . . ."

"Probably," Mikk smiled prettily and the Magna snorted. The Vyzanian certainly knew how to flirt with the camspecs. "Extra years do not guarantee extra wisdom."

". . . and a romantic."

"Oh, I hope so! With all my heart!"

"The gods know why," the tribune said. "It is a terrible liability."

Mikk shook his head with good-natured indulgence. "Come now," he said. "What am I, after all? An investment broker? We are professional romantics, tribune. No truly practical person would get into this business."

"Please, Master Mikk," the tribune said, softening, "I am on your side. I know you are not a dangerous criminal."

"You do? How very disappointing."

"Ah!" The Egagee-motar slapped his withered hands together in exasperation. "I can do nothing if you are like this! I do not know where to go."

"Don't feel bad, tribune. You never were very secure without a strong director."

Surprisingly, in spite of the gallery's snickers, the Egagee-motar was not insulted. "Perhaps that is the reason I am here and you are there," he said thoughtfully.

The Magna switched off the optitube and rubbed his complaining sacrum.

"Contact our agent at the Kekoi jail. We've got to find out how Mikk is getting salt."

And it would be nice to know what's going on in the Droos' head, he thought, but reptiles are even more exasperating than hydras.

Chapter Sixteen: The Return to Droos

It had been a wait of a hundred years, but Thissizz still held back in the shadows of the Great Cavern as his young nieces and nephews, a dozen bright yellow wriggling and chattering limbless ones, swarmed around Mikk. They rubbed up against his hip and curled around his legs, extremely excited because they had heard the word on this remarkable performer and his surprise tunic.

"Pocket for me, Mikk! Pocket for me!" they cried. Some poked their noses and blue tongues right into the hidden openings of the tunic.

Mikk did his best to control the chaos by handing out circles that the Droos children flung up to hover and jingle or caught on their noses and the tips of their coils. The pups fell all over themselves chasing after the toys, and some accidentally tied their bodies into knots. Mikk helped undo them.

"One at a time now!" he cried. "Oops! Watch your sister there. That's right. Don't they sound nice? Of course you can have one of your very own. Yes! I really was there when you were born. Do you remember me?"

Thissizz remembered Mikk and recognized him, but how much he had changed! His letters had said nothing about this even though the Droos had begged for a description. Mikk was tall now and although he'd remained very lean—he had a marvelously small waist and narrow hips—he was strikingly sinewy and well muscled. All his rigorous dance and gymnastic training showed in the gracefully elegant way he moved, and it brought the heat to Thissizz's face. His long-lost friend was in the flower of First Adulthood.

Thissizz had also grown up. He was full size and the rich jewel blue of the young male. On the whole, he was much calmer than he had been, but the sight of his "pretty red-haired pup" as a young man moved him deeply, and when his nieces and nephews finally wiggled off with their new playthings, Thissizz's hold on his emotions slipped and he sighed. Mikk, who was on the other side of the Great Cavern, looked up, eyes narrowed and searching, a half smile of expectation on his lips.

It is no use hiding, Thissizz thought. Mikk will find me with his sharp senses. I will try to be decorous.

Thissizz unfurled himself from the shadows and slinked with studied nonchalance toward his friend. When Mikk saw the Droos, his features froze for a moment in amazement, then opened into a wide, joyous grin. Thissizz abandoned his assumed apathy and raced to him, nearly knocking the young man down.

"How I missed you, my friend!" Mikk cried. He embraced the Droos fiercely, and Thissizz worked his long blue tongue through the apprentice's tousled shock of flame-colored hair. "Look at you, Thissizz! How splendid you are!"

"You also are very beautiful," the Droos said with great feeling. Mikk's cheeks briefly turned pink.

"Just taller," he said softly. Then, he continued excitedly, "People tell me you've become a fantastic singer! I can't wait to hear you. Will you sing this evening?"

"Yes! And there have been so many good words about you I can't recount them all. Is it true you won the Upsilon Vega Comic Arts Award?"

Mikk rolled his eyes and groaned. "What a nest of fry that was!" he said, slipping into Droosian slang. "Three hundred judges from ninety-two worlds—I nearly upped my swallow."

Thissizz laughed and rubbed his cheek against Mikk's shoulder. "I wish I'd been there. How I would love to tour with you!"

"That's one reason we're here! Master Huud wants to hear you sing so he can decide if you're ready. Didn't you know?"

"I did, but papa tried to hide it from me. He didn't want me to get nervous."

"Are you nervous?"

Thissizz switched the tip of his coils back and forth. "Maybe a little . . . no, not really." He cocked his head at Mikk. "You're performing from *Bakak D'lu* tonight. Are you nervous?"

"Maybe a little," Mikk smiled, echoing Thissizz closely enough to momentarily confuse the Droos. "No, not really."

Thissizz quietly studied his friend's playful aurora-colored eyes, then grinned, slowly displaying his now complete set of four hundred teeth.

"Happy you here I . . . oh, no . . ."

Mikk chuckled and ran his hands down Thissizz's side, which made the Droos shiver and darken in color.

"Yes, I know." He embraced Thissizz again. "I couldn't sleep at all this week. I still feel I'm going to explode."

"Are you hungry?" Thissizz asked and, unable to resist its smooth, pure whiteness, he softly kissed Mikk's neck, an echo of the apprentice's parting kiss of long ago. The young man blushed again, a wider spread of color, and explored his cheeks with his fingertips as though he expected to find them altered in texture as well as temperature. Thissizz was charmed by the phenomenon and dipped his wedge-shaped head down and around Mikk's face to inspect it from every angle.

"Oh, my!" Mikk said. "I seem to be doing that a lot lately."

"I think it's pretty."

"It's embarrassing. Vyzanians aren't supposed to blush." He raked his hand through his hair, a gesture Thissizz remembered fondly.

"Maybe not all Vyzanians," the Droos said softly. "Just you."

A group of five identical turquoise females entered the Great Cavern. When they saw the friends, they squealed dramatically and began to torment Thissizz while displaying and shaking their hoods coquettishly.

"Thissizz, will you sing for me?"

"Thissizz, you forgot my birthday."

"Who was that I saw you with last night in the snow?"

"Is that your friend? He's cuter than you are."

"When are we going to ribble, Thissizz?"

At this last comment, Mikk feigned a look of scandalized shock and Thissizz ducked his head under a fold of his hood and hurried into a side tunnel with his friend in close pursuit.

"Who were they?"

"The Ahshessa sisters," Thissizz mumbled.

"They are very smitten."

"They are very deluded."

"I see."

"It's not funny."

"Of course not." Mikk put on a dour expression that he could not hold and quickly covered his mouth with his sleeve. "I am sorry!" he laughed. "But I think it's marvelous. Maybe you should marry them."

"I have no desire to marry!" the Droos protested, but he smiled in spite of himself.

"Never mind," Mikk said. "I was joking." He curved his arm around his friend. "You can't blame them, though. You are a ruggedly handsome Droos."

Thissizz tossed back his head. "I know."

That afternoon they toured the city, revisiting all the places they knew from Mikk's first visit, and at each new turn in the tunnel the apprentice became more excited. He chatted feverishly about his work, laughing at everything around him, and Thissizz became more and more quiet in response, too overcome to say a word.

"Dear gods, Thissizz!" Mikk cried over a slice of frozen melon, briefly breaking off his high-speed story about Somal. "I don't know what's the matter with me. You must think I've gone completely mad."

Thissizz merely gazed in delight at Mikk's glowing face, a face as familiar as his memories and yet unknown, a secret in spite of its open animation. Both of them had changed and it was their first meeting all over again—in reverse. This time, Mikk was the crazy one, skipping over the surface of every subject that came into his head, and Thissizz the bashful mute, trying to decipher the real meaning of what his friend was saying. The apprentice didn't stop talking until the Droos quietly slipped the tip of his coils around his ankle, at which point the young man became very still and a brief silver flame flashed in his pale lavender eyes.

"Mikk?" The flame flared up again and the Droos felt a deep heat in his bones as though Mikk's eyes had set his marrow on fire, a fire that melted away the tunnels, the Ahshessa sisters, the years of separation—everything. There was only himself and his friend. Nothing more was needed.

The young man suddenly looked up at the vault of the cavern where a small skylight, similar to the one over the hot pool, let the day in. "Oh, dear!" he said, and his dismay was a palpable weight on his voice. "It's late. I have to help Master Huud with the sets for this evening's program."

"Please stay. I, I want . . ."

Thissizz wanted to explore that silvery flame. It came from someplace new, beautiful, and mysterious and reached inside him to touch a place equally strange and thrilling, unlike any sensation he had felt before. Unfortunately, he did not know how to describe it and felt too shy to try.

Mikk slowly got to his feet and Thissizz's heart raced when he saw the frustration in Mikk's eyes framing the silver.

"Yes," Mikk said. "But . . . later."

He turned and dashed away down the tunnel, feet barely touching the ground as he dipped in and out of the crowds of Droos until Thissizz could no longer see him.

But he could feel him.

The Great Cavern filled quickly that evening and was soon sultry with the heat from hundreds of Droos. Backstage, Huud Maroc raged over how the performers' makeup was already beginning to soften and run.

"Great Beast on a bun!" He stormed back and forth as Mikk darted in and out of his path like a gleaner fish between the fangs of a banmiir eel. "I look like an Ichtian court buffoon! The eye frost is melting down my cheeks faster than lactfat!"

"You look wonderful, Master Huud," Mikk said with a quick nod of reassurance to the young Droos girls of the chorus. "Better than a man half your age."

"Dung balls!" the veteran thespian roared sonorously, and Mikk knew that even though the master did not for an instant believe his compliment, he nevertheless enjoyed it. "Don't be a fool, boy! I'm a wreck! We all look terrible! Even you look as though you've contracted some horrible infectious disease! Take that paint off and redo it."

Mikk made no move to change his very minimal makeup. The master often put on quite a show of jumpy yips before a program, and the apprentice was convinced it was exactly that: a show, part of the ritual Huud Maroc used to key up his theatrical energies.

Sure enough, the master suddenly stopped pacing and Mikk, following at his elbow, almost banged into him.

"What does it matter anyway?" Huud Maroc sighed. "After all, which is more important? The makeup or the performance?"

"The performance," Mikk dutifully answered. "Always."

"Even so, it would be nice to get some cooperation around here!" The master had found his second wind and waved furiously at the bank of theater lights. "What does that fool think he's doing stringing out the hot colors in a row like dried fish? Woff! Get your raggedy Kekoi butt down here! I want to scream at you . . . !"

Mikk shook his head. No one was safe from the performance *before* the performance. Even he felt a bit on edge. The apprentice rarely exhibited the same precurtain madness as the master, but tonight an unfamiliar effervescence fizzed in his limbs and made his skin hypersensitive, as though he'd burned it and the assaulted nerves were raw to every ion in the air. I've been performing for people for a century, he thought. Why be anxious now?

At the risk of really spoiling his makeup, Mikk dipped a sponge in some chilled alcohol and dabbed his temples, then sucked on the sop so the alcohol's tasty sting would distract him from his inner fire. He peeked out at the mass of limbless, a dazzling sea of sinuous colors, rolling and shifting with oceanic hisses and rumbles as it settled into place for the performance.

I'm finally performing for Thissizz. That's why I hurt.

On cue, his eyes found the great blue Droos coiled down front and the blood froth tripled its volume. All nine valves of his heart seemed to open at once then contract in a sudden gush that distended the veins in his hands and left him feeling steadier and clearer than he had in hundreds of theaters, on hundreds of worlds throughout the galaxy.

"For you," he murmured. His friend was a still and introspective presence in the middle of the storm of Droos, his enormous black orbs wide under a tense blue brow.

"For you, everything."

* * *

Thissizz had arrived early and was too agitated to pay attention to the opening choral medley or Huud Maroc's solo ballads. However, the piece that followed, a scene from a Terran kabuki play about a woman who was really an enchanted white bird, snared the Droos' interest and gathered it into a point. The onnagata was astonishing, completely convincing as a young wife torn between her love for her husband and her true wild nature. She floated weightlessly across the stage, girlish, knowing, and sorry all at once as she made her gold and white fan dance like one of the giant butterflies of the flower forest. In spite of the onnagata's height, Thissizz thought Huud Maroc had played a trick on the audience and cast a real woman in the role. He gasped when, at the conclusion of the scene, the onnagata removed his wig and that glorious red hair flipped down over his forehead.

Next, the troupe of Mrkusis performed acrobatics, and, as a well-planned surprise, in the middle of their most elaborate tumbling patterns, Mikk flew out of the wings and crashed through their routine with a reckless series of comic rolls, dives, flips, and spins. He quickly demolished the Mrkusis' pyramids and scattered the acrobats in all directions. While everyone had a good laugh, Mikk stole a fast bow and an "angered" Huud Maroc yanked him offstage with a braided hair lasso.

"Oh, my friend!" Thissizz murmured under the tail pounding and whooping cries of the Droos crowded around him. "I happy am you lost no longer are!" He decided he would try to get backstage at intermission.

However, when intermission arrived and most of the Droos sipped sweet fruit drinks from large geode bowls to lower their temperatures and cool the nearly steaming Great Cavern, Thissizz discovered the outworld press had gotten backstage first.

"Master Huud! Master Huud! A word please, sir!"

"Sir! Congratulations on your return to Droos! Can you tell us why you delayed it so long?"

"How about your apprentice, Master Huud? We hear he's the talent to watch on the galactic circuit. What's his story?"

Thissizz withdrew even though he would have loved to hear

what the master had to say about Mikk. Forcing his heavy coils through the journalists would have been rude, even dangerous, and the young Droos was unusually sensitive to the vulnerability of smaller species. Nevertheless, he was determined to see Mikk again this evening. He had to. No amount of chilled nectar could lower the fever in his bones, but perhaps Mikk's fingers . . . that was what he had missed most of all! It was strange but, when they touched, it was as though he understood what it was like to have limbs for embracing. It made him feel almost as close to his friend as he was to himself.

The first act after intermission was a short Belian ballet, an abstract simulation of crystals growing and spreading their patterns at the bottom of a mineral pool. It was lovely, but Thissizz wanted Mikk and, when the dancers withdrew, he got his wish. The apprentice strode out alone onto the stage and, without any musical accompaniment, sang an Ichtian myth cycle aria.

Thissizz reeled back in astonishment. The whispery timid voice of this once delicate-looking young boy had broken free and become shockingly powerful. It was an enormous voice, passionate yet controlled, with a marvelously elastic range and incredible brilliance. It seemed to slice open the vault of the Great Cavern and let in the uncharted distances of the galaxy. The phosphor globes shivered and flickered as the sound soared past them.

Thissizz shifted about and rewrapped his coils in a dozen configurations. This was special! Something unique and compelling. The lonely decades of separation had hidden the gestation of a true voice. The voice of a master.

If I succeed only half as well tonight, Thissizz thought, I will have outdone myself for all time and maybe Mikk will take me with him. Oh, I would die of happiness!

Still, the evening was far from over. Huud Maroc returned to recite classical Droosian sonnets that many of the elders, some of them hard of hearing, loudly agreed were incomparable, but which the juveniles had no patience for. Thissizz watched the young ones slip two by two into the dark antechambers to whisper, munch on soft fermented fruit, and gossip about the opposite sex. However, they quickly stashed their illicit delicacies and returned to watch Mikk in the finale even though it was a scene from an ancient Belian tragedy.

Thissizz liked *Bakak D'lu*, but he was nervous. Every actor in the galaxy either wanted to, or did, cut his teeth on the role of the prince, but Huud Maroc's portrayal was legendary, widely available on optitube reissues, and routinely studied as an example of how the classics should be performed. It would require enormous audacity to play the same role opposite the master's king, and none of his previous apprentices had dared. Was Mikk good enough for such a challenge? What kind of test did Master Huud intend this to be?

Thissizz hunkered down on his tight stack of coils and rubbed his brow against them.

Patience, Thissizz, he told himself, you will soon find out.

The cavern darkened, the stage brightened, and the magic began.

Dressed in a clinging black sleeveless dance suit, Mikk came onstage, a tense, rangy shadow looking for a place to crouch in wait for the king. Thissizz had never seen anyone move with such natural animal edginess except an actual animal, and instantly he found himself in another time, another place, watching someone he did not know, someone he feared.

The prince soliloquized about his lust both for the crown and his stepmother, the young queen:

"I will have them though I must carve through the flesh on my father's bones to reach them."

He pulled a dagger from his slipper and licked it. Thissizz shuddered. The expression on the prince's face was terrible, a blend of hatred, desire, jealousy—and regret. Although tormented and oppressed, this prince was preparing to kill someone he loved as much as despised. Not even Huud Maroc had considered such an interpretation. At least, not before Mikk.

Now the master, as the king, entered swathed in a voluminous belted robe of gold that trailed along the stone floor behind him. Unaware of the prince, he removed his crown and set it on a small glass table as though laying aside a serious burden. He spoke about his queen:

"My morning star, grace of my twilight years, without you there is no dawn and I cannot rise to grasp the reins of my dominion. Had I greater power, I would spur you to my chamber and forbid your absence from my side another day! My thirst for you is a desert. I would have rain."

Then Mikk produced the most startling invention of the evening. When he crept out of the dark to deliver the famous mocking lines about the sexual and political pretenses of age, he did not speak in his usual voice but, with the alteration of a couple words, dressed his lines in the higher, more penetrating tones of a woman, presumably the queen herself:

"Rain indeed, my sometime spouse! Spur my sides so I rest by your side? Your reign has slipped, oh king of nothing! You fall through the night of mortality dismounted. Do I return that you may mount again? A fond fancy, old man! Let nimbler legs and stronger backs ride your throne and your queen."

The king panicked at the voice and tried to escape, but he could not get a clear look at his attacker because the prince moved too quickly, flitting in and out of the shadows behind him. The prince laughed, caught his father, and spun him around. Face to face with the truth, the king shrank in the prince's grasp and seemed to age a hundred years.

No! Thissizz thought. This is too cruel! But the prince had always killed the king and always would. With electric speed, the young murderer sank his blade into the king's throat and twisted it, a Vyzanian form of assassination, and rescinded all the moral pretenses of his class. Nobility was dead and the corpse sagged in the prince's embrace. He clutched a lock of the king's silver hair in his fist and the wiry muscles of his arm stood out, but trembled. The new order had triumphed, but was not as stable as what had gone before.

The scene could have ended there, but this was a new kind of prince. Mikk's pale, ice-eyed triumph suddenly cracked and darkened as he realized what he had done, and he lost his grip on the corpse, which dropped in an awkward heap to the floor. He stared at it, transfixed, then, with a choked howl, flung down his dagger and fled the stage. In the ensuing silence, the lights winked out.

How great your power, my friend! Thissizz thought. Gods steady me! What am I to do?

A deep roar rose from the audience, and when the lights came up, brightening on the lone, grim-faced performer, the acclaim visibly startled the apprentice. He seemed to hover in the half light of the performer's "squeezed sponge," unable to distinguish between himself and the character. His hand flew to his mouth and his eyes turned a turgid violet, but they cleared quickly and he broke into a relieved grin.

Thissizz was beside himself and almost missed Huud Maroc's invitation from the stage, a subtle nod when the noise at last began to abate. The Droos quickly mopped the tears from his eyes with his tongue and wended his way up the coil ramp to the stage to take his place in the solo point, the acoustic sweet spot off center and to the right. He decided to sing his favorite song, a paean to love and youth and he caught a glimpse of Mikk, a parka over his dance suit, standing with the master in the wings. The young man stuck out his tongue and pinched it with his fingertips, a Vyzanian theatrical blessing meaning "choke up and bleat." That was all Thissizz needed to re-ignite his courage and he shook out his hood, took a deep breath that greatly expanded his large blue body, and started to sing. His intoxicated thoughts revolved around his friend's brilliance, his smile, his lavender eyes, the seductive grace of his body. Mikk was beautiful and Thissizz's voice carried the depth of his affection out into the Great Cavern and back into the wings where the object of his ardor was in trouble.

In spite of Mikk's carefully honed ability to distill and discipline the information entering his ears and eyes, Thissizz's song was too much for him and his sensory defenses collapsed. This wasn't mere music, this was a gorgeous flood that passed through him and washed every shred of loneliness from his soul, replacing it with a fabulous, excruciating desire. The young man shuddered and clenched his jaw over a groan that, nevertheless, escaped in muffled pain. Huud Maroc quickly came up behind his protégé.

"Steady, lad," he whispered.

"I . . . it's . . . oh, help . . ."

Mikk's chest heaved and he began to rock involuntarily to the music. His lips parted and the master clapped a hand over the apprentice's mouth. "Cover your ears, Mikk," he said, but Mikk vigorously shook his head.

"Not again," Huud Maroc sighed. "Worse than Somal." He locked his free arm across Mikk's chest as the young man started to writhe in earnest. Subduing him was not easy—the apprentice was much stronger than the master.

"Shh, boy. Don't fight it. It'll only make it worse. Move if you want. The Droos are. See? Sway with it. That's it. Good. Easy. Easy."

Not that the master was immune to Thissizz's voice. It was wondrous, light years away from the sweet but undeveloped sounds Thissizz had made on their last visit. However, Huud Maroc wasn't as gifted, or as cursed, as Mikk. As he struggled to contain that slim bundle of flexing, stretching, twisting muscle and bone and tendon, he didn't know whether to count his blessings or be wildly jealous. What did Mikk hear? What did he see? Huud Maroc had been Mikk's master, mentor, nurse—everything—for a century and he still didn't understand how the apprentice experienced reality and what it meant to him. He doubted he ever would.

Thissizz ended his song and Mikk went limp. Huud Maroc thought he had fainted, but Mikk gently pushed the master's hands away and, shielding his eyes with his arm, slipped backstage and disappeared.

Thissizz had seen Mikk's gyrations, saw him leave the wings, and became frightened. After accepting the vocal accolades and heavy thumpings from his fellow Droos, he rushed to Huud Maroc to find out what went wrong.

"Master Huud! What did I do? Did I hurt him?"

"Not at all, my young friend. You overwhelmed him. If I didn't take you along on our tour next year, I think he'd kill me and it would be eminently justified."

"Yes? You liked it?"

"Well done, Thissizz," the master said and the Droos quivered all over with pleasure. "Go find your friend."

It was dark in the tangled catacombs behind the stage, but Thissizz easily located the distraught apprentice. Even before he saw him, he sensed his friend's heat, a wordless but eloquent message in the isolated chill of the back caverns. Mikk was leaning against the wall in a corner, his face to the polished stone. When Thissizz approached, the young man slowly turned around and the two friends gazed at each other in silence.

Thissizz came closer and, using the tiniest corner of his tongue, straightened Mikk's hair and licked the tears from his face.

"What troubadour could resist a prince?" he whispered.

Mikk slid his arms around Thissizz, rested his cheek against the Droos' warm, smooth scales, and let himself be carried out a side tunnel, up a steep coil ramp, and into a private burrow lit by three small phosphor algae night lamps. Thissizz gently set him down, kissed his mouth, then drew back to look at him with the tip of his coils curling and uncurling excitedly. Mikk flashed a sudden, self-conscious grin.

"What if Master Huud found me here?" Nevertheless, he removed his parka and began to peel off the black dance suit.

"I doubt he'd mind. How do you think he and papa became such good friends?"

Mikk giggled and Thissizz had difficulty believing the young man had ever been the benighted murderer prince. As he had the day he first came upon the strange boy with the wet red hair, he circled Mikk and let his eyes feast on the patterns of light and shadow playing over the clean, hard contours of his friend's body.

"It's cold in here," Mikk said.

"Clothing is such a strange thing," Thissizz mused, "especially when you pull it off. It's like shedding skin."

"Oh! Does that distress you?"

"No," Thissizz said. "It's very stirring." He stopped, lowered his head, and passed his scaleless cheek over the hilly pattern of Mikk's stomach muscles. "As though you're transforming into a limbless one."

"Gods in the sky! That feels wonderful . . ."

"Your eyes are full of silver, my beautiful friend."

"So are yours."

Thissizz ran his tongue along Mikk's jaw and was delighted by the subtle saltiness of his skin and its faintly spicy aroma. Oosmoosis had told him that when Vyzanian males became adults, they transferred their silks from plain unadorned wardrobes to fragrant merro wood chests and cabinets. The long-lasting scent clung to their clothing and skin and was considered the perfume of manhood.

Thissizz sifted his trembling coils between his friend's legs. Mikk a man! The Droos became almost too aroused to remain in control, but he had to. Now that they hovered on the lip of intimacy, they could no longer ignore certain anatomical discrepancies.

"Mikk," he said and the young man pressed his thighs together, squeezing the Droos and almost shattering his concentration, "I have had male partners before, but I've never ribbled with a biped."

"And I have never experimented with the limbless."

"What is to be done?" Thissizz breathed, a long hot gust that stirred Mikk's hair. "I do not want to split you open."

Mikk was silent a moment, then smiled. "That is why the gods gave me strong legs and hands, my friend, and you such a flexible tongue."

They laughed together at that, then Mikk became serious.

"Thissizz, all my life I've been set apart, strange . . ."

"Special."

"It can be the same thing in the end. No matter how close I get to someone, no matter how intimate, I can never reach their true selves and they can never reach mine. It remains hidden."

"That's the special sadness of all sentient creatures," Thissizz said. "The recognition of the rift between 'me' and 'thee.'"

"Yes, but with you, Thissizz, I want to cross that rift. I want to share all that I am with you." His voice softened almost to inaudibility, but its resonance was vastly greater than his timid childhood whisper. "All these years, the thought of you sustained me, steadied me even when things got so bad I didn't know where or who I was. You were always there in spirit. Now we're finally together, I want . . . I want to touch that sacred flame I see in you with the one I feel in me."

Thissizz, his huge black eyes wet with emotion, curved his hood around Mikk's shoulders, a protective shield of shimmering blue.

"My beautiful friend, you already have . . ."

* * *

"Is Thissizz ready to tour?" Oosmoosis asked.

"It'd be criminal for him not to," said Huud Maroc. "Perhaps next year, after Belia."

Oosmoosis nodded and tongued a chunk of crystallized nectar from his bowl.

"That odd little Academy fry turned out to have considerable marvels inside. But what a gamble, Huud Maroc! Especially after you swore you would not take on another apprentice."

"Do you know when I realized I hadn't made a mistake about Mikk? When I saw him covered with birth slime. Here was a boy who had never been outworld, let alone seen a Droos, and yet he plunged in as midwife. That showed real courage."

"So your premonition proved true?"

Huud Maroc laughed, took a sweet from his own bowl, and chewed it thoughtfully. "It hasn't been nearly as bothersome as I expected."

"You're fond of the young man, aren't you?"

The ring of phosphor lamps in the burrow added a greenish glow to the Droos' now coppery bronze scales, and the master sighed. Time passed much too quickly.

"Don't tell anyone or my reputation is ruined." He leaned back on his elbow. "He frightens me sometimes, Oosmoosis. I've never known any apprentice who was this fiercely dedicated. I swear he knows what I'm trying to say before I know it myself, and there are times he gets an idea in his head that nothing, absolutely nothing, can shake. Like the surprise tunic." The master picked up another sweet, tossed it high, and caught it in his mouth. "Performance masters often forget about the children," he said. "I don't mean they aren't friendly to them or forbid them to come to performances, but it's rare for one to create something uniquely *for* children. Mikk's the first performance master in my experience to do so."

"Is Mikk a master now?"

"He doesn't know it yet. After Belia, he will."

"A triumph in a major role or exceptional concert in another people's art on another people's world. That's how you defined it once."

"Exactly. You become a master when an outworld audience

acknowledges that you are." Huud Maroc's craggy face became wistful. "I'm going to hate to let him go, but it's time. Half my troupe wants to join him and I'll give them my blessing. Mikk's a warmer-hearted and more intuitive performer than I ever was."

"Don't say that! You're very well loved."

"I'm an institution," Huud Maroc grunted. "Not a particularly comfortable thing to be."

"You're just feeling old tonight thinking of the young ones." The elder Droos edged closer and gave his friend a provocative smirk. "I wonder where they are now?"

"Don't play ignorant with me," the master rumbled affectionately. "Where else would they be given their behavior this evening?"

"Like master, like apprentice?" This time Oosmoosis helped himself to a sweet from Huud Maroc's bowl.

"Nonsense. This is much more complicated. Why do you think I kept away from Droos as long as I did?"

"Undoubtedly for the same reason I never until now authorized the import of telewaves with image screens."

Huud Maroc's blue-purple eyes burned at the elder. "You *knew*?"

"I'm a Droos," Oosmoosis smiled. "We know serassi must be kept apart until they can embrace without losing their identities."

"Serassi," the master whispered, and, for a moment, he thought all the phosphor lamps in the burrow had winked in unison. "Most races don't have a name for it at all."

"It's beyond the bonds most races recognize." Oosmoosis' black eyes focussed on something far away, something invisible. "Even beyond friendship and love. There have been 'dark' serassi who hated each other but could not bear to live without the physical or psychic presence of their 'heart twin.' The bond does not respect age, sex, or, in Mikk and Thissizz's case, species. They are two as one, one made of two." The elder arranged his coils in a more comfortable pattern that, coincidentally, encircled his friend's reclining body. "I knew when Thissizz saw Mikk again everything would change. You knew the same about Mikk."

"Yes, that's so." Huud Maroc shook his head. "Incredible!"

"There is a Droosian folk belief that genuine serassi find each other only in their last incarnation because only then can they fully experience the wonder."

"Do you believe that?"

Oosmoosis shrugged, a little painfully. The osteoporosis in his upper coils had become worse in recent years. "First incarnation, last incarnation—we cannot see these things."

Huud Maroc drummed his fingers on Oosmoosis' scales. "Is there anything we can do to help them?" he asked.

"We've already done what we can, my friend." Oosmoosis rested his head on Huud Maroc's thigh and closed his eyes. "Do not fear for them. They are 'light' serassi. Blessed. They should live a very long time."

Early the next morning, while sipping a bowl of sisi, a spicy Droosian vegetable broth, Huud Maroc felt a curious warmth pass through his hands and, when he glanced up, Mikk stood just inside the entrance to the burrow, shoulder resting against the stone, arms crossed. The master slowly set down his bowl. Mikk seemed under the lingering influence of a life-enhancing elixir. The serenity and assurance of his long, lithe, muscular body, his almost incandescent well-being, frightened the master. This was no apprentice.

The transfigured young man smiled.

"Mikk? Something?"

"I know why you did it," Mikk said softly. "I understand."

"You do?" The master hardly knew what this vision was talking about.

"Yes, and I forgive you."

The master understood. "You had to know you could survive the pain, lad. Life is too capricious. It often separates us from the ones we care about."

Mikk unfolded his arms and, with a grace that all but stopped Huud Maroc's heart, crossed the burrow, bent over him, and kissed the top of the elder master's silver head.

"Thank you, but Thissizz and I are never separate, even with half a galaxy between us."

He straightened and flowed out of the room. The master was dumbstruck, paralyzed by his first stare state in nearly three hundred years. He had just been granted a glimpse into the unfathomable, his reward for the years of cruel kindness.

"Serassi," he at last whispered in prayer. "Holiest gods, it's true. The soul and the flesh are kin."

Chapter Seventeen: The Decision

If Mikk had let his discipline slip and missed a rehearsal or two, been late to cast meetings, or dashed in at the last moment before curtain, Huud Maroc would have understood. What the master did not understand was why none of this happened. Mikk seemed more eager to work than ever and, in spite of what must have been very late nights for him, overflowed with happy energy.

"When serassi are together," Oosmoosis said, "they are most themselves."

"Wonderful," the master groaned. "The lad's wearing me out."

"You should see Thissizz," the elder chuckled. "He sings in the tunnels and kisses everyone he meets."

Nevertheless, for one moment, the master thought he had caught Mikk being irresponsible, or at least distracted. Early one evening he came upon the friends wrapped together asleep next to the hot pool. Mikk was naked and both were completely covered with mud. Even Mikk's hair was thickly coated in black ooze. The mud was volcanic and therapeutic, but Huud Maroc doubted the pair had ended up in such a state out of a shared desire for organic skin care. It was nearly time for Mikk to perform, and the master considered waking him, but decided against it. The in-name-only apprentice was an adult and had to accept the consequences of his actions.

However, less than an hour later, Mikk was not only clean and dry but singing for a group of teary-eyed elders and outworld diplomats who had petitioned the master to let the "fine young one with the fiery hair" perform for them at a party clinching a new trade agreement. When Huud Maroc gave Maya a questioning lift of his eyebrow, she straightened her body and crossed two of her tentacles in front of her.

"Mikk quick," she said proudly.

"Maya too," the master winked.

The cephalopod slipped him a thick parcel. "New sketch," she whispered.

"Good!" The master made sure he and the costumer were out of sight of the sharp-eyed apprentice, then opened the parcel and flipped slowly through the colored drawings.

"Excellent!" he said as he handed them back. "Your best yet."

"Of course." Maya tucked the parcel under three of her legs.

"Make sure Mikk doesn't see them. I don't want him to find out until the proper time."

"Maya silent. Sleep on sketches. Mikk respect Maya bed."

"Smart lass." The master peered out of their hidden corner. "Look how he enjoys himself, Maya. He's got them sobbing like babies."

"Mikk happy. Shining."

Huud Maroc crouched down to Maya's height and her six jellies widened—she was surprised by his gesture.

"Maya, what do you think of this situation between Mikk and Thissizz? I know how you feel about Mikk . . ."

"Maya fine," she said with a casual wave of her foot. "See before."

"You have?"

"Eldest sister youngest brother."

"Gods in a barge!" the master gasped. "Within your own family? Siblings?"

"That not odd. Werevan not particular. But—outcome strange."

" 'Dark' serassi?"

Maya nodded. "Eat each other."

Huud Maroc stood abruptly and cleared his throat. "Um . . . lovely . . ."

"Master have nervous imagination." Maya toddled away with her sketches. "Thissizz vegetarian."

The rest of the troupe, not as familiar with serassi, was exceedingly curious about the attachment between the apprentice and Oosmoosis' youngest son, but no one had the nerve to confront them about it.

"I don't understand, Master Huud," Oo-aika said. "It disturbs me that something this unnatural seems so natural." She flexed her hands and caused the knotted cords in her forearms to bunch up. They were at a special postperformance cast supper to celebrate the retirement of one of the Kekoi jesters, and since Oo-aika had given herself a new tattoo for the occasion, she wanted to see how it moved. "What exactly is this relationship? We Ti-tokans know about boys who love boys . . ."

"Mikk's a man, Oo-aika."

"Yes, of course, but Thissizz isn't even a biped."

"Why don't you ask Mikk to explain it?"

"I'd rather not," Oo-aika said stiffly. "He's already outwomanned me once."

"Really?" the master smiled. "When was that?"

"That's between me and him. I do not wish to discuss it."

As an experiment, the property crew had rigged the large cavern with prototypes for the new anti-mag lamps, fist-sized cubes of opalescent mineral glass that not only gave off a soft pastel light in shifting colors but, when positioned over small pyramids of the same material, bobbed and jiggled in the air, suspended in an antagonistic magnetic field. One of the Belians discovered that the blue component in her skin disrupted the field when she passed her hands through it, and she improvised a ballet for her departing fellow trouper in which she manipulated the lamps' movements by whipping her arms and feet in and out between the cubes and pyramids.

The younger Kekoi jester, to honor his comrade, performed a condensed overview of the elder artist's routines. The troupe nearly choked on their fruits, greens, and sauces as they laughed at the one-liners, pratfalls, and unique facial mugging, which included a moue the junior artist could not quite duplicate. The older Kekoi had to demonstrate and sucked in his entire face until it resembled a collapsed furry melon.

Huud Maroc picked Mikk and Thissizz out of the merry group. The apprentice was leaning back against the coils of his limbless friend and, although laughing as heartily as anyone else, had that familiar piercing gleam in his eyes. He was absorbing the Kekoi's routine, analyzing it. The master chuckled. Mikk could not shut off his professional curiosity even at a party. Although the young man had passed the hypothetical standard of "fifty mastered arts" long ago, he seemed bent on adding to his knowledge at every turn.

He watched Mikk and his serpentine friend kiss during the applause for the young jester and the apprentice caressed the Droos' slick blue nose. A deceptively delicate hand, Huud Maroc thought, remembering Oo-aika's discomfort. Given his H'n N'kae martial arts training, Mikk probably could thrust that hand through a stone wall without getting a scratch and, given his basically self-effacing nature, he'd undoubtedly apologize for it.

When the clapping died away, there was a lull in the entertainment, but it didn't last long. Mikk lowered his hand and without taking his eyes from Thissizz's face began to sing with him. At once, the other performers stopped chatting to listen. Huud Maroc did not think any of them had ever heard the friends sing together, and even he was shocked by the complementary nature of their voices. The blending of Mikk's ringing, rapier clarity with Thissizz's warm angelic sweetness bordered on the supernatural. The longer the master listened, the more difficulty he had telling which voice was whose. Mikk and Thissizz had become one instrument playing two notes.

Oo-aika jabbed him with her elbow and pointed to the anti-mag lamps. When Mikk and Thissizz began their song, the lamps stopped bobbing and hung perfectly still. Now, as the music progressed, the cubes slowly descended, violating the repulsion of the magnetic poles, until they touched the pyramids, point to point. They stayed in this impossible contact until the song ended, when they floated back up to their original positions. The company was stunned. Some of them, skewers of food at their lips, held them there as though they had completely forgotten they were eating.

"What, gods shield us, was that?" Oo-aika whispered.

"I don't know," the master replied, "but it wasn't a trick. It was real."

The retiring Kekoi jester fluffed out his silver ruff and howled.

His younger colleague followed suit, and before long everyone was whooping and hollering their praise for the strange young couple shyly curled up together on the floor.

I've lost another half dozen performers at least, Huud Maroc thought, and the lad isn't even officially a master. It's time he knew where things stand.

At the end of the evening, the master caught up with Mikk and Thissizz just as they were about to turn in. "May I borrow this young man for a while, Thissizz?"

"Of course, Master Huud," the Droos smiled. "I'll know where he is."

"Let's go for a walk, Mikk."

When they stepped out into the darkness, the drifts were as deserted as they had been that evening years ago when Mikk first encountered the silent powdery ice.

"It went well this evening, Mikk. *Sass Roori Mesh* is not an easy play."

"The Droos are a very enthusiastic and forgiving audience."

"Nonsense, lad, you have a flair for comedy. Remember, the first time I saw you, you did something funny." The master puffed into the chill and watched his own heat steam and freeze. "But, to be honest, I think you're at your best with tragedy. You understand it better than most young men I've come across."

Mikk gathered up the collar of his parka and brushed some snowflakes from his hair, but did not look at the master. "Thank you," he said quietly.

"We'll be leaving for Belia in a couple of weeks. Do you feel you're ready?"

"Yes. Thissizz has a new telewave."

"I was referring to our new production."

"You haven't yet told me what you plan to do."

"Are you curious?"

Mikk stopped and gave the master one of his unsettling, crystalline stares, the kind reserved for pinning down a phenomenon and consuming it. "Of course," he said coolly, "but you haven't shared your intentions with anyone except Maya."

"How did you know?" the master asked, deeply surprised.

Apparently aware of how threatening his eyes looked, Mikk shifted them away to the tightly closed flower trees, but nothing disguised the tension of his body. "It's not kind of you, Master Huud. Lying to me is a terrible strain on her. She's broken out in a brown rash that hurts so much she can't sleep."

"I'm sorry, lad. She said nothing to me."

"You know she wouldn't! You know how proud she is. You told her to keep something secret, and by the gods she'll kill herself doing it!"

"Don't be angry, Mikk. I wanted it to be a surprise." A wistful smile wrinkled the master's cheeks and he rested his fingers on the young man's arm. "There's a reason I had you learn that scene from *Bakak D'lu.*"

Mikk's lips parted and a small cloud formed and melted on the air. "We're going to do the entire play?" he whispered. "On Belia itself?"

"Yes. Of course, you will be the prince."

The gem-like hardness dissolved from Mikk's eyes, which quickly turned a liquid purple, and he took a step back.

"Don't stand there gasping like a beached swamp grouper, boy. Say something. Do you understand what this means or not?"

Mikk uttered a small, soft cry and bit his glove. With tears congealing on his red lashes, he quietly put his arms around the old performance master and held him a long time.

The next morning, when Thissizz found out about *Bakak D'lu,* he covered Mikk's face and hair with kisses and told the young man to climb on his back and close his eyes.

"Where are we going?" Mikk tightened his grip on Thissizz's coils and heard the rustle of the brush and the startled flight of birds as the Droos carried him into the depths of the flower forest.

"Don't peek. You will be able to tell soon enough."

"I could walk at your side. I can hear where you move and follow."

"And deny me the pleasure of carrying you?"

"Droos are not beasts of burden."

"You're not a burden, except when you're being argumentative. Now hush!"

Mikk grinned, kept his eyes closed, and held on. As the branches parted, he tried to remember the rise and fall of the land, the sound of soft loam followed by stone followed by grasses as they passed under Thissizz's undulating coils. Gradually, the quality of the sounds changed, opened as though no longer contained by the canopy of flowers, and the air cooled. He heard the skree-caw of kites.

"I know where we are!" he cried.

"Where?"

Mikk gave Thissizz a squeeze. "The Rainbow Ravine!" He opened his eyes, hopped lightly off the back of his friend, and ran out to the grassy ledge. He stretched his arms triumphantly over his head.

"How bright it is! Like a chest of jewels. It's exactly as I remember . . . but different somehow. Why is that?" He looked over his shoulder, his expression joyous but puzzled. "How can something familiar be completely different, too?"

"I think you see things differently now." Thissizz wound elegantly up to his friend. "Perception changes."

"Yes," Mikk said thoughtfully. He returned his gaze to the yawning crags and flashing colors of the ravine. "But it really just changes its clothes or its color, as we do."

"Are you sorry for that?"

"Oh, no! I want the different colors. I want to remember them. I want to remember everything." Mikk smiled again, this time with confidence. "This will always be my favorite place," he said. "Every time I come here, I want you with me."

Thissizz nuzzled the young man's shoulder and Mikk lowered his eyes.

"There is something I always wanted to share with you, Thissizz, but I couldn't write it. It was too . . ." His eyes darkened.

"What? Please tell me."

Mikk sat on the grass. "I've remembered the basket."

Thissizz listened to Mikk's story of childhood terror, then laid his head in the young man's lap and wept. "My beautiful friend! All those years burdened by a memory you couldn't even see!"

"I am not burdened now. I feel as light as one of the kites, diving and soaring without effort."

"I'm going to ask my mother to adopt you," Thissizz sniffed.

"I don't need that!" Mikk laughed. "Such a sweet Droos . . ."

"What do you need, Mikk?" Thissizz turned his long head, the better to see his friend's face.

"Nothing. But I *desire* everything. I want to be the best performance master ever." Mikk became thoughtful again. "Such a strange way to live, don't you think? Running all over the galaxy, performing for others. Long ago, Vyzanian actors traveled in flatboats from town to town and didn't actually live anywhere. It's the same for me, except that I know where I live and it travels with me."

"Where is that?"

"Here. In you. You are my home, Thissizz, wherever you are."

The Droos curled the tip of his coils around Mikk's ankle and the young man's eyes flared silver. "Sing for me, Mikk. Something warm that I can feel low in my coils."

"You're the one with the miraculous voice."

"I can listen to myself anytime. Please? Make my heart travel."

Mikk squinted into the bright distance as he tried to think of an appropriate song, but another kind of entertainment occurred to him.

"I have an idea!" he said and stood up. "I'm not very good at it yet, but I think you'll like it. Let go of my ankle, Thissizz."

"You're going to sing with your feet?"

"Something like that. At least, if I had more experience . . ." He moved a short distance from Thissizz and limbered up, contorting his back in such a way that his friend thought he was trying to tie himself into a bow.

"Is that it?"

"No, silly," Mikk grinned, "but watch closely and don't laugh or I'll lose my concentration."

As Thissizz watched, Mikk took the meditation stance then carefully began a Somalite songdance ballad, the only one he felt secure enough to perform. In fact, Thissizz was Mikk's first audience for songdance, although the apprentice had discussed many of the moves with Master Huud.

Thissizz knew of songdance from Mikk's letters, but had never seen or heard it performed. He sucked in his lower lip, gathered his brow into tiny blue ridges, and held this comically worried expression for the entire ballad.

When he'd concluded, Mikk returned to the meditation stance, then looked anxiously at his friend. He even rubbed his foot against his ankle. "It . . . it's partly because of you that I decided to study songdance in the first place," he said, "but I want you to be brutally honest. What do you think?"

"I don't know," Thissizz murmured. "The air stopped. I couldn't breathe."

"It did? You couldn't? I didn't mean to . . ."

"Oh, Mikk!" Thissizz flung his coils about his friend and snatched him in close. "How beautiful!"

"Thissizz, please! I'm only a novice!"

"Care I n-not!" the overexcited Droos stammered. "Beautiful, b-beautiful Mikk!"

Thissizz's tongue lashed out and ran down the young man's neck and under his collar to slide over the sensitive skin of his shoulders. Mikk, arms pinned to his sides by his friend's ardor, arched his back and cried out. His voice bounced off the walls of the ravine.

"Why?" he sang as Thissizz pushed his nose into his tunic and tore the silk. "Why do I love this so much?"

"We are serassi," Thissizz hissed. "We are different eyes in the same face." He wrapped his long lips around Mikk's throat and worked his silky slick tongue over the heated pulse just under the skin.

"We are much more than eyes, my friend," Mikk whispered fiercely. "We have become new creatures." He rocked and swayed in Thissizz's embrace as though he, too, was a Droos.

"I never believed in reincarnation," he said, "but I do now."

Chapter Eighteen: Ahva

Bakak D'lu was not the only great Belian tragedy, but it was the most familiar and the most strenuous, especially for the actor playing the prince. Huud Maroc put Mikk on a special diet during the weeks of rehearsal and imposed a severe curfew.

"If you want to carouse and carry on like a cheap cabaret crooner," the master said, forbidding Mikk to do things the young man never did anyway, "do it when you can afford to, not while preparing *Bakak D'lu.*"

So Mikk took his vitamins, upped his intake of salt sticks, and went to bed early, but the strain still took its toll. He became irritable and restless and began to sniff about for a way to distract himself from the rigors of the production. With Thissizz on Droos performing a series of concerts on eight continents, that distraction had to be local. It turned out to be Ahva.

"Ahva" meant "flutter," an unusual name for a Belian, but Mikk thought nothing could have suited her better. Ahva was cast as the young queen, the bone of contention between Bakak D'lu and the prince, and she extended the flirtatious manipulations of her character into her daytime life as well. She had the willowy, hairless, androgynous blue body of all Belians but knew how to move it in the most suggestive manner. She drove Mikk out of his mind with her "accidental" brushings up against his arm and bumpings of her knee against his during supper, for which she apologized with soft throaty vowels and soulful sidelong glances from her large, deeply slanting sapphire eyes. She also made a habit of dropping by Mikk's dressing room to ask him for something when he was half-dressed or even naked. Ahva herself, like all Belians, wore nothing at all.

Mikk got angry at her, publicly, and pushed her away, but both of them knew he enjoyed her attentions and one day he cornered her against the looking glass in his dressing room, blocking her escape with his arm, and stroked her forehead, a highly erotic gesture on Belia. Ahva uttered a tiny scream, ducked under his elbow, and ran off.

I'll have to be more devious if I'm to get the benefit of that soft delectable blue skin, Mikk thought. He began to stalk her during the afternoon rest periods.

The Grand Imperial Theater, an edifice that resembled a spiky ice fortress, was part of a park complex in the Belian capital. Belians liked their parks ordered but overgrown, and the straight rows of mildly incandescent silver-blue and gray-blue firs intertwined their branches overhead in a thick, glistening canopy. It was the perfect place to play "ounce and doe" with a heartsick young man. Ahva would slip out of her room and escape into the park, and Mikk, leaping down from his second-story window, would follow.

Belians not only built the fastest spacecraft in the galaxy, they were pretty fleet themselves. Ahva would wander over to a tree, lean against it, and wait until Mikk, who moved like a feline through the cool afternoon mists of the deserted park, was right behind her. Then she would bolt soundlessly, a startled sylph, for another tree at the opposite end of the park. Mikk was quick, as Maya had said, but he could not catch Ahva even at a dead run. After a short sprint, he had to drop back to another predatorial stalk. Within a couple weeks, in concert with the health food, this high-speed afternoon chase nearly doubled Mikk's stamina, but it trebled his frustration as well.

"Where did you find that kinked-up air of danger for the prince?" Huud Maroc asked him. "It's perfect."

"Must be the diet I'm on." Mikk went to bed with an ice-water-soaked cushion between his legs to kill the pain.

The game continued all the time the troupe was in rehearsal. The afternoon before opening night, Ahva, as usual, snuck out and Mikk, as usual, followed.

The mists were especially heavy in the park that day and the soft glow from the trees hung in the moisture like haloes around their trunks and branches. It was lovely but made Ahva and her luminous powder blue skin especially difficult to find even with Mikk's powerful eyesight. When he finally did, his damp hair and clothing clung to him unpleasantly. It was the last afternoon before the premiere, he was agitated beyond endurance already, and when she darted away, he called to her with the ache of pure full-blaze desire. "You're tearing my heart!" he wailed. Ahva stopped and whirled around, her face pale.

"If the prince pleases my people tonight, perhaps I please the prince tomorrow." Then she vanished.

Mikk would have given the performance of his life regardless. Even without the master's startled admiration, Mikk knew he was superbly suited, physically and intellectually, for the dark prince. Nevertheless, his agony of soul went beyond anything he had shared with the Droos. The Belians broke into song for him during the curtain call, an honor reserved for their most beloved heroes, and Huud Maroc kissed him, right on stage.

Mikk felt powerful three times over. He had triumphed in one of the most demanding roles in the galactic repertoire; could now, with conviction, consider himself a performance master; and the young blue-skinned beauty watching wide-eyed from the wings was his.

But when Mikk dashed out to the park the following afternoon, he could not find her. The mists were light so that wasn't any hindrance. She simply wasn't there. He ran from tree to tree and circled the park half a dozen times—no trace of Ahva. He cursed and kicked his heel in the ground, furious with himself for being duped by such an obvious tease. Unfortunately, the sweet pain refused to go away. Mikk could not pretend that what he felt for Ahva was love, but it was definitely something more than lust. It was a visceral, even spiritual, craving for validation of his desires. Thissizz loved him and so did Master Huud, but what Mikk wanted more than anything his first day as a performance master was proof that this exasperating young Belian desired him because he was desirable in essence, not because he was gifted, favored, or in any way set apart by talent or circumstance.

Perhaps that's too much to hope for, he thought. If Ahva does, by some miracle, show up, it'll probably be because I'm Mikk the performance master, not Mikk the young man. Performance is my life, my identity, now more than ever.

He had crouched down during these ruminations and picked absently at the frosty blue grass with his slim white fingers, but now he looked up and saw Ahva standing not more than a couple of arm's lengths away. He rose slowly.

"Why did you come?"

"I was curious. You are very strange." Her multifaceted eyes softened to velvet. "I think you're beautiful."

He approached her and drew invisible spirals on her forehead with his finger. Ahva sighed and folded her arms behind her head as Mikk clutched her to his chest and kissed her shoulders over and over, surprised and delighted by the sweet-tart savor of her skin.

Mikk began that evening's performance with an effortless assurance that attracted Huud Maroc's pleased attention. "I see the first night yips are gone."

"I feel very strong," Mikk smiled.

"Good! Because Councilor Oplup is here tonight checking up on the new master."

"Don't worry. I'll give a performance to satisfy even his appetite."

Things went well until halfway through the third act, when Mikk began to feel a peculiar burning sensation in a rather private place. He dismissed it as a side effect of the supplements he had been taking. That kind of dosage could be very irritating. However, the burning intensified. By the fourth act, Mikk had to fight to disguise the pain and the difficulty of his performance increased arithmetically.

"Well done, Mikk!" one of the minor players whispered backstage after Mikk had finished a scene and slumped shaky-kneed against one of the thin transparent pillars that supported the roof of the theater. "Your torment looked incredibly real!"

Between their scenes together, Ahva watched him closely, obviously puzzled by his behavior, but he was too busy with costume changes and touch-ups to his fever-melted makeup to explain his distress.

By the sixth act, Mikk was in agony but it was too late to bring in a stand-in. Besides, that globally proportioned Councilor Oplup was sitting right down front, his fat spilling over the armrests of the modular float chair, his thick-lidded watery eyes fixed unblinkingly on Mikk.

During the final seventh act, Mikk "swam the waters with the Beast" and felt as if his psyche had split in two: one piece the performance master creating a stunning portrayal of the prince in *Bakak D'lu*; the other a flayed, but living, mass of quivering raw meat. The inside of his mouth also began to burn, but it hardly mattered. He had left mere pain behind centuries ago. The vertical light bars suspended between the pillars bent and twisted before his distorted vision and he wished he could shed his hot clinging costume and perform naked, in true Belian style, although he doubted it would give him any relief.

The curtain call was nearly as uproarious, and as long, as the one the night before, and Mikk endured the endless acclaim with a tight, hard smile, blackened eyes everyone seemed to assume were the result of the intensity of his performance, and sweat running down his temples in rivulets. The minute the soundproofing screen closed, he collapsed.

"Mikk!" Huud Maroc cried. He bent over the young man, who was in too much pain to speak. "What is it? What's happening?"

Mikk could barely whisper, so Huud Maroc put his ear next to his lips, only to straighten quickly a moment later in anguished rage.

"When did you have time to do *that*?" he roared. "Gods in heat, Mikk! You can't bed with Belians! Their body fluids are slow acid! Whatever possessed you?"

Mikk looked up at the old master with streaming, panicked eyes, and Huud Maroc realized the young man didn't need any more psychic punishment than he was already inflicting on himself.

"Never mind, lad. You didn't know and, contrary to how it feels, it's not terminal. It should pass in a few hours, no lasting damage done."

Then the master heard an unmistakable leaden thud coming up the side ramp.

"Beast breath!" he hissed. "The Councilor! That jealous bucket of guts will have you drawn and quartered if he finds out you've been having interspecies sex. Foobiss! Don't just stand there, give me a hand."

With the prop master's help, Huud Maroc spirited Mikk out a side panel, down around the gusting ornamental steam fountains behind the theater, and up a utility lift to Mikk's room before the Councilor could see him. He then gave Maya special instructions.

"Don't let anyone in except me, understand?" He turned with a sad, tender smile to his young colleague. "I don't know how you made it through the performance, Mikk. You must love this crazy life more than I do."

Mikk floated in his hammock on a sea of choice, particular cruelty. The master may have said he was not going to die, but Mikk was far from sure. He was almost afraid to breathe because the slightest movement sliced through his groin like a glowing spear. The action of his own heart filled his ears with rapid thumping.

Or did he hear another kind of pounding? There were voices outside his door.

"Good evening, uh, madam," came a greasy baritone. "I would like to see Mikk." Dear gods . . . Councilor Oplup.

"Mikk sick," Maya said. "Come back tomorrow."

"But I want to discuss his performance with him."

"Have to wait."

Mikk smiled in spite of his pain. He could imagine what their little scene looked like: the diminutive cephalopod, who barely reached past Mikk's knees, facing down that mountain of stored calories.

"No one see Mikk tonight."

"See here, fish!" the Councilor boomed. "Do you know who I am?"

"Maya not care! Maya different union! Now out, you, out!"

The heavy footsteps echoed away, noticeably faster than during their approach, if still ponderously slow, and the room became quiet again. After a moment, the door slid open and Maya entered with a glass basin and her kit.

"Maya get rid of big lard." She set the basin and kit on Mikk's side table then pulled herself up on it as well.

"Thank you," Mikk said, wincing as the blisters on his lips protested every syllable. Maya looked him over with her tentacles crossed in front of her.

"Hunh, Mikk sore?"

"Yes. Mikk sore."

Maya stepped onto the basin, arranged her tentacles around the rim, and squatted. A clear sticky fluid dropped out of her abdomen.

"What are you doing?" Mikk asked.

"Maya juice base. Kill acid Belian juice."

"You amaze me, Maya. Of course," he added, remembering the Droos birth slime, "it won't exactly be the first time."

"Take off clothes."

Mikk raised himself painfully, peeled off his soaking wet costume, and swore under his breath. No, nudity would not have been a good idea. He looked ghastly. The irritation had scribbled a web of dark pink streaks down the full length of his thighs and up his groin to his stomach.

Serves me right for listening to my body and not my soul, he thought. The gods know a fool when they see one.

Maya took several makeup sponges out of her kit, dipped them in the basin, and swabbed her own body fluids over Mikk's inflamed flesh. The burning subsided dramatically and Mikk moaned with relief.

"Oh . . . you take such good care of me!"

"Maya always good."

"My mouth hurts, too."

"Ugh! You do filthy kind sex things." Maya dabbed the bitter, pungent substance on Mikk's lips. Her half-dozen eyes became sly. "If Mikk want wife," she said, "Maya available."

Mikk laughed and patted her gratefully down her dark soft body to her tentacle legs.

"I'll consider it. I couldn't do better."

"Damn true."

"That dresser of yours is a vile creature."

Councilor Oplup had appeared bright and early the next morning while Mikk was eating alone in his room.

"She's very loyal."

"I see you've recovered from your ailment." Oplup eyed Mikk's breakfast dubiously. "What *is* that?"

"Grains and fruit."

The Councilor shuddered throughout his fat. "How dreadful! Not a man's meal at all."

"You wanted to discuss my performance, Councilor?" Mikk was in no mood to suffer much of the man's contemptuous arrogance.

"A dazzling display of thespian skill," Oplup said and Mikk cringed at the Councilor's puffed-up language. "Truly remarkable. Let me be the first to congratulate you on your official entrance as a performance master into the universe of theatrical arts."

The pomposity made it difficult for Mikk to keep down his breakfast, but he smiled at Oplup and thanked him, in its way a much more gruelling piece of acting than the prince in *Bakak D'lu*. The Councilor gave Mikk one of his own menacing smiles and dropped a sweaty, spongy arm on the young man's shoulders. Of all the ways friends and strangers had touched or assaulted Mikk's semiclairvoyant upper back, this was the most unpleasant. He couldn't wait for the Councilor to leave so he could bathe again.

"I'm sure that now you're a full member of the Association, you will maintain a friendly, and respectful, relationship with the Council."

"Of course."

The Councilor tightened his arm. "We do understand what that means, don't we? It means knowing who your friends are and avoiding the wiles of your enemies."

"I'm not aware of any enemies, Councilor," Mikk said sweetly.

"Sometimes they are hidden. Hidden deep inside. Waiting to turn our judgment away from the proper path."

Mikk stiffened in spite of his efforts to remain cordial. He did not like being threatened this early in the morning. "I'll keep that in mind."

"Good!" The Councilor pinched Mikk's bicep, a little too eagerly to be friendly. "Hm, what a meager body you have, Mikk. Not a man's physique at all."

Mikk pursed his lips in poor imitation of contented good humor and ushered the wobble-fleshed Oplup out the door, locking the panel open when the Councilor was gone. He wished he had some

Ichtian incense to fumigate the room, and he gave up on his break-fast, pouring himself a cup of grass broth instead, so rich in min-erals it was more a medicine than a food. He needed all the fortification he could get this morning. "That wretched Garplen is a chronic virus," he muttered.

As Mikk raised the cup for a final sip, Ahva appeared in the open doorway. He set his drink down. The actress seemed unchar-acteristically shy and hugged the oval jamb, averting her long sap-phire eyes.

"I didn't know," she said. "Please forgive me."

"I'm responsible, too."

"I shouldn't have teased you like that. You were working very hard. It only made matters worse for you."

"I came after you willingly."

Ahva's eyes shone on the young performance master. "Do you like me anymore?" she asked.

"Yes! I still want you even if I can't have you."

Ahva padded up to him and delicately danced her spidery five-jointed fingers over his face. "I want you, too. I want to know more. I want to know everything."

"That's because you're Belian. Perhaps you'll have to learn what it's like *not* to know me so well." Her fingers tripped over his lips and he kissed them. "You're a very fine actress, Ahva. Would you like to join my troupe?"

"I couldn't. Not after this. It would hurt my soul to watch you day after day knowing I can never lie with you again. If I can't have you, I won't have you."

Mikk slowly passed the back of his hand over Ahva's forehead. "If that's what you want, I won't insist, but we can at least see each other this evening on the boards and pretend."

"Yes. I am glad of that."

At the end of a year, at the end of the run, Mikk stripped a proud and misty-eyed Huud Maroc of fully two-thirds of his troupe, col-lected Thissizz for the Droos' first voyage outworld, and headed into the future.

Entr'acte: Kekoi Kaery: Martin

When Martin cleared his throat, Fod, who was on desk duty that evening, looked up from his platter of smoked swine, eyed the Terran's rumpled suit and balding head, and gave a short, contemptuous laugh. "You must have been the runt of the litter," the black-furred rookie said in guttural Belian.

Martin was not amused. His wide blue eyes narrowed into a sour squint and he pulled a pack of nicotine-free cigarettes from his coat pocket.

"No smoking, Terran," the Kekoi barked. Martin ignored him.

"I'm here to see Mikk," he said, and proceeded to light a cigarette. The guard leaned out over the desk and plucked the weed from Martin's fingers.

"No interviews," he said, and crumbled the cigarette between his claws. The bits dribbled onto the floor.

"I don't want to interview him!" Martin cried, his face purpling all the way up into his receding hairline. "My name is Martin Brannick and I . . ."

"I don't care who you are." Fod pushed himself back into his seat with his knuckles and discovered he'd accidentally lain across his platter of food and gotten grease on his new uniform. He wiped his hands over the stain and only managed to spread it around. "No one can see Mikk," he growled. "Nobody."

"You don't understand." Martin pressed up against the desk in spite of the swine's strong, rancid stench. "I have a special vested interest in your prisoner. His well-being is of the utmost impor—"

"How many times do I have to tell you, Terran?" Fod scooped

up a slice of swine, slurped it into his mouth, and chewed angrily. " 'No' means no. Go away before I call one of the security dogs."

Martin was about to dig in and escalate this exchange into a full-blown Brooklyn-style shouting match when a clawed hand gripped him by the back of his collar, lifted him almost off his feet, yanked him down the corridor to a private corner, spun him around, and shoved his back up against the wall.

It was Raf. The gray officer put his nose against Martin's and raised his hackles.

"What did I tell you?" he snarled. "We do it my way or not at all! You can't barge in here and demand to see Mikk. You'll get yourself thrown off the planet."

"Your way is taking forever!" Martin hissed. "I've been here over three weeks and nothing's happened."

"These things take time."

"You think *Mikk* has time?"

Raf slapped a furry hand over Martin's mouth. While they glared at each other, the harried Terran slipped a new tin of caviar into Raf's pocket. The guard grunted but otherwise hid any sign that he'd noticed.

"I came twenty-six light years to see Mikk," Martin continued when Raf removed his hand. "I've been sleeping in the same clothes since I got here because your gifted shuttle terminal personnel lost my luggage, your cuisine has knotted up my intestines in braids, there's no decent place to sleep because the city's infested with media hyenas, and you tell me you need more time to sweet-talk a professional party entertainer in a cheesy goatee?"

"Yes! Unless you can come up with something better. The Council is nothing to fool with. Pairip knows that and so should you."

He let Martin go and the Terran patted down the strands of hair spanning his shiny crown. Raf straightened his coat for him. "Odd material. Not very practical in this climate. You should get yourself a doublet."

"No, thank you," Martin pouted. "I've no interest in looking like a German mercenary from the sixteenth century. Why do you people wear so much clothing? You have fur."

"Why do you?" Raf retorted. "It's not as if you Terrans have much to hide!" He looked over his shoulder at Fod, who had returned his full happy attention to his dinner. "They've stopped Master Mikk's salt, you know," he whispered. "When the Freen went to the lab this morning, the head researcher wouldn't let him in. Even threatened to bite him." Raf sighed. "Your black fish eggs are the only salt Mikk has had today."

"Did he say anything? A message for me?"

"He doesn't know you sent the eggs."

"What? Why not?"

"Keep it down!" Raf grimaced, then his tone became sympathetic. "Look, this is my world. Kekoi law takes precedence if I get caught, but you and Mikk are outworlders. I can't stop the Council if they want to hurt you." He gave Martin a friendly pat and smiled wearily, displaying his broken left canine. "Why don't you get something to eat? Bathe, clip your nails, whatever it is you Terrans do to feel comfortable. There's nothing more to be done this evening."

Raf shuffled away, passing down the corridor to the officer's mess as fast as his bow-legged gait could carry him.

Martin strolled dejectedly around the periphery of the courtyard and worked his way undisturbed through three cigarettes although there was still a considerable crowd milling about, reluctant to end the unusual day and head home.

What a place! he thought. Fifteen years ago, if anyone had told me I'd be on Kekoi Kaery trying to help an outworld performance master escape certain death, I'd have said he was crazy.

He pulled his last clean handkerchief from his pocket and blew his nose. Still bloody. This was the longest period of space lag he'd ever had.

"I'm too old for this," he muttered, and scanned the courtyard. Except for the white lozenge-shaped, tridecker hover tram waiting outside the stone Stock Exchange Tower for afternoon commuters, he could have been standing in some weird outworld theme park based on a painting by Breughel. Instead of peasants and burghers, there were hirsute street vendors, merchants, and government officials dressed like peasants and burghers. Instead of foreign sailors and village idiots, there were outworlders in scales, skins, shells, and feathers. Some wore special adaptive suits and toted portable mechanical atmospheres of diverse designs.

A female Kekoi with a yoke over her shoulders, from which two small pups in baskets dangled as if on swings, brushed past him.

Sixteenth, maybe seventeenth century, Martin thought, complete with witch trial.

A new fight was developing at the embassy end of the courtyard, a row of tall, narrow buildings squashed shoulder to shoulder like medieval guild halls and painted many colors. Martin decided to go watch. A fight would be an excellent diversion. It fit his grumpy mood perfectly, which depressed him. Had he sunk so low?

As Martin approached, he realized that, small as it was, this altercation, like the morning's already famous "bird picnic," involved outworlders and could prove explosive. Some Lambdans and a group of unsavory, sallow bipeds, who looked very human but weren't, had cornered a tawny young Kekoi in jester's rags and were badgering him unmercifully, shoving him and threatening him with brightly glowing blue heat knives and what looked like brass knuckles festooned with silver spikes. Curiously, the Kekoi did nothing to defend himself although he was a tall strapping male with a full ruff. No one in the crowd seemed to want to help him either.

One of the sallow bipeds swiped at the Kekoi with his spiked knuckles and slit open both the jester's nose pad and his left ear. The jester stumbled back toward Martin, a hand cupped over his bleeding nostril. The outworlders taunted him in Belian.

"Serves you right, you bastard!"

"Next time, the whole ear comes off, Aro!"

The Kekoi wiped his nose on his sleeve. Martin offered him his already soiled handkerchief, but the jester shook his head.

"Don't help me, Terran," he panted in gruff but excellent Belian.

"You don't deserve it."

"Yes, I do." Aro hacked up some bloody saliva. The outworlders had gotten in a few punches before Martin showed up.

"Aro, I know who you are."

"Then you'll want to come at me, too, won't you? Be my guest."

"No. I'm Mikk's . . . friend."

The Kekoi laughed, a deep, ironic rolling in his chest. "Everyone is now that he's in jail! And they're all after me for putting him there." He winked at Martin. "Better get your licks in before there's nothing left of me to lick, Terran."

"Don't be stupid, Aro. *Your* songdance wasn't proscribed and it won't be the last no matter what they do to Mikk. If it hadn't been you . . ."

"But it *was* me," Aro said fiercely, glaring in pain at Martin. "Nothing can change that, ever. What was that Terran's name? Judas? I'll bet he pleaded bad timing and bad judgment, too. Well, not me. I have my pride. I'll face my punishment standing up."

With that, the Kekoi stiffened his back and marched resolutely into the square. Several people, including a couple of Kekoi security dogs spat on him as he went by, but Aro never broke stride, never turned his head, and never said a word.

Once Aro had moved on, the security dogs quickly cleared the streets in their usual inimitable fashion. "Off!" they barked and snapped their strong, sharp teeth at the sleeves of stragglers who growled in response but moved on, ears folded back flat against their scalps.

"You, too, Terran!" a security dog added in Belian.

"Yeah, yeah, in a minute," Martin said. "Can't a man have a leisurely smoke without being harassed by the local constabulary?"

"Make it fast. There's a curfew."

"Since when?"

"Since the likes of you showed up! Get on with it!"

Without further comment, Martin lit a fresh cigarette. He'd learned that the Kekoi respected a little rude defiance, up to a point, and he'd reached that point when the security dog's lips curled back over his canines. Dealing with these people was like dealing with Park Avenue attorneys. Level of threat meant everything, and he didn't want to get on the bad side of a seven-foot-tall wolf man.

The sun dipped behind the jail and the courtyard darkened to a cold gray.

An ugly piece of masonry, Martin thought as he studied the jail. High, featureless walls, tiny windows—a fortress. No place to be locked up alone.

Something brushed against his trouser cuff, and he glanced down to see a funny little chipmunk creature with rabbit ears and scarlet racing stripes. It hopped a few listless paces, squeaked, and coughed a phlegmy hair ball onto Martin's Italian loafers.

"Face it, Brannick," he sighed, "you were too old for this fifteen years ago."

Part Three: Master

[C.Y.S. XII: 1058–1060]

Chapter Nineteen: The Invitation

It was a torrid Tenth Day holiday afternoon in the Season of Fruit, and the insects were thick in the steaming gardens of Mikk's Wynt home. Nevertheless, the corridor was cool and shadowy as Briin, Mikk's young butler and household manager—and a would-be actor—quickly padded along the tiles toward the hearth room. An important letter had come over the telewave.

However, when he got to the hearth room, the door panel was shut and, judging by the muffled thumps and sighs that escaped this attempt at secrecy, Mikk and Thissizz were engaged in intimate exercises.

Briin dutifully positioned himself next to the door panel, ear close to its smooth white surface, and waited for something to crash. When something did, he took a moment or two to interpret the sound, pensively rubbing his short round nose, then flipped open his notebook and shook the ink in his stylus.

"Let's see," he said in the fussy accent that belied his upbringing on a cargo flatboat with fifteen siblings. " 'Ti-tok, Vine Dynasty ewer: insured.' Dear me, there goes another one. 'Crystal: replaceable,' lucky for us." He stuck the stylus in the dense brown curls that lapped against his ear and listened stoically for the next drop in inventory.

Mikk emerged a couple hours later, hair in disarray, but lavender eyes glowing with private satisfaction. The performance master was just shy of his half millennium, in what Vyzanians called the True and Beautiful Life. Rumor had it he had started to live backward, which was why he didn't seem to age.

Briin pocketed his notebook and helped put to rights his employer's woefully mangled garments. He didn't believe in the rumors. He was more inclined to believe in the beneficial effects of these bouts with a full-grown Droos. They would keep a Garplen lean and feisty.

"Sir, you might consider a separate room for yourself and Thissizz, one without furnishings."

"That's an excellent idea, Briin! I wonder why I never thought of it myself."

Perhaps you enjoy the sound of breaking objects, Briin mused.

"By the way, sir, this came while you were occupied." The house manager handed Mikk the sheet of cellulose. "It is not from a fan."

Mikk quickly skimmed the small, tight outworld type, nothing like the wild squiggling dance of Vyzanian script. His eyes darkened a shade, but the pigment fluttered, a sign he was struggling with mixed emotions.

"What is it, sir?" Briin asked.

"An invitation to tour that feverish blue-green world orbiting Sol."

Thissizz lifted his rosy orange head from the desolation in the hearth room and sneezed. "Terra?" He wiped his nose with his tongue, and Briin actually performed a small hop in his excitement.

"Oh, congratulations, sir!" he gushed. "Could you bring me a hat?"

"A hat?" Mikk's eyes still hadn't settled down, and Briin decided to adjust his enthusiasm to a cooler cheerfulness. He refrained from hopping a second time.

"Yes, sir. I understand Terran gentlemen wear hats."

Mikk arched his red eyebrows. "I don't see why not. Did you have a particular style in mind?"

Briin whipped the stylus out of his hair and deposited it in the sleeve of his chartreuse and purple tunic. "Choose something you think would suit me, sir." He smiled brightly and marched off to the kitchen to hector the cook. Mikk peered over his shoulder at the grinning ceramic-shard-dusted Thissizz.

"It's a good thing he gave me the commission and not you," he smiled. "The gods know what kind of headwear a Droos would find appropriate."

Thissizz shook himself off and rippled gently up to his friend. He glanced at the invitation.

"Isn't Terra the world where serpents have two penises?" he asked.

Mikk's eyes darkened completely and he groaned. The Droos kissed his neck.

"I know," Thissizz sighed. "It's all right. I'll stay with my family next year."

"It's not all right! This will be my Terran debut." He ran his long hands slowly down the Droos' folded hood.

"Diplomacy is a slow art, my beautiful friend. You don't need a Droos to impress them. Everything you do will be new and amazing." He grinned. "Come—I feel like a swim in your terrace fountain."

"I'm very upset about this, Thissizz."

"You won't be once you're working, and when you come back, you can tell me all about your Terran adventures."

Mikk hiked through the trees to Huud Maroc's estate with a bottle of mullt Briin had pressed some years before and which promised to have reached its peak alcohol burn. When he arrived, the performance masters went into the atrium, a sheltered, sun-dappled space enclosed by stone lattices carved in imitation of the sacred friezes in the First House. Pink vines curled in and out of the myths of First Arrival and, where the light was brightest, draped long bunches of tart green berries.

"Master Huud, why are yours the only 'creeping arteries' south of Hei to bear fruit?"

"Magic." The old master opened the mullt and sniffed it. "Hm!" Once he had decanted the spicy, pale green vine cider into two tall, narrow flutes set on a low stone table, he carefully, painfully lowered himself onto a pile of canvas cushions.

"May I take some cuttings?" Mikk asked, joining him.

"Yes, but only because you brought the refreshments." Huud Maroc sipped the mullt. "Excellent burn, Mikk! Well concentrated. Tell Briin he's a genius."

"I will not!" Mikk laughed as he took up his own flute, "but you're right. This is lovely." He pursed his lips. "Do you suppose getting drunk on alcohol is the same as getting drunk on corthane?"

"It may look the same, but take care," the master said sternly. "If the Terrans find even one vial of corthane in your troupe's belongings, they'll expel the lot of you."

"Don't worry, Master Huud. My troupe wouldn't think of breaking the law."

Huud Maroc snorted ironically, then squinted at his former apprentice with eyes faded from their once piercing blue-purple. Mikk thought the old master was long overdue for retinal surgery, but the mere mention of anything connected to the medical profession sent Huud Maroc into a rage much more dangerous to his well-being than advancing astigmatism.

"You know, Mikk, it's just as well Thissizz can't go. A Droos would probably frighten Terrans."

"Thissizz? He's the gentlest soul in the galaxy."

"You and I know that, but Terrans judge by appearances." The old master freshened his glass. "We're talking about a very insecure people. Terrans still consider first contact a military rather than a diplomatic issue. They'd just as soon dissect a new outworlder as talk to him. I learned most of their performing arts secondhand and, when I finally met their masters, none of them except the Nipponese kabuki actor were willing to teach me anything in person."

"But that was almost two hundred years ago, Master Huud. It could be very different now." He set his flute down and steepled his long fingers. "Maybe Terrans have trouble accepting outworlders because their lives are too short to gain a true understanding of the interconnectedness of all species."

Huud Maroc laughed heartily.

"You're tedious when you get metaphysical, Mikk! And you're wrong. Why don't you give up that never-ending study of songdance and rejoin us lowly mortals scrabbling about in the here and now?"

Mikk smiled indulgently at his former master. "I've been thinking a lot about songdance lately, Master Huud, and I realize that although it may have started as a way for me to explore how I feel about Thissizz, it seems to have become a way to explore how I feel about myself." He shrugged. "It's become a habit I can't give up."

"To each his own addiction, boy. What a lot of . . ." For once the master let Mikk imagine his own expletive.

"Be honest, Master Huud. You miss it, don't you? You're upset because you want to go with me."

"Nonsense, lad, I'm happily retired."

"I see. Is that why you keep telewaving Veern Illist at all hours with ideas for his Mummers' Pilgrimage?"

"I never did that!" the old master roared, the veins in his forehead swelling. "I called him once! Once! Ask him yourself. It was merely a friendly chat between colleagues!"

"Shh! Master Huud, please! I don't care whether you called him once or a hundred times. Veern could use some shaking up, but," the younger master shook his head sadly, "you have to look after yourself. You cannot tour anymore. You have to stay here."

Huud Maroc scowled petulantly. His eyes were full of smoldering intelligence in spite of their failing acuity, and Mikk's soul grieved.

When the mind remains strong, but the body does not, that must be the greatest cruelty the gods can inflict on a performer, he thought.

"I want them to know how great you are, Mikk, that's all," Huud Maroc muttered.

"If I can't convince them, I'll donate five thousand zyrr toward the new theater you and the Crown are building."

The old master's interest jumped. "Indeed! And if you can?"

"Twenty thousand."

Chapter Twenty: The Man in the Balcony

At precisely eight o'clock in the evening, the house lights of the Rose Kirkby Theater in the New Embassy Convention Center downtown went out, quitting all at once like snuffed candles, and in the startled murmurs and rustlings a new single light hovered in the darkness of the empty stage, a small rectangle composed of four narrow parallel strands of pure white energy.

The sound followed, a cross between a violin, a hammered dulcimer, and a weeping girl, a sound that skipped about the theater as lightly and exuberantly as sunlight over new aspen leaves. Whatever that instrument with the glowing strings was, the musician playing it was an expert, confident enough to risk crossing into unexpected emotional territory.

As the music became more elaborate, the lights came up on stage to reveal Mikk, resplendent in a short, gold-flecked, belted crimson jacket and black leggings. His long white fingers danced feverishly over a slim oblong box made of a strange milky wood slung over his shoulder on a silver string. The performance master bowed, dipping the long loose lock of red over his forehead, then walked across the stage to the far corner where he continued to play his light-strung box.

The music quickened and a large turquoise sphere, about three feet in diameter, floated into the light from the opposite wings. It passed slowly down front, keeping about a yard and a half above the stage, hesitated, drew back, hesitated again as though searching for the source of the music, then headed directly for Mikk and stopped just behind him. The performance master ignored it and continued to play, eyes now closed and a peaceful smile on his lips.

238

The globe nudged Mikk like a pet wanting attention. Mikk still didn't stop playing, but he looked over his shoulder and the globe rose over him and came down in front, blocking his view. The performance master leaned to one side to peek around it and the globe followed, again blocking his view. Mikk crouched to look under it and the sphere dropped gently to the floor.

The performance master then surprised everyone by leaping up on top of the ball, which promptly lifted above the stage, drifted down front, and sailed out over the audience. It flew into the cavernous theater, finally stopping to hover dead center in the deep space above the orchestra, on a level with the people in the loge.

Mikk never stopped playing.

The audience held up their small children so they could see better, and the applause was heavy, but Mikk's illusion was not over. The music changed key and slowed to a sinuous, rhythmic, evolving arpeggio, and the performance master, after casually lifting each foot to inspect the soles of his slippers and demonstrate there was no adhesive on them, began to walk down the side of the globe. Several people shouted in alarm, but the performance master, held to the globe by some mysterious hidden gravity, took a stroll around the equator, his body parallel to the floor many feet below, then he walked underneath the globe and stood at its nethermost pole—upside down.

The crowd was so wild now they drowned out the music, but at its conclusion Mikk threw wide his arms and the lights briefly went out again. When they came up a moment later, the sphere and the performance master had vanished.

Up in "Freen heaven," at the front of the balcony, above and away from his journalistic colleagues, a weary Martin Brannick watched the premiere through his binocular specs and wished he could smoke one of his nicotine-free cigarettes without getting thrown out. He didn't usually feel the need for a cigarette while he was working, but he was exceptionally agitated this evening, and the more he watched, the more ill at ease he became. Since he was a professional, he tried to define the source of his distress, but was having difficulty.

It wasn't the material. Other critics might have trouble with outworld theater merely because it was "foreign," but not Martin Brannick, theater critic for the *New York Times* for the past five and a half years and roving arts correspondent in London and Paris for two years before that. He was a sophisticate, a Yalie. A dose of unknown languages was not enough to stir the queasy heat in his gut and the craving for the weed.

Martin adjusted his specs and felt a tiny pinprick at his left temple, the unmistakable prelude to a migraine.

"Shit," he muttered; the Belian next to him, a legal resident judging by the dull aluminum alloy "red card" hanging on a leather cord around his neck, stared. Martin pretended not to notice and returned to his uncomfortable ruminations.

It's not the performances either, he thought. They're damned good. He checked his pocket watch and shook his head. He would have to get his review in immediately after the performance to make the morning edition. Instant communication for instant people. He hated having to watch and compose copy at the same time.

Very well. What exactly was this show, this first of five completely different programs? Was it a sampler like a box of chocolates? Martin doubted that or his head wouldn't hurt.

As he watched, Belian dancers skipped and contorted on crisscrossed gossamer threads over the audience's heads, Vyzanian singers made light change color with their voices, and Kekoi clowns and Mrku jugglers shrank to teacup size, emitted green sparks from their fingers, and performed feats of levitation.

The red-haired performance master was in the thick of it—or could there be two of him? Mikk popped up in so many places, in so many unlikely guises, Martin began to see him where he wasn't, or, at least where he shouldn't have been. One minute he was making dozens of small gold balls circle his head horizontally like planets orbiting a sun—by far the most unexplainable form of juggling Martin had ever seen—the next he was playing a ba-sik, a Rogoine zither the size of a small canoe. He had to work the strings with his feet as well as his hands. Soon after that, he was back on stage in a short Belian ballet.

Doesn't this man ever rest? Martin wondered.

It was during the ballet that Martin began to discern the theme of the program, if not the cause of his discomfort.

Mikk performed in a pure white dance suit that made him look both nude and neuter. He also looked blind, dead-eyed. Colored lenses probably.

Martin briefly stopped composing copy. There was something wrong with that assessment, but he couldn't get a sharp enough focus on his specs to verify his error. Mikk's eyes weren't artificially tinted. Somehow, they *were* black.

Martin shuddered and clicked back into his critic persona.

Mikk had returned to exact revenge on his Belian murderer who was seducing his Belian wife. Blue, blue, and white. Why not give the role to another Belian? Martin wondered. Could this be a purely aesthetic choice? I don't see why . . . Damn! The man's a reptile! And yet weightless. A real ghost.

Martin leaned forward in his seat and his eyes hardened. Every act challenged a boundary of some kind. The proscenium was meaningless; performers inhabited the entire space. Gravity didn't exist; dancers flew. Incompatible phenomena mixed; Kekoi jesters blew themselves up and survived. The dead killed.

Mikk cupped his partner's soft blue chin in his white fingers— a moment of panicked realization in her eyes—and snapped her neck.

Perfect, Martin thought. Cold and merciless.

He filed away this batch of data and tried to stretch his legs, at least as far as the narrow space in the balcony allowed, but he kicked the wall of the rail in front of him, rather loudly, and got another glower, this time from a Freen a couple seats down from the Belian. A Freen with delusions of grandeur. His chunky gray body was stuffed into a double-breasted DiMarco suit.

"Sorry," Martin whispered. The Freen lugubriously blinked his leathery double eyelids and turned away.

The Mrkusi acrobats returned to perform more lunatic daredeviltry, hanging from each other's hair and throwing each other from the catwalks. Martin closed his eyes, determined to play professional hooky until intermission, but after the applause for the acrobats, there was a stir of surprise and delight from the males in the audience and Martin woke up. Hegron, the Ichtian actress, had just come on stage, closely pursued by Mikk.

This is an Ichtian? Martin thought. If I'd known, I'd have booked passage years ago!

Hegron was a sable-skinned siren, petite, voluptuous, with hip-length medusa braids and oriental eyes. Martin was captivated and, at first, didn't notice that, like Mikk, Hegron was in a doublet and hose: not Vyzanian silks, not Kekoi jester's rags, but the garb once worn by well-bred gentlemen of the court of King James.

Hegron rounded on Mikk with a charming pout and the performance master's happy, almost vapid, grin dissolved.

"Why, how now, Orlando, where have you been all this while?" she scolded, the lines from Shakespeare's *As You Like It*, "You a lover? An you serve me such another trick, never come in my sight more."

Poor Orlando blinked ingenuously and pressed his fingertips against his bosom in gentle denial and protest.

"My fair Rosalind, I come within an hour of my promise."

"Break an hour's promise in love?" the mannishly attired Rosalind cried. "He that will divide a minute into a thousand parts and break but a part of the thousand part of a minute in the affairs of love, it may be said of him that Cupid hath clapped him o' th' shoulder, but I'll warrant him heart-whole."

Martin's British colleagues had told him about this scene. Apparently, Mikk was using it to introduce Hegron and her talents in a way that would be understood by the local audience. In Japan, he'd done something similar with a recreated scene from a classic Kurosawa film.

Martin wasn't sure how to react. On the one hand, the woman was absurdly beautiful and dramatically clever, teasing every bubble of wit out of the words, and he was tempted to surrender his judgment and declare her the successor to Dame Candace Everton. On the other hand, the actress's accent, although not unpleasant, was noticeable. So why use Shakespeare? Why not an Ichtian play? With this crowd, did it matter?

If you want to impress an American audience, Martin thought bitterly, you should use something from *Road-Kill Raceway*.

As for Mikk, the Bard's English might as well have been his native tongue. He spoke it with a clean, rich music that rendered his dense earnestness all the more ridiculous. The audience laughed more lustily than Martin would have expected.

His migraine began to travel, seeping around his skull to his right temple and through his sinus into his eyebrow, which started to twitch.

I've got to splash my face before I get sick on someone, he thought. Unfortunately, the row was blocked with various races of knees and rapt stares. He didn't dare.

Orlando placed a solicitous white hand on Rosalind's sable cheek. Perhaps his naïveté in the face of her masculine disguise was not entirely genuine.

Martin wiped the sweat from his lip.

Intermission, he swore to himself. The washroom during intermission. If I last that long.

After Hegron's final bow, Mikk returned to freshened acclaim. He carried a long crystal wand and a clear globe about the size of a soccer ball. The globe held what looked like a pretty little rubbery tumbleweed.

Mikk came down center to address the audience.

"Thank you," he said in bright, pure Anglo-English. "You are very generous."

With a small flourish of his hand, he stood the slender wand on end and set the globe on it. It balanced perfectly.

"In my years as a performance master, I've met many wonderful singers, but Yii is unique. Not only is her gift impossible to describe, she is the first of her people to leave her world, the first to perform for outworld audiences. Yii is a Qo, one of a rare race who lives on a chain of distant asteroids with a very thin atmosphere. She has to stay inside this pressure sphere or the air would crush her. Needless to say, this makes it difficult for her to travel."

He stroked the globe gently.

"Qo live about twelve Terran years. Yii is ten so this is probably her only tour."

The performance master hesitated, and when he spoke again his voice was softer.

"Please be as generous with her as you have been with the rest of my troupe. I know you will be very pleased."

Mikk withdrew into the shadows. The Qo, alone in the spotlight, gave off a pulsating radiation and, at first, that was all, but gradually a sound began to rise from the globe, increasing in volume and clarity. Some of the Qo's tendrils started to vibrate rapidly.

The sound became a voice, a female voice, soprano, sustained beyond the bounds of any human voice or acoustical instrument Martin had ever heard. A second sound, another voice, joined in: mezzo-soprano. A third voice, a fourth voice—all added their special resonance as more and more of Yii's tendrils began to shiver and tremble. In only seconds, an entire celestial choir sang from the vibrating Qo in the transparent globe.

The theater held its breath as the sound floated into the wide darkness, caressed the air, and rebounded from the pilasters. The putti on the proscenium seemed to abandon their perches to flit about the chandeliers as the voices moved from one side of the theater to the other, hung over the middle, swooped around the balconies, and spread themselves into every corner.

Martin couldn't tell whether the Qo sang five minutes, fifteen, or five hours. When the song finally slipped away and stopped, the long silence allowed him to hear his own heartbeat. Not one sigh, one cough, one rustle of a program disturbed the silence until, at an indefinable but palpable moment of communal release, the audience opened its voice and cheered. Martin tapped the readout on his pocket watch. Yii had sung for a little over three and a half minutes.

Mikk reappeared and lowered his head while the audience showered its euphoria over the delicate creature in the globe. Then he picked up Yii and the wand and carried them offstage.

Chapter Twenty-one: The Washroom

The washroom was crowded, overrun with outworlders, but Martin pushed his way in, the drumbeat in his head intensifying.

A trip to the washroom used to be an impersonal, businesslike experience before the Outworld Public Rights and Sanitation Act gave Belians, Freens, and other outworlders the right to invade public restrooms. Martin agreed it was a better answer than the ill-kept outhouses outworlders had had to use and infinitely preferable to forcing them to squat or spray outside, but it transformed what was supposed to be a serene interlude in one's life into an unnerving exercise in stoic endurance.

The Belians weren't bad, but they talked incessantly, and the new arrivals liked to stand close to you and watch, sometimes asking personal questions. Also, Martin could not be certain all of them were males. He didn't understand how most people could easily tell Belian men and women apart. Both sexes' organs were hidden internally except at the height of sexual arousal. Martin had committed a number of faux pas over this and had earned a minor reputation as a well-intentioned bumbler.

Even so, Freens were much worse. They played with the water, loudly compared the size and output of each other's personal equipment, and spilled soap dust all over the floor. As Martin bent his face down into the weak little basin fountain, one of these overly familiar outworlders clapped a thick wet hand on his coat sleeve, leaving a sudsy print on the cashmere.

I'll bet the women have it better, he thought, staring unhappily at his reflection. Only thirty-six, but his hair was thinning and the lines and puffs under his round blue eyes were those of a news-paperman ten years his senior. His small body was starting to get soft, which was especially irksome. What was the point of love handles if one didn't have a lover to handle them?

Martin splashed his face then pumped out a portion of soap dust and began to scrub his hands briskly. That wretched Vyzanian didn't have any superfluous flesh around his middle, but he doubted that was what bothered him. Why, when the program was excellent, did he feel almost compelled to write a scathing and bitterly personal review?

A man in a tuxedo, Terran, stepped up to the basin next to Martin's and yelled to another man in the softly whirring sani-stalls.

"Hurry up, Frank! I don't want to miss the second half."

"I'm coming, I'm coming. The vacuum outtake is backed up." The man in the tux swore through his teeth.

"Damned Freens. Still, show's great, isn't it?"

"This your first time?"

"Almost. Last live thing I saw was the Nipponese versus the Mets."

"Don't remind me. I should have bet in yen."

The man in the tux laughed.

"Incredible, isn't it? Me, in a theater! I thought the only stuff worth watching was on the tube."

Martin shook his head. It wasn't easy being the lone voice of sanity in an asylum. Even though subscriptions were strong and the advertisers happy, the *Times* was in trouble. He was convinced the grand old journal of the Big Apple was engineering its own demise by continually changing format and hiring and firing staff at whim, all in the name of "keeping current." It angered Martin because he believed in theater, believed in the tradition of pithy writing the *New York Times* had once been famous for, and believed in the civilizing effect of art—*real* art. These days, all anyone wanted was a quick rundown of the plots of optitube programs and sordid columns about celebrity sex lives. Why such information continued to fascinate was beyond him.

Frank finally came out of the sani-stall and joined his friend. Look at them, Martin thought. Prosperous businessmen. Smiling, joking—and culturally illiterate. To them, theater ranks somewhere between exhibition baseball and sitcoms.

Martin held his hands under the infrahood and felt the warm reddish light draw the moisture from his skin.

I'm swimming upstream. Fighting the tide while the happy dead drift past me to the pools of ignorance.

"Good lord, Marty, you look terrible!" came a cheerful voice tinged with urban New England.

Oh, no. Perry Matthews of *Boston Today*. Martin forced a casual smile. "Migraine. How are you, Perry?"

"Couldn't be better," his sanguine, portly colleague said with a friendly series of pats on Martin's back. Martin found the man extraordinarily tedious because he was genuinely upbeat, an abomination among critics.

"Nice coat!" Matthews whistled. "An early Christmas present from your aunt?"

It became harder for Martin to maintain his smile. "Ha, ha."

"Don't be touchy, Marty," Matthews smiled sympathetically. "We should all have such generous burdens in the family. Are you enjoying the master's show?"

"Read my review and find out. I never divulge my opinions ahead of time."

"Not intentionally, perhaps, but I detect a whiff of hostility." He folded his arms and gave Martin a twinkly eyed scowl. "What's the matter, my son? Mikk of Vyzania is one of the best performance masters in the galaxy."

"Oh, I love that!" Martin sneered and absently began washing his hands again. " 'Performance master!' What the hell does that mean? The man's in everything and he's running himself ragged as a result."

"But that's what a performance master does, Marty. He's a generalist who's as accomplished in each art as a specialist and, frankly, I've never seen anyone as tireless as Master Mikk. He's absolutely phenomenal. The epitome of energy."

Martin winced. He hated hyperbole.

"By the way, Marty, are you going to the reception tomorrow night?"

"I haven't decided." When hell freezes over, he thought.

"Well, if you do, there are a couple of things you should keep in mind." Matthews glanced about the emptying washroom with an air of dark but thrilling conspiracy.

"Vyzanians can be pretty tricky. A friend of mine in the diplomatic corps calls them 'white scorpions.' Cold and polite, smooth as their skin, but that reserve can vanish in an instant and you'd never know what hit you." Now he whispered in Martin's ear. His breath smelled of garlic and basil—Matthews had a weakness for Italian food. "Whatever you do, don't bring up the Black and Red War."

"Why would I want to discuss ancient history?"

"Vyzanians don't consider it ancient. The war might as well have ended yesterday, they're that sensitive about it."

Martin didn't bother to refry his hands under the infrahood. He shook the water from his fingers and several drops darkened Matthews' silk cravat. "All right," he smiled, "forget the war. How do Vyzanians feel about interspecies miscegenation?"

He had finally succeeded in dampening his colleague's good cheer. Matthews' rosy color went from Miss All-American Beauty to Chrysler Imperial.

"Marty," Matthews said coolly, "performance masters are a rare breed, guardians of the cultural flame. There are less than a thousand of them in the entire galaxy. Maybe it's the migraine that's put you in this belligerent mood, but you'd better do something about it or it'll skew your review." The entertainment editor for *Boston Today* headed for the door. "Don't pan Mikk of Vyzania, Marty. You'll regret it."

Now alone in the washroom, Martin was overcome with nausea and ducked into a sani-stall to vomit, after which his headache subsided to a dull hammer.

"I don't want to pan Mikk," he murmured as he emerged, "I want to hurt him . . . and it makes me feel filthy."

His mouth felt filthy as well and he weighed the pros and cons of braving the crush at the bar to get a drink.

I shouldn't, he thought. I promised.

The Vyzanian's image reappeared before him, the expressive marble white hand caressing an ebon cheek.

Damn it, auntie! I'm thirsty . . .

Chapter Twenty-two: Yii

Backstage, Kekoi prop masters, massive males in soiled leather jerkins and thick belts hung with heavy keranium tools, swaggered past carrying coils of cable, shoving scenery flats, and pushing crates of props on floating airfoil dollies. Belians, Mrkusis, Vyzanians, outworlders of every description bustled about, some half in, half out of costume, others naked, a few eating exotic foodstuffs from small silver boxes. The air throbbed with languages, music, and laughter, and the smells of paint, dust, hot phosphor resin, sweat, fixatives, and cosmetics slammed into the nostrils.

With Yii's pressure sphere tucked under his arm, Mikk steered through this maze of disparate activity with the smoothness of a seal negotiating a kelp bed. Close on his heels, Maya had trouble keeping up.

"Why Mikk lie?" she panted. "Yii thirteen."

The performance master didn't answer. He passed down a long dressing room, all lights and mirrors and boxes of strange pigments and half-eaten meals, to a small softly lit chamber where he set the Qo on a table next to a flask of water. He gently placed his hands on the pressure sphere and felt the hum of Yii's life force. Qo burned very brightly but he could detect an unsteadiness, a fluctuation in her energy.

"Mikk?"

"Shh, Maya. I hope the light in this room will feed her, but it's already so late . . ."

As Mikk stroked the globe, the Qo shivered and her light brightened, but the performance master still wasn't happy. "This tour has been a terrible strain on her."

"Yii well?"

Mikk shook his head. "She could die anytime."

Maya scowled. "Then why come?"

"It's what she wanted. She's enjoyed singing for people. She told me it was the most wonderful experience of her entire life and she doesn't regret it at all."

Maya craned her eye stalks up over the table's edge to see better. "What happen when die?"

"Her life force will go out and she'll break up into crystals." Mikk became rueful. "Something like salt."

"Yii in pain?"

"Not in any way we can understand." Mikk hesitated uncomfortably before continuing. "When she's dead, she wants me to dissolve her crystals in this glass of water—and drink her."

Maya stared at him dubiously. "Why?"

"She said if I took her inside myself she could still live and sing." Mikk ran his hand through his hair. "I promised I would."

"Hunh. Strange."

"Maybe not. She's quite right about continuing to exist in another form. It's rather poetic when you think . . ." He stopped speaking and his eyes blackened.

"What? Maya hear nothing."

"She . . . she's saying good-bye," Mikk whispered. He wiped away a few tears. "Damn! She didn't want me to cry . . ."

"Mikk . . . look . . ."

The Qo's light flickered irregularly and, as they watched, became fainter and fainter—and went out. Another beat, and the delicate tumbleweed form in the globe collapsed into a small pile of sparkling powder.

At first, neither Mikk nor Maya could move. Then the performance master braced his hands on the globe and gave it a sharp twist, opening a seam at its equator with a small hiss. He removed the top and carefully poured the crystals into the flask of water, tapping gently so that the very last dust fell in. He lightly swirled the flask and the crystals dissolved.

He was raising the flask to his lips when Maya put a tentacle on his arm.

"Wait." She made a short double prayer gesture over the flask, four tentacles steepled together. "Now."

Mikk's brows knit and something vaguely like a smile tilted one corner of his cheek, but he didn't comment. He tipped the flask and drank. His eyes were far away when he finished, but lighter, returning to their pale lavender.

"Mikk all right?"

"Yes," he nodded. "Let's go."

When they came out of the chamber into the long dressing room, the troupe was waiting for them and looked anxiously at Mikk. Hegron was crying. Mikk gazed sadly at them a moment, then sighed.

"Two minutes to curtain, everyone."

Chapter Twenty-three: Finale

It may have been Martin's imagination, but the second part of the program seemed more intense than the first and Mikk surpassed even the formidable standards he had already set for himself.

Near the end of the evening, the lights brightened on a stage completely barren except for a long line of upended crystal goblets in close formation, like a rank of soldiers, stretching from one end of the stage to the other, and a clear, heavy polyglass barrier set far upstage.

There were no musicians. In deep silence, Mikk emerged from the wings dressed in the simple gray-green uniform of a low-ranking enlisted man of the Black and Red War. He wore soft tight black leather boots that hugged his feet from toe to ankle to knee and carried a half-empty goblet of pale green mullt, the fermented Vyzanian vine cider.

Martin tapped his lip with his finger. The story behind the glass dance was simple enough. A soldier of the Black and Red War had invented it when his commanding officer was killed during a suppertime raid. After the dust cleared, the soldier discovered the officer's glass of mullt was intact, not a drop spilled. The irony maddened the soldier and he drank the mullt, turned the goblet over, and, according to legend, danced on it. It became a way to honor the dead and, since there were a lot of dead, there were a lot of overturned goblets.

Martin didn't quite believe the legend and yet Mikk's bearing sent chills down his back. The performance master carried himself with upright, regal grace, but his expression was grim, sad beyond sadness, and fierce as an eagle's. He strode across the stage behind the goblets and stopped at the midpoint, where he slowly, delicately, drank the mullt, then whirled around and flung his empty goblet at the polyglass barrier. The crystal shattered with a loud ringing crash.

Mikk briskly turned back to the line of upended goblets and with a click of his heels leapt lightly into the air and landed on the center glass on the very tip of his right boot, making a sharp, clear bell tone. He held this pose, like a statue of Mercury on an ice cube, before he snapped into the air again and began his tapping, leaping, spinning ballet down the line of glasses, not once returning a foot to the ground.

Martin became confused. How could a grown man dance on goblets, let alone dance as though he was insane with grief, without breaking them? No one had that kind of control. It had to be another illusion, and yet the cold fizz in his blood told him very clearly it was not.

Mikk's flying feet picked up tempo as he spun and leapt and danced over the dangerously frangible crystal and made it sing, a percussive chiming that filled the theater. One false move, one misplaced or overly sharp step, and the goblets would fall or break under Mikk's dancing weight, but he tore across the slick surfaces with the abandon of a man running on concrete. He defied gravity. Cries of anguish rose from the audience as Mikk became a spinning blur and the ringing from the goblets became continuous. People jumped to their feet, waving their arms, and the Belian next to Martin burst into tears.

On and on Mikk danced, opening invisible, half-understood wounds in Martin's memory, hallucinations of fiery fields and phantom corpses. Mikk was the Death Angel, master of the invisible, the ringing one sustained scream that throbbed on the ear like a siren.

In a final frenzy of calculated rage, Mikk hooked the toe of his boot under each goblet as he passed and flung them in rapid succession at the polyglass barrier, a glass machine gun going off. Down the line he flew, the shards spraying off the barrier in bright, shimmering arcs, until, at last, at the far end, he flipped the final goblet high into the air and, with a flying kick, neatly split it in two with his heel. He caught the halves, one in each hand, and flung the pieces at the barrier to join their brothers.

The Belian sitting next to Martin broke down and actually rested his head in the critic's lap. Others had jumped to their feet and were screaming their praise. Mikk stood on the debris-strewn stage, chest heaving, and watched with black-eyed detachment as masses of flowers landed at his feet. Then he closed his eyes and let the sound wash over him.

At some point during the pandemonium, Martin pulled off his binocular specs—and lost them. Had he dropped them under the seats? Had a light-fingered Freen snatched them as they fell? It didn't matter. They would come out of his paycheck.

Martin might have cared more if he'd had the energy, but his migraine had renewed its onslaught and the visual doubling it caused was the reason he'd removed the specs in the first place. Two outworld demons skipping across crystal were more than he could bear.

I can't review this show, he thought. The words would die on the page. Why is he doing this to me?

Mikk had one last act to perform that evening: an encore. After a quick change, a clearing away of the broken crystal, and the installation of a piano, the master returned, completely recovered, in superbly tailored white tie and tails. This time he was grinning. He sat down at the keys, ran his hands grandly back over his hair, flexed his fingers, scowled, then pounded out a riff of hyperactive Chopin that rapidly deteriorated into manic Mozart and finally collapsed entirely under the rubble of some very creaky Chuck Berry. The crowd tittered and Mikk jumped from the bench and stalked angrily once around the recalcitrant instrument. He swore at it in Vyzanian, a cascade of unintelligibility that sounded like Russian-made-Dutch-through-an-Italian-lilt, before resuming his seat to play Gershwin's "Three Preludes."

No, please! Martin's beleaguered senses pleaded. Not Gershwin!

The audience sighed with happy recognition and settled back to enjoy the music. Martin clenched his jaw and endured.

A few more bars and it will be over . . .

However, the music segued into a very different piece, something equally familiar to Martin if not to the bulk of the audience.

> "Che gelida manina,
> Se la lasci riscaldar . . ."

"Jesus!" Martin hid his face in his program so no one could see who had cried out.

What a voice! You could sculpt marble with it and yet it seduced the soul as well as the ear with its enthralling sensuality, transforming the aria from *La Bohème* into molten platinum. Martin's eyes filled with tears.

Actor? Dancer? Comic? Singer, too? Four completely different programs to come? What kind of man are you? What species of artist does everything?

Several women leaned on the rail of the balcony, ring-encrusted fingers digging unheeded into their cheeks, and gazed dreamily at the Vyzanian performance master. At his soaring and rapturous high C, one of them dropped her program and it fell into the loge, landing on another woman's head. The injured party didn't even flinch. Martin did not have his binocular specs, but he could have sworn Mikk's smile broadened. The performance master seemed to be aiming his shamelessly naked sword of a voice directly at the balcony. Thrusting his power right at them. This was more than seduction. This was domination.

Are you an eater of cultures? Martin wondered. Swallowing up the arts of the galaxy all for yourself? Look at these people! They're standing in the aisles, sitting on the steps. God knows how many of them snuck in to see you and still you want more! No one could get these people into a theater but you, a man with no compunction whatsoever about playing Ichtians, Belians, in works from worlds that are not your own. All works! Any form of performance! Audacity like that borders on arrogance—it *is* arrogance! But here they are, packed to the rafters to see you, perhaps their only visit to a theater in their lives. Why you? Why does it have to be you? An outworlder. Not human.

The people gave Mikk another ovation. The women waved and blew kisses. One of them ran down the aisle below and tried to get up on stage but a Kekoi caught her and carried her off.

Martin did not stand. He was ill.

Oh, you bastard . . .

Chapter Twenty-four: The Telewave Call

"I cannot find fault with Mikk's rendering of the traditional Vyzanian glass dance," the performance master read the next morning after his solitary four-hour dance session in the theater's upper rehearsal room. He'd returned to his suite for breakfast.

"The outworlder is an adept and profoundly gifted master of this treacherous art, and no people who have ever suffered the cruelties of war could misunderstand the pain and fury of the flying steps and shattering glass. However, I question the appropriateness of the Gershwin and Puccini that closed the program. This is not material I would include in an evening devoted to outworld forms. Terran music is born out of the unique sensibilities of human beings. Mikk is a fine performer, but he is not a human being. By definition, he cannot comprehend the source of our music's spirit. What other peoples might feel about Mikk's commandeering their art for his own purposes, I can only speculate."

Mikk took a lemon from the hand-thrown bowl on the dining table, a gift from the Nipponese emperor, and began to slice the fruit into thin slivers with a Ti-tokan dirk, a short but nasty saw-toothed blade the customs officials at Koch Airport had threatened to confiscate until Mikk showed them his Certificate of Gift and Right signed by the Sultana herself. He squinted pensively into the weak winter sunlight filling the suite. All the members of his troupe were housed in the New Embassy Convention Center only a few steps away from the theater and their rooms were identical, with one exception: Mikk's suite had many more windows. He had insisted on as many panes of double-glazed polyglass as possible, which meant he'd had to be moved to the Inner-Circle Club level—and so had Maya, which did not please the concierge. Once resettled, Mikk had gone through the suite and removed all of the louvered blinds from the windows and stashed them deep in the closet.

Mikk skewered one of the lemon slices, wrapped his tongue around it, and zipped it into his mouth, peel and all. The fruit stung his mouth and nostrils with a pleasant acid freshness, but he did not smile.

Almost without exception, the American media had raved about the show, falling all over themselves to find superlatives to describe the show's wonders, so Mikk was intrigued, and a little puzzled, by this review in the newly revamped *New York Times*. Hidden under a veil of urbanity that contrasted strongly with the rest of the paper's creeping insipidness, the theater critic's words bristled with a hostility that had nothing to do with the quality of the performances themselves, which he had evidently liked. Rather, his rancor seemed to stem from a poorly supressed xenophobia toward outworlders, but it had a distinctly personal edge, as though the man felt directly threatened. Mikk would have liked to know why, but the review was no more revealing than a passing conversation.

Mikk chased his lemon with a sip of Earl Grey tea sweetened with date sugar, another gift, this time from the Egyptian ambassador to Paris.

He'd read worse. On some worlds he'd even been threatened with bodily harm for displeasing reviewers. Still, he usually shrugged off critical barbs as though they were stinging flies, troublesome but not fatal. For some reason, this one stuck and drew blood.

Mikk got up and took his lemon-sticky plate into the kitchen, put it in the Rotowash, and pressed "sterilize."

It must be Yii's death, he concluded. We've a hit on our hands and all I feel inside is a thick, featureless cloud, like the view out the windows.

Only fifty Terran years had passed since the city fathers had given up on the old Manhattan, evacuated the buildings and tenements, razed the entire island, and rebuilt it. Late night comics called it "Renewed York," and Mikk agreed it was a remarkably clean and bright city, but it seemed to have lost something in the overhaul. What had happened to all those colorful neighborhoods he had read about? The merry mishmash of a hundred cultures' music, smells, arguments, and laughter? New York was now row after row of polite red brick townhouses and unassuming steel and stone towers with neatly manicured miniparks and plazas decorated with officially commissioned sculpture. It was the most homogeneous, lackluster mass habitation Mikk had seen since the Spairan capital, and he missed the piled-up, rattletrap centuries of Paris, London, Berlin, even Tokyo.

And other, more underground places. When he'd finally made it home from the premiere for his two hours of sleep, instead of slipping inside his nice satin-sheeted king-sized bed, he'd curled up naked on the parquet floor instead. Cold as it was, it reminded him of the smooth, hard burrows of Droos.

"Droos," he said aloud and his limbs warmed several degrees. Communications treaty or no communications treaty, he was going to telewave Thissizz.

Mikk moved to the parlor sofa, a lumpy white life raft whose cushions listed drunkenly at the slightest pressure, and positioned himself before the wall-sized telewave unit, a special feature of the Inner-Circle Club suites. He picked up the button box.

"Let's see," he said, talking himself through it to control the sudden trembling he felt at this illegal act, "forget about direct codes and resort to operators. Authorized ones first."

He entered the first code on his button box and got a pretty young blond.

"Guten Tag, hello, this is the interworld operator. Your tele-wave destination, please."

"Belia," Mikk said with his most charming smile. "Eastern continent."

"Hold please, I'll connect. Auf Wiedersehen, good-bye."

Mikk took a quick breath and released it slowly. Now the fun started.

The Belian operator appeared and, as Mikk had hoped, recognized him.

"Mr. Mikk! Good day, sir. Where are you calling from?"

"Terra, my friend. I'm trying to reach Droos."

"I wish I could help you," the operator said, "but Terra doesn't have communications clearance with Droos."

"A pity, isn't it? I've been trying to find a way to introduce Thissizz to them, but they balk at the idea of the limbless."

"Thissizz?" The Belian's cobalt eyes took on an excited luster. "He's my favorite! I have everything he's ever recorded. Those Terrans don't know what they're missing."

Mikk recognized the subtle invitation to a business transaction, but pretended not to notice it in order to define the terms. "If you can't get me Droos, how about Bar Omega Sept?"

The Belian chewed his sharp middle finger and let his long eyes drift archly upward. "They only have a priority one treaty with Terra," he said with deliberate slowness. "Is this call of galactic importance?"

Mikk shrugged and revealed his offer. "Is getting you a copy of Thissizz's as-yet-unreleased chip before everyone else of galactic importance?"

The operator popped his finger out of his mouth. "Bar Omega Sept, coming up."

Not bad, Mikk thought, considering the chip is so new it's not even recorded.

Priority one codes tumbled down the screen in flickering parallel columns, then the Bar Omega Sept operator appeared.

Mikk showed no emotion before the brilliantly plumaged, mask-visaged Septan. In spite of intense diplomatic ministrations, most performed by Mikk's inscrutable father, the inhabitants of the "Bird World" had not officially forgiven the Vyzanian Crown for a slight committed by an ancestor six thousand years before the monarch's birth. Besides, the Septans were deeply offended that the young Crown Prince kept an aviary. Mikk had to be careful how he comported himself. Almost anything, even a misplaced vocal inflection, could set off an interworld incident.

After a ceremonial wink of each eye in greeting, Mikk launched into the droning melodies of Septan speech, accompanied by the appropriate, and highly elaborate, gestures.

"Good pleasure and great luck, dear Septan brother," he said, his hands winding gracefully. "It would be a clear sweet breeze to sing to the people of Droos."

"You sing from Terra," the Septan replied. He bobbed his pink and blue feathered head then tilted it completely upside-down. "You are a clever one, my Vyzanian brother. The waters of Droos do not flow like a brook through Terran fields."

"So true," Mikk continued with a twitch of his shoulder and a ripple of his spine that ended in a snap, "but my heart cries for the smile of my friend Thissizz, who serenades the gods."

"On the shadow side of our claspings, we are brothers with the Vonchoi. These wanderers care not from whence a song flies."

"Ah! I, too, can sing in the dark."

Mikk had been lucky. He now had a pirate frequency. The Vonchoi were adventurers who didn't respect anyone's borders. Although he didn't particularly relish the idea of dealing with them—you never could predict what a Vonchoi would want in an exchange, and fairness played no part whatsoever—Mikk was certain if anyone could get Droos frequencies, the Vonchoi could.

The Vonchoi operator, a slick slate-colored amphibian dressed in red leather shreds studded with gold rings, leaned on her soft, squashy palm and grinned at Mikk, exposing a mouth full of needlelike teeth.

"Why, if it isn't Mikk the Vyzanian," she trilled. "To what do I owe this pleasure, you gorgeous hunk of male brightness?"

"I'm trying to contact Droos, my love," he replied with an extra touch of smoky chest voice to elevate her interest.

"What's it worth to you?" she pouted and toyed with her rings.

"What do you want, sweet one?"

"What I want, I can't have, unless you climb into that machine and telewave your pretty self here."

"Wish I could . . ."

"*Don't* you?" she chuckled, then her eyes became slits and another rung in her rack of teeth revealed itself.

"Maybe just a peek?" Aggression rasped under her words.

Mikk's use of a sexy voice had backfired. The pirate queen wanted him to remove his clothes, strip for her like a Gadelon Guild prostitute. Mikk was violently offended but, nevertheless, calmly rose to his feet and, to the Vonchoi's great surprise, undid his belt.

"You . . . you'll do it?" The Vonchoi had lost her leering bravado.

"This is nothing if it means I get Thissizz." Mikk flung away his tunic and it landed behind the optitube console.

"But you're a performance master!"

"I don't care." Mikk untied the lace on his leggings and swiftly slid them down his thighs to his ankles. He kicked them off and straightened. His skin felt cold and tight as he watched the operator's shocked face without blinking.

"Are you satisfied?" he asked.

The Vonchoi gulped and made an awkward attempt not to let her eyes wander, but she succumbed quickly and looked Mikk over with nearly surgical intensity.

"Far from it," she said after several minutes of mute distress. "I won't be able to sleep for weeks."

"Do I get Droos?"

The Vonchoi's olive eyes were glassy.

"Do I get Droos?" Mikk repeated.

The pirate shook herself. "Yes. Whatever you want."

The codes flashed on the screen. Mikk pulled up Thissizz's, waited, and the familiar bright form of his limbless friend materialized on the wall of the Terran suite.

At first, they looked at each other in rapt silence: Mikk nude, the button box still in his hand; Thissizz swaying gently, huge eyes burning on his friend.

Mikk slowly set the box on the floor, lifted his arms to the Droos, and mimed embracing him, nuzzling him, rubbing his body up and down his coils. Thissizz rumbled softly and hissed.

"I knew you would reach me sometime." His great face loomed close. "I miss you."

Mikk ended his long-distance love making and choked on a sob.

"Did Yii die?" Thissizz whispered and Mikk nodded.

"It's w-winter here," Mikk sniffed, quickly collecting himself. "I wish we could lie together."

"Do the Terrans like you? My father says they're an eager but confused race."

"We're quite a sensation," Mikk smiled. "The Nipponese were especially pleased. Their Emperor showed me some temple gardens the Crown would envy."

Thissizz cocked his head quizzically. "Is it true Terrans have hair on their bodies? In the still shots, some of the males even have fur on their faces."

"Well, yes," Mikk said, unsure why Thissizz was bringing this up, "not like the Kekoi, but . . ."

Thissizz gave Mikk a sly sideways leer that let him know exactly what his preferences were, and the performance master blushed faintly across the bridge of his nose.

"Shall I sing for you, serassi?" Thissizz asked.

"Yes. A morning song for a gray morning."

Thissizz shook out his hood, cleared his vocal cords, and sang about wanting to be out and about now that dawn had come, the sun was warm, and the flowers had opened their massive petals. Mikk's fingers twitched as the glorious vibrations moved from his ears into his skin and cheekbones and through his nervous system. He closed his eyes and hummed softly in harmony.

"Such a vast distance," he sighed at the song's conclusion, "and your power remains greater than anything I've ever known."

Thissizz spread his hood to its fullest dimensions and shivered so that the skin and scale fan buzzed slightly. Mikk's jaw muscles worked nervously and he slid his hands down over his groin to soothe its swollen veins and unquiet organ.

It's not my imagination! he thought. I can smell his heat! Even taste it . . .

"Please hurry home when this tour is over," Thissizz said. "I want to touch you."

"Yes, my friend. This is much too long a time without you."

"Much too long."

"Could you call Briin for me? Tell him I found his hat."

"What kind is it?"

"A boater."

"A boater?"

"It suits him. You'll see." Mikk again raised his hands and pretended to caress the face on the wall. Pretended . . . and yet registered a real sensation of slick, warm skin.

"Say hello to your wives and children for me. I love you."

"I love you, too." The screen went blank.

Mikk wandered over to the bank of windows and frowned at the congealed fog obscuring most of the skyline. Anyone glancing out the rows of polyglass eyes in the office building opposite the Convention Center could have gotten a free fishbowl view of what had humbled the Vonchoi, but no one did.

Maya banged through Mikk's unlocked door and shimmied toward him with a new tunic draped over her tentacles. "Terran silk no good," she squeaked irritably. "Maya have to rip seams *twice!*"

She scooted up to the performance master and poked his hip. "Hunh! Not dress?"

Mikk came out of his reverie.

"I'm sorry, Maya. I didn't mean to be rude." He glanced down at the tunic. "Is that for tonight?"

"Tonight future. Now *now*. Mikk brood. Need get out."

"Not a bad idea, Maya! It's Tenth Day. Nothing to do until the reception. Maybe I should find a children's hospital." He smiled crookedly. "Or a reptile house."

In the end, Mikk went to the Convention Center's amusement park and was mobbed by children wielding sticky green cones of SpunSweet. The tenacious candy ruined his surprise tunic and Maya screamed at him for over an hour about how she didn't have time to keep making him "damn hobby clothes," but his soul felt stronger. He prepared himself for the reception.

Chapter Twenty-five: The Reception

Martin did not want to go. Snow threatened, the streets were icy, and the only optitube program he thought worthwhile, *West End Theater Showcase,* was presenting *The Alchemist*, one of his favorite plays.

Martin did not have to go. He was the theater critic, not the society columnist.

Martin went. He had to meet this blood-haired outworld polymath face to face. Unfortunately, when he arrived late at the New Embassy Convention Center's banquet hall, he realized he was too agitated for this kind of soirée. The sheer number of people and outworlders unsettled him, and he began to wonder just what he intended. A confrontation? Exorcism? An apology for the only negative words out of forty-seven legitimate journals in New York City?

Martin stamped the slush from his boots. No. No apology. Someone had to be the slave at the charioteer's elbow: "You are mortal—you are wrong."

However, when he picked out the Vyzanian across the room, he briefly lost his momentum. Mikk resembled an outworld reinterpretation of a Botticelli. He was taller than Martin had expected, perhaps six foot two, and splendid in silver-shot turquoise, although the belt, a tightly cinched ash-colored rag, didn't match at all. Still, the so-called tunic, which looked more like a happi coat or smoking jacket, emphasized Mikk's impressive breadth of shoulder, his narrow waist, and his eerie, even ethereal, dancer's carriage.

If it's true Vyzanians age only eight years every century,

Martin brooded, then this is the youngest forty-year-old man I've ever seen.

Belians lived a long time, too, of course, but because they looked less like human beings, their aging, or lack of it, was more abstract—and infinitely less irksome.

I'll bet he's had treatments, Martin thought. All performers have. Synthosteroids, surgery, the works.

However, no treatment in creation could explain what he'd seen and heard the night before. Nothing enhanced performance to that degree, not even the highly dangerous, and universally banned, cell rejuvenation compounds. Mikk's blood plasma would have broken down long before the chemicals could have given him what he apparently already had. Martin's skin tingled into gooseflesh. The man was a freak.

That beautiful dark actress was with the performance master, hanging on his arm and watching the ebb and flow of glitterati with serious eyes and jumpy reflexes. Everything startled her: a tray of hors d'oeuvres thrust in her face, a curious Belian hand on her shoulder, a sudden laugh or a snap from a still cam. At each new shock she glanced quickly at Mikk and the sight of his smile would relax her, if only slightly. A couple of times she grasped Mikk's hand, lifted it to her mouth, and—Martin couldn't believe it—licked the performance master's fingers with her long purplish tongue, sucking on the tips as though they were licorice.

The performance master did not react the way Martin would have if a darkly gorgeous, exotic actress had started to slurp on his digits. He remained calm, gently disengaged himself, and whispered something to her that she seemed to find illogical—her brow puckered prettily—but respected. She left his fingers alone until the next buildup of crowd induced anxiety.

Martin had seen enough. The critic snatched up a drink with a "nonalcohol" green flag on its swizzle stick, and sallied forth to do battle. He strode boldly across the room and shook the performance master's hand, a hand that, for all its obvious vigor, felt unnervingly like a young woman's. A strange spicy scent hovered around Mikk like some kind of woodsy cologne. Martin's nostrils flared in protest—he hated perfume.

"Martin Brannick. *New York Times.*"

"Ah, yes!" Mikk said pleasantly. " 'Brannick on Broadway.' I'm sorry. I didn't realize you had two names."

His accent, and teeth, are perfect, Martin thought and he gave him a hard below-the-nose-only smile.

"I don't use both in my column." He sipped his tonic water, eyes fixed unwaveringly on the performance master. "It's an affectation. Like *your* name."

Mikk's genial expression became "the grin"—it pained Martin that Perry Matthews, in a typical burst of gleeful overkill, had seen fit to flatter the performance master with quotation marks.

"Very good, Martin. Dispense with the pleasantries and get right down to business."

He nodded to Hegron and she reluctantly withdrew.

"Not until we're both properly armed." Martin took another drink, a strong red-flagged martini, from a nearby tray and handed it to Mikk. The performance master shrugged, downed it, and set the glass aside.

"Good burn, but a strange flavor," he said thoughtfully. "Similar to the tonics I was given as a boy."

Martin's sloping shoulders drooped lower in dismay. He had just lost his bet with Perry. "Vyzanians are immune," his colleague had said. "It's probably an adaptation to the decaying plant starches in their lakes. No one knows for sure. Their entire world is alcoholic. They call it 'the Intoxication.' "

"That is patently absurd. I'll bet they spread that tale to cover up an unusual sensitivity."

"You really want to make a wager? Fine. The loser treats the winner to lunch at the New Russian Tea Room."

"I hate that place."

For his part, Mikk was concerned about this fairly young but unhealthy looking man with the wide stare. Martin had not removed his beautiful hair coat or animal skin gloves even though the room, crowded as it was with hundreds of guests, was stifling. The critic obviously did not feel at home, and Mikk suddenly wanted to befriend him. He was feeling particularly brittle himself this evening and wore a Vyzanian mourning sash although no one outside his troupe seemed to know what it was.

But Martin did not want to be befriended. Without further ado, he violated Perry Matthews' warning. "So, how bad *was* that little Black and Red conflict of yours?"

My God! Martin rocked back a step. What's wrong with his eyes?

Mikk lowered them quickly as though he also was upset by their pulsing flares of dark pigment. "We butchered about a million of ourselves every year for three lifetimes."

"But, one of your lifetimes is . . . that's three billion people!"

"Three point six."

"You call that a *civil* war?!" Martin cried.

"All wars without outworlders are civil wars."

"That's not how we define it."

"It should be."

"Well, no matter what you call it," Martin said, determined to prevail in spite of his opponent's unnerving physical distractions, "that's extraordinary carnage over fishing rights."

"It was more complicated than that. . . ."

"Was it? I heard the war started because a palace guard hacked a man to death with a sword for trolling in the king's ornamental pond."

Martin expected a reaction of some kind to this salvo, something at least as extreme as the alteration in eye color, but Mikk must have recovered himself. His eyes, lavender again, remained pale and he merely released a delicate moan, as though the story was a current piece of overworked gossip, not long-buried history.

"I don't think you can blame an entire war on the actions of one man," he said.

"Maybe not," Martin said, going for the kill, "but one man can do an awful lot of damage."

Mikk did not take the bait. He changed the subject. "This is a lovely space, don't you think?" He glanced up at the high, bald concrete walls. "Cool and spare. Nataki XII designed it, didn't he?"

Martin recognized the diversionary tactic, but hated the building too much not to comment. "That man has massacred good design!" he spluttered. "He's holding an entire generation of architects hostage to his success. Schools won't even listen to alternate concepts of proportion or layout, let alone give students grants to experiment. Someone needs to cut through the nonsense and call this fraud by its real name: pretentious greed."

"An emancipator for enslaved architects?" Mikk asked, picking up the civil war theme again.

"Precisely! Art dies without the free exchange of ideas."

Mikk grinned slowly at Martin, who suddenly realized what he had implied.

"Touché," he said frigidly, "you son of a bitch."

"Ah, so you've identified my species! Thank you. I was wondering where you fit me in your pantheon of culture."

"Don't put more malice in my words than is already there. I am not that crude and you are not that worthy. An actor hardly has the right to exploit Civil War references."

Mikk's smile faded. "What is your quarrel with me? How am I a threat to you?"

"You're a cultural thief, sir. A myna bird collecting bits of glass and snatches of conversation. You think you can planet-hop about the galaxy, appropriate people's entertainment, and claim its magic for yourself." Martin took a deep breath and straightened his back but remained well over a head shorter than Mikk.

"It does not work that way," he continued. "It's form only. Mere imitation. You delude yourself if you think you can know the soul of a foreign people's work and yet you pretend to it all the time. A very destructive pretense. Your practices will ruin what you rob."

"Not true," Mikk said, and Martin was struck by the keen, cool intelligence in the performance master's expression, the direct opposite of the dark-eyed agitation he'd displayed over the Black and Red War. "I'm not taking anything from anyone. A performer can only claim as his what he brings *to* a performance, and what he brings he also shares. A work belongs to every person who experiences it. It grows with exposure."

I see now why people are so easily fooled by this outworlder, Martin thought. He looks good, he sounds good, and he knows how to persuade. He is certifiably dangerous.

"I think the pieces I've chosen can bear the stress of performance," Mikk continued, "even a bad performance, and you have yet to say I have performed anything badly." He tried to put his hand on Martin's arm, but the critic pulled away. "Martin, I would never pretend Terran art isn't Terran. In the first place, it would be impossible, and, secondly, if I wanted to call anything 'mine,' I'd write it myself."

Martin did not reply for some time, but his wide blue eyes continued to sit on Mikk, which distressed the performance master, not because of their cold hunger, but because of their look of isolation. They were the eyes of a man staring out of an empty house at a city miles away.

"Very fine words," the critic murmured at last, "but they don't address the issue at all."

"I see. What are we talking about?"

"It's a question of identity. Who, after all, are you?"

"Who are *you*?"

The critic calmly dropped his drink, which hopped on the floor and splashed Mikk's slipper, then walked away. Since he'd never removed his coat, he didn't need to retrieve it. He was through the heavy swivel door panels and out of the hall in an instant.

The reception continued in noisy merriment, but the silence in Mikk's mind was unbearable. As soon as he could, he escaped and went upstairs to the Inner-Circle Club suites and tapped on Maya's door. Maya did not like crowded parties full of strangers so Mikk knew she would be home.

When she opened the door, the dresser took one look at Mikk, and let him in. Without a word, the performance master disrobed, lay face down on the parquet, and Maya gave him a massage, wriggling up and down his back with her eight flexible feet. He groaned.

"Good," she said. "Maya work it out. What happen?"

"Nothing really."

"Uh-hunh." She gave him a stinging slap. "You poor liar. Tell Maya."

"I got a glimpse into someone's personal hell," he sighed. "It frightened me."

"Why? Not *your* hell."

"I don't know. I know he's wrong, that he's caught up in his own prejudices, but it still bothers me. This one man in particular."

"Hunh, you soft in head. Master need hide like dune lizard."

In spite of himself, Mikk smiled. "What—and hurt your little feet?"

Maya smacked him again. "You lucky Maya like job," she said as Mikk's quiet laughter lightly bounced the cephalopod. "You really *ugly* biped. All Maya can do not spit up."

"Keep flirting like that and people will think we're lovers."

"Not possible. Maya too beautiful for you."

Mikk reached back over his shoulder, grabbed one of Maya's tentacles, and kissed it.

"Yech!" she cried. "Such nasty habit." But her six eyes glowed with secret pleasure.

When he was dressed again, Mikk went back to his own suite. The day's fog was gone, but the light from the city bounced dull and rusty off a solid ceiling of suspended ice, casting a faint yellow glow over the skyline, the furniture of the parlor, everything. He pressed his nose against one of the windows and his breath frosted the polyglass.

What if I *am* a threat? he wondered. That little man was terribly upset. . . .

Outside, the air began to fill with tiny drifting flakes.

"Ah! . . . dear gods . . . snow . . ."

Mikk stepped back from the window and, in honor of this gentle visitor from his past, softly practiced a Somalite songdance ballad, one of Whees-aru's most poignant and mysterious about a villager watching his house burn to the ground.

Hegron, who had finally grown too uncomfortable to stay with people who did not speak her language, had found her way to the Inner Circle with only three false turns on lower floors. She was about to enter Mikk's habitually unlocked room when an amazing sound came through the door and she nearly fainted. She closed her eyes and pressed her hands against the wall to steady herself.

In all her years as a slave entertainer, she'd never heard anything this sad and lovely even though her owner had been one of her country's richest warlords before the revolution, a man who could purchase the services of any artist he desired. Any artist, that is, but Mikk. For his talents, the warlord had had to give up Hegron, and this new master kept telling her he was not her master in spite of everyone's calling him "Master" Mikk.

"How can I explain to you, Hegron?" he'd said. "I do not own you."

"But I was sold to you."

"No. I bargained for your freedom and now you have it."

"You're the master!"

"It's not the same," Mikk said, exasperation angling his voice. "It's a title. I'm a master of performance, not people."

"But everyone does what you say," Hegron persisted.

"I'm their employer!" Mikk cried. "And they *don't* always do what I say!"

Hegron still didn't understand, but she understood his power and wanted to express her gratitude for it. Her previous owner had insisted on being pleasured, especially by her licking his fingers. Over the years, she'd grown to enjoy it herself, first because it distracted him from other, more painful "pleasurings," then because it made her feel safe. No one could touch her or hurt her while she was licking the master's fingers. No one dared.

Mikk was trying to wean her of the habit. He'd push her hand away, without roughness, and whisper in Ichtian, "Save that for a lover, Hegron."

Hegron had had many sexual partners, but no lovers. Even so, she recognized the broken heart in Mikk's songdance and, cowering in the hallway, her nose against the wallpaper, she began to cry. The songdance stopped and Mikk opened his door.

"Hegron?" His smooth, young-looking face was etched with concern.

"M-master!" she sobbed. "You sound so s-sad! What could m-make you so sad?"

"It's a sad song, Hegron."

"N-no. There's more." She wiped her nose with one of her braids. "S-something more than the song. I heard it."

Mikk bit his lip. She was right. He'd been thinking of the first time he saw snow, his first visit to Droos, and the pain of absence had returned. It had little to do with the lyrics of the song or the gestures of the dance, but, as Whees-aru had told him, "Songdance is never about itself alone. It's a pebble thrown in a pond. The ripples reach in all directions."

"I miss Thissizz," he said softly. "Songdance is a way for me to embrace him even when he isn't here."

"But why sing something sad? Doesn't it make you hurt more?"

"Not at all. It makes me feel better."

Hegron's lovely black brows puckered. She obviously did not understand.

"It's like the old Terran music I played for you the other night," Mikk said. "Do you remember? The blues pieces."

"Yes!" Hegron grinned. "They were wonderful! I could feel them in my belly."

"You see? If you can turn your pain into music, then you have power over it and can release it. A lonely song can help you feel less lonely."

"I can make you feel less lonely, Master Mikk."

Mikk quickly looked away in embarrassment. "Hegron, don't . . ."

"Why not, Master Mikk? You find a Droos beautiful."

The actress's lip trembled and she lowered her head. She was close to tears again. Mikk took her hand in his.

"I think you're beautiful, too, Hegron, but that doesn't mean I have the right to possess you."

"Even if I want you to?"

She lifted her head and looked directly into Mikk's eyes. Their silver glitter was not a reflection of the light in the hall. The source was inside Mikk.

"Even if you want me to. People are not possessions."

"But you've had other lovers, Master Mikk. I know you have."

"Not for very long, Hegron. I travel too much and . . ."

"I don't need a long-time lover, Master Mikk."

"You deserve one, Hegron, and you deserve one who can bare his soul to you without fear." Mikk sighed and gave her a sad smile. "I can't do that."

Hegron's confusion altered to concern, and Mikk regretted having shared even this much of his pain. The former slave had a very tender, empathetic heart that bled as much for others' misfortunes as for her own. He'd have to explain his words or she'd worry herself into a fever.

"Long ago, before you were born, I was . . . damaged, Hegron. It left me afraid of getting hurt, and, as a result, I have always been especially careful not to let people see too far inside me."

Hegron's brow relaxed. She understood this, which wasn't surprising considering her own experience. Slaves had to find ways to protect their inner lives, too.

"Thissizz is the only one who has been able to reach past that fear and find me. With him, I'm safe. With him, I have the strength to be defenseless."

Hegron was quiet a moment, then nodded thoughtfully.

"That's what was in the music," she said. Mikk's pale eyes widened.

"Yes!" he said softly. "I think so." He stroked her braids affectionately. "That's exactly what it was."

His smile was so kind that Hegron decided she would someday give him something he truly wanted—and he startled her by reading her thoughts, or seeming to.

"You're a generous person, Hegron, and there are many ways to say thank you. Maybe someday you can bring me a wonderful piece of news that will make me very happy."

Hegron grinned then stood on tiptoe and kissed his cheek, which was surprisingly soft and slightly salty.

"You need sleep if you're to be ready for tomorrow," he said. His face looked pink.

"Yes, Master Mikk."

She turned to leave, but stopped and looked back. "Master Mikk? Why have you never performed that song in public?"

"Because I'm not yet good enough."

Hegron was puzzled, but decided the master knew best. "Well, good night, Master Mikk."

"Good night, Hegron."

When Hegron was gone, Mikk undressed and retrieved his green silk robe from its temporary resting place under the dining table. He wrapped it tightly around his long body.

"I'm such a mess when I travel," he muttered. "No Briin to keep me in line, I suppose."

After mixing himself a glass of salt water, he went into the bedroom and flipped on the tabletop telewave, turning it toward the bed so he could sit on the pillows and have one last look at business before surrendering to his night phantoms.

He quickly regretted his decision.

"Not again!" he howled. "How can those Beast's bastards do this?"

The Council had raised the performers' tithe again, almost double what it had been, and it had to be paid before the next General Council meeting, mere weeks away. Delinquent Association members would lose their licenses to perform and would have to return to their home worlds.

The new tithe would not affect Mikk much. He was an established performance master and could easily absorb the cost, but he knew hundreds of young, adventurous galactic performers who would be deeply hurt by this increase, probably to the point they couldn't tour at all—undoubtedly exactly what the Council was after. They didn't need the money. They wanted to curb experimentation.

Mikk smacked the telewave with the flat of his hand. Half of his own troupe was young talent just starting out, and Hegron! Hegron certainly couldn't pay this! In fact, since she became a member of the troupe, Mikk had secretly . . .

He grinned. A blaze of startled inspiration.

Why not? he thought. Nothing in the Council Rules prohibited it, although it was highly irregular, definitely improper, and would draw an enormous amount of attention. Still, his patience had been stretched very thin by the events of the last two days. Mikk's fingers began to enter the codes almost before he realized he'd made the decision.

"No tiptoeing behind their backs, this time," he whispered, drunk on his own defiance. "Martin Brannick and the Galactic Council can say what they want, write what they want, tax what they want. No one is going to close my show. No one is going to silence the music."

Chapter Twenty-six: 19,999 Zyrr

"You agreed to review all five shows," Martin's editor said. She straightened her peach plastic scarf.

"I've changed my mind."

"Why?"

"One's enough, don't you think?" Martin reached into his pocket for his nicotine-free cigarettes. A meeting in his editor's office was like an audience with Lucrezia Borgia, and the Hectorine Armendariz triptych on the wall behind her, "Ice Cream Social in the Style of Francis Bacon," didn't help.

"After all, there are local companies, good ones, who never get any press and—"

"You already have one lit, Martin."

"Oh." He set the cigarettes down. "I think we need to support our own a bit more. How is Broadway supposed to come out of this latest slump if we continue to focus our energies on foreign productions?"

"Martin, dear." The editor perched her renipped, retucked, and refluffed body on the corner of her black marble desk. "What's the matter with you? Mikk's troupe isn't just the hottest ticket in town, it's the *only* ticket in town. What local companies do you mean? The audience participation dinner theater on 42nd? The soap opera discos? The zillionth revival of *Fiddler on the Roof*? Broadway hasn't been Broadway since the rebuilding. We have to take what we can get, and you said it yourself: Mikk and his performers are damned good. For me, that's what matters."

"It's not right, Betty."

"What isn't, Marty?" Her gold-plated fingernails clacked on the marble.

274

The critic pinched the bridge of his nose. If he read the signs right, this new headache was going to be special. "What he's doing," he said. "Mikk performed Gershwin . . . and Puccini, for Christ's sake! Unbelievable! An outworlder doing Italian opera . . ."

"At least someone is. I think he did a wonderful job, too."

Martin looked up, shocked out of his attempt to massage away his vascular pain. "You didn't tell me you were going to be there," he said quietly.

"Some Belian friends of mine got house tickets." The editor eased off the desk and slapped smooth the tight skirt of her paper foil sheath. "I think you should know, Marty, I was going to fire you for that review you wrote."

"*Fire* me?! For speaking my mind?"

"No one agrees with you, not even your aunt, although she did talk me out of it." The editor's implanted eyelashes batted slowly in studied sympathy. "You really should do something about those headaches. They're clouding your judgment."

"I've a right to my own opinions!" Sure I do, he thought. As long as I've okayed them with auntie dear. Damn it! When will someone treat me like an independent adult?

"Don't be a pill, Marty. I want four more reviews out of you and I want them to be short and upbeat, understand?"

Perfectly, Martin thought. The wavy lines dancing around his head turned red when he rubbed his eyes, as red as that theatrical brigand's unnatural hair. Would four forcibly cheery reviews exorcise this devil from his psyche? Would he be rid of Mikk and his graceful excellence forever?

No. Mikk was his spiritual migraine and migraines had an unfortunate habit of recurring when you were least prepared for them.

"Excuse me, Betty," he said as he rose to his feet. "I have a date at the New Russian Tea Room."

"You hate that place."

"That's why I'm going."

Across town, the performance master telewaved Vyzania.

"Gods, lad, what a miserable transmission! Are there sunspots?"

"At least, but I suspect other interference as well."

"The Council?"

"It's not important, Master Huud. What is important is that I've decided to donate 19,999 zyrr to the new theater."

"Excellent! But what happened to twenty thousand?"

"We've outdone all my expectations, Master Huud, but I did fail to please someone."

"I see. Well, if you ever manage to win this someone over, give him the one zyrr. Critics keep us strong, Mikk."

Chapter Twenty-seven: The Threat

It was a golden, balmy day on Droos, a day between performances, and the two friends decided to get away to their favorite secret place, the small grassy ledge overlooking the Rainbow Ravine. There they ate fruit, sang, but, on the whole, were happy just to rest against each other and watch the diving kites swoop in and out of the brilliant quartz bands.

"Perhaps Mr. Brannick needs a companion," Thissizz said. "Someone to help him feel less a stranger in his own skin."

"My generous Droos!" Mikk stroked Thissizz's smooth side. "You could be right."

The Droos smiled and started to hum gently. Mikk closed his eyes. "I'm very sorry my presence upset him so much," he said.

"Maybe you'll meet again and get a chance to start anew. The gods bring people together for a reason."

"Yes," Mikk breathed. "Yes, they do."

The performance master suddenly opened his eyes, sat up, and looked back at the thicket.

"What is it, Mikk?"

"I don't believe it," Mikk groaned. "How in the name of the gods did he know to look for us here?"

"Who?"

"Councilor Oplup. I'd recognize that wheezing snort any-where."

"Has he seen us yet?"

"I can't yet see him myself, but it sounds as though he's using a bush blade."

"That's forbidden! This is a park."

"I doubt Oplup cares." Mikk's spine stretched taut as he strained to pinpoint the distant bush blade's location. "My guess is he's at the Clustered Sisters."

"He'll never make it around them. The path is too narrow." The Droos scowled. "I hope he breaks his blade on their quartz flanks! Imagine! Cutting down protected trees." He put his lips against Mikk's ear. "Let's run away before he gets here."

"To the Beast with him!" Mikk settled back against his friend. "I'm not going anywhere because of that gar-wart."

Thissizz chuckled. Mikk had never called anyone such a thing before, but it was highly appropriate considering the gar-wart's size, smell, and stupidity. "Then I shall stay, too," he said.

Soon Thissizz as well could hear the small, high-pitched motor of the bush blade as the rotund Councilor laboriously hacked his way through the dense Droosian thicket. When Oplup appeared, his wiggling rolls of gelatinous fat had sweated greasily through his tentlike summer clothing.

"I'm going to up my swallow," Thissizz said. "Don't look until you're very ready. He's twice as big as last time."

"Lovely. Praise the gods."

Oplup cut the motor on the bush blade and rolled and rocked on his stumpy legs to the reclining performers. He retrieved a rag from between the lumps of flesh on his left arm and mopped his forehead.

"A hot day, Mikk," he said, rudely neglecting to greet Thissizz at all.

"It's marvelously comfortable over here, Councilor," Mikk said with a quick glance at Thissizz, who smiled. The performance master regarded the reeking Oplup with the placid calm of a man perfectly at home, perfectly at ease, and perfectly aware of his power.

"There wasn't time last night to speak with you," said the

Councilor. "Your performances go on for an unconscionable length of time. You must be exhausted."

"I've never felt better." Mikk was obviously in superlative health. The sunlight glowed on his skin and, even at rest, his body exuded a supple, energetic strength. Still, Mikk's fine condition did not impress the Councilor. Oplup caught sight of the tip of Thissizz's coils curled around the performance master's ankle and he frowned darkly.

"I understand you paid your performers' tithes for them in flagrant violation of Council protocol," Oplup said.

"Many performance masters have," Mikk smiled. "Protocol is not law."

"You were the first."

Thissizz beamed proudly at Mikk then kissed him tenderly on his mouth, right in front of the Councilor.

"How revolting!" Oplup said, spitting the words at Mikk. "At our next General Session, I'm going to recommend that performance masters be forbidden to pay their troupe's tithes for them."

"You'll do no such thing," Mikk said calmly. "We both know the Council is much too greedy for that."

Oplup's chin sank into the rolls of fat around his neck and he puffed irritably. "You certainly are sure of yourself," he sniffed. "Like a damned H'n N'kae."

"My goodness, Thissizz! The Councilor is full of compliments today!"

Without the need to discuss it first, the friends immediately launched into the chorus of the blatantly martial H'n N'kae anthem.

Oplup hated the H'n N'kae, hated everything about them, including their language and music. He dropped the bush blade and attempted to cover his ears, but he had grown too fat and the extra flesh on his arms prevented his hands from reaching past his shoulders. Mikk was embarrassed to find this grotesque phenomenon moderately fascinating.

"I am sorry, Councilor," he said. "We're in a playful mood today."

"I'm warning you, Mikk," the Councilor said, popping his rigid jaw now that the singing had stopped, "your attitude has not gone unnoticed and your . . . perversions will be your downfall."

"Don't be absurd, Councilor." The lavender brilliance of Mikk's eyes rivalled that of the quartz in the ravine. "I've never *gutted* and *eaten* my lovers."

Oplup's extensive flesh turned yellowish gray. "What a foul imagination you have, Vyzanian," he said in a steady but poisonous voice.

"It's a gift."

"You can't possibly have any proof."

"Gods flying, Councilor!" Mikk cried impatiently. "I'm glad I can't prove it! I may therefore be able to convince myself it isn't true."

"Better make sure you succeed," Oplup said. "That kind of rumor has a way of flying back to foul the nest where it hatched."

"What a nice metaphor! May I use it?"

In spite of his severe annoyance with the performance master, the Councilor was genuinely flattered by the request and utterly failed to pick up on the sarcasm. "Humph," he said, lifting his blunt nose disdainfully. "How pathetic. Begging for material like an Ichtian panhandler. You really are working too hard, Mikk. Be careful. That's when you could make mistakes. Serious mistakes."

His sense of superiority restored, Oplup bent down for his fallen bush blade, couldn't reach it, and abandoned the attempt with a self-righteous smirk. He waddled off to find the tunnel he had already cut in the otherwise unviolated Droosian forest.

"You took a terrible risk, Mikk," Thissizz said. "He might retaliate."

"He'll have to retaliate against half the Association. It's a very widespread rumor."

"Is it true?"

"I sincerely hope not," Mikk sighed. "I have enough trouble accepting that kind of behavior from Venwatt spiders." He caressed the coil around his ankle.

"In any case," Thissizz said as he nibbled Mikk's shoulder, "I'm glad you never converted to Oplup's religion. You are much more beautiful in your leanness."

"We mustn't be intolerant of another's beliefs." Mikk's smile eased into dreaminess. "I'm sure there are many on his world who find his devout gluttony remarkably attractive."

"I am in no hurry to meet them." Thissizz slipped his soft tongue inside Mikk's loose tunic. "How lovely your back is! A wonderful country for me to explore."

Mikk wrapped his arms around the Droos' neck and the need for further words died away as the special serenity of their bond flooded his heart.

When we touch, his eyes told the Droos, *our gods lay down their weapons and I can forgive every trespass, even Oplup's.*

Entr'acte: Kekoi Kaery: The Second Day

"I am afraid your salt pendant must go empty again, Mikk-sir," Bipti said.

A new freezing dawn had entered the cell, and Mikk's slow breath clouded around his face as he leaned back against the wall under the window, arms crossed, staring stonily at the Freen. In spite of the cold, Bipti was sweating and had to dab his brow and upper lip with his sleeve.

"I tried the chemist as you suggested, but he would not give me salt either. He said he didn't have any."

Mikk narrowed his eyes. In reality, a portion of his displeasure was fabricated. He still had half a tin of caviar hidden in his surprise tunic.

"And the spice vendor?"

"She did not set out her wares today. The, uh, the broadsides, Mikk-sir . . . It is too crowded to sell anything."

Mikk decided to let the Freen suffer a bit more by forcing the pigment into his eyes, enough to make them a shadowy violet. Bipti quickly glanced away and scratched his ear.

"Would you like me to tell you what the pictures are, Mikk-sir?" he asked meekly.

"No. I can guess."

"I am very sorry about the salt." Bipti started to twitch under Mikk's unforgiving stare. "What will happen if you don't get any?"

"First, I will become very thirsty as my body loses its ability to retain moisture."

"Couldn't you just drink a lot of water, Mikk-sir?" The Freen's inner eyelids fluttered.

"Oh, I certainly would, Bipti, but without salt, my chemistry cannot function properly and my body cannot process it. I'd still lose moisture, rapidly."

"And . . . and then?"

"My hands would begin to shake, then my entire body." Mikk darkened his eyes another shade for dramatic emphasis and the Freen whimpered. "Finally, I would go into convulsions . . . and die."

"Oh! Mikk-sir!" The Freen covered his mouth, aghast. "You would? You would die?"

Mikk was tired of being cruel. He closed his eyes. "It may not be such a loss, Bipti. One dead entertainer. Tell me." His voice dropped as his true, troubled spirit revealed itself. "Do you know what the Somalite Peace is?"

"N-no," Bipti stammered. "N-no one knows that b-but the Somalites, M-Mikk-sir, and they cannot t-tell us."

Mikk opened his eyes, their unforced darkness now melancholy rather than angry. "Perhaps they want me to join them, Bipti. If so, it won't matter whether I get salt or not. Today, tomorrow—it's not your fault."

The guard shook his head quickly, obviously eager to remain blameless. "Are you thirsty, Mikk-sir?"

"Not yet, Bipti."

"But soon?"

"Yes."

Martin's skin crept when he saw the broadsides. Plastered to the buildings and fences of the courtyard with a quick-drying resin, they bore a startling resemblance to the incendiary cartoons issued during the upheavals of nineteenth-century Europe and had the same grotesque elegance: finely etched lines depicting, in graphic detail, some of the nastiest images Martin had ever seen. One of the mildest showed Mikk blithely walking off the edge of a cliff taking a motley train of blissfully unaware performers with him. At the bottom of the cliff awaited a nest of giant hungry drax larvae, one of nature's most stomach-turning inventions, all mucus and bloody fangs. Another broadside depicted Mikk relieving himself, in an exotic fashion that paid little attention to the realities of Vyzanian anatomy, over the heads of well-known Council members. A variation, a rebuttal of sorts, had the Kekoi press in the Council's place happily catching the filth in their mouths. Yet another showed the Council dissecting Mikk and eating his reproductive organs stewed in a pot of gon, the classic gamey Kekoi casserole.

The artists of these broadsides seemed especially fascinated by Mikk's long, sinewy body, so unlike the typical burly Kekoi's, and exaggerated his leanness until his image resembled an anatomical drawing, all flayed muscle and bone. Martin dejectedly conceded the artists had a point. The Council was out to "skin" Mikk.

The captions to the broadsides were in Belian for universality, but Martin had never seen these particular words in print and had only rarely heard the Belians say them.

The Kekoi print journals were cleaner, but every bit as extreme in feeling as their counterparts on the walls. They tended to fall into one of two camps: those who not only wanted Mikk vindicated, but wanted the Council rounded up and executed, and those who feared Mikk's actions would trigger a reign of retaliatory terror that would destroy the domestic, as well as galactic, entertainment community.

No one defended the ban itself, and Martin was not surprised. No self-respecting Kekoi would even think of such a thing.

Martin paid for his papers, tucked them into his cashmere coat, and headed back to the broadsides, determined to choke down their excesses so he would be better informed, when he saw Mikk's diminutive cephalopod costumer standing before the worst ones, crying. He'd seen her before when a gaggle of out-world journalists had tried to interview her for the optitube and had been delighted when, instead of answering their questions, she'd scared them off with some well-aimed snaps of her beaky mouth.

A feisty little thing, he'd thought. Far from pretty, but—interesting.

Now her public grief alarmed him. She sounded exactly like an abandoned child.

"Maya?"

"Bad things," she squeaked. The thick tears seeped from her six eyes and dropped to the ground like heavy syrup. "Filthy."

"Hey, now, calm down." After a moment's hesitation, he reached down to give her a reassuring pat on her head—or was it her back? "There's still hope."

Maya flipped the goop from her eyes. "Maya go to room," she sniffed, "watch Mikk things. Not come out forever."

Before Martin could say more, Maya scuttled into the crowd and disappeared.

"Are you Mr. Brannick, the critic?" someone behind him asked in Belian.

"Who wants to know?" Martin said belligerently, in English, without turning around.

"United Galactic-ah Press," came the response, also in English but cadenced in a way that turned Martin cold. He was used to Mikk's flawless Queen's English, but could still recognize the pseudo-Russo-Dutch singsong. Martin glared out of the corner of his eye at the camspectacled outworlder: a Vyzanian.

"I unnert-stand you have-a bin to zee-a Mikk," the journalist said. "Doos he rilly sink he can-a beat da Council? Would he con-senn to an innervoo? If-a so, we can-a joost make dee afternoon deadleen."

Martin stared at the Vyzanian without answering. The man undid the camspecs, removed them from his face, and blinked curiously at him. The journalist's eyes were deep magenta, a very rare eye color Vyzanians called "monarch purple." The journalist was a member of the royal family.

"You ought to be ashamed of yourself," Martin said. Pushing the journalist aside, he forced his way through the crowd and into the courtroom.

*   *   *

Mikk was "on" again when the Kekoi guards brought him back into the courtroom. He'd primed his defenses and felt ready for anything. Unfortunately, the next tribune, a timid, sallow hermaphroditic biped from Odmah, a minor world on a far-flung arm of the galaxy, did not. Et opened ets tiny O-shaped mouth and whispered something in a humming, buzzy language that made Mikk start, then turn angrily to the High Tribune.

"High Tribune, Mohemma does not speak Belian!"

Pairip's heavy flesh shifted ponderously as he leaned forward. "That is not possible. The Council chose the tribunes very carefully. They must know Belian because the proceedings are galactic."

"Well, no one made that clear to Mohemma."

Mohemma drew in ets mouth until et was invisible and looked mournfully at Mikk, who shrugged and said something in the outworlder's low burr of a language.

"Beast!" Pairip cried. "We'll have to get an interpreter."

However, it quickly became evident that the only one present who knew Mohemma's tongue was Mikk and, being the defendant, he was forbidden to translate.

"But Mohemma must be allowed to give ets presentation and ask ets questions like any other tribune," Mikk said, "or the validity of these proceedings is voided."

"That is true," the Spairan interrupted in her clean monotone. The outworld journalists were so surprised by the unfamiliar voice they swivelled their camspecs and overhead receiver cones every which way trying to locate the speaker, and optitubes across the galaxy were treated to several seconds of bouncing courtroom ceiling shots.

"However," Counsel 6 continued, "it is also true that you cannot be the interpreter of a tribune's words. You are not impartial."

"So, what do we do?" Twee the Borovfian whined, tapping his mouthpiece impatiently on his knee. "We can't drop everything while we look for an interpreter. That could take weeks!"

Mohemma looked questioningly at Mikk and Mikk softly translated the predicament. Mohemma turned to the High Tribune and, gesturing alternately at etself and Mikk, said something much louder this time, much more impassioned.

"What did et say?" Pairip asked.

"You're going to trust *him*?" the Borovfian tribune snapped. "I move we continue without the Odmahi tribune's testimony."

"You can propose nothing of the sort!" Pairip rumbled with a sharp glance of his keen black eyes. "Now—what did et say?"

"Mohemma is willing to have me translate for et. Et says et has only one question to ask me."

"Unacceptable!" said Twee. "Mikk would do anything to further his case, including alter a tribune's words so they are advantageous to himself."

"*You* be silent." Pairip imperiously pointed out Raf, Fod, and Korl. "These guards would be just as happy to throw a Borovfian in jail as a Vyzanian. Happier probably." He smoothed his beard. "I will allow Master Mikk to translate Mohemma's question."

Mikk translated Pairip's pronouncement for the Odmahi tribune, and Mohemma launched into a careful stream of sound, accompanied by minute, fluttery gestures of ets hands. Et folded them when et had concluded, and Mikk translated for the High Tribune.

"Mohemma says, 'We hear so much of Somalite generosity because the Somalites allowed everyone to visit their world. However, they never offered to help any of these pilgrims reach the Peace. I believe they were actually very selfish and their desire to end songdance proves it. Therefore, Master Mikk, as beautiful as songdance is, does it deserve preservation? It is the child of a rarefied, insular culture willing to leave others floundering in darkness. Why risk death to hold on to something few will ever understand? Something its creators did not even want people to have?' "

"Hm." Pairip nodded. "Your reply?"

Mikk smiled gently at Mohemma and answered. He was careful to include the slight nasality and politely hesitant starts and stops of "artist's class" Odmahi. Mohemma cocked ets head and, at the conclusion of Mikk's answer, sighed and looked away.

"Well?" Pairip asked.

"I told et that all peoples are flawed, but that does not mean their artistic and philosophical strivings are without merit. Perhaps, if we were gods, we wouldn't need to reach beyond our natures, but even the gods like to invent things. I won't condemn songdance merely because its creators were imperfect, and although I certainly don't want to die for this art, I will if I have to."

"You're a damned fool," Twee muttered.

"Am I? And what would you die for, tribune?"

"Not some dance, I assure you."

Several of the tribunes, the Lambdan in particular, chuckled at Twee's comment, but others, including Pairip himself, seemed embarrassed by the Borovfian's lack of shame. Encouraged, Mikk looked down the dais at Thissizz—and his hope withered. The Droos' eyes were open, but he seemed as inert as ever.

How fine is the line between love and hostility? Mikk wondered. You are here, my friend, but where are you?

The Magna shook his head and tossed aside his infrashades.

"This is ridiculous." He hacked the loose mucus from the back of his throat and swallowed it. He'd caught an ague experimenting with an ice soak for his bad back.

"Damn performance masters! They're too shrewd for ordinary interrogation."

His coelenterate assistant hop-sucked into the room.

"What is it now?" the Magna growled as he carefully turned in his settee.

"Your granddaughter is here, sir."

The Magna's sour mood altered instantly. He cut the volume on the optitube and grinned until his jaundiced cheeks almost broke apart under their load of dry wrinkles. "Show her in at once!"

The assistant slupped away and a moment later a small Hrako girl in sock-footed orange coveralls scrambled madly into the room.

"Gapi!" she cried and joyfully bounded into the Magna's bony lap and threw her arms around him. He crushed her close against his sharp collarbones and kissed her yellow bristle brush hair.

"Iki! My little star fly! How are you?"

The girl was homely even by Hrako standards. She had huge buck teeth, prominent scallop-shaped ears set so low in her head they resembled fins, and spindly limbs covered with the scabs of juvenile swamp pox. However, to the Magna, she was the dearest, most beautiful creature in the galaxy.

"I missed you so much, Gapi!"

"I missed you, too, Iki."

The girl wiggled around into her accustomed forward straddle position on her grandfather's lap.

"Oh!" She pointed at the optitube. "It's Mikk the Pocket Man."

The Magna cringed. He should have turned the optitube off Too late now.

"Gapi, why are those people looking so mean at Mikk?"

The Magna stroked her stiff hair. "He did something wrong, little one."

"Are they going to spank him?"

The Magna smiled sadly. How precious this simple view of life! And how short. "No, Iki. His punishment will be much greater than that."

Iki's yellow eyes widened, uncomprehending. She obviously couldn't imagine anything worse than getting spanked. "But what did he do?"

"He broke the law, child."

Iki looked back at the optitube. When she spoke again, her whisper was almost too low to hear. "If he says he's sorry and promises not to do it again, will they let him go home?" She turned hopefully, fearfully, to her Gapi.

"I don't know," the Magna fibbed.

The girl slid out of his lap and walked soberly up to the optitube. She stood rigidly before it, then touched Mikk's image, pressing her small scabby palm against the screen.

"Be good, Pocket Man," she whispered. "Don't be scared."

Nabu never should have let her steal from the master's tunic, the Magna thought, silently cursing his son. "Iki, dear? Why don't you run down to the aquarium and look at the baby eels? I'll be there shortly."

The girl's misshapen face lit up and she dashed out of the Magna's chamber.

The Magna shakily boosted himself from his settee. "Your days are numbered, Vyzanian," he muttered to the remote visage on the screen. "I swear it. You . . . will . . . die."

"Very interesting Kekoi broadsides about you, Mikk," the Venwatt tribune said when the session reconvened that afternoon. "Very ugly. Very offensive."

Mikk doubted someone with four arms and tufts of hair that

looked like basting brushes was qualified to judge, but he did not say so.

"That depends on one's point of view, tribune."

"So it's a matter of opinion?"

"Yes."

"Is your opinion more valid than the Council's?"

"Are they cracking down on Kekoi broadsides as well?" Mikk asked sweetly and got a smattering of laughter from the gallery.

"Would you object if they did?"

"Yes."

"But they're horrible," the Venwatt said.

"It doesn't matter, tribune. They're part of the Kekoi culture of free speech."

"That's hypocritical of you, Mikk," the tribune smiled with a snap of his double row of masticator plates. "You yourself have deliberately flouted a world's cultural expression."

"Have I?"

The tribune cast his eyes over the packed courtroom. "I'm a little reluctant to bring up this subject on this particular world, but I trust our furry friends will hear me out."

"Go on, tribune. Show some backbone."

"You disapproved of that new juggling on Ev-Mobix 'Gar."

"Yes."

"Would you have imposed a ban on the practice?"

"Yes!"

"Then you *do* condone some forms of censorship!" the Venwatt cried triumphantly.

"This is hardly the same thing at all. Porquille is repugnant beyond belief."

"Hear, hear!" a Kekoi cried amid widespread murmurs of approval.

"That is not a universal opinion," the Venwatt said. "You have set yourself up as a spokesman for free expression, refusing to submit to a ban yourself, and yet you would impose one on others."

"Only if I could, but I cannot. It is not in my power, nor should it be. However, I *can* protest."

"That is not a universal right either!"

"Tribune," Mikk raised his loop-bound hands to emphasize his point, "people will protest whether they have the right or not. It's the nature of thinking creatures. I guarantee I will do my best to convince people not to patronize such foul entertainments."

"You would let people decide for themselves?"

"Yes."

The tribune chuckled and slowly shook his head. "All those widely different species on vastly different worlds with very different views of morality and truth? Where would that leave you and other galactic performers? Where is the safety net if you run afoul of a dangerous government?" The Venwatt picked something out of his hair and ate it.

"There isn't much of a safety net now," Mikk said coldly, "or the Ev-Mobiks would not have been allowed to punish me without a hearing."

"That is an unacceptable argument! You broke the rules."

"*What* rules?" Mikk's voice started to rise. "The Ev-Mobiks have never answered to any code of behavior but their own, and the Council has never protected anyone from it. I took my chances and paid the price. I owe the Council nothing!"

"You, sir," the Venwatt shouted over the increased agitation of the crowd, "are quite mistaken. Do you realize the kind of chaos there would be if every world set its own standards for galactic performance? Could you manage hundreds of Ev-Mobix 'Gars? Artists must not be above the law no matter how fierce their dedication to their craft. There has to be a limit. We have to agree on something at the expense of *someone*."

"And the Council wants to mark that limit between me, one miserable performer, and songdance, a *sacred* art!"

"Sacred to whom?"

"Sacred to *me*!" Mikk cried and his fury broke free. "They've singled *me* out for special harassment. Why? Why does the ban apply only to *me*? Does that sound like something a Somalite, even a dying one, would ask for?"

"This is hardly the place to—"

"The Council imposed this absurdly unfair ban as punishment for my daring to stand up to its abuses and hypocrisies!"

"Control yourself, Mikk! I don't think—"

"I wouldn't be in the least surprised," Mikk continued at a high but controlled volume, "if this ban also represented a pitiful attempt on the Council's part to punish my master, too. Well!" He shook his manacled fists at the tribune. "If anyone deserves to be called celestial, tribune, it's Master Huud. The Council never could touch him and it never will!"

Mikk's voice reached a thunderous level near the end of his speech, and, in the silence that followed, the tribunes fidgeted in chastened discomfort. Hudd Maroc's name seemed to have unnerved them and, for the moment, no one knew how to continue.

Thissizz had not moved or even blinked.

"Are you . . . quite finished?" Pairip asked Mikk.

"Yes."

"Tribune?"

"I suppose so."

"Well, are you?" Pairip pressed irritably.

"Yes. But I reserve the right to comment on future tribunes' presentations."

"That is understood."

"And I think the Borovfian's objections should be listened to," the Venwatt added.

"I thought you were finished." Pairip's bottomless voice reverberated under his weight. The Venwatt huffily crossed all four of his arms and looked at the ceiling.

"So," the High Tribune said, "we will hear from the Bar Omega Septan tribune."

Mikk groaned. Don't they know Amda ar'k is insane? he wondered. Don't they care?

Amda ar'k shook his feathers at Mikk and many of the ragged plumes dropped to the floor.

"Swim, Vyzanian," he squawked. "The waters are getting deep."

That was his entire presentation. The court waited politely for a few minutes, but when it became obvious that Amda ar'k was not going to elaborate, Pairip adjourned the session for the day and Mikk was taken back to his cell.

On the way, he happened to glance up at the grate in the tunnel. He stopped. The coney was there, staring wall-eyed at him, nose twitching.

There's something odd about that kit, he thought. It doesn't know enough to head for the mountains.

"What is it, Master Mikk?" Raf asked with a sharp look at the surprise tunic. "Are you unwell?"

"Lookee!" Korl giggled, pointing his sandy-furred claw. "A bun-kit!" He reached for the grate.

The coney bit his finger and fled.

"Yow!"

Fod slapped his broad thigh. "How did you ever make lieutenant, Korl?" he laughed. "Did you lose your real uniform and steal this one?"

Raf grabbed both junior guards by the scruffs of their necks and heaved them ahead down the tunnel.

"One more word out of either of you and you're both on report!" he barked, then lowered his voice to Mikk. "More fish eggs tonight."

"But you're not on duty. Bipti is."

"Trust me."

Part Four: Trials

[C.Y.S. XII: 1074–1075]

Chapter Twenty-eight: Ev-Mobix 'Gar

If Briin was not around to stop them, the kitchen felines ventured beyond their usual diet of vermin and raided Mikk's larder for cultured milk and dried herbs that made them sneeze and dance in rapid circles. The pedigreed tumble puppies also knew they could get away with more in Mikk's company, and one wet evening during the Season of Wind and Rain a brindled gray was merrily destroying one of Mikk's best dance slippers as the performance master sat on a cushion in the parlor and composed a rondo on the zimrah.

When the small light on the telewave screen lit up to let him know the evening installment of galactic news had arrived, Mikk set aside the zimrah, separated the tumble puppy from his ruined slipper, and carried the soft little ball of speckled fur, which began to munch Mikk's finger with its tiny teeth, to the telewave with him.

Mikk scanned the governmental announcements and editorials and skipped the screen after screen of financial reports to settle into the arts and entertainment section. There was a long review of a Mrkusi acrobatics exhibition on Spaira—as usual, the Spairan writer discussed only the satisfying mathematical precision of the tumbling patterns and didn't mention their beauty or danger at all—followed by shorter reviews from all over the galaxy. There was also an article about a new form of juggling on Ev-Mobix 'Gar, which Mikk read closely. The more he read, the more horrified he became, and he clutched the tumble puppy to his breast as though protecting the fragile creature from the atrocities on the screen.

"This is as bad as the barbarities committed on Circlorax-9J," he breathed.

Mikk knew Ev-Mobix 'Gar housed more than its fair share of shady characters. The galactic free port trafficked in everything from rare birds to counterfeit gems, from drugs and prostitutes to stolen sculpture, weapons, and spacecraft. Its sprawling Central Bazaar seethed every hour of the day and night with jugglers, pickpockets, fire eaters, carnival barkers, madmen, comics, beggars, military personnel on leave, musicians, acrobats, pimps, hustlers, murderers, and students. Even so, this ghastly entertainment, dubbed "Porquille," slang for an impromptu barbecue, was vicious even by jaded Ev-Mobik standards.

"We needed something fresh to attract new business," the article quoted the enterprising cabaret owner responsible for the new form of juggling, "so I hired a street artist to come up with something."

What the juggler came up with was a variation on the traditional three-man flaming brand toss: he used live animals.

"It's a real crowd pleaser! You should hear the ladies scream when the beasts fly over their heads."

"What happens when an animal dies?" the journalist had asked.

"Oh, he throws it away and gets a new one."

Mikk buried his face in the wiggling tumble puppy and wailed into its fur. The muffled vibration tickled the warm little beast, which shivered all over in ecstasy and licked Mikk's nose.

How could people be so cruel merely for the sake of novelty? There were plenty of other, more benign entertainments they could have tried—bolba juggling, for example. So far, not one of their jugglers had had the patience to take it up. Gods' mercies! Mikk would be glad to teach them! Anything to make them abandon this terrible animal toss.

There was only one problem: The one thing Ev-Mobix 'Gar did not import was outworld performers. The only reason the world had a Council charter at all was so its native performers could travel, not so people like Mikk could bring in a troupe or even perform solo. On this point, the Ev-Mobiks were violently protectionist and the Council had not felt the need to impose its own sanctions. Enough horror stories circulated about hapless performers who had taken on the Ev-Mobik authorities to create a kind of natural ban. In Mikk's case, it was possible that merely showing his face at Ev-Mobik customs might be construed as an act of provocation, he was that well known.

He returned the telewave screen to neutral and set down the tumble puppy, which instantly bounded off to further the disintegration of his slipper. After a moment's glum rumination, he got up, unlatched one of the crystal-paned garden doors, and stepped into the pouring rain.

Mikk didn't mind that he was almost instantly soaked to the skin. It was late in the season and the storm was warm and revivifying. The rains had filled the lakes and ponds, low and inactive during the Dormant Season, and had swelled the vegetation in preparation for the Blossom Season. Mikk had not needed a salt stick in weeks.

He strolled in the bluish darkness down the flagstones of the gently curving path through the masses of sleeping shrubs, the fruit trees, and the climbing vines, all bristling with tight green, black, and purple buds, to the main fountain, shut off for the season. He watched the rain pelt the surface of the trapped pool, creating rings within rings that broke through other rings, endlessly. The image made him think of his mother.

He could see her again, as true as the present, hiccupping after her tears, the melted eye frost discoloring her cheeks and fingertips.

"If you can't be talented," she had said, "at least be inconspicuous and don't humiliate me in front of my guests."

"Well, mother darling," Mikk replied to the fountain, "I *am* talented and I intend to humiliate a great many people."

Mikk hoped that the brothel section of the Central Bazaar on Ev-Mobix 'Gar, with its tangle of multileveled streets meandering around a fetid warren of tenements, was not only difficult to police, but barely policed at all. That seemed to be the case. Mikk wandered the highways and alleys, a blue scarf over his nose and mouth to cut the stench, plugs in his sensitive ears to reduce the din, not seeing a single red helmet or jackboot. The crowds reassured him: a convenient mass of swirling anonymity to dive into if the situation got ugly.

Considering the confusion of the streets and the sameness of the buildings, the cabaret was remarkably easy to find. Mikk set a gem worth several years' business into the palm of a scrawny Gadelon Guild prostitute and she happily took him there by the hand.

Mikk took out his earplugs and shook his head in disbelief. He'd been to some seamy places in his career—not every world had the time, patience, or wherewithal to keep itself running in some semblance of order—but the cabaret brothel was a cesspool. The walls sweated from the dank, sticky heat of outworld tourists and slumming natives crammed to near immobility in the room. People on Ev-Mobix 'Gar smoked bantroots rather than chewed them and the air was green with the sickly sweet stink. A couple in the corner, members of an amphibious race similar to the Vonchoi, openly copulated next to the boxes of sliced, and rotting, melons used to flavor the vials of intoxicants being shared indiscriminately by the patrons, each person touching his, her, or ets tongue to the stoppers before passing them along. The floor was tacky, even gummy, and when Mikk examined the sole of his slipper, it was stained with a viscous red-brown glop he realized had to be the doomed animals' blood, urine, and feces.

Porquille itself was worse than he had expected. The shrews were conditioned to expect disaster the moment they were brought into the cabaret, and the animals tore about, squealing and chewing the splintery slats of their cages, long before the juggler heated up his pail of pitch.

The man's work was hot, and he and his anemic assistants went about shirtless and streaming as they stirred the pitch and snatched up the first animals to be painted. As Mikk gagged in the shadows, the jugglers wrestled with the panicked shrews and coated each of the animals with almost enough of the thick gelatinous material to kill them before the juggling even got under way. The head juggler then took the smoking bantroot from his mouth, touched it to the primed fur until it caught fire, and flung the first shrew to one of his partners. When nine of the shrews were thus suffering immolation, the jugglers, in protective gloves, performed the three-man toss. The burning animals flew through the air, flailing, pissing, shrieking, and trailing a blur of tight, smoky flames.

Mikk ripped off his scarf and pushed his way outside so he wouldn't vomit on anyone, but once he caught his breath, the nausea disappeared. He was too angry to waste time being sick. He double-checked the side pouch of bolba balls he had smuggled past the immigration officer by "accidentally" hinting it contained gray-market aphrodisiacs, then squeezed back into the cabaret.

Mikk doubted outrage at the cruelty of the practice would have much effect on these men, so he aimed his blow at their egos. At the height of their performance, while everyone was laughing and clapping at the spectacle, Mikk committed the performer's sin. He struck a contemptuous pose and, projecting over the crowd, voiced his dissatisfaction.

"This is unbearably tedious. Nothing but cheap sensationalism when all you're doing is a pathetic little three-man toss."

The lead juggler dropped an animal and glared at Mikk.

"If this is the floor show," the performance master continued, "I can imagine the abysmal quality of the entertainment upstairs."

The juggler flung down the smoldering creatures he was holding, and his partners, without a third, had to stop as well.

"You have a better idea, Vyzanian?"

"Even one-handed I'm a finer juggler than you are." Mikk stepped forward and the crowd started to murmur.

"That's Mikk the performance master."

"Are you sure?"

"I saw him on H'n N'k."

"What's he doing here?"

"Damned if I know. I'm surprised the authorities let him in. People would pay money just to watch him walk down the street."

The lead juggler spat. "You wouldn't dare," he snarled at the performance master.

Mikk eased the side pouch from his shoulder. "I put it to you as a challenge. We'll let the crowd decide."

"Go on."

"You can do any solo combination you like and I'll use my bolba balls with one hand only. If the people here think that what I do is more interesting than what you do, you'll leave the animals alone, at least until you've given bolba juggling a good sixteen months' study and a chance here in the cabaret."

"And if they prefer me?"

Mikk cleared his throat. This was difficult for him, but he had to stick his neck out if the Ev-Mobik was to accept the challenge.

"If they prefer you," he said, "I'll torch a shrew myself."

The Ev-Mobik juggler broke into a cold yellow grin and the cry went up. There was a down and dirty spate of wagering, which did not make a lot of sense to Mikk considering this was a contest of opinion, not determinable outcome, but, as the saying went, "Ev-Mobiks will bet on whether their double suns will come up in the morning."

The Ev-Mobik juggler fished around behind the shrew cages for a motley assortment of fruit, construction tools, knives, cooking utensils, and even a rusty double elbow valve from a latrine. Apparently, he was what was known in galactic tossing circles as a generalist. He looked at Mikk.

"It's your world," the performance master said with a bow. "Be my guest."

Mikk had to admit the man was pretty good. He handled the disparate, misbalanced objects with a rough-hewn muscular dash that smacked strongly of his street origins but was, nevertheless, quite appealing. What he lacked was finesse—something Mikk was famous for.

The crowd became boisterous when the juggler finished, whistling and calling out his name, slapping him on the back. Mikk remained calm. He cradled a dozen of the bolba balls in the crook of his arm while a burly gentleman bound up his free hand with a long, heavy drax-skin belt.

"That's tight enough, thank you." He positioned himself in the middle of the room, and the hubbub died to whispers. Several of the ladies from above stairs, naked except for the Guild brands on their left hips, came out and hung languidly on the railings to watch.

With one snap of his arm, Mikk flipped all twelve balls into the air and his white hand flashed with the fine, swift precision of a hovering nectar thief, the tiny insectlike bird on Vyzania that fed among the flowers. He snatched and tossed the balls in a dizzying sequence of varied rhythms, passing them behind his back, around his legs, catching two in a stack on the tip of his nose, and rolling them across his shoulders.

Such a display had never been seen on Ev-Mobix 'Gar even if some of the tourists had watched Mikk do similar work elsewhere. The Ev-Mobik juggler's jaw dropped and his competitive posturing fell away, replaced by studious fascination. The performance master nodded to him. A true juggler knew real art when he saw it and the Ev-Mobik was, in spite of his failings, a true juggler.

Mikk brought his performance to a close with a sweeping flourish and caught all the balls back in the crook of his arm. The patrons of the cabaret pounded their fists on the tables and the ladies on the railings held their breasts up with their hands in tribute, which made Mikk blush. The Ev-Mobik juggler smiled and shrugged grandly, acknowledging the performance master's superiority without further protest.

However, the crowd quickly hushed when out of the shadows behind Mikk came the familiar click-clatch! of government-issued flak rifles.

Mikk had not counted on undercover police.

The Ev-Mobiks beat the performance master with his pouch of bolba balls until the canvas gave out, then expelled him from the planet in a casket-sized beacon pod.

"If you ever set foot on our world again," they warned, "you will be drawn and quartered and fed to drax larvae."

Mikk was in no condition to argue. Luckily, a passing Belian freighter picked up the flashing pod and its nearly hysterical occupant and delivered the performance master to a colonial hospice to recover.

"No, I won't accept that!" Oplup thundered at the hastily convened regional Council debate. "Mikk must pay for offending our Ev-Mobik brothers."

"Don't you think the revenue lost during his convalescence is punishment enough?" asked a fellow Councilor, a mousy little biped from Ohri 12. "He was about to go on tour and had to cancel all his engagements."

"That is not sufficient! The damage he has inflicted on the Council's reputation has set our relations with Ev-Mobix 'Gar back centuries. Centuries!"

"Councilor, I don't think that's quite . . ."

"Enough! Mikk must be publicly chastised or I withdraw my support from this chapter effective immediately."

Faced with such a tremendous financial catastrophe, the regional Council chapter devised an appropriately humiliating act of contrition: live from his hospice room, via optitube to 462 worlds, Mikk burned his visa and apologized in fifty-three languages to the Ev-Mobiks—while coughing up blood. Thissizz, who knew nothing about Mikk's troubles but had been inexplicably anxious and fretful for days, howled when the images appeared on his touch-sensitive Belian wall optitube. He sobbed and thrashed violently on the floor of his burrow, and his wives and children fled in a panic. They peered at him from the outer tunnel and begged him to stop before he hurt himself.

"Thissizz! Please!"

"Daddy, you're scaring me!"

The littlest ones began to cry and crumpled themselves up in tight balls.

"Where?" Thissizz wailed. "Where hospice? Where Mikk?"

They couldn't tell him until he'd beaten himself to exhaustion and was covered with blue-black bruises. Even in this sorry condition, he left immediately.

The light was low in the room where Mikk lay draped with gauze on a faintly incandescent heat bed. His sensitive eyes, seriously irritated by prolonged pigment impregnation, could not tolerate any glare. They had drained but were laced with engorged blood vessels.

Thissizz slinked silently up to the pale yellow bed and smiled shakily down at his friend.

"Hello," he said tenderly, and Mikk raised an unsteady hand to the Droos' soft cheek. Thissizz rumbled low in his coils and kissed the fingers. Mikk's lip was swollen but, on the whole, his face was free of injury.

"They spared your nose."

"They were very considerate," Mikk replied hoarsely. "They hit me where it wouldn't show much, but the pod . . . I thought I was going to die."

The Droos gently laid his head on the performance master's chest and enormous tears rolled out of his great black eyes.

"Why did I do it, Thissizz?" Mikk rasped. "I knew how they felt about outworld performers. What is wrong with me?"

"You have a flaw in your psyche." Thissizz nuzzled Mikk's throat, which was warm and moist from the heat bed. "I've known about it for a long time."

"What kind of flaw?"

"You worked terribly hard to focus your scattered talents and succeeded beyond everyone's expectations, even Master Huud's. However, part of you was not freed by that focus but imprisoned in it. Sometimes, your will becomes willfulness."

Mikk swallowed uncomfortably and rested his hand on Thissizz's head. "That is a very serious flaw," he said mournfully. "It could get me killed."

"It stands out because otherwise you might be perfect. It is serious, yes, but I don't think I could love a perfect man."

Mikk quietly, painfully, put his arms around the Droos. "Please take me home," he whispered.

Thissizz carefully worked his coils under and about his battered friend, lifted him from the heat bed, and carried him out of the hospice. The Belian attendants, although intensely curious, forced themselves to keep working and tried to ignore the fact that one of their patients was leaving bound up in the affectionate coils of a great hooded serpent.

Thissizz engaged an Ichtian herbalist, and for a few weeks Mikk's house reeked of vile funguswort brews and burnt pond slime, but the performance master improved rapidly. Soon he was strong enough to throw the unsavory herbalist and his noxious concoctions, plus a sackful of coins and semiprecious stones, bodily out of the house.

"Leech!" Mikk cried.

"Oh, yes, yes, yes, yes," bobbed the troll-like herbalist as he gathered up his booty. "That's what I am, oh, yes, that's what I am. And look at all this lovely money! Thank you, thank you, oh, yes, yes, yes!"

"Beast on crutches!" Mikk slammed the door. "A miserable

specimen for an Ichtian," he said to Thissizz. "Still, I am feeling better. That was a lot more fun than it should have been."

"I am glad you, at least, are recovering," the Droos said, and his depressed tone alarmed Mikk.

"Why? What has happened?"

"A servant just came from Master Huud's house. The master is dying."

Chapter Twenty-nine: The Whir Crickets

The day Mikk was arrested on Ev-Mobix 'Gar, Huud Maroc got up from supper and dropped back down again, his entire chest aching, although it was not quite the wrenching stab of an attack. The master protested that all he needed was rest, but, for once, his house servants defied him and brought a specialist up to the estate, a black-haired young doctor in a crisp new physician's gold-spotted blue tunic. Huud Maroc glowered at him disdainfully and muttered under his breath about "young pups think they know everything" while the doctor examined his broad chest with a pocket sono-probe.

"I'm afraid you've an irregular heart action," the doctor concluded. "Fairly advanced. It's affecting at least six valves." Now the doctor was the one to scowl. "You should have contacted me sooner."

"To what purpose? So you could drug me with your abominable poisons?"

"You might have lived longer."

"Damn it, man! I'm 1,250 years old! How long would you have me go on?"

The doctor looked stunned.

"Twelve hundred—?"

"I see I've shocked you. Good! I doubt I'd have lasted if I'd given myself over to the ministrations of your evil profession."

"It's not an evil profession!" the young man cried, deeply wounded. "You may not have needed a doctor before, but you need one now."

"Not any more." Huud Maroc's cloudy eyes flashed dark and furious at the doctor. "I'm dying. Save your skills for others and let me finish out my days with some dignity."

"That's just the point! You need medical attention so you *can* pass your days with dignity. Dying is not easy!"

"I know that!" the master snapped. "I've done it thousands of times! Now get out before I have you thrown out!"

The young doctor went away, and Huud Maroc retired to his rooms to put his affairs in order, determined to face his future without further interference by "the infernal legions of medical mountebanks," but things did not turn out the way he planned. Simple chores became increasingly difficult. Merely bending over to retrieve his slippers or an ink stylus caused him to gasp and his heart to race. By the time Thissizz brought Mikk home from the Belian hospice, the old master was bedridden, and a few days before Mikk heaved the Ichtian herbalist out of the house, Huud Maroc had a real, critical attack. The master, now helpless and in great pain, grudgingly sent for the unhappy young physician although he was convinced the "pup" would refuse to come. To Huud Maroc's surprise, not only did the doctor return, but when he saw how far the master's condition had deteriorated, he volunteered to contact his family for him.

"My apprentices are my family," the master said. "There is no one else."

Remarkably, all of Huud Maroc's former apprentices were in the sector, and they dropped everything to journey to Vyzania.

Finally, a servant was sent round to Mikk and arrived just as the Ichtian herbalist sailed head over heels into the street. Since the performance master was occupied, the boy spoke to Thissizz instead and Thissizz told Mikk.

Mikk took the news in silence, a vague disquiet tensing his features, as though he had misplaced a pair of spectacles or a favorite jacket but had not yet begun to panic. Thissizz was not fooled by this seemingly mild distraction. "The master is declining rapidly," he said. "Shall I go with you?"

Mikk started to run his fingers through his hair, but stopped mid-stroke. He shook his head and Thissizz planted a small kiss on his neck.

"I will be here when you return."

Mikk had never seen all of them together in one place, but when he arrived, there they were: all thirteen of Huud Maroc's former apprentices. Vaan Reegan, Huud Maroc's first apprentice, another Vyzanian, now a snowy-haired elder statesman of the arts himself, was there as was Ok Roe-ii, the Ti-tokan master who had introduced a new dance form into her world's ballet cycles. Hom the Longchild had arrived early and was weeping inconsolably in the arms of his most recent guardian, a tiny Mrku woman made entirely of dark brown wrinkles. Upr the Kekoi epic poetry singer thoughtfully stroked his chin fur and N'l-v'n-k'k, the H'n N'kae tragedian swayed in the center of the room and moaned softly through his sorrowful prehensile lips. Mikk hated to see the great performer in such despair and pulled some sticky sugar candies out of his surprise tunic and held them under N'l-v'n-k'k's mouth so the massive insectoid could slurp them into his digestive tract.

"Zanch oo," he said in ragged Vyzanian, and Mikk gave him a friendly tweak on the antenna.

One by one, in the order in which they had become apprentices, the performance masters went in to see Huud Maroc. When Hom the Longchild emerged from the sickroom, he ran to Mikk and clung to him, sobbing like a new orphan, which, in a way, he was.

"What am I going to do, Mikk-mikk? Who's going to write my bedtime stories now?"

"I will, if you like. Now, take this and blow your nose. That's it. Good lad. Don't worry. We'll make sure you always have guardians."

"Master Huud chose the best."

"I know." Mikk glanced at the Mrku woman. "We'll do *our* best."

At last, the doctor signalled to Mikk, and the youngest performance master went into Huud Maroc's bedchamber.

Master Huud's servants had arranged the room beautifully, letting the loveliest of the flowers and silks sent by the great performance master's colleagues and fans spill down the walls and over the floor so the room resembled a fantastic garden. The scrolls, letters, and telewave transmissions were neatly stacked in one corner, and the ritual baskets of merro fruit the master could no longer eat were arranged in a colorful pyramid near the window, which was open to let in the fragrant Blossom Season breezes.

The doctor had just swabbed the dying master's face, but withdrew into the flowers so Mikk and Huud Maroc could have some privacy.

Even at his advanced age, the master was still handsome, but Mikk was horrified by how exhausted and listless he looked, motionless in the low hammock, and was chagrined by his own shock. The man was near death. Look the Visitor in the face, he told himself. This is no time to be faint of heart.

But self-chastisement failed to keep Mikk's grief at bay. The pigment flooded his irises unchecked and his tears flowed freely. As he leaned over his master, several of them dropped on the dying man's cheek. Mikk moved to wipe them away.

"Leave it, Mikk," Huud Maroc said, his deep bass voice weak and labored. "Your tears mean a lot to me."

Mikk grasped Huud Maroc's hand and squeezed it hard.

"You are my last apprentice, boy," Master Huud said, ignoring, or even forgetting, that Mikk was a grown man and an experienced performance master himself. "My last and most special."

Mikk shook his head.

"It's true," said the master. "The others are marvelous people, they warm my soul, but you took my elder years and erased them. Made me a young master again."

Mikk looked away and palmed his eyes with his free hand.

"You know everything I know," Huud Maroc continued, "even more. But there is one thing I never told you and I want to tell it to you now."

Mikk lowered his hand and again turned his wet black eyes to Master Huud's faded blue-purple ones.

"It takes a lot of work, a lot of dedication and love to be a performance master," Huud Maroc said, "but it is not enough to have this love, this dedication. You can learn everything there is to know about performance, call yourself a master, and no one will dispute it, but you're never really a performance master until you achieve something beyond the boundaries. The boundaries cannot be defined until you run up against them. Ok Roe-ii found a boundary in Ti-tokan dance and broke through it. The uproar was tremendous. Some intolerant ones even wanted to kill her."

"I remember."

"But she didn't falter. She faced her detractors and triumphed. If they had killed her, she still would have triumphed, do you understand, boy?"

"Yes, Master Huud," Mikk said, slipping into the deferential accents of the apprentice.

"That is what makes a true master, Mikk, and it is rare indeed. I am unsure I fit that description myself."

"But you do, Master Huud," Mikk protested. "Of course you do."

"Hush, lad, my ego doesn't need that." Huud Maroc closed his eyes and Mikk briefly panicked, thinking he'd lost him, but the master's lids fluttered and his dim eyes reopened. "Mikk, I may not be that truest kind of performance master, but I've wondered for years if you are."

"Oh, no, no! Please! Half the time I haven't the faintest idea what I'm doing."

"Don't give me that!" A spark of Huud Maroc's old irascibility flared beneath the cataracts. "That annoying modesty of yours rears itself up at the most inconvenient times."

"My apologies, Master Huud."

"You think your surprise tunic was a freak accident, boy? Even that mess on Ev-Mobix 'Gar reveals a significant restlessness, a straining against the seams."

"I thought it was a flaw."

"It isn't a strength *or* a flaw, lad. It's simply there. Your hidden sword. How you use it and in what context—that's what makes it a strength or a flaw."

Mikk stroked a lock of silver hair from Huud Maroc's forehead. The master's skin felt clammy. "You always believed in me even when it didn't make sense to do so."

"If I had any sense, would I have gotten into this business in the first place?"

Mikk laughed, but wept, too. "You're dying and you're killing me."

"That's a terrible pun," the master pouted. "Don't ever use it again."

"All right."

They fell silent, and the breeze from the water lily garden stirred the flower petals and silks in the room. The afternoon slowed and Mikk swore he could count the individual clicks of the buzzing whir crickets. He saw the doctor shake his head.

"Shall I ask the others to come in?" Mikk asked softly.

"No," Huud Maroc said. "They don't need this as much."

"I don't understand."

"Yes, you do." The master's voice dipped to a level even Mikk had difficulty hearing. "They're just former apprentices. You are my son."

The life was leaving Huud Maroc's eyes the way the glow leaves cooling embers and Mikk felt an important part of his own life dying as well.

"Keep warm, Mikk. I love you."

"I love you, Master Huud."

The clicking of the whir crickets waned to a largo feebleness and ceased. Mikk cupped the master's face in his hands and kissed him. Huud Maroc was dead.

Chapter Thirty: The Somalite Disaster

A couple weeks after Master Huud's ashes were mixed into the mortar of the new theater, now to be named after him, the two friends went to the dance room at the top of Mikk's house to watch the sunset over the russet roofs and tall, swaying, slim-branched widow trees of Wynt. The wide curving windows glinted in the pink-gold light, and the performance master rest-lessly toyed with a bolba ball, dancing it over his fingertips and catching it on his elbow.

"How many bolba balls can you juggle now?" Thissizz asked.

"Twenty-nine."

Thissizz cocked his head. "That is not true, Mikk. I saw you practicing this morning with thirty-two."

"You will never see me perform in public with more than twenty-nine," Mikk said simply, but with an edge.

"I see. You say so to honor Master Huud, but I think that's very foolish."

"What do you mean?"

"Don't you think Master Huud would have wanted you to sur-pass him some day? Why train such a fine performer if he is only going to do what has been done before? You're a wonderful bolba juggler, Mikk. Thirty-two balls!"

Mikk shot his friend a scorching look, took up the box of bolba balls at his feet, and upended it. Flipping balls up two at a time with his toe, Mikk began to juggle a triple loop and kept adding balls until there were none left on the floor. Forty-five of the gold spheres danced in the afternoon light and Mikk's breathing remained steady, his movements sure.

He dropped the balls in a rapid-fire single stream back into the box.

"I want to tour again as soon as possible," he said fiercely.

Thissizz's brow ruffled in consternation. "Isn't it a bit early to return to work? You haven't given yourself time to rest."

"I don't need it. I'm as strong as ever." To prove his point, Mikk stood on his hands and walked around his friend on the tips of his index fingers.

"Your body may be fine, but your soul is vulnerable. No one would blame you if you took a year or two off to tend to this lovely garden."

Mikk righted himself and brushed off his hands. "I appreciate your concern, serassi, but I'm all right. Work steadies me. It's the best thing after a loss."

Thissizz sighed and withdrew his objections. In spite of Mikk's words, tiny lines under the performance master's eyes betrayed a psychic distress considerably greater than he let on. Thissizz did not want to agitate him further with a lecture about his will. If Mikk believed work would make him feel better, so be it.

However, the very next day, as Mikk began the complicated task of tracking down the available artists of his troupe, the tele-wave news box for "galaxy-wide" lit up. He switched over from "personal."

"Oh . . . dear gods . . ."

Thissizz, who was coiled up across the parlor close to the garden doors and working his way through a large bowl of fruit, stopped chewing. "What is it, Mikk?"

"Something terrible has happened to the Somalites."

Before Thissizz could ask for details, Briin entered to announce Marshall Larr was in the front hall and wanted to see Mikk.

"Marshall Larr? Are you sure, Briin?"

"It's rather difficult to confuse him with anyone else, Master Mikk." The servant fiddled delicately with the woven belt of his loud yellow and red tunic. As he had virtually every day since Mikk brought it home, he wore the English boater.

"That's true," Mikk said thoughtfully. "Please bring the Marshall here."

"Yes, sir."

"I wonder what he wants," Mikk said to Thissizz. "Vyzanian statesmen do not casually drop in on entertainers."

In fact, when the self-assured former merchant admiral strode into the solarium in his official silver-embroidered maroon tunic, it was the first time a Vyzanian official above the rank of attaché had been in Mikk's house. "Ah! Lovely solarium, Mikk," he said, somewhat vaguely. "Just the place to relax on a hot afternoon."

"Uh, yes. Briin? Could you bring something cool for the Marshall? And de-alcolate more fruit for Thissizz."

"Very good, sir." Briin exited as quickly as he'd entered.

The Marshall finally noticed the full-grown Droos lounging on a mountain of cushions, a bowl of alcohol-cleansed Vyzanian fruit before him.

"Great Beast! Thissizz! I must be very distracted indeed. How do you do? I've admired your work for a long time."

"Thank you. You resemble your stamp."

The Marshall whooped with laughter, but Mikk did not join in. He knew Larr had not come for pleasure, and when Briin brought in a drink for the Marshall and a fresh bowl of sanitized fruit for Thissizz, the official set aside his party humor and became grave.

"I assume you've heard something of the tragedy on Somal?" he asked.

"I only now pulled up the story," Mikk said. "I haven't had a chance to read it. Something about a global disaster?"

"A *terminal* disaster. They're all going to die, Mikk."

The Marshall's words fell heavily on the room. The only movement was his gentle swirling of the fragrant nectar in his tumbler.

"It couldn't have happened at a worse time," he continued. "It was their season of Meditation Silence, and not only were there no ships in the area—actually, that may have been a blessing—but they were maintaining telewave silence. Their nearest neighbors . . ."

"The Rogoines."

"Yes. It was weeks before they knew something was wrong and then only because the Somalites did not reestablish contact. The Rogoines asked a Belian flagship to investigate, and they discovered the Somalite sun was deteriorating and sending out waves of radiation." The Marshall sipped his drink. "It was too 'hot' for anyone to go in, but you know the Belians, always the heroes. They didn't care that the Somalites refused to leave. They pulled off about a thousand of them and took them to the Santman hospice, and they lost twenty-six crewmen doing it."

"Didn't anyone see this coming?" Mikk whispered.

"You know how the Somalites were about advanced technology, Mikk."

"But surely the Belians . . ."

"The Belians' best estimate didn't foresee first deterioration for another 10,000 years." The Marshall shrugged, his once rock-edged features, softened by age and rich cuisine, sagging in an expression of grand resignation. "This kind of prediction is far from an exact science," he said.

Mikk looked at the floor and drew a small invisible circle with his toe. Thissizz's heart ached. Mikk's anguish, carefully concealed, nevertheless agitated the Droos' senses, a crackling sting under his scales. He wanted to wrap himself around his friend and ground out this bad psychic electricity, but he didn't know how the Marshall would react.

"The rescued Somalites?" Mikk asked. "They're dying?"

"Every last one of them. It's only a matter of days, weeks perhaps, at best."

Mikk's hand fluttered distractedly to his mouth, but he snatched it away and crossed his arms tightly in an effort to focus his attention.

"The Somalites were special to me."

"That's why I'm here. The Santman hospice contacted me directly. The Somalites are suffering terribly, emotionally as well as physically. They're completely lost without their home world."

Mikk averted his eyes. He seemed to be staring out the crystal doors at the tiered fountains in the garden, but Thissizz knew he wasn't looking at anything—at least, nothing present in the garden or solarium.

"The hospice administration wanted me to ask you personally if you would be willing to perform Somalite songdance for the survivors. The Santmen think it might lift their charges' spirits, and, the gods know, the Somalites can no longer entertain themselves."

Mikk returned to the Marshall. The performance master's black irises looked like holes in his face.

"Yes, of course. I'll get ready immediately."

"Thank you. You've eased my mind. The Santmen are the greatest philanthropists in the galaxy and close allies to the Crown. I'm sure the Somalites will appreciate your special skills."

The Marshall took his leave and Mikk dropped into the cushions next to Thissizz.

"Mikk, Marshall Larr . . ."

"I know what you're going to say." Mikk shielded his stressed eyes with his arm. "Marshall Larr is a self-interested politician who couldn't care less whether the Somalites live or die, but *I* care. I owe them a fealty he couldn't possibly understand."

Thissizz dipped his head over his prostrate friend.

"Mikk," he hissed softly in Droos, "you've already had a heavy dose of pain this year. Here is an entire hospice full of death."

Mikk removed his arm and gazed seriously at the glowing orange face above him. "I'm going, Thissizz."

"Take me with you. You shouldn't be alone."

"Nonsense. Why should you suffer as well? I've kept you from your family long enough." Mikk managed a bent smile. "Your youngest wife is having her first brood soon, and if you're not there when they're born, she's liable to recruit her other husband to play daddy to *your* children."

Thissizz grinned bashfully and his color deepened. He loved being a daddy. "The pups miss you, serassi. They haven't seen my 'special spouse' in months, and my wives have saved up so much gossip they're getting dizzy with it."

"I know, but I still have to go." Mikk sat up now that his eyes were back to normal. "Besides, you're due for a molt and I don't think you'd enjoy being in that condition on a distant world." His smile took on a touch of seductive heat. "You'll look wonderful in emerald."

"Oh, I give up!" Thissizz said, flustered. "You best know."

"Thank you. I'll take Maya with me. I couldn't be safer if I traveled with an army." Mikk stood and stretched and this time really did look out at the fountain. He eased into sadness. "The last time

I saw Whees-aru was after my Terran tour. Barely fifteen years ago. He said nothing about this."

"Maybe he didn't see it coming."

"Thissizz, he was at Peace. Something as serious as the death of the sun could not have escaped him." Mikk rubbed the back of his neck, and Thissizz began to massage his shoulders with his nose.

"All those centuries of peace and contemplation," Mikk mused, "then this . . . and their suffering is as acute as anyone's."

"Perhaps the gods became jealous and decided to reclaim their children," Thissizz said, and Mikk nodded.

"Whees-aru never told me in so many words, but I think I got as close as any outworlder to understanding songdance and I still wonder if I know anything about it at all." He turned in the Droos' half embrace and leaned his cheek against him. "What do you suppose it's like to be at Peace?"

"You probably have to be Somalite."

"Then, as usual, we have to search for our own answers without a compass."

"I'm sure, long ago, that's how the Somalites started."

Mikk laughed and kissed his friend's throat. "You always cut through my ramblings and find the truth!" His smile fell. "You really think I look tired?"

"Yes, but you will go to the hospice."

"But, not tonight." Mikk slid his leg around Thissizz's body and tightened it. "Will you stay with me? One more evening?"

"You do not need to ask."

Chapter Thirty-one: The Santman Hospice

The Santman complex was nothing like the cozy Belian colonial hospice. Mikk gasped when the shuttle cleared the horizon of the large red asteroid and he saw it for the first time, an enormous, gleaming white edifice rising from the bottom of an extinct caldera. Enclosed in an atmospheric shield as large as a small world, the hospice's hundreds of floors piled on top of each other in a steep, bristling cone of contagion wards, experimental atmospheric tanks, and one-of-a-kind isolation chambers. It was a very impressive facility, undoubtedly the best possible place for the Somalites, but it terrified Mikk. He had performed in hospices before, but this pure white temple to pain vibrated with the music of death like no other.

The Santmen padded about in soft white booties, passing along the shiny white unadorned corridors like revenants. Mikk shuddered. No wonder most of the cultures he had encountered considered white the color of mortality and his own starkly pale people preferred bright clothing. Mikk, true to type, wore the supple, deep blue dance suit and loose scarlet tunic he favored when his courage needed a boost. He felt he was the only spot of color and highly conspicuous until a surgeon covered with slick yellowish blood emerged from a cutting room and brushed brusquely past him. Mikk decided not to begrudge the white its disturbing, but abstract, purity.

When he was ushered into the south quadrant lobby, he saw the only thing that could have upset him more than the hospice itself: Councilor Oplup and a small coterie of his "business associates," Lambdans with smarmily self-important expressions of boredom on their gold faces.

What is *he* doing here?

Mikk's mind raced over the recent past as the fraudulently lugubrious Councilor greeted him and limply shook his hand with a mushy paw.

"Such a sad time, Mikk. A disaster of galactic proportions."

"I never expected the Council to take an interest in the Somalites," Mikk said, thoroughly dismayed that it had.

"The death of an entire people is of enormous interest."

There are especially colorful names for ghouls like you, Mikk thought sourly, and I know them in at least 250 languages.

"I heard about your invitation to perform for these unfortunates and thought I could be of some assistance." Oplup smiled.

Now that Master Huud is beyond your harassment, you've decided to turn your torments on me, Mikk thought, but I suppose it's best to be civil.

"That won't be necessary, Councilor. I'm to perform alone."

"Oh, Mikk!" Oplup chuckled. "You're always so amusing. *I'm* not a performer!"

No, thank the gods! But your acting ability is beyond remarkable.

The Santman administrator, a faceless figure sheathed in an antiseptic aura of quarantine as well as all-powerful white, drifted into the lobby. It was time for Mikk to see the Somalites.

As they passed down the empty corridors, each the same as the last, the premonitory chill agitated the fine nerves of Mikk's shoulder muscles.

"Must I change into white, too?" he asked.

"No." The Santman stopped at a door fitted so perfectly into the wall its edges were almost invisible even to Mikk's keen eyesight. "It doesn't matter. You won't get anywhere near them."

The door slid silently open, Mikk stepped inside, and the panel sealed up behind him.

The glare was, if anything, worse than it had been in the corridors, and Mikk blinked rapidly to combat the sudden flash and sting. Once his eyes adjusted, he saw he was in an empty chamber as high and cavernous as a small shuttle bay, but disturbingly free of echo. There wasn't a single piece of furniture or equipment or any visible source of light. The room was an empty box whose ceiling, floor, and three of its walls were identical, featureless . . . white. The fourth wall, a sheet of heavy polyglass, separated Mikk from the horror he had been trying, in vain, to prepare for.

The fifty remaining Somalites hung at various levels in the moist, sterile weightlessness of an isolation chamber to protect their traumatized bodies from further injury. Anchoring them to the softly pulsing equipment on the floor, hundreds of thin colored tubes snaked through the emptiness and pierced the Somalites' hands, feet, throats, genitals, and a dozen other places, feeding them, removing wastes, and coaxing their contaminated blood through their veins. A tethered Santman in a puffy white shield suit glided among his charges like a diver in an aquarium, dabbing pus, vacuum-siphoning away floating globules of vomit, and reinserting tubes that had pulled out of disintegrating flesh. Most of the Somalites were missing patches of skin that had sloughed off in heavy strips, leaving raw, suppurating wounds, many as deep as the muscle, and all of these dignified, once beautiful people were naked. The isolation chamber bore a ghastly resemblance to a Kekoi hunting lodge during the Wild Season.

There were no Somalite children or Somal Freens. All of them had already died.

Mikk crept up to the polyglass and rested his hands and nose against it. Pigment slowly eclipsed his shimmering irises as he stared numbly at the gently bobbing Somalites and searched for the woman from the riverbank.

"My daughter is dead, Mikk," came a hoarse, whistling whisper.

Mikk barely recognized the speaker. The elder's rich green skin had become a sickly dirty olive, his clear gold eyes dull bronze, nearly blind, and his stately form was blistered and rent, a burnt corpse.

"Whees-aru," Mikk murmured in Somalite.

"I am not what I was," the elder said. "Why are you here?"

"The Santmen invited me. They thought it might be of some comfort if I performed songdance for you."

"I'm not sure of that," Whees-aru sighed painfully, "but you have come a long way and you were always a sincere scholar of our art. You have my permission to perform."

Mikk drew back from the polyglass and stood in the preparatory meditation stance, knees slightly bent, head erect, eyes closed, hands softly clasped before him. Because of his agitation, getting centered took somewhat longer than usual, but, at last, he opened his eyes and slowly spread his arms. At the same time, he began to sing the difficult, sustained syllables of one of the oldest, most traditional Somalite ballads. As the song progressed, he moved through the accompanying dance, every subtle bend and flex, every ripple and sway saturated with centuries of revelation.

Except for rare "symposia" before Peaceful Ones, whose only reactions had been laughter, obscure riddles, or silence, Mikk had never performed songdance for an audience larger than one: Huud Maroc or Thissizz. The late master and the Droos had always loved Mikk's self-described "fumblings," which was why the growing moans and cries from the isolation chamber shocked him. The more he sang, the louder, more agonized the protests until he had to abandon the movement consciousness altogether. He was hurting them.

"Whees-aru, I-I'm sorry. I've offended with my ineptitude."

"No," the Somalite wheezed, "your performance was excellent. By far the most beautiful harmonic web any outworlder has ever created. That is why we grieve."

"I don't understand."

"You must forget our art. Never perform it again."

Mikk was dumbfounded.

"Forget . . . ?"

"Yes. As though you had never heard of us."

"But I can't do that!" Mikk cried. "I'm Vyzanian! I've spent two and a half centuries committing your songs and stories to *memory*. Do you know what that means? *Vyzanian* memory!"

The white box, although climatically controlled, nevertheless seemed to produce a terrific draft that reached up inside Mikk's tunic and gripped his belly.

"Gods above! Songdance is exquisite, so full of meaning. Why would you want me to forget it?"

"We will soon be extinct. We are already severed from the world that nourished our soul. As you said, our songdance is full of meaning. Only we truly understand that meaning and we will be gone."

"But . . ." Mikk suddenly had to arch and twist his back. The tremor in his shoulders had become a deep, searing burn. "But people can still benefit from your knowledge. Surely some memory is better than none at all. Many races have died and their art lives."

"No." A thin line of dark spittle ran out of the corner of Whees-aru's mouth. The Santman attendant floated by and wiped it away. "You do not understand. Yours is likely to remain the only nearly perfect version of our art after we are gone. Future people might confuse your songdance with our own, and we would rather vanish from universal memory than let that happen."

"What about those whose interpretations are even less pure than mine?" Mikk fought the urge to sound desperate, but his control was slipping.

"No one could possibly confuse their work with true songdance. Their way will die quickly. They do not concern us nearly as much as you do. Therefore, you must promise never to perform the ballads again."

Mikk winced as the psychic lightning corkscrewed up his spine. Cold sweat beaded on his brow. "I beg you . . . don't ask this of me."

The Somalite smiled and it split his blistered lips wide open. The Santman sailed past again and sponged away the yellow blood.

"I am sorry for your pain, my unhappy friend, but we cannot be swayed on this point." The elder swallowed, a wet clicking, and continued in a thick mucusy gurgle. "Do not despair. Who can say where our darker fortunes may lead us? Consider it a challenge for your soul. What will you do to accommodate this burden?"

"I don't want this burden," the performance master said huskily.

"Perhaps . . . you . . . need . . . it." Whees-aru choked suddenly and his chest caved in a little as though his ribs had softened and could not withstand the shock. The Santman gently opened the

Somalite's mouth and siphoned out a quantity of curdled brown slime, part of the lining of Whees-aru's lungs.

The Santman administrator took Mikk to a mourning room because the performance master, although quiet, was dangerously close to hysteria. His eyes were as black as pitch and his breathing rough, bordering on hyperventilation. Surprisingly, the mourning room was pink rather than white and had a view of a formal volcanic rock garden ringed by narrow conifers.

Once alone, Mikk beat his fists on the soundproof walls and howled. He wanted to damage something but the walls were keranium, and finally he just curled up next to the polyglass window and sobbed.

The performance master had been censored before. Ev-Mobix 'Gar was not the first resistant culture he'd encountered, and every galactic performer had to deal with the wayward tastes of the Council, but Mikk had never been asked by a dying race, a race for whom political and social considerations had become meaningless, not to perform their art again. The Somalites wanted oblivion and insisted he help them—which was like being recruited to assist a suicide. Mikk could not bear it. He rocked and moaned in his corner with the grief of the exile: actor, thou shalt not act.

He was still crouched in great distress when the door parted and let in Councilor Oplup. The invasion of privacy offended Mikk strongly, and he did not attempt to disguise it. He unfolded himself slowly and stood up, blackened eyes smoldering.

"I assume you have a damned good reason for coming in here."

"Naturally." Absolutely unfazed by the performance master's threatening stance, Oplup maneuvered his girth into the room. "This is of the utmost importance. I have been to see Whees-aru."

"I'm sure that was pleasant for both of you," Mikk sneered. "Tell me, what appealed to you most? The floating blobs of blood and vomit? The lacy patterns of shredded skin?"

"You seem to have decided I am much more hard-hearted than I appear," Oplup said coldly.

"Dear me! I can't imagine how I got that idea."

"It's irrelevant anyway," Oplup sniffed. "I'm here merely to pass on information. Whees-aru has asked me, in my capacity as

Councilor, to impose a galactic ban forbidding you from ever performing Somalite songdance again."

"Don't toy with me, Councilor!" Mikk snarled. "It's one thing for me to make a gentleman's promise to Whees-aru, it's quite another to impose a galactic ban! Whees-aru wouldn't want a performer to die or be exiled for indulging in songdance. That would be a bit excessive, don't you think?"

"Not just any performer. You. You are the one they consider dangerous so the ban applies only to you."

The jolt shook Mikk as though he had been injected with a synthostimulant. The flesh of his shoulders and upper back seemed to be tearing from his bones. "What?" he gasped.

"Furthermore, you are never to demonstrate this art or teach it to any student or apprentice, and you are never to speak a word of the Somalite language."

"Whees-aru said nothing about using their language!" Mikk took a step toward Oplup, who rippled back but remained calm. "He merely asked me not to perform! This is insane—he would never insist on such a ban and on me alone! Let me speak with him."

"That's going to be quite difficult." Councilor Oplup's mouth puckered into a small ugly moue. "Whees-aru became celestial not half a minute after we spoke."

"Died, you mean!" Mikk clenched his teeth against the murder he felt.

"The Council prefers that . . ."

"I know what the Council prefers! They prefer everything neat and tidy and that I keep my mouth shut."

The Councilor frowned. "You shouldn't challenge me, Mikk," he said blackly. "Your status with the Council has been shaky since Ev-Mobix 'Gar. Accept the ban. Don't force me to make it even more restrictive." He put his pudding-soft hands together and patted his gargantuan stomach. "Consider it an embellishment on that gentleman's promise you made. Of course, you would first have to *be* a gentleman."

"Get out!"

The Councilor unhurriedly waddled and rolled out of the mourning room.

* * *

"Mikk!" Maya chased after the performance master as he hastily packed up his things. They had been in the hospice only a few hours, and his behavior made no sense at all. "Mikk! What happen? Great fat thing here before you—Maya bite ankle. Know up no good. Stop or Maya bite Mikk ankle, too!"

Mikk threw down his load of silks and crossed both arms over his face in an unfamiliar gesture of anguish. Maya swelled her soft body to furious, livid proportions.

"Ee-ga! Fat thing die! Maya see to it."

Mikk shook his head, held out his arms, and Maya vaulted into them. She wrapped her tentacles around him as he sobbed.

"Mikk all twist in knots. Need Maya dance on back."

"They put a ban on me, Maya. A galactic ban. I can't perform Somalite songdance anymore."

Maya's six eyes swivelled on Mikk's face. "Ee-ga!" she said, much softer than before. "Maya smell bad things in this. Very bad. Want Mikk close. Keep things out."

"That may be impossible, my love." Mikk stroked Maya's slowly deflating body with trembling fingers.

"Maya do impossible all time." But the cephalopod did not sound confident. "Now untie Mikk muscles. Lie down, you."

"No," Mikk said picking up his fallen clothing. "We have to get away from this place as quickly as possible. I can't endure it another minute."

"If Mikk say, so then, but soon as on ship, submit or Maya break things."

"Agreed. Be merciless."

Maya worked on Mikk's back until pink bruises appeared in his white skin. Her efforts exhausted her, and the performance master carried her curled-up little body back to her cabin with its already messy nest of bedclothes. He set Maya in it, carefully arranged the rumpled wads around her, then returned to his own cabin and tele-waved Droos. Oosmoosis appeared on the screen.

"I am sorry, Mikk. Thissizz is in deep molt and must not be disturbed."

"Please," Mikk begged. "We hurt."

Oosmoosis smiled at Mikk's natural, and entirely unconscious, use of "we." At that moment, both serassi were indeed in great pain.

"I know, my friend, but it is very dangerous to interrupt a Droos in molt. You know that."

Mikk wiped his eyes and nodded.

"However, Thissizz made a voice chip. Would you like to hear it?"

"Please."

Oosmoosis discreetly switched off his screen so Mikk could hear the recording privately through the aural decoder, and Thissizz's caressing song opened like a flower in Mikk's cabin. The performance master's eyes filled again. The song was a duet, a conversation between lovers. As Thissizz reached the points in the song where the second voice was to respond, he paused, leaving silences of appropriate length for his unseen partner. Mikk softly began to fill in the gaps, singing the answers to Thissizz's questions.

When the song was over, the screen came back on.

"Was the message clear?" Oosmoosis asked.

"Yes. Thank you. Please tell Thissizz I got it."

"I'm sure he already knows."

"And tell him I love him. I wish with all my heart I could say so in person."

"Take care, my friend."

When the transmission to Droos ended, Mikk telewaved Wynt. "Briin?"

"Oh, yes, sir! How are you, sir? We didn't expect to hear from you so soon, sir!" The house manager was as buoyant as a Mrku gas kite.

"Uh, is everything all right there, Briin?"

"Couldn't be better," the young man said brightly, "although we did have to take out that merro tree. It was a root virus after all."

"I see," Mikk said, briefly saddened by the news. "Well, if there isn't anything else, Maya and I will be heading home."

"Yes, sir. You did receive an invitation from Terra/Belia Holidays."

"A *cruise line*?"

"Yes, sir. Some kind of multinational politicians' junket masquerading as an economic conference."

"Oh, no, no, no." Mikk massaged his eyes with his fingertips. "Call them back and tell them I have a previous engagement."

"Very good, sir."

Mikk lowered his hands and the house manager twitched. He was hiding something.

"Briin?"

"Yes, Master Mikk?"

"What else?"

"Sir?"

"Briin, your eyes went dark the moment you saw me. They're still black."

"They are?"

"Don't play games, Briin . . ."

The young man looked away then drew up closer to the tele-wave. He was openly distraught this time.

"The ban came through," he said.

"Already?"

"It's a good thing you used the code you did, sir. The others are jammed with press wanting to know what's going on."

As he spoke, the servant gestured to the performance master in Freen sign language. "I've hidden your notebooks and texts on songdance," he signed, and Mikk gestured back, "Thank you." Clever, Briin, Mikk thought. If the line was tapped, it was unlikely the Council would interpret the signs as anything but nervous fingerplay. The Council did not recognize the Freens as people, let alone people sophisticated enough to invent sign language.

Mikk chewed the knuckles of his left hand. There was only one way a galactic ban could have come through this quickly. Oplup had to have set the machinery for one in motion long ago and then waited for the right opportunity to impose it. The bastard! The last hours of one of the most gentle and mysterious artists in the galaxy burdened—ruined!—by the vengeful connivings of a, of a . . . Hundreds of languages at his disposal and Mikk could not find an obscenity strong enough to match his wrath.

"Sir?" Briin asked meekly. "What do I tell the journalists?"

"I don't know. Tell them I'm unable to discuss it at present, which is true."

"Gods preserve us, sir! What happened?" The house manager was near tears.

"They were out for blood, Briin. They cut a piece out of my soul."

"Oh, sir . . ."

"It's done. We have to find ways to live with it, although I wish I didn't have to. Not now. I feel too . . . Wait a minute! Briin, are any of those press transmissions from the Terran sector?"

"Not yet, sir."

"When did that cruise line want me to come?"

"As soon as you could get there. The vessel is already under way."

Mikk almost laughed. He couldn't believe he was actually going to do this, but he needed a place to run. Just for a while. Just until Thissizz was out of molt.

"Tell them I've decided to come," he said. "I'll leave immediately."

"If that's what you want, sir."

"I might as well. I can't face the media."

"I understand. Will Maya accompany you?"

"I'll send her home. She hates tourists."

Entr'acte: Kekoi Kaery: Night Visitors

"Martin!" Mikk jumped from his pallet. "You came! How are you?"

"I'm sick, thirsty, my nose is bleeding, I have diarrhea, and there isn't a single decent room available in the entire city, no thanks to you. They've lost my luggage, I need a bath, and a Kekoi coney upchucked on my shoes."

Mikk looked puzzled. "Did it have red stripes along its back?"

"Why? Is that dyspeptic rodent a friend of yours?"

"Well, I . . ."

Martin sneezed dramatically, almost doubling over, and Bipti glanced up from his cross-legged squat in the shadows. The harried Terran patted his coat pocket.

"Ah, hell," Martin sniffed, "dropped my stylus . . ." With a low grunt, he crouched on his hams and passed his hands over the dark, cold floor. "A man in his fifties shouldn't have to put up with this," he grumbled to Mikk. "Of course, when you were fifty, you were still playing with finger paints, weren't you?"

From his crouch, he saw Bipti settle back into the shadows and close his eyes. Martin quickly pulled a tin of caviar from his pocket and set it in the low radiation-free meal slot in the steadily gleaming energy grid.

"Ah, here it is," he said, retrieving his deliberately fumbled writing instrument. "Gift from my aunt, you know. If she found out I'd lost it, she'd subject me to 'the look' and I can't bear 'the look.' "

By the time Martin straightened, the tin was gone. Not only hadn't he seen Mikk take it, he hadn't seen him cross the cell—

but the performance master's pale eyes shone unusually brightly.

Martin coughed self-consciously. Mikk did not look as grand and confident as he had in the courtroom. He looked drawn, even a bit smaller, and Martin realized for the first time that much of Mikk's public behavior on Kekoi Kaery had been a performance—an especially gruelling one.

"How are they treating you?" he asked gently.

"They've been civil, although it's very cold in here."

"I'll speak to them about it." Martin rubbed his hands together. Mikk was not exaggerating.

"I haven't seen any of your troupe. I should think they'd be here in force, storming the courtroom."

"I had Maya contact them and tell them not to come. If things turn out badly, I don't want the Council to think there was any complicity. They punish that sort of loyalty."

"But Maya stayed."

"Maya is Maya."

Martin nodded and decided not to tell Mikk about the costumer's tears. He nervously pinched his fingertips. He hadn't expected the sight of Mikk in jail to upset him this much. "What a fine mess you've gotten us into!" he blurted angrily.

"Laurel and Hardy!" Mikk grinned. "Very good."

"I've been sizing up the opposition, Mikk, and it looks like the Council chose tribunes from the most conformist races in the galaxy, and Thissizz doesn't seem . . . oh, Jesus, I'm sorry!"

Mikk had abruptly turned into the shadows, but the shaking of his shoulders betrayed him.

"I apologize, Mikk. That was thoughtless."

The performance master raked his fingers through his now shaggy hair and managed to collect himself. "It's all right, Martin. I'm beginning to think Master Huud was wrong and that song-dance is 'death lily' after all."

Martin grunted knowingly. He was familiar with the Belian death lily's sweet, dangerous duality.

"I auditioned for the role and I got it." Mikk smiled shyly over his shoulder. "Unusual casting, don't you think?"

"No," Martin said feelingly, "not at all. I might have thought so once upon a time. Hell, I still think you're the most aggravating bastard I've ever met . . ."

The performance master laughed, but his eyes remained black. ". . . but I've never been so . . . Mikk, I was the only Terran in that courtroom and yet, for the first time in my life, I knew I was among allies. It was the most wonderful feeling." He moved closer to the gate and scowled at the bands of light. "By God, I wish I could get you out of here!" he said and pretended to shake the grid.

"I wish you could, too. I'm not fond of confinement."

"I'm going to get the Kekoi to warm up the cell. It's barbaric to keep you in cold storage like this."

"Maybe . . . maybe you could also get them to send in a Belian to change the pattern of the grid." Mikk looked at the floor. "I've asked several times."

"The pattern?"

"Yes." The performance master rubbed his right ankle with his left toe. "It's too much like a basket."

"A basket?"

Mikk nodded, still moving his slipper up and down his ankle. The gesture was a humiliated schoolboy's and Martin felt embarrassed for him.

"I'll see what I can do."

That night, Martin had trouble falling asleep in his room in the pensione on the square. For one thing, he shared the space with three other persons, Kekoi, who, once they'd introduced themselves, piled together in one bed like a litter of wolf pups.

"Care to den with us?" one of them asked Martin in Belian.

"Uh, no, thank you."

"There's no catch, Terran. It's for warmth, pure and simple."

"I'll pass, all the same," Martin said, then, worried he might have offended the trio, added, "Allergies."

Frankly, there was only so much cultural exchange he could tolerate, and he still had to listen to their snores and contend with the fact that there were no blankets. The pensione was very cheap, and the management must have assumed no one but pack-loving natives would stay there. Martin tucked his feet up under his coat, determined to make the best of it, and had just

drifted off when he heard a commotion below the window and
jerked awake.

"Now what?"

His companions were still asleep, snorting and snuffling in each
other's fur. Martin wrapped his coat around his not-getting-any-
younger body, padded barefoot across the cold stone flags of the
drafty room, and peeked through the slatted shades. Directly
below, a clump of familiar tawny fur shivered in the midnight
gloom. Whoever else had been in the square had fled before
Martin got to the window.

"Aro!" he whispered as loudly as he dared. The young Kekoi
turned one eye in his direction and Martin gasped. One eye was all
Aro had.

"Who?" Martin asked in Belian.

Aro, bloodied and ghastly as he was, grinned giddily. "You
wouldn't believe me."

"Stay where you are! I'm coming down."

"Don't worry. I'm not moving."

Martin filled a basin, snatched up some extra towels—these, at
least, the pensione did have even if they were dingy and chewed
up, probably literally—and hobbled in the dark down to Aro.

"Ev-Mobiks," the jester said.

"What?" Martin gingerly dabbed the oozing wound with a wet
towel. "Why?"

"Tourism is down sharply on their world since they threw
Master Mikk off."

"But wouldn't they go after him? Not you?"

"You dumb Terran!" Aro chuckled. "They already did and he
already apologized. You must have seen it."

"Um, yes, but . . ."

"The Ev-Mobiks are lucky the Vyzanian Crown didn't retaliate. Trust me. They don't want any more negative publicity. It's
not Master Mikk's fault porquille came up at the tribunal."

"It's the Venwatt's, right? Either that or Mikk is still to
blame for there being a tribunal at all." Martin rinsed out his rag
and took up a clean one. Thank God it was too dark really to see
the blood. The entire front of Aro's jester's rags was one damp
shadow.

"Not the way the Ev-Mobiks figure it. They're gangsters. They understand enforced silence. In their eyes, I'm at fault for forcing Master Mikk to break his vow so they're shredding me, one slice at a time."

"Mikk didn't have to break the ban," Martin said. Aro fixed his remaining eye on him.

"Terran, only a fool, and I was a terrible one, would think that." The Kekoi pushed away Martin's sponge. "I didn't know enough about songdance. I didn't know enough about Master Mikk."

Martin got up and offered his hand. "You're bleeding too much. Come on. I'll get you to a vet— . . . doctor."

Aro leered crookedly and Martin felt hot.

"I can stand." The jester pushed himself to his feet by clawing the wall. "You know, the nearest doctor *is* a veterinarian. Probably as good as anyone under the circumstances."

"I'm sorry."

"Forget it," Aro said amiably. "You're Terran."

"My name is Martin "

"Really?" Aro snickered into his sleeve.

"Is that funny?"

"In Kekoi, mar-tan is a kind of sweetmeat."

"Yeah?" Martin took the jester's furry arm over his shoulders.

"It's good. You should try it. It's got swine blood in it."

"Thanks, but I'm dieting."

"Hey! Not bad! You're pretty funny for an amateur."

The same research veterinarian who no longer supplied Mikk with salt blocks came to the door of the lab—which to Martin's nostrils smelled like dead skunk—and, at first, would have nothing to do with Aro.

"Go away," he said, "you're bad luck."

However, Aro was twice his size. A brief snarl and bristling of hackles convinced the veterinarian to back down.

"Tell a soul and I'll put out the good one," he muttered.

"Better not," Aro said. "The Ev-Mobiks hate to be upstaged."

The veterinarian quickly cauterized Aro's wound with a hand laser and slathered it with a thick, oily antiseptic. He did not use any anesthetic because he did not have anything appropriate, but Aro didn't even wince. Martin, however, couldn't watch. The glare of the vet's lab revealed the gore's true deep burgundy, and, through the entire operation, Martin trembled with animal panic.

"Where are you staying?" he asked when he finally took a peek.

"Here and there. At least until people stop treating me like rancid meat."

" 'Scapegoat' we call it. It's senseless."

Aro shrugged and cautiously poked the spider floss filling his empty socket. "People are afraid. They expect trouble if Mikk is condemned."

"He may be vindicated."

"That is the second dumbest thing you've said tonight." Aro pulled on his torn and bloody jester's rags.

"If you have no place to go," Martin said, "why don't you stay with me? One more won't make any difference, and apparently I've been going against custom."

"Thanks, but no. If the Ev-Mobiks catch up with me, they'll finish the job and shred anyone with me who could be a witness. Still, that's generous of you. I wouldn't have expected a Terran to share his bed with a Kekoi."

"Neither would I. It's a first for me."

Aro's tawny ears pricked forward. "He's gotten to you, hasn't he?" he smiled, and Martin heated up again.

"I don't know what you mean," he said stiffly.

Aro snorted ironically, then turned up his collar, fluffed out his fur, and headed into the cold city night.

"I didn't have to come here, you know!" Martin called after him. "It's not as if I owe Mikk anything!"

Nothing important anyway. Just my life . . .

Chapter Thirty-two: The Luxury Cruiser

Erect, platinum-haired, and urbane, Captain Dupré of the *T.S. Ariadne* was an immense relief after the ugliness in the Santman hospice.

"I'm surprised you decided to come, Master Mikk." He sipped his grainy scented beverage. "The best this boat usually offers is second-string floor shows and comics either too new or too old for a real following."

"I was available." Mikk smiled, barely touching his own drink. "And I needed some . . ." He paused. No one on the luxury cruiser had asked him about the ban, and he suspected they had not yet heard about it.

". . . some diversion."

"Well," Dupré sighed, "diversion you may get. Politicians are not my favorite."

Mikk looked out the polyglass viewport in the captain's private quarters. The luxury cruiser hung serenely in the darkness, a slow, swollen craft the size of a small city.

Not a bad place to get lost, Mikk thought, as long as the guests keep busy with their own problems and don't become curious about mine. "It was kind of you to contact the shuttle personally," he said. "I thought it was the purser's duty to inquire after a guest's needs."

"You're more than a guest, Master Mikk. I came down from Montréal to see you when you toured America. It's hard to believe it's been almost fifteen years."

"Has it?"

"I'd never seen anything like the show you put on, Master Mikk. You *deserve* special consideration."

"Thank you."

"Also—I've been to Somal."

Mikk's blood hissed in his ears. His discomfort must have shown because the captain rested his hand on Mikk's breast and hooked his index finger on one of the surprise tunic's pockets, rather intimate contact for a first meeting.

"Don't be concerned," he said quietly, and Mikk was intrigued by the half tone of unspoken passion in his voice. "Press aren't allowed on this cruise, and your fellow passengers are too self-absorbed to care. All they want is to be entertained."

The captain dropped his hand, finished his drink, set the glass on a small chrome sideboard, and led the way out of his cabin. "The delegates made me promise to give them and their charming spouses an after-supper tour of the ship, and they wanted you to come along so they could pester you with their requests."

"That's why I came, captain."

"Yes, of course. Still, we do have some lovely Belian flotation chambers nobody ever uses . . ."

"Is that an invitation?"

The captain paused at the door and looked at Mikk as though abstractly amused by this question, but he didn't reply.

This could be more diverting than I anticipated, Mikk thought.

Once the economic delegates, their spouses, and bodyguards had gathered together in the main concourse, Captain Dupré herded them through the ship like an indulgent schoolteacher and expanded on his list of amenities.

"The *Ariadne* provides the discriminating traveler with unparalleled facilities and services for every exigency," he recited with what Mikk immediately recognized as counterfeit enthusiasm. "She has fourteen decks, three formal dining rooms, a grand ballroom, four bars, six snack areas, two gyms, a botanical garden . . ."

Mikk had seen larger, but didn't say so.

The touring party shuffled into the shopping plaza and stopped at its large central fountain; the water, lit from within, resembled a shower of crystals. Several of the delegates approached Mikk with requests for the evening performance, asking almost exclusively for selections from their own native arts, nothing unfamiliar. One of the women, the wife of President Carlo of Bolivia, glided up to Mikk and curled her long-nailed fingers around his arm.

"I'll bet you've been to lots of worlds, haven't you, querido?" she asked in Spanish, her breath strong with the familiar scent of a pond in the Dormant Season.

"A few, señora."

Señora Carlo tightened her grip. She'd painted her lips a dark berry maroon and smeared one corner. The color rode up on her cheek.

"What pretty amethyst eyes, you have!" she said. "And your hair! Is that natural?"

"I'm afraid so, señora."

"Oh, don't be afraid." She pushed her face up under Mikk's chin. "Many, many worlds . . . You're very brave to travel so far from home."

Señora Carlo as well? Mikk mused, remembering the captain's enigmatic greeting. She seemed about to ask if he'd encountered any exotic sexual practices on those worlds.

However, Señora Carlo suddenly became morose and her brown eyes puddled.

"Is there a world where a woman can be alone and not have to do anything for anyone?" she whispered. "Not have to smile when she feels like screaming?"

How was he to answer? His spirit was bent under the weight of a galactic ban. He had no real hope to offer anyone, himself included.

President Carlo himself then materialized and, laughing easily, apologized to Mikk.

"She's just tired." He maneuvered his lady away. Mikk was grateful, but didn't think the president needed to pull his wife's hand like that. Drunk or not, she didn't deserve to be treated roughly.

He turned his attention to two other delegates who were arguing in English.

"That's right," one with a bronze face said indignantly, "a second-rate power, prematurely old because it has always lacked a soul."

"Oh, really, Emir?" the fleshier man, an American, replied with a sarcastic smile. "Your country has been a flea-infested backwater since India's control of fusion! Without their investment along your coastline, you wouldn't be able to afford this little junket."

"As if you would turn down a handout from anyone!" the Emir cried. "Tyrants, murderers, madmen—they're all the same to you as along as they have money!"

The American thrust his belly at the Emir.

"And what about your little agreement with the Midslavian czar? That rattlesnake's got the heads of butchered Muslims decorating the walls of his trophy room. What does that say about *your* priorities, pal?"

The bickering degenerated into fisticuffs, which the bodyguards quickly broke up by quietly engulfing the combatants in constricting masses of ill-dressed, muscular flesh. Captain Dupré, who had finished describing the workings of the fountain to the German delegation and had returned to Mikk, shook his head. "Sometimes I wish I'd joined the merchant marine, but the luxury lines serve better food."

"Oh, thank you!" Mikk laughed. "There's no better tonic than dry Terran wit."

"Is that so?" came an unwelcome voice out of Mikk's memory. "Maybe we should bottle it and export it to the great galactic unwashed."

"I was under the impression the media were not allowed on this cruise," Mikk whispered to the captain. Dupré's brows met, an angry platinum bar.

"Our cruise director has much to explain."

Mikk doubted he could accommodate another emotional shock in such a compressed timespan, but it was too late now. He turned to recognize the twenty-thousandth zyrr. The man he had not pleased.

"Martin." Mikk offered his hand. The critic did not take it. He looked the performance master up and down and grunted.

"You haven't changed at all."

Mikk would have said the same, but time had not been kind to the critic. He looked noticeably older, tired, and he still smoked those supposedly non-habit-forming nicotine-free cigarettes. His hair had continued its retreat, exposing a bare spot of scalp at the crown.

"You retain your ability to express disapproval while professing admiration," Mikk said, wondering where he had found such measured, even baroque, language. "I'm glad. There's nothing worse than a sentimental critic."

Martin almost smiled. "They told me you were on this cruise. I didn't believe them." He gave a crisp flick of his cigarette. "You've sunk to a new low, Mikk, undoubtedly to take another stab at imitating our performers."

Mikk sighed heavily. He did not want this conversation, did not want this man's company, no longer wanted to be on this floating resort.

"Martin, I'm not interested in arguing with you. I'm here by special request to entertain heads of state. I don't think they would have asked me to come if they didn't consider me a true artist."

"True artist? I heard the dying Somalites forced you to vow never to perform their works again because you weren't good enough."

The blow was unexpected and the pigment forced its way into Mikk's eyes.

"Ooh, now," the critic said softly, but with a hint of happy malice, "take it easy."

"What happened between me and the Somalites is none of your concern," Mikk said, his voice becoming abnormally constricted. "They thought my work was too similar to theirs and feared other peoples would be confused by it. They preferred no memory at all."

"Uh-huh. A race who wanted oblivion." Martin flipped his cigarette into the fountain.

"I tried to convince them otherwise."

"Sure you did, and the personal ban the Council slapped on you was just a technicality. I guess Ev-Mobix 'Gar wasn't enough for you, was it?" Martin scratched his chin in mock wonder. "Tell me. Who did you offend this time, Mikk? The elders? The *children*?"

Mikk passed his hand over his throbbing eyes.

"Mr. Brannick," the captain said, "that was uncalled for."

"I call them as I see them!" Martin snapped.

"Excuse me," Mikk said. "The Indonesian delegation has asked for some traditional dances this evening. I must get ready." Still shading his eyes, he ducked past the bodyguards and headed away from the delegates.

The critic's sour benediction followed him: "Knock 'em dead, sweetheart."

As Mikk strode briskly out of the Fountain Mall, down the ramp to the Stardust Promenade and the stage, he took several deep breaths and felt the fluid seep back out of his eyes. The malice of the man! And to what purpose? The critic certainly didn't care about the lost art of a people from the far end of the galaxy, that was obvious. The Somalites were an excuse for a personal attack, but why? If Martin found him so disagreeable, he easily could have avoided him in a ship this size. Why, in the name of the gods, was the critic even on board?

Mikk stopped outside the stage door and rested his shoulder against the cool, slick wall. He was panting.

"It doesn't matter," he said aloud to convince himself. "There's the work. Remember the work, lad. The gods above and the Beast below can't stop it. It's our life. Our breath."

As he remembered Master Huud's words, Mikk did breathe easier and his anxious pulse slowed. He picked up his fallen ego and went into the theater.

Chapter Thirty-three: The Entity

Well into the middle of the cruiser's artificial night, Mikk suddenly awoke, the patter of the nine valves of his heart in his ears. He had no idea what had wakened him. The atmospheric ducts hissed softly in the well-insulated room, and he was marvelously comfortable in the ample pillows and quilted coverings of his bed. He rolled over and punched the small button that opened the window panel. All was still outside except for the distant beacon satellite marking the boundary of the shipping lane.

Usually a view of open space, with its masses of stars, worlds, souls, comforted Mikk because it reminded him that nothing in the galaxy was ever lost. Everything returned to the hearts of new stars, new worlds. The master, the Somalites, Mikk, Martin—all of them would be changed and emerge in unforeseen forms in the distant future. Their souls would find other houses. But tonight, all this vast jeweled emptiness just hammered home his loneliness, and he wept into his pillow. It was all very well to speak of continuities and passings and the web of existence, but nothing eased the pain of real, tangible extinction, the death in your arms.

"Damn you, Martin!"

Mikk would have wrestled with another circuitous black market telewave call if he hadn't sensed deep in his joints that Thissizz was still in molt. How terrible not to have access to his friend's gentle wisdom at such a time!

"I am only half myself without you," he murmured. "The lesser half."

Mikk sat up and the premonitory frisson raked a quick claw across his back. He'd heard something—a sound that, well, wasn't a sound. He got out of bed, slipped on his robe, and released the door seal. It parted to show the empty carpeted hallway between the deluxe suites. The heart of the giant cruiser hummed a heavy bass note and he felt the faint vibration in the walls, but there was nothing more.

Mikk knew he wouldn't be able to get back to sleep just yet so he went to the closet to find his salt pack and discovered that the cruiser's deck staff had misplaced it.

"My apologies, sir," the steward said when Mikk complained over the personal voice com in the sitting room. "We're working on it. We've narrowed down its location to somewhere in decks five through nine."

"I'll have to start wearing a salt pendant if this kind of accident happens again."

"Sir, it's highly unusual for us to lose a passenger's belongings. Please understand. Your arrival at such short notice . . ."

"Never mind," Mikk smiled benignly. "I'll manage. Thank you." No point in making the steward miserable too.

Mikk padded barefoot into the hall and down the steps to the lift tube. At this time of "night" all the main kitchens were closed, but the snack bars would be open and maybe he could find something appropriate to his needs.

The nearest snack bar was in the observation deck under the dome at the very top of the cruiser. Mikk tapped in the coordinates and the lift tube shot him up in an ear-popping schuss of warm air to deck fourteen. When he arrived, he shook his head and yawned several times to counteract the dizziness. Too bad these newer luxury cruisers did not have stairwells. He detested being thrown through the air by any propulsion other than his own.

Few people were in the observation deck, mostly couples gazing at the stars and each other. The lone man at the empty white curve of the snack bar was the first Freen Mikk had seen on board doing something other than mopping decks or cleaning lavatories.

"Good evening, Mikk-sir! What would you like?"

"Do you have anything salty?"

"Not much." The Freen rummaged about below the counter. "You know these Terran souls and their high blood pressure, Mikk-sir. They like potassium-based substitutes."

"Hm . . . I really do need some sodium, my friend."

The Freen popped back up and scrunched his flat features together in concentration. "I have mustard. It's a condiment, not usually eaten alone, but it's salty."

"I don't think I can afford to be picky. My fingertips are numb."

The Freen handed him several packets of the yellow sauce and Mikk gamely tore one open. After all, it couldn't be as bad as the captain's bourbon, could it?

It was, but it was salty, so Mikk squeezed the condiment onto his tongue and forced it down. His fingers regained sensation.

Then—what *was* that? The stargazing couples had noticed it, too, and looked up at the crystalline dome just as he had. It was not quite a noise, more a small shock, a ripple of static, but it came from a particular direction, like a noise, and vibrated on the ear, like a noise. It also created a brief optical distortion outside the dome and made a patch of stars jiggle and swim.

The officer on duty in the observation deck, a rangy arrow of a man with more buckles, belts, and buttons than seemed necessary, hurried to the security voice com, opened the panel, and spoke into it. Mikk knew something odd was going on. He got a cup of water from the Freen as a mustard chaser and decided to head back to his room when, once again, the nearly silent crackle passed overhead, this time accompanied by a thin streak of blue light that danced across the outside of the observation deck and disappeared. A second Freen, startled by the phenomenon, dropped his tray of dirty tumblers with a melodramatic crash and froze in an attitude of despair, inner lids half-closed, hands twisted back on themselves in cruelly unnatural positions. Mikk cradled the catatonic Freen in his arms and laid him on the floor.

"He's all right," he said to the knot of anxious spectators. "It's a kind of light-sensitive epilepsy. Many Freens have it."

The officer's voice com conversation became more urgent. Mikk picked up every word in spite of the secretive whisper but could not make sense of them. The officer seemed to be speaking in an intravessel code.

"Ten tiger, Base Nine. We'll wash out the jeepers on this end before they break and dash, but hang a six-plus on this one and stand by."

Give me a little more and perhaps I can decipher it, Mikk thought, but the officer closed the panel and addressed the people in the observation deck.

"The captain tells me we've encountered a minor, if eccentric, energy field. It's perfectly natural and nothing to be alarmed about. However, he encourages you to return to your suites. We could experience some minor power outages in those decks nearest the upper and lower hulls and he doesn't want anyone tripping in the dark."

His words sounded reassuring and, unless the officer was a better actor than Mikk, he had not lied. He sauntered back to his post as though nothing in the galaxy were amiss. He even yawned and loosened the holster strap across his chest a notch.

"I'm more space-lagged and depressed than I thought," Mikk murmured. "I'm imagining disasters."

The Freen on the floor opened his eyes and scowled at Mikk. "What are *you* looking at, swamp stork?" he asked in surprisingly fluent backwater barge Vyzanian.

"Pond scum," Mikk replied, standing up. "Next time, remember your medication."

He padded back to the lift tube and flew to his own deck. Once again in his suite, he dropped gratefully onto that welcoming tender tangle of bedclothes and fell instantly asleep, only to be awakened a minute later by the buzz of the tiny voice com over the headboard.

"Beast! Now what?"

It was the chief purser. "The captain wants to see you in the deck seven rec room, Master Mikk."

"Why? Does one of the delegates need a partner for midnight racquetball?"

"This is an emergency, sir. Please see the captain at once."

Emergency or not, Mikk was not about to visit Captain Dupré wrapped in a robe. It would be unseemly, or misinterpreted, so he hastily dressed in his dance suit and surprise tunic.

When he opened the door panels, he found a security officer waiting for him, a tall, muscular Pan-African woman who led Mikk to the security lift tube, a faster, more direct line than the one for passengers, and they were jettisoned directly to the deck seven recreation room.

The bright, high-ceilinged space with its polished wooden floor was empty except for the captain and a knot of security people at the far end of the clearwall, the side of the room that was not keranium but a single curving slice of polyglass. The captain saw him.

"Ah, good, Mikk, here you are." Dupré sounded tense, but he hadn't lost any of his easy sophistication.

"Understand, Mikk," he said when the performance master joined him, "for a Terran I'm hardly a babe in the woods. I've taken guests to twenty different worlds and read up on many more, but I've never seen anything like this."

"I'm no scientist," Mikk said.

"No, but you're better traveled than I am. Come look out at the air lock down there."

From the clearwall, the smooth white hull of the ship bulged in a broad arc then tapered to a point. Its shape reminded Mikk of a water sow, a warm-blooded ocean creature of Vyzania's Great North Banks. The rec room had the best view of this angle of the ship.

"That's the electrical anomaly that flitted over the observation deck a few minutes ago," the captain said. "What do you think?"

Near the bottom of the seventh deck as it started its outward swell was a circular emergency air lock, outlined in red, and hovering tightly over it was a shifting, multicolored, semitransparent mass that threw off bands of blue and yellow current. Mikk had seen a lot of curious phenomena, cloud forms that were really plant colonies, sentient energy fields, even bodies of fluid that had a mind and flowed uphill, but this was new. A jellied vapor.

"I wish I could say, captain," he replied, "but I have no idea what it is. It seems organized if unsettled." He looked Dupré in the eye. "I think it's alive. Perhaps even intelligent."

"Merde," the captain growled, briefly reverting to Québecois French. "A load of tiresome government conventioneers and we run into an unidentified outworlder."

"Sir!" a frantic voice cried from the captain's pocket voice com. "Something's entered the deck seven air lock."

Outside, the thing seeped through the metal skin of the hull and disappeared.

"Is the seal broken?" the captain asked.

"No, sir. It passed right through like a ghost. It's in the ventilation ducts now."

"Where is it headed?"

The officer down by the air lock didn't need to answer because the entity suddenly issued out of the rec room's ceiling fan and hovered before them. Mikk nearly locked into a stare state when he saw the thing, which lent him a moment of objective curiosity.

He decided the entity wasn't ugly so much as incoherent, as though it couldn't settle on any particular molecular configuration or density. Perhaps that was how it had gotten through the hull: it had accidentally stumbled on a density that could penetrate metal and now, in its rapid-fire shiftings, was trying to find a form appropriate to the atmosphere. If so, it was not doing very well. It fluttered and writhed, a jumbled mess of semisolid, semifluid energy and gas-impregnated muck that hissed and crackled with great jolts of static electricity. Mikk couldn't even be sure how large the thing was. It fluctuated between the size of a Terran pilot whale and a small personal space shuttle.

The security officers immediately raised their side arms and fired on it. The thing twisted in on itself and shot back a bolt of blue lightning that reduced the officers to ashes and burned a neat round hole in the floor. Mikk, shaken out of his contemplation and too close to the line of fire for comfort, did a back flip out of the way just in time and tried to grab the captain's arm as Dupré drew his weapon.

"No, sir! Please don't die too!"

The captain didn't get a chance to fire anyway. The entity shrank up with a tiny squeal, shot across the rec room to the service lift tube, and exploded up the draft out of sight.

That thing certainly can move quickly when it wants to, Mikk thought. *What is that strong, musky odor? Strange. It smells frightened.*

Mikk, with his long legs, reached the service lift tube first.

"What are the coordinates?" the captain asked.

"I can't tell. The controls have melted. I'll wager the lift went back to the coordinates it came from." Mikk looked up. "Who last used this tube?"

"I did."

"Where did you come from?"

"I, well . . . hm." Captain Dupré reddened. Incinerated security people notwithstanding, this was the first time the performance master had seen the elegant Canadian genuinely discomposed.

"Where did you come from?" Mikk asked again.

"Nom de Dieu! Just follow me." Mikk accompanied the captain to the security lift tube and it deposited them on the pink-tiled deck of the aft pool.

To conserve energy and staff power, the aft pool was supposed to be closed at "night," the bays of its lift tubes locked, so Mikk was surprised to find that not only were the lights on and the heaters working, but a huddled group of terrified nude swimmers at the diving end of the blue Olympic-sized pool were screaming and pointing at their uninvited shape-shifting guest. The only one who could have let them in at this hour was the captain himself. Mikk guessed Dupré's dislike for politicians didn't prevent him from allowing the occasional private pool party.

The performance master recognized two military attachés, the Emir, a Viceroy, a couple of ladies who looked too young to be anyone's spouses, President Carlo's depressed wife, and who was that cowering in her arms? To judge by the wet bald spot, it was Martin. Mikk had never seen a Terran blush that far down his body. Señor Carlo was not present. Neither were the bodyguards.

The amorphous unknown itself hovered almost anxiously over the water.

"Get out of the water!" Captain Dupré cried as he ran to the hysterical swimmers. "That thing has an enormous electrical charge."

Mikk helped pull people from the pool and personally fished out the critic who, frightened as he was, couldn't refrain from delivering yet another barb.

"Already one too many *aliens* on this ship," he snarled, with special emphasis on the pejorative epithet.

"Under the circumstances, I will ignore that," Mikk said.

Once everyone was out of the pool, they backed slowly away from the water and closer to each other. The unidentified young ladies hugged each other and whimpered.

The entity, which transmuted irregularly as though distressed by its own confusion, drifted toward the deep end nearer the swimmers and tentatively sent down a fairly solid tentacle to touch the water. A huge yellow spark erupted from the surface of the pool and the tentacle snapped away only to visibly change composition and extend again. This time, when it touched the water, the tentacle set up a churning vibration that echoed all the way down to the bottom of the pool, and, to the horror of the observers, the entire artificial lake began to slosh and whirl and spin up the tentacle into the entity. Thousands of gallons of safely sanitized water roared and gurgled out of the bowels of the pool and disappeared in an inverted funnel into the hovering thing, which did not increase in size at all. In a matter of minutes the pool was dry, a pale blue cavern twenty feet deep at the diving end where the shivering band of bipeds stood.

As for the entity, it still hung over the pool, shimmering and shifting, but it seemed sluggish and the electrical discharges were not as frequent.

"It's resting," Mikk said.

"How p-perceptive!" Martin stuttered through chattering teeth. "What do we d-do now? The lift t-tubes are on the other side of that d-damned thing."

"Perhaps if it's distracted, most of you could get to the lift tubes before it noticed," said Dupré. "I'll head for the tanning deck and see if it follows."

"Most of us?" asked one of the military attachés. "Are you crazy? You've seen how powerful it is! Sucked up the pool like it was drinking through a straw. None of us would get ten feet."

"Maybe we should try talking to it," Mikk said. The others stopped shivering and stared at him.

"We should try *what*?" asked the Emir.

"Talking to it," Mikk repeated. "It might be intelligent."

"Talk about what?" Martin asked. "The weather in the intergalactic vacuum?"

"Doesn't matter. If we can get a linguistic link, we might put it at ease, or at least distract it, as the captain suggested."

"You're the one with the facility for outworld languages," Dupré said. "If you honestly think that—whatever—is intelligent . . ."

"I don't know," Mikk said, but the idea was becoming strangely attractive to him. "I'd like to try. I need to."

"You feel the need to get us all killed?" Martin scoffed.

"Shut up, Brannick!" the captain snapped. "I don't hear you coming up with a better idea!" He turned to Mikk. "This thing could be about as sentient as a sponge, you know."

Mikk nodded. His back and shoulders had been heavily taxed lately, their intimations and accompanying half images more jumbled than usual. The compelling desire he felt could be the allure of his own death. He moved gingerly out along the pink tile toward the hovering entity but hadn't gone five steps when he abruptly stopped and the sweat at his neck turned cold.

Gods of the stars! he thought. What do I say? Peace be with you? What if it doesn't understand the idea of harmlessness? What if it doesn't understand anything? He dabbed his throat with the back of his hand.

What would Thissizz say? he wondered. What he always says, probably: Are you hungry? Oh, dear . . .

He giggled nervously. He doubted the thing was thirsty in any case, but it could be in pain. He decided that was as good a thing as any to ask and ran rapidly through twenty different languages and gesture patterns with no discernible response, although he was sure the entity was watching him.

After another twenty questions, Mikk turned to the others and shrugged helplessly.

"I can continue," he said, "but . . ."

The entity launched a new long thin tentacle that whipped across Mikk's shoulder, sliced through his clothing, and cut into his flesh. He yelped and clutched the wound. The edges of the tears in his clothing and skin were singed and the stinging was terrific. Astonished, Mikk gaped at the entity. In spite of its previous behavior, he honestly hadn't expected an outright attack and the pigment pumped into his eyes. The thing shrank back.

"Mikk!" cried the captain.

"Keep away! I've got its interest now."

"Interest like that could be fatal."

"I'm aware of that!" Mikk barked. Then he added, barely whispering, "Very aware."

Through his tears, Mikk clearly saw the intricate inner workings of the amorphous creature, its churnings and reconnections
and spreading fermentation of matter. It was beautiful, a self-
contained organic nebula. Why did the gods make so many
dangerous things so attractive? He could love this creature if it
understood.

There was the musk scent again. Mikk took a deep breath. He
had to try again. He opened his mouth for a fresh round of difficult
foreign phrases and the thing rushed him, stopping only an arm's
length away. It leaned its bulk over him and released a harsh
reverberating moan that was anything but friendly.

"Ho . . . ah!" Mikk's breath blew out of him and he gazed up at
the twitching, glittering mass, transfixed.

This is my death, he thought. It'll watch me a moment, then
strike. Probably won't even know what it's doing. I annoy it. Oh,
serassi! What should I do?

Well, Beast! answered his trouper's sense of recklessness, I'd
better go out in style! Mikk pulled some small bolba juggling balls
out of his surprise tunic.

"Once a performer, always a performer," he said softly and
began to toss and catch the balls, humming to himself.

The entity yanked its matter up straight, ceased its tortured per-
mutations, and froze into an irregular semisolid blob the color of
the awful condiment Mikk had choked down earlier in the
evening. The change shocked him and he almost dropped the
balls, but he hung on and kept juggling although his hum became
a one-note rasp.

It seemed to last forever, this suspended animation punctuated
by Mikk's simple rhythmic manipulation of the gold balls. The
musk scent was gone. Why is it so still? he wondered. Curiosity?
Pleasure?

Suddenly, the balls flew from his hands and were caught in a
field of blue light in front of the entity, where they began to repeat
the circles Mikk had just made with them. Inside the entity itself,
tiny white sparks flickered.

Mikk laughed. The thing was juggling! Juggling exactly as he
had. The air around the entity twinkled with pure childlike delight.

Then, the most incredible change of all. Keeping the balls suspended, the entity collapsed and began to reshape itself, this time

with a sense of particular design. It bunched in its material, smoothed and stretched its form and altered its color until—

Mikk was staring at himself, an exact duplicate down to the crazy squiggles of bright embroidery around the pockets of his surprise tunic. Even the wound in his shoulder was copied and, once achieved, his double winced and dropped the bolba balls. It examined the injury with amazement. It hadn't known it had hurt Mikk: that was clear from the chagrined half smile, half frown it gave the performance master. Mikk reached into another pocket of his surprise tunic, retrieved a second set of bolba balls, and held them out in offering to the Mikk-disguised entity.

It may have resembled the performance master, but it behaved like a much more emotionally simple creature. It grinned ecstatically at the present, grabbed the balls, and hugged them close, barely able to control its excitement. The thing's touch was cool, completely without electrical sting, exactly like Mikk's own fine, smooth skin. The performance master wiped his eyes, moved that such an uncomplicated intelligence could, at the same time, be a genius at molecular recombination. A galactic idiot savant.

It reached out and gently stroked the performance master's hair, as charmed by it as most children were. No longer concerned about assault, Mikk let the entity play with his crimson locks all it wanted and twitched when the thing inadvertently pulled it. The entity drew back its hand in alarm, but Mikk smiled and it relaxed.

"I wish we could talk together," he said. The entity watched his mouth, enchanted. "But the bolba balls will have to do at present."

The entity moved its lips in imitation, but made no sound, and finally dismissed the activity with a perplexed grin. It clutched its gift and, without further ado, disintegrated, bolba balls and all, into its relatively stable yellow mass. Gliding swiftly above the tanning deck, it passed through the walls and out of the ship.

Mikk's leftover strength abandoned him and he dropped to his knees. He considered fainting but heard a sound that reminded him he was not alone in this place—there were witnesses. He turned his head.

The Terrans were applauding. Even Martin.

Chapter Thirty-four: The Twenty-thousandth Zyrr

Mikk was treated like a hero—and hated every minute of it. However, he smiled and mumbled his thanks. By now, the ban was all over the airwaves, and if the delegates found it more amusing to toast him at the captain's table, recommend him for field decorations as if his mollification of a frightened entity was "distinction under fire," and shower him with other unnecessary tokens of esteem rather than question him about the Somalites, so be it. Captain Dupré repeated his comment about the flotation chambers but continued to hide his motives. Mikk, eager to keep his life from becoming more complicated than it already was and disappointed that Dupré refused to speak to the point, pretended not to know what those motives were.

A few nights after the poolside epiphany, nights during which the theater critic was conspicuously absent, Martin appeared at Mikk's door with a small elegantly wrapped box and a subdued demeanor. "You know," he said without quite looking Mikk in the eye, "redheads are supposed to bring *bad* luck, but I guess that doesn't apply to space vessels." He handed Mikk the box. "The Nipponese delegation told me this was an appropriate token of apology. I hope you think so."

"Please come in." The circles under the critic's eyes stirred Mikk's empathy. "Can I get you some refreshment?"

Martin shook his head. He sat on the viewport bench and leaned his elbows on his knees, his hands hanging limply before him. Mikk pulled up the leather ottoman and joined him. The critic looked too dejected to speak yet, and Mikk quietly undid the rice paper wrapping on the box.

Inside was an ivory netsuke of two children wrestling with a puppy. It had to be at least seven hundred years old and worth a fortune. A theater critic could not well afford this.

"The Nipponese cut me a deal," Martin said, embarrassed.

"It's beautiful." Mikk cradled the piece in his hand. "I don't know what to say."

"I don't want you to say anything. I came to say some things to you." He patted his pocket, looking for his cigarettes, Mikk supposed, but gave up and returned to his attitude of depression. "What do you think that thing was?" he asked.

"I don't know. The Belians call unknown space travelers 'messengers.' "

"Yes, I know. Why is that?"

"Because they tell us something we didn't know before."

Martin nodded and rubbed the ridge over his right eye as though it pained him. "Then you're my messenger," he said. "You taught me something about myself I didn't know before, or at least didn't want to acknowledge." He laughed weakly. "Me, of all people!"

"I don't understand."

Martin finally looked at him. His round blue eyes were bloodshot. "My ancestor was Commander Richard Kirkby."

"Gods in the sky, Martin! I had no idea you were so well connected."

Martin snorted in self-contempt.

"I don't go around advertising it. It can be a burden being related to the man who made first contact. The Belians even built a shrine to him, can you believe it?"

"The Belians have always enjoyed being first," Mikk said philosophically.

"But that's beside the point." Martin pushed himself up from his slouch, but grimaced and squeezed his eyes shut a moment. "Do you remember how he died?"

"Heart failure, wasn't it?"

Martin shook his head. "That's what the government wanted people to believe. He committed suicide with an overdose of a synthostimulant. Got it from a doctor friend who needed the money."

"I'm very sorry."

"Would you like to know why?"

"I wasn't going to pry, but I'm curious, of course."

Martin made another, more thorough search of his jacket, and, once again, gave up. Mikk detested cigarettes but would have liked to offer him one anyway, for hospitality's sake.

"The Commander always maintained that first contact was a great step in human progress," Martin said, "that a treaty with the Belians was the forerunner of what he hoped would be many productive and peaceful relationships throughout the galaxy, but he was troubled. It's a terrible blow finally to *prove* yours is not the only intelligent life in the universe. It upsets all your assumptions about ultimate good, natural laws, even God."

Now Martin massaged his neck with his thumbs. He was definitely in some kind of physical distress, but Mikk didn't know whether to ask him about it since the critic kept talking through his agitation.

"Of course, my ancestor was an atheist, a military science officer who believed in the rational pursuit of rational answers. He expected to find someone like the Belians and surprise! He found them! What a leap for mankind, eh?"

Mikk didn't reply. He sensed the critic was opening doors in himself that, perhaps, had never been opened.

"He said, 'We're not alone anymore. There's someone else we can talk to,' but the Belians showed us that, not only are we not alone, but the galaxy is crowded. There are hundreds of peoples out there, some friendly, some hostile, most of mixed morality, all as complicated and contradictory as human beings."

It's a headache of some kind, Mikk thought, a bad one. I wonder if I should call the ship's physician . . .

"I think it overwhelmed the Commander. He became obsessed with the idea of identity. In a universe of so many, what is it makes a particular people or a particular person unique? He wrote some, uh, rambling treatises on the subject. They were suppressed for years."

Mikk had tried to read one of the treatises, but it was too disturbing. The thoughts of someone thrashing with the Beast himself.

"The Commander was a great man," Mikk said. "Great men are often plagued by the greatest demons."

"Then I must have inherited a demon myself. The Somalites

may have celebrated the concept of universal oneness, but it scares the hell out of me. That's why you frightened me so much."

"I frightened you?"

"Of course. You're too damned good. You really do steal the fire of every culture you visit and make it your own. I didn't understand what a performance master was, what you do, and I took the theft personally. I neglected to remember that, like a human artist, you keep the work alive, and I was jealous. I know that's irrational . . ."

"Martin, I . . ."

"Let me finish. It's my failing, not yours. There's not much left in the galaxy we can call our own. Maybe it's because I'm human, but it terrifies me."

Mikk smiled sadly. "Would it make you feel better to know it even terrified the Somalites?"

"What do you mean?"

"I didn't invent that story about their wanting oblivion. They really did want me to stop performing songdance because *it wasn't theirs*. If they couldn't have true songdance anymore, they didn't want anyone else to think they had it either."

"What do you know?" Martin said. "Selfishness—from the Somalites."

"Nothing as terrible as that. Probably simple fear. They were dying far from home, something their faith had never confronted before."

Some of the strain faded from Martin's face. "So, in the end, they were just like us."

"Oh, no! If I were allowed to perform one of their works for you, you wouldn't say that. They were some of the wisest, most profoundly gifted people in the galaxy. It breaks my heart that I can't share their songdance."

"Is it at all like glass dancing?"

Mikk laughed softly. Lately, he'd been comparing the two arts himself. "I've always felt they were mirror twins of each other. Light and dark aspects of the same god, but, I don't know."

"Do you think you could explore your theory right now? I wouldn't tell anyone."

"I believe you, but," Mikk glanced significantly at the ceiling, "the Council might be monitoring this suite and neither you nor I would know it until they came and carried me off in keranium wrist shackles."

"Fascists," Martin muttered with grand disdain, then fell silent. Eyes on the floor, he seemed to be meditating.

"You're not a bad sort at all," he said at last, "and you saved our lives talking to that whatchamacallit."

"I'm glad I could help."

"Too bad you can't help an unemployed theater critic. The *Times* fired me last month."

"Oh, dear! I'm very sorry, Martin."

"Don't be. Actually, I'm pretty pleased with myself. I finally told them what I thought of their editorial policies and they couldn't take it. Of course, they can't take much at all anymore. The paper folds at the end of the year." Martin's blue eyes became wet and swimmy. "My aunt was supposed to go on this cruise, but she didn't want to. She gave me the ticket thinking it would cheer me up."

"There must be other papers. Perhaps telewave news?"

"Perhaps, but I'm sick of spouting opinions no one gives a damn about—present company excepted. For once, I'd like to go to a show and watch it, just watch it, like everyone else."

Mikk picked up the netsuke and turned it about in his hands, letting the highly sensitive skin of his fingertips play over the tiny details of the carving.

"You could be my Terran agent."

"What?"

"You could be my Terran agent." Mikk set the netsuke back in the box. "I enjoyed my Terran tour very much. I'd like to come more often. You know what's going on and could get me the best dates. It would be quite lucrative for you."

Martin's eyes widened. "Are you serious? That would be . . . that's a fantastic idea!"

"I'm glad you think so. When I return from the Kekoi Elections . . ."

"The Kekoi Elections? I've heard about them. Don't they riot in the streets?"

"I think someone mistranslated. 'Revel' is more like it. Long ago, the Kekoi decided their politicians were terrible communicators, absolutely unable to discuss issues or questions in any kind of forthright manner."

"All politicians are like that," Martin grunted.

"But the Kekoi are Kekoi. Their politicians *agreed*, so now they hire armies of entertainers to fight their campaigns for them. It's much more amusing."

"Don't you have to do a lot of research on the candidate you're stumping for?"

"We have to research all of them. Performers are shuffled around every few days. That way, no one can say a candidate had an unfair advantage because a particular actor was on his side."

"That's nuts."

"Perhaps, but it works. People do go to the polls knowing who they're voting for, although that doesn't mean they have better choices." Mikk folded his arms. "It's true everywhere. Those who want power are usually the least qualified to hold it."

Martin actually smiled in spite of his pain. "You know, I'm kind of sorry now I brought up that war when we first met. Got us off on the wrong foot."

"That's not your fault," Mikk said. "Vyzanians live a very long time and forget very little. It makes it difficult to forgive, especially to forgive ourselves, so we're a bit touchy."

"Were any of your relatives in the war?"

"Oh, yes."

"Which side?"

"Both."

"Uh-huh. Foot soldiers?"

"Alas, no," Mikk sighed. "Officers. I hope you don't think less of me because of it."

"I'll try to overlook it."

Now it was Mikk's turn to smile. "You know, Martin, you could represent my friend Thissizz as well once the treaty with Droos comes through."

"Thissizz? Who is he?"

Mikk pulled a recording chip from his tunic pocket and dropped it into the black cylindrical audio box on his bedside table. "I play this when I'm feeling especially lonely," he said.

As Thissizz's voice filled the cabin, Martin blanched and the lines of pain around his eyes vanished. "You mean to tell me this is the voice of an actual living creature?" he whispered.

Later, Mikk wrangled his way through some shady frequencies to get Droos on the telewave, and Thissizz himself, who was finally out of molt and a brilliant iridescent green, answered. Mikk was too overcome to speak and Martin talked to him instead, in Belian.

"What a delightful . . . person," he told Mikk when the screen went dark.

"I've always thought so." An especially full, hot blush fanned out across Mikk's cheeks. Martin's quick squint told him he understood that blush, but was puzzled. Still, the former critic had the grace not to make an issue of it.

"Mikk, representatives from half the civilized Terran world are on this ship. After what you did the other night, it shouldn't be difficult to persuade them to push that treaty through."

Mikk cried out in delight and embraced the startled critic. Then he "found" a hexagonal gold coin behind Martin's ear and handed it to him.

"What's this?"

"The twenty-thousandth zyrr," Mikk said. "I've wanted to give it to you for fifteen years."

Entr'acte: The Third Day

"Sir, we think we've discovered who is smuggling in Master Mikk's salt."

The Magna, who lay on his bed wrapped from head to foot in a quilted pink Ortho Cocoon and was trying to visualize his vertebrae free of pain, would have murdered his assistant with insults for this interruption if his news hadn't been unusually good.

"Yes? Who?"

"Raf the Kekoi guard, although we don't know where he's getting it or in what form." The hydra hop-sucked up to the bed. "He rarely leaves the jail complex and then only to eat or sleep in the guard house."

"And he's the one in charge of searching visitors. Hm . . ."

The assistant leaned over the Magna's face. The Magna scowled.

"Do you mind? I'm trying to slow my heart, not shock it into fibrillation."

The assistant retreated and twiddled his polyps anxiously. "Sir, should we have Raf reassigned?"

"No. If we meddle further in Kekoi bureaucracy at this point, we'll draw too much attention to ourselves. Let him be for now. That way, we can find out his source."

"Yes, sir. Very wise, sir."

"Tell our agent to watch Mikk's visitors closely. The master is exceptionally light-fingered. Even with the grid, he could pick a visitor's pocket without anyone noticing."

The Magna squirmed in the cocoon. Now that his concentration was broken, he'd developed an itch and couldn't reach it. "Help me out of this thing, will you?"

The assistant gingerly approached the bed again, searched the length and breadth of the cushiony cocoon, but could find no way to open it.

"Is there a special key or fastening, sir?"

"Of course! On the left. Hurry! I have to scratch."

The assistant searched again, in vain. "I don't see anything, sir," he said, starting to whine, "unless you mean this toothed seam. Does that come apart?"

The Magna, now rippling like an insect ready to hatch, screamed at him.

"Yes! Pull the tab! Beast! I've thrown my hip out . . ."

The slippery-"fingered" assistant wrestled awkwardly with the tab and finally tore open the cocoon. A cloud of pink flocking sprayed into the air, and the Magna immediately doubled up and wriggled his fingers into his crotch.

"I knew this was a bad idea," he said, "but that damned physician! 'Try it! You'll love it!' Remind me to contact the Galactic Medical Council to have his license revoked."

After a feverish raking of his nails, the Magna sighed and lay panting on his side. His assistant had pushed down his jelly and resembled a squat, transparent bush, a stance full of chastised depression.

"Does our bumbling friend understand about the roochi?" the Magna asked.

"Yes, sir. He balked at first, but when I explained that roochi, although corthane-based, would not kill the master, only disorient him, he agreed to do it."

The Magna grunted.

"He's slow, but usable." He rolled over onto his unrelieved back. "I guess his species really does care for its young after all."

"How are the little ones, sir?" The assistant solicitously extended his eye stalks.

"Healthy enough, but they cry too much. I had them moved to another cell across the compound. The sound was upsetting Iki."

"Perhaps, sir, if you let them all play together . . ."

"What?!" Transported by fury, the Magna bounded out of bed with an agility he did not legitimately possess. "My grand-daughter in the same room as . . . You must be insane!"

The mortified coelenterate's eyes dangled and his internal organs slowly drifted down through his body to his soft "foot."

"My apologies, sir. I was not thinking."

"As usual!" the Magna cried. He was suddenly alarmed to find himself vertical and that alarm triggered new spasms in his back and hip. He clutched them with his bony hands.

"Go away before you 'not think' yourself into a cell of your own!"

The assistant listlessly slipped out of the room.

The Magna crawled painfully back into bed on top of the rumpled Ortho Cocoon. He gathered together a small mountain of pink and draped himself over it, face down, buttocks in the air, and was almost comfortable for the first time all day.

I just hope I last longer than that damned Vyzanian, he thought. At least we're getting close. Stop the salt and we can slip in the roochi.

The Magna picked at the flocking. Naturally, he hadn't told his soft assistant that no one really knew what roochi would do to a Vyzanian. Its only legal function was as a dart poison for killing birds in the Mrku rain forest. Even there it was rarely used because a substantial part of the flesh around the wound had to be cut out and burned before the rest of the carcass was safe to eat. Corthane tolerance notwithstanding, roochi would probably do much more than "disorient" the performance master.

"But it won't matter," the Magna told himself. "We can pin the blame on Raf, or even Bipti. The Kekoi knows nothing, and who's going to believe a Freen?"

The rolled-up cocoon provided a lovely pressure against his belly and groin, soothing in its yielding passivity. The Magna closed his eyes. At the moment, he didn't even care about the tribunal, which had begun its third day light years away.

Martin, who had successfully fought for a seat down front behind the rail, felt sorry for Féqé-ad, the Rogoine tribune. He had been the last of the tribunes to arrive on Kekoi Kaery and had landed in the infirmary with a severe toxic reaction to the world's pollens. He still looked haggard, but was trying to weigh the issues with a cool, impartial head.

"I wish they'd let you perform songdance for us here so we could decide its value and be done with it," he muttered to Mikk. "That's the only way to settle this mess."

"Or unsettle it," Mikk said with a gentle smile.

"That's the real issue, isn't it?" The tribune squinted his reddish, catlike eyes. "How *do* we judge your performance? There is no one left alive qualified to determine the authenticity of anyone's songdance, let alone yours." Féqé-ad blew his small black nose into an already bloody square of pale blue silk.

"There are no more ancient Rogoines, either, yet you perform their epics. Is your work authentic?"

"A good point, but your challenge—" here Féqé-ad held out his rugged paws as though begging for a measure of rice "—your challenge, regardless of the details, attacks the foundation of the Council's power and therein lies a great danger. The worlds of the Association, through their charters, have clasped hands and agreed to work together. It isn't a perfect alliance, but it works. You would uncouple all of those clasped hands by ushering in dissent, factionalism . . . chaos."

"Everything passes around the wheel to its beginning, tribune," Mikk said, almost lyrically. "Everything rises to its own collapse."

The Rogoine rubbed the strainer hairs over his mouth, and his sensitive ears, like small black membranous cones on either side of his head, sagged. "You worry me, Mikk. I don't think you know what you're doing."

"Yes, I do. I'm committing murder. I just don't know the victim yet."

"High Tribune," Féqé-ad said, "I yield to the next questioner. As far as I'm concerned, there's no point to this tribunal, but I will sit it out and not put a weight on the hours by asking more."

"As you wish." Pairip yawned spectacularly, as though he had unhinged his jaw and cracked apart his skull. "The tribune from Nyan Sewpa has the floor."

The Nyan Sewpan, a singer named Bythr, looked almost human, but was the second of the two tribunes who required special apparatuses to breathe. Two tubes ran into his nostrils from a large soft pack resembling a polystyrene bubble strapped to his back. Martin had already noticed how, over the course of a day, the bubble gradually collapsed in on itself. He had no idea what kind of gas it contained.

"I detest you, Vyzanian," the Nyan Sewpan said with a charming smile.

"The feeling is mutual, tribune," Mikk replied with an equally lovely display of teeth.

The better to eat you with, Martin mused sourly.

"But we must set aside personal feeling," the tribune said, "and take in the broader view of the issues before us."

"Spoken like a politician," Mikk quipped.

"Flattery will not help you." Mikk gave the tribune an arch expression of amazement, which he ignored.

"Your arrest for breaking a galactic ban may be the most fortuitous thing to have happened to the galactic entertainment community in centuries," the tribune continued, "similar to bringing up a racketeer on tax delinquency charges. It gets you into custody and, maybe, while we have you, we can run down your other crimes."

Interesting, Martin thought, I didn't know these tactics were so universal.

"Other crimes, tribune?"

"Oh, yes," the Nyan Sewpan nodded, wagging his nostril tubes. "Serious ones. Ones that question your very status as an upright man." The tribune picked up his notes, a sheaf of lime green cellulose squares, and riffled through them.

"Are you not, Mikk, a shameless engager in interspecies sex?"

The crowd's interest jumped dramatically and the journalists in camspecs practically crushed each other vying for a better angle. Mikk's eyes narrowed.

"My relationship with your fellow tribune is common knowledge," he said evenly, but Martin felt the crackle of suppressed ire filling the air around the performance master. "The Council has never challenged me on this issue before, and I have never heard that affection between sentient species is a crime."

The gallery buzzed softly, and the optitube remotes slid together on their rack and trained their snouts on Mikk's face.

"I'm not talking about Thissizz," Bythr said. "I'm referring to your liaison with Ahva, the Belian actress."

Mikk was obviously stunned. He stared at the tribune, seemingly unable to speak.

"It is true that interspecies relations are not officially a crime," the Nyan Sewpan nonchalantly strummed his nostril tubes with his fingertips, "but such practices cast a cloud over your moral character, especially considering you are in frequent contact with children."

"Where . . . who did you . . . ?"

"We, that is the Council, of course, persuaded the lady in question that her new life was more important than her silence."

The pigment jetted into Mikk's irises for all the galaxy to see.

"What have you done!?" His voice pushed past the controlled projection of the previous day to a sonic boom. The tiny oculus of the dome could not stand the stress; it shattered and rained crystal shards all over the floor between Mikk and the tribunes.

"If you've harmed her in any way . . . !"

"You'll what, sir?" Bythr asked mildly. "Really now, don't you think one galactic offense is more than sufficient?" He glanced contemptuously at the debris. "I suggest you keep your voice down."

Mikk didn't reply, but his rigid posture told Martin he was barely holding on to the trappings of civilization.

"Furthermore," the tribune said, again picking through his notes, "it seems you also had a tryst with one Oo-aika, a Ti-tokan dancer, right under the nose of your then master Huud Maroc—but excuse me. I am in error. Not a tryst. According to my notes, she attacked you with intent to rape."

The tribune looked over the tops of his thick ultraviolet quadrifocals and his smile twisted into a leer. "Almost raped, Mikk? By a woman?"

"You seem to find that amusing, tribune. It was not."

"But—a *woman*? What poor excuse for a man almost gets raped by a woman?"

"Forgive me, tribune," Mikk said, "have you ever seen a Titokan woman?"

"Females are females."

"Are they?" Mikk turned around and scanned the gallery. "Ah!" He pointed to the upper balconies. "There we are." Then, as the crowd rustled and squeaked in their efforts to follow his gaze, the performance master spoke to an unseen person in a strange language of elastic vowels and short, crisp consonants. His tone was respectful and the person deigned to rise as requested so everyone could see her.

The last time Martin had seen such a physique was on a decathlete who had been suspended for synthosteroid use. The Ti-tokan's extensive tattoos only heightened the impression of massive, and overbearingly confident, power, and the courtroom hummed with agitated whispers.

"Tribune," Mikk said, "I'd like you to meet Oe-aa Kay. She was kind enough to explain that she has been ill, which is why she looks so frail."

The agitation increased, especially among the males in attendance. Oe-aa Kay grinned handsomely at Bythr, then said something to Mikk, who looked surprised and smiled sheepishly in response.

"What did she say?" the tribune asked as he fumbled with the tight collar of his puffy coat and took a deep whiff of his portable atmosphere. "Was it a threat?"

"That . . . depends," Mikk said with an innocent little wave of his loop-pinioned hands to the giant woman in the balcony. "Oe-aa Kay thinks you're cute."

"What?! You tell that, that bitch monstrosity I'll . . ."

"Damn you, tribune!" Mikk cried, all of his fury returning. "It took me seventy-two of your years to convince the Ti-tokans I was something more than an especially talented house pet! I am not going to undermine my efforts by translating your rudeness. If you want to call her names, do so yourself, but if she makes you too nervous, maybe you should reconsider your slanders of me. Remember, Oo-aika did not rape me, although she certainly could have. Ask yourself why not."

The Kekoi at Martin's side started to clap, then another joined in, then a few more, all in fierce, sharp rhythm. Soon the entire crowd was clapping and the rhythm dissolved into applause. Martin slumped back in his seat. Once again, Mikk had regained control, but he was tiring, and Martin recognized the fraying edges of an actor who had been in a role a bit too long.

* * *

"Always the same, isn't it, Mikk?" Martin asked when he returned to the holding cell that evening. " 'My, my, what about the children?' "

Mikk smiled wanly, but was silent.

"Well, I have something that might lift your spirits," Martin continued. "Rumor has it there's a huge pile of telewave mail to you squirreled away in the courtroom basement. The Council won't let the Kekoi give it to you, but *I* got something that came in on my code at the pensione." He moved closer to the grid, the better to see Mikk's reaction and block Bipti's view.

"I think it's from a child," he said as he reached into his coat and withdrew an envelope—and a new tin of caviar—which he slipped under the meal slot so Mikk could reach them, "but I'm not sure. Whoever wrote it actually sent it to, well," he glanced at Bipti, "let's just say our only ally in this tank, and he sent it on to me. That would have been pretty sophisticated detective work for a kid."

The tin vanished as though it had never existed and Mikk opened the envelope to read the blue-inked message on the thin, slick paper:

Mikk-mikk—

I saw you on the optitube and wondered why those performers were being rude to you. You are *much* smarter than they are and a better entertainer, too. W'gang said it's because you broke a promise and she told me the story. So that's why the Council is angry!

But maybe you broke the promise because you *had* to, that songdance was more important. I don't know why because I can't do it myself, but I've seen it and it's very pretty.

Master Huud told me that we are the flutes that play the music and flutes break but new ones are made so the music won't stop. Maybe you're breaking yourself, but I think it's good for the other flutes and the music.

—H—

Mikk pressed the letter to his eyes and Martin saw his throat working.

"You don't need me to tell you, Mikk of Vyzania, that you have a power the Council cannot control."

"But they control my body," Mikk said huskily. "They've kidnapped my freedom." He looked up and some of his tears were blue with the ink from the letter. "I go into that courtroom every day and their henchmen gleefully carve up my character like so much swine flesh. This power you say I have has done nothing to spare me this injustice."

"Wait and see. Maybe a groundswell in your favor is on the horizon."

Mikk grinned shakily. "Don't tell me *you* are having premonitions."

"I must be spending too much time around Vyzanian performance masters. I've given up wondering what's going on. I actually offered to share my bed with Aro last night."

Mikk's melancholy returned, but it was darker, quieter, steely with anger on Aro's behalf, and, at that moment, he looked much stronger. "The Ev-Mobiks are after him, aren't they?" he whispered.

"How did you know? They put out one of his eyes."

Mikk's reaction to the news was shocking. He hissed, body curled like a cornered jaguar's, eyes flaring violet-pink in the darkness of the cell. He snatched up the stool next to the washbasin and with one blow smashed it to kindling against the wall.

Bipti sprang out of the shadows and roughly shoved aside Martin, who fell.

"Mikk-sir, please! Don't do that! The Kekoi will be angry."

"Leave him alone!" Martin said, picking himself up off the floor. There was something magnificent about Mikk's rage. It quickened Martin's adrenaline. "If he wants to wreck the jail, let him! What difference does it make?"

"You don't understand!" Bipti wailed. "They'll take it out on me, not Master Mikk!"

But Mikk's fit of violence was already over. He leaned on the washbasin and his arms and hands trembled.

"He's right, Martin," he whispered. "Perhaps you should go."

"If that's what you want." Martin brushed off his coat. Odd. He thought he'd brought a spare tin of caviar, not just the one he'd slipped to Mikk, but he didn't feel it. No use worrying about it now, though. The Freen was watching. He pointed to the fallen letter in the middle of the cell. "Don't forget the letter. That young fan is duplicated all over the galaxy. You have got to hang on!"

He limped down the corridor, stopping now and then to curse and massage his knee.

When Martin was gone, Mikk retrieved Hom's letter and reread it. Then he folded the fine paper very small, pulled the empty salt pendant from under his surprise tunic, and put the letter inside. He turned his face to the wall.

"Mikk-sir?"

"Don't talk to me, Bipti."

"But . . ."

"Not—a—word."

Bipti withdrew to his corner and sat down—on something smooth, round, and cold. He picked it up and turned it over in his blunt hands, his double eyelids flicking back and forth rapidly.

On the black lid of the little metal box were a beautiful pink and silver image of a water creature and strange spiky letters in gold. Native or outworld, the words were meaningless to Bipti, but he tucked the tin in his belt anyway.

Entr'acte: The Fourth Day

After all that juicy pulp about Mikk's sexual misadventures with Ahva and Oo-aika, Martin knew the broadsides this morning would be special, salacious beyond his worst intoxicant-addled college nightmares. The security dogs would have to roll in by the caravan load to break up the rioting.

However, when the dawn light filtered through the slatted

shades of his room and woke him, all Martin could hear were the morning birds and the comfortable snuffles and snorts of his sleeping roommates. Alarmed, he dressed hurriedly and practically tore the shades from their fixtures.

There was indeed a mob, of hundreds, but they were silent and hovered at a distance around the only—the only—piece of paper plastered to the courthouse wall. Incredibly, every broadside of the previous days had been removed. The fences and masonry were bare except for this one image, which Martin could not make out at this distance. He stumbled down the stairs, tucking in his shirt, and trotted across the square.

The picture was a large still shot of Mikk and Thissizz entwined in a duet. It was a close-up, and the expression in their faces, especially their eyes, was clearly visible.

Martin felt the hair on his neck rise. There was something there, something he recognized in his bones but could not name because, in spite of the recognition, he had never seen it before. Anywhere. Not even his aunt and late uncle, the most incorrigible romantics he'd ever met, had shared such light. It wasn't just love, it was—music! Physical and emotional music.

"Someone put it up late last night."

Raf stood at his side, furry hands on his off-angled hips. He munched a bantroot.

"But where are the broadsides?" Martin asked. Raf took the twig from his mouth.

"There are some things," he said quietly, "that even we will not touch."

"I don't understand."

"It isn't something you understand. It's something you feel."

Martin studied the picture again. "Why aren't Thissizz's wives jealous?" he asked.

"Look at their eyes, Terran," Raf said. "Are *you* threatened? Or inspired? Think about it." He turned away and started a zigzag path back to the jail.

"Come by after the morning session. The master could use some more outworld 'support,' if you know what I mean."

But before Raf reached the jail, he became rigid and his ears cocked forward. Creeping around the gutter beneath the courtroom wall was that damned coney again, and, for a moment, the bail-iff looked as though he was fighting the instinct to chase it. He shuddered, even whined a little, and the coney bolted, disappearing under some rotting roots abandoned by a produce vendor days before.

Raf shook his ruff, scratched his ragged ears as though they alone were the source of his agitation, and continued toward the jail.

It was a short session. The Lambdan tribune, a young actor, gold-skinned, gold-haired, handsome and very aware of it, began with much the same points his fellow tribunes had touched upon in much the same words. Mikk answered curtly, which Martin knew was the performance master's restrained way of registering disdain. The Lambdan, however, seemed to interpret it as jealousy and preened, checking his hair, the fall of his transparent body suit, the condition of his fingernails.

"Come on, Mikk," he said, "your stubbornness will make it hard on all performers. Can't you see the signs of the times? The crackdowns, the increase in the tithe. They've got us and we might as well accept it. If you back down now, maybe they'll be lenient and sentence you to exile. It's simply not worth it."

"If it's worth it to the Council to punish the performance of a ballad by exiling the singer," Mikk said coolly, "then I think it's worth it to put up a fight. Obviously, it's already become hard on us, tribune."

"It could become much worse."

"Tribune, I live three times longer than you. Not much is worse than exile for life."

The Lambdan seemed pleased by this reference to Mikk's antiquity, although the performance master did not look any older than he did. The actor threw back his shoulders and stretched, the better to display his youthful physique.

"What about death?" he asked.

"They already have that one on the books," Mikk said, "or have you forgotten?"

"The Council could pardon you."

"You think so, tribune? I'm a performer. I'm here because I

performed. If they pardon me, I'll perform again. And again! Don't waste our time talking about a pardon. I'm condemned or I'm vindicated. You know that as well as I do."

"What about the promise you made to the Somalites?"

"We've already been over this!"

Careful, Mikk, Martin pleaded silently. Don't lose control.

"The promise was voided by the acclaim given the Kekoi jester. Perhaps you know something about my sense of hearing, tribune. I guarantee you it is no pleasure to hear that many dead knocking from their graves."

"You may have misinterpreted what you heard, Mikk," the tribune said. "The Somalites were a very spiritual people. The ban may have been a way to test your soul, and what you heard were the doors of paradise being slammed against you."

"Dear gods, tribune!" Mikk said with convincing wonder. "Where does a porno star from Lambda 5 get such an evangelical spirit?"

"Porno star!" the tribune spluttered, spittle sticking to his dimpled chin. "I'll give you pornography, you Vyzanian pedophile . . ."

"Call me that again," Mikk interrupted softly, "and, so help me, I won't care about another galactic crime."

In the dead hush that followed, the Borovfian's methane tank gurgled feebly, the only sound. The arctic menace in Mikk's voice seemed to have arrested the air and suspended the act of breathing for every person in the courtroom. The Lambdan, whose golden features had suddenly tarnished, quaked as though the performance master was a Mandan bush predator that would tear him apart if he as much as blinked.

Pairip cleared his throat, loudly, and rang the bell around his neck.

"We will recess for three hours," he said, then quickly muttered to Raf. "Get Mikk back into the cell immediately. Tell Fod to keep close and have his weapon ready."

"But, sir, I don't think—"

"Do it! The master's angrier than I've ever seen him and he has a Gold Wing in H'n N'kae personal warfare."

Martin didn't know what that meant even though Pairip had spoken in Belian, but the bailiff's jaw dropped.

"Are you serious?" Raf whispered. "We've been joking with him in the hallways! We even took the loop off so he'd be more comfortable."

"Well, don't do it again! Now, get him out of here."

Raf, a bewildered Korl, and Fod, remarkably sober and professional now that he had his firearm drawn, escorted the performance master back to his chilly gated cell. Mikk made no aggressive moves whatsoever in spite of his dark mood, but they watched him anxiously and continued to loiter outside the energy gate after safely locking him up.

"Have I grown a beard or something?" Mikk growled. "You're gaping like pond spawn! I'd prefer to be left relatively alone, if you don't mind."

The guards retreated and Fod cautiously took his place outside the unhappy performance master's cell.

"What's with the guards?" Martin asked when he arrived two hours later. "The way they looked at me when I asked to see you, you'd have thought I'd volunteered to swim in a tank full of crocodiles." He glanced at Fod, who was squashed against the wall as if trying to meld his black bulk into the gray of the stone.

"I don't know." Mikk hugged his knees as he sat on the pallet. It was especially frigid in the cell that day, and Martin produced his one bit of good news: a rough brown hair blanket, which he pushed through the meal slot.

"It's a saddle blanket," he said. "That's all I could find."

The depth of gratitude in Mikk's eyes affected Martin curiously. He almost wept, something he hadn't done since he was fourteen years old and a young girl had smiled at him. Mikk wrapped the blanket around his shoulders, and Martin got as close to the energy gate as he dared. "I went back to my room to get more caviar," he whispered, "but someone broke in during the morning session and took every tin. None of my roommates saw anything. They slept right through it!"

Mikk stroked the blanket and nodded as if he'd expected this news for some time. "What about the media?" he asked. "What are they saying?"

Martin wanted to bark back that he considered the lost caviar much more important to Mikk's well-being than any meddling press hounds, then remembered Fod and bit his tongue. What if the reason he'd been robbed was because one of the under-guards actually understood English? He hadn't considered that before.

"Um, the press is seriously divided, Mikk. It's impossible to get a handle on opinion one way or the other." He shrugged. "In any case, everyone has forgotten about those damned elections. The candidates have been debating each other personally on the opti-tubes, and no one is watching."

Mikk's eyes glittered steadily from the shadows. "I'm not going to be vindicated, am I, Martin?"

"I honestly can't say. The longer this drags on, the quieter people get. I'm sure you've noticed. They're not laughing in the galleries anymore."

Mikk rested his head back against the masonry, and Martin was shocked by how lean the performance master looked, even for him. Those first Kekoi broadsides had not been far from the mark. Stress had sucked in Mikk's skin and made the tendons and veins in his neck stand out too prominently.

"I'm tired, Martin. Confinement is affecting my senses. I can't trust them anymore. I'm having trouble anticipating the line of argument and reading people's behavior. I can't, I can't even see . . ." He lost the end of his sentence.

"I know. I wish I could help. I feel useless here. Are you sure we can't get other levels of galactic authority involved?"

"It would cause more trouble than it's worth. You help consid-erably just by visiting me."

"I tried to visit Thissizz, too. That and the break-in are why I'm late."

"You're not late."

"They wouldn't let me see him. Something about tampering with a tribunal."

"Oh, Martin . . ."

"Damn it, Mikk! Thissizz is next! What does he think he's

doing up there? Maybe they threatened him somehow to force him to be a tribune, but his silence isn't helping you at all!" Unable to beat his fist on the burning gate, Martin kicked his heel on the floor instead. "Why doesn't he say something? I thought he loved you!"

Mikk was silent. His eyes, although pale, were blind, dull, focussed on nothing, and Martin realized the performance master had asked himself these same questions many times and could not answer them. Or maybe, on some level, his pleas had reached the Droos—and been refused.

"Forgive me, Mikk, but I saw something in a still shot that I didn't understand. You and Thissizz. It's . . . I don't have a name for it."

"The Droos do," Mikk whispered. " 'Serassi.' It means 'heart twin.' Briin says that when Thissizz and I are asleep, we breathe in unison."

Martin stared at the performance master. "If you aren't vindicated," he snarled, "I'm going to make sure those bastards pay and pay dearly."

"Martin, don't—"

"Forget it, Mikk! It's all or nothing now. I've had it with the Council."

He hurried out of the jail before Mikk could say anything to stop him.

Chapter Thirty-five: The Election Games

When he reunited with Thissizz for the Kekoi Election Games, Mikk told him and Maya about his adventures on the luxury cruiser, but did not discuss the ban. Since Maya was there when

Mikk first learned of the ban, Thissizz went to her for details, but she was almost as tight-lipped as the performance master.

"Bad things," she muttered.

The Droos sensed as much by the half-articulated burning in his nerves. At night, when the Kekoi moons spotlit them in their warm, entangled embrace on the floor of their simple quarters above the market square, Thissizz tried to get his friend to unburden himself. "There's a terrible shadow in your heart, Mikk. Let me lighten it."

Mikk turned his face away, but the Droos curled his tongue under his friend's chin and gently forced him to look at him. "Please?"

Mikk's moon-frosted eyes clouded with grief. "Oh, Thissizz!" he whispered, almost the whisper of his childhood. "Why wasn't I born a Droos?"

"Don't wish for that. You are exactly what you are supposed to be and I wouldn't have you any other way. Would you want me to be Vyzanian?"

"No! You are much too splendid a creature as you are. Forgive me."

"You degrade yourself when you think you don't give me as much as I give you." Thissizz's head dipped close to Mikk's, almost touching. "You give me more. You give me the rest of myself. When you're not with me, I think of you to remain steady. You lift me above myself just as I give you a place to land."

Thissizz worked his body around his friend's and curled the tip of his coils around Mikk's ankle.

"I love all of my wives, all of my children, every one of my friends," he murmured, "but you are the flame at the base of my heart. I knew, from the first instant I saw you, I knew. That shy, slender red-haired boy was mine and I was his."

Thissizz felt his friend's breath catch and he licked the wet red eyelashes.

"It isn't healthy, serassi. You must share this with me."

"Seven million souls!" Mikk cried. "Lost!"

"Let it pass," Thissizz urged. "There is nothing you could have done."

"I wish I had never gone there as an apprentice! I wish I had never learned their songdance! It beats in my brain every minute of the day trying to get out. Forget? How can I forget? I'm Vyzanian!"

Thissizz shifted his scales so they massaged Mikk's skin from shoulder to hip. "Do not lose heart, my friend. We will face everything together."

Mikk rested his hand on the Droos' head. "I'm frightened, Thissizz. This pain will never end."

"*We* will never end! Songdance is a great and noble art, but mine is not a pure and noble soul. If I had to choose between the loss of songdance and the loss of my beautiful friend . . ."

"Please, Thissizz. Don't say any more . . ."

"I must, serassi. You are too important to me. Listen, I'm going to whisper a story in your ear."

The silver light in Mikk's eyes jumped.

Still a child, Thissizz thought tenderly. You love stories.

"I remember a day many years ago when I was a small pup, a baby. I was chasing my tail when suddenly I was filled with a wonderful white blaze of intense longing. I didn't know what to do with myself. I couldn't eat, I couldn't sleep. I cried all day and into the night because I couldn't contain this inexplicable joy." He kissed Mikk's ear.

"I recently found out why that day was so special," he said. "Do *you* know why, my beautiful friend?"

Mikk shook his head.

"That day was the day you were born."

Mikk gazed at the Droos with shining eyes.

"Don't ever turn away from me, Thissizz. Whatever happens . . ."

"Never, my beautiful one. Never."

The performance master sighed raggedly. " 'Lie with me when the wind has died,' " he murmured, quoting Brock-ell, " 'And listen to the nine drums beat . . .' "

Thissizz lay his head on Mikk's chest and listened to him sob instead.

The Kekoi Elections were an outdoor festival. Every morning, Mikk and Thissizz joined the other performers, most of them native Kekoi, in the market square of the capital city for the dusty drum and bell procession out of town, up through the trees and granite passes, to the Place of the Hairy Heart, the windy natural amphitheater where the "Games" took place. As the performers marched by, prosperous burghers, well brushed and attired in costly but conservative quilted jackets and trousers, and scruffy-furred gypsies in thick boots, jingling jewelry, and gaudily patched vests and wide pantaloons lined the footpath to cheer them on. Vendors cried out from booths and tents where they sold everything from hot food to wooden toys, inflammatory fly-by-night newspapers, astrological forecasts, and reeded noisemakers that sounded like bleating goats. Splinter pods of unofficial entertainers amused the crowds with puppet shows and stilt-walking acrobatics, and the smoke from roasting meats hung thick and pungent in the treetops long before the sun had made it over the towers of the city below.

Every day there was a fistfight, every day the security dogs with their Belian stun pistols carted away the more belligerent partisans, and every day the Kekoi pups nearly shredded Mikk's surprise tunic with their clawlike nails before he got to the roped-off performance circle.

"Maya sick mend tunic," the cephalopod grumbled. "Make Mikk sew holes." But she dutifully threaded her three needles.

On the fourth day of the seventh round of the Kekoi Elections, Mikk and his cohorts were laughing and jeering from the sidelines as their opposing number extolled the virtues of their candidate in a series of allegorical scenes in which one Kekoi, dressed as the hopeful politician, vanquished all manner of sociopolitical ills in the form of papier-mâché monsters animated by other performers. Heckling was sanctioned at the Kekoi Elections, and Mikk indulged himself in the rare, wicked pleasure of bad etiquette.

"Even a child wouldn't believe this rot!" he cried, and the lead Kekoi threw him an obscene gesture. Mikk laughed then began to imitate the Kekoi's posturing.

"No fair!" the fuzzy jester cried. "It's not his turn!"

"He's not in the performance circle," one of Mikk's partners said, "and none of it is his material. He's copying you!"

"No, he isn't! He's *mocking* me."

"Just get on with your scene," Mikk said. "Didn't anyone ever tell you to ignore hecklers? For the gods' sake, at least act like a professional!"

The Kekoi shook his fist at the performance master. "It'll be your turn soon!"

"I'm looking forward to it!"

Thissizz, who had gone to fetch refreshments, returned with a small skin bag—and three Kekoi pups clinging to his tail. They promptly abandoned their reptilian transport and attacked the surprise tunic.

"Squash fruit," he said as Mikk took the pouch. "They were out of frozen berries."

"The Games must be very popular this year." Deliberately ignoring the pups, Mikk bit into one of the juicy red fruit and handed another to Thissizz, who swallowed it whole.

"It's because of you, my friend."

"Don't be absurd!"

"How are we doing?"

"Not bad." Mikk tried to catch some juice that trickled down his chin, but Thissizz licked it away for him. The pups ran off with their toys. "I've shaken up this jester pretty thoroughly. Put him off his form. If Aro is anywhere near as easy to fluster . . ."

"He always is . . ."

". . . we should look quite good tomorrow in comparison."

Thissizz gave Mikk a quick peck on the ear, pleased to see his friend enjoying himself. No one on Kekoi Kaery had mentioned the ban, not even the media, certainly a welcome respite for the beleaguered performance master, but a bit odd considering Kekoi outspokenness. Thissizz supposed the ban had so offended their hosts that they had agreed, for Mikk's sake, not to bring it up. This kind of pack consensus prevented unrest. Without it, Thissizz had a feeling the security dogs would be carrying weapons more serious than stun pistols.

At last the scenes were over, and Mikk and the other performers applauded heartily. After all, in a couple of days they might end up on the same side. The jester Mikk had hectored waved to the performance master and shuffled off.

"What is Aro going to do?" Thissizz asked.

"I have no idea, but our spies think he'll present more material in praise of his candidate's virtues."

"I wish they'd get back to the satire," the Droos sighed. "It's much more fun."

The burly, tawny-furred young male strode into the performance circle and Mikk's partners hooted and chanted in a guttural, childish singsong:

> Aro, Aro, wider than a barrow!
> Tried to dance, tore his pants
> And all could see his bare-oh!

"You pick on me more than anyone else!" the young jester cried.

"Naturally," Mikk said sweetly. "You're a rookie. It's a rite of passage."

"Enough is enough! I know you, Mikk of Vyzania! You're the worst of them! All smiles and soft words, then yow! Just like a scorpion!"

"I'm not doing anything, puppy."

"Stop calling me puppy! I'm a grown dog!"

"Yes, that's true," Mikk said soberly. "It's unfair of me to belittle a colleague. You're fully licensed now, aren't you?"

"Damn right, I am!"

"Don't be angry, Aro. I promise I won't tease you anymore."

"I don't trust your promises."

"Then let's join hands on it, in Kekoi fellowship. What do you say?"

Aro hesitated, twitched his ears, then shrugged. He approached Mikk and they clasped each other's forearms.

"Swear," Aro said.

"Oops, just a minute," Mikk said, letting go. "I need to get rid of these first." Out of his sleeve he pulled Aro's underknickers, discreetly snatched the moment the jester got close enough to Mikk's magician fingers. The performance master tossed them to his howling comrades, and they waved them over their heads like a flag.

"You are pipgip shit," Aro growled softly.

"Oh, Aro!" Mikk laughed. "What did you expect? It's the Election Games! Surely you have some mischief in store for me as well."

The jester's brown eyes narrowed.

"Do your worst," Mikk said. "I'm ready."

At least, he thought he was, but the sudden half vertigo that swept up his shoulders, passed through his neck, and swam in his ears told him something wasn't right. Aro gave him a hard, canine grimace, and Mikk realized that the Kekoi was angrier than he had intended to make him, possibly too upset to accept an apology, and, before he could give him one, the jester faced the crowd. He brushed some straw from his sleeves, closed his eyes, and took up a familiar stance that caused Mikk to drop his piece of squash fruit. As the horrified performance master watched, Aro swayed to the left and began a Somalite song-dance ballad in praise of a wise man, ostensibly his candidate. A ballad penned by Whees-aru.

"What the Beast does he think he's doing?" cried a gold-toothed gypsy goodwife from the lower terraces. "We swore an oath! He's going to ruin everything!"

The Kekoi crowding the dirt sides of the amphitheater began to draw together in growling displeasure, and the security dogs trotted down the hills, unlocking the safeties on their stun pistols as they came. Someone threw a roasted root at Aro and soon half-chewed knuckle bones and squash fruit pits pelted the dust at the jester's feet.

Mikk himself might have leapt into the ring and throttled Aro for his insolence if the jester's performance hadn't been woefully inadequate. Aro was not breathing properly, his balance was off, and his singing had a pronounced nasal whine that, to Mikk's ears, sounded as close to a Somalite half whistle as a rusty hinge. He shuddered.

"Easy, my friend." Thissizz slipped a restraining coil around Mikk's thigh. "It's nothing. A case of very poor manners." But Mikk wasn't listening. He stared at the Kekoi jester the way he would stare at a baby who had suddenly croaked out an obscenity.

"He can't possibly expect anyone to accept that," he said through his teeth. "It's horrific! They'll hoot him out of the grounds."

The security dogs apparently expected much worse and put on their black and gold riot helmets, but just as the crowd seemed ready to transform into a mob, the tumult died away. People with their arms cocked, ready to hurl edible missiles at the singing jester, relaxed and ate their weapons instead. The Place of the Hairy Heart became quiet.

Mikk knew what had happened. Even bastardized, songdance had considerable power. He had once seen a Somalite child put a pet marmot to sleep by singing the refrain to an evening prayer without any of the requisite movements at all. Still, it wasn't proper songdance. Neither was this, but Aro's ballad had persisted long enough to charm the crowd in spite of its mediocrity. When the jester finished, they gave him loud, long—and sincere— applause.

Smiling from pointy ear to pointy ear, Aro skipped around the circle to accept this tribute, but stumbled when he saw Mikk. The Kekoi hunched in his shoulders, grinned, and laid his ears back in submission, but Mikk's grim demeanor did not change. Aro backed away, blew one last kiss to the crowd, and hopped over the rope, out of the ring.

"Mikk, please. Don't do it."

"You saw what happened, Thissizz." It was a much cooler night, and the moonlight through the shutters was watery and broke unevenly over the silk of Mikk's tunic as he paced the floor. "They applauded, and not because they thought it was funny."

"They don't understand. They don't know any better."

"Exactly!" Mikk furiously confronted his friend. "They don't know better! They think what they saw was authentic Somalite material the way it was meant to be!"

The tip of Thissizz's coils briefly knotted itself. "Mikk . . ."

"Well, it wasn't." Mikk's darkened eyes began to tear. "It was a travesty. This isn't what the Somalites wanted. They wanted a true songdance or nothing at all!"

"The Somalites didn't love you!" Thissizz cried, and the sharpness of his sudden anguish stung Mikk. "The gods' curse on that terrible promise! *I* love you and I-I not you see h-hurt again!"

Mikk quickly put his hands on his friend's face in an effort to console him. "Please understand," he said tenderly. "I have to. I can't submit to this ban another minute. It'll eat away my life."

"Your life! Take away your life they, they mustn't!"

"Thissizz, please listen to me! This struggle *is* my life! The ban—it's like everything else: the false words, the fear, *the basket.*" He massaged Thissizz's slick eyelids. Their common pain burned all over, but especially the eyes. His own had to be pure ink.

"I must be free, serassi. An actor *acts*. He does not sit by and do nothing."

Thissizz shook his head and pulled away.

"Thissizz!" Mikk reached for his friend, but the Droos swung his body around and hissed. His hood flared, then crunched together in a tight wrinkled mass along his spine.

"No, Mikk! Too far this time! My heart tears away!" He stifled a furious sob. "Watch you hurt again! Can't! Sacrifice you, sacrifice *me*!"

"Thissizz! Please! Wait!"

But Thissizz couldn't. Eyes averted, the grieving Droos hurried out of the performance master's room, his coils rippling irregularly behind him.

Mikk gazed at the empty space where his friend had been. A satellite pod of jesters passed in the street below with a crowd of revellers in their wake, and their cheerful shouts and laughter seemed to mock the performance master.

"Gods of the st-stars," he stuttered. "It's f-freezing."

He looked at the empty space again and tried to will a Droos where there was no Droos. He marked out a tight circle, walked it three times, then sat on the floor. The jesters were gone now and the room was quiet.

"What have I done?"

Chapter Thirty-six: Arrest

In the morning, Maya trimmed Mikk's hair but, contrary to her usual practice, did not give him the morning gossip. Thissizz had not appeared at breakfast, and the glassy transparency in Mikk's eyes, the unfamiliar rigidity in his shoulders, frightened the usually fearless cephalopod; she dreaded what kind of altered sounds would issue from his throat if he spoke to her. Mikk spared her that trauma by saying nothing from the time he rose to the time he left for the day's performances. When he was gone, Maya packed away her shears and sponges, folded Mikk's clothing, and tidied his chamber. It calmed her.

Thissizz was still missing when the "army" counted up its number for the new round.

"What happened to your friend?" they asked Mikk.

"He's not feeling well," he replied. "He . . . may not come."

"That's bad," said the master jester, a deep brown individual with especially heavy chin fur. "We were counting on his satiric song cycle to really tangle their hair."

Mikk fingered the embroidery on one of his pockets. "I doubt after today it'll matter much," he said.

"What's gotten into you? You look gray. Are you sure you're not unwell yourself?"

"I'll be up for the festivities, I assure you."

The sun came out, the banners snapped open in the wind, the vendors hoisted the awnings over their stalls, and the fifth day, seventh round of the Kekoi Elections began. The performance ring was swept, the ropes tightened, and the souvenir hawkers put new cock feathers in their soft hats. Everything was back to normal, as though Aro's indiscretion had never happened.

Everything except the children. When the performance master climbed the hill with the others, the pups hid behind their parents and would not come out. At the ring, Mikk stood with his arms folded across his chest, eyes on the ground while his colleagues pranced and paraded and savaged the claims made the previous day by the opposition. The brightness of the sky, the color of the carnival, and the low comedy of the jesters did not penetrate the performance master's mood, and, in spite of his surprise tunic, none of the young ones touched him or came close.

"I don't understand," one baffled mother said. "It's Master Mikk, puppy. Don't you want a surprise?" The pup shook her head.

"He's not playing."

"Not playing?"

The pup buried her face in her mother's skirts. "I want to go home."

Mikk's partners finished their political ribaldry and cartwheeled out of the circle, and he unfolded his arms and stepped over the rope. The crowd greeted him boisterously, but, after a minute during which the performance master remained still and did nothing, the noise died down, replaced by nervous mumbles. Mikk caught the eye of Aro, who sat on an empty barrel munching some roast fowl, and the jester's face fell. The hand with the ragged drumstick hung in the air, lost on its way to his mouth.

Mikk took the meditation stance, breathed deeply a few times, and began to perform the same ballad Aro had performed the day before.

When the audience realized what Mikk was doing, they called to him to stop.

"No, Master Mikk!"

"What are you doing, you fool?"

"For the love of the gods . . . !"

But Mikk ignored them and soon the beauty of the movement consciousness subdued them, enveloping them in the Somalite music of the spheres. Freed of the strain of suppressing what was constantly on his mind, Mikk gave a performance straight from his soul. His body embraced songdance the way it embraced Thissizz after a long absence and he undulated as delicately as an underwater plant, as sinuous as a Vonchoi rock adder. His voice curled around the people's faces, licked their ears, and floated away on the wind, a visitation from another, higher reality. His heart and mind lifted themselves above the crowd to dance in the smoke, and, for one hallucinatory moment, Hom was there, holding his hands, telling him again "everything he knew," but the words were strange, altered:

> *"When you sing, launch the bird. When you dance, love the Droos. When you play music, pour the flames, and, when you act, laugh at god."*
> *"But, Hom. I'm not acting."*
> *"Of course you are, silly! This is an act of willfulness."*
> *"Thissizz?"*
> *"You are releasing a very great anger."*
> *"Whees-aru?"*
> *"Hush, lad. Of course you want to terrify people. Make them tremble all the way to the depths of their souls."*
> *"Master Huud?"*

But the vision faded and Mikk could no longer see who had spoken. He had reached the middle of his performance, the peak of its emotional intensity, and had lost all sense of who or what he was. His mind fell silent. He continued to dance and sing—in fact he saw his performance as though he moved around himself in invisible camspecs, a performance of chilling, otherworldly perfection—but his consciousness had evaporated, leaving behind a diamond-pure emptiness. Mikk was out of himself, nothing, nowhere.

He recognized the invitation. The line was well drawn and he saw both sides with the dispassionate clarity of an angel. There was nowhere else to go. It was time to choose.

He did not cross. At the final instant, with his soul wavering like a leaf over the lip of a pond, he declined. Whatever lay on the other side, he knew it would not appease his restlessness. It was too pure. If it was not death, it was also not life, at least not for him, and Mikk turned his back on it. He returned to the pungent smells of hay and dust and sweat and manure, the vital cries of the crowd at the conclusion of the ballad. The divine ice melted from his eyes, and they met the large black orbs of his dearest friend, who swayed far up behind the Kekoi. Thissizz's great, lonely eyes stayed on Mikk until several helmeted security dogs surrounded the performance master and shackled his wrists behind him. Then the Droos lowered his head and was lost in the roiling anonymity of the crowd.

"I'm sorry, Mikk," the tallest dog said. "You know I have to do this."

"Yes." Mikk spoke languidly, distantly. "Of course."

The crowd, not yet free of the spell of Mikk's performance, protested loudly at his arrest and, once again, threatened to become violent.

"Don't touch him, you beasts!"

"Let him go! He's the voice of god!"

"No, I'm not," Mikk said. "Please. Let us pass."

Aro wrestled through the masses toward Mikk. "Mikk! Blessed stars, Master Mikk, please!" he cried. The performance master, now being led away, stopped and looked at the Kekoi with a mildness that only anguished the jester further.

"It was a joke!" Aro sobbed. "A wicked, vicious joke! I never thought . . . !"

"Control yourself, Aro," Mikk said. "It was bound to happen sooner or later. Don't blame yourself for the action I now take." A shadow of distress flitted across his face.

"Please ask Maya to take care of my things. I don't want anyone to touch anything."

"Yes, all right," the jester sniffed. "She'll eat them alive."

The security dogs marched Mikk briskly down the hill, a river of people licking at their heels. The crowd followed them into the city, across the market square, and washed up onto the steps of the courthouse. There, Mikk was separated from them and taken inside.

With nothing better to do, the mob chanted outside the jail and set six bins of vegetable peelings on fire. The security dogs used sonic whistles to clear the streets, very effective on the Kekoi's sensitive canine hearing—and on Mikk's as well. Although Raf, too, was suffering, he muffled the performance master's ears by embracing his head in his furry arms. He had to stop Mikk's screams before they broke all the windows in the courthouse.

Entr'acte: Thissizz's Questions

Gapi had told her not to, that the tribunal was "unhappy" and for "grown people only," but Iki had to find out what was happening to the Pocket Man. While her Gapi took his nap—she could hear the slow, sad moan of his snore from the dark cave of his bedchamber—she tiptoed on scabby feet into his cool, silent office with its polyglass cases of strange scrolls, instruments, and boxes of colored lights. She tapped on the optitube and scooted up close so she wouldn't have to raise the volume above a murmur. The image of the Kekoi courtroom blossomed on the screen.

Iki jumped guiltily and glanced behind her. Gapi's coelenterate assistant was in the doorway, his body waving gently as though he were under water. She expected him to rush off to tell Gapi about her misbehavior, but he didn't. After watching her a moment, still swaying benignly, the light from the hall a diffused yellow-green as it passed through the membranes of his vitreous body, he hop-sucked into the office and stood quietly next to her.

They watched the session together.

When Mikk returned to the courtroom with his trio of wary Kekoi guards, his agitation showed in spite of what must have been heroic efforts to appear as calm and ready as always. His eyes were an unstable purple and he clasped his hands together so tightly when Thissizz rose from his coiled position that his fingertips turned pink. Martin leaned forward to get a better view. The Droos blinked, but seemed detached, even indifferent.

"Mikk," he said, and at the sound of his friend's melodious voice, the performance master trembled slightly, "my fellow tribunes have made much of the unfortunate incidents on Ev-Mobix 'Gar and Belia, using them as examples of your chronic recalcitrance, your moral degeneracy, and your potential threat to the well-being of children."

He doesn't sound natural, Martin thought. This isn't a lover's vocabulary.

"That appears to be the case . . . tribune," Mikk said carefully. "I disagree with their conclusions and characterizations, but I do not claim to be perfect."

"No." Thissizz brought some of his coils around front and wrapped them in close. "That would be foolish. I believe you have been 'imperfect' in this manner more than once."

The shock in the performance master's face had to be genuine. Martin didn't care how skilled an actor Mikk was: no one could fake that kind of intense visceral pain.

"In what instance, tribune?" The startle pigment fluctuated wildly in his eyes.

"Did you invent your surprise tunic on Spaira to entertain the Spairan children?"

"Yes, but—"

"Spairans? Counsel 6 will forgive me, but aren't Spairans devoid of humor and a sense of play?"

"Yes. If I may speak—"

"Didn't your master, Huud Maroc, advise you *strongly* against attempting to amuse the Spairan children?"

"Yes, please—" Mikk was really trembling now, and the Freen next to Martin began to quiver in bioelectric sympathy.

"Huud Maroc, the greatest performer of his generation, warned you not to use your surprise tunic with the Spairan children?"

"Yes."

"But what happened, Mikk?" Thissizz asked. "Did you take his advice?"

"No."

"I see." The Droos gently rocked his head as though working out a kink. "You went against the advice of a seasoned and acclaimed professional and performed for the Spairan children in your surprise tunic."

"Yes! Damn it . . ."

"Were they amused?"

"No," Mikk sighed. "They were politely confused, but, no, they were not amused."

"So, since your surprise tunic was a failure, did you abandon this invention?"

"No. As you can see," he added with a small smile, "I'm wearing it now."

"My, yes! Such stubbornness!" Thissizz nodded toward the gallery, but nobody laughed. "Tell me—if the Spairan children had been hostile rather than confused, would you have given up your tunic?"

"No."

Martin squinted. Something was happening, but he was not sure what. These questions were headed somewhere very specific.

"Why not?" Thissizz asked.

"I thought children on other worlds might enjoy the tunic even if the Spairans did not."

"But how could you be sure? One of those worlds might have put a ban on your tunic or executed you outright for offending them with such childish nonsense. Wouldn't it have been safer to drop the whole idea, as, no doubt, Master Huud suggested?"

Ah-ha! Martin smiled to himself. I think I know where you're going.

"Master Huud did *not* suggest it," Mikk said, "but, yes, it would have been safer and I would have been a poorer artist for it."

"How do you mean?"

Mikk was still struggling to hold himself together, but this question appeared to steady him with its appeal to a more intellectual response. "Art is not static," he said. "It dies without innovation."

My God! Martin thought. Almost my own words . . .

"Some inventions work, some don't, but invention must continue. Change is part of anything living."

"Art is a living thing?"

"Most definitely."

"But what a dangerous and unseemly living thing this surprise tunic is!" Thissizz flipped the edges of his hood as though ridding himself of an irritating dust. "All those children pawing over you in their greed, some of whom have claws. What abominable behavior you encourage! Not to mention the real risk that you could be injured."

"It's a risk I accept willingly."

He's shaking too much, Martin thought. He's too upset to see what Thissizz is doing.

"Then art is not only a living thing but dangerous?"

"Sometimes." Mikk's back straightened. "Sometimes it must be."

"Don't grandstand, Mikk," Thissizz said. "You seem willing to loose a potentially dangerous creation, dangerous *idea*, of dubious merit on the public, apparently without considering either your chances for success or possible tragic consequences."

Mikk's inked eyes were ghastly, as black and shiny as ripe olives. His stagecraft slipped away and the overhead remotes broadcast, in close-up, how weary and gaunt he'd become. Thissizz turned sharply to the High Tribune.

"No more questions." He quickly coiled himself on his cushion.

"Very well. We will—"

"Thissizz," Mikk interrupted, and something in his whisper startled Pairip. The Garplen gestured to the guards, and they edged forward.

"They mean to separate us, but they cannot."

The guards hesitated. Pairip had not yet adjourned the session and, therefore, they did not know whether to secure Mikk against violent behavior or escort him back to his cell. The High Tribune studied the performance master, who, in turn, did not take his eyes from Thissizz, and the courtroom settled into stasis. Martin slowly looked back over his shoulder at the quiet masses in the gallery and was amazed. Not one person was looking at the dais. They either stared at the floor or at each other, voiceless, guilty.

Pairip broke the spell by uttering a sound somewhere between a bass groan and a wheeze. He rang his bell. "We will reconvene tomorrow afternoon."

"Tomorrow afternoon!" cried the Borovfian, losing his mouthpiece. "Why the delay? I move we hear the last questions now and get this over with!"

"Twee," Pairip rumbled, "I have already decided that your claim to honorable membership in an intelligent race is fraudulent and that you lack all taste, generosity, and proper appetite. Don't tempt me to place you any lower on the food chain."

Twee fiddled nervously with his mouthpiece.

"Any more objections?" Pairip asked. "Good. Tomorrow afternoon."

Iki tapped off the optitube and picked at the crust under her nose. She had not understood much of what she had seen, but what she had understood upset her. Her Gapi had been right. The tribunal was "unhappy." She raised her face to the silent see-through person at her side.

"What's your name?" she asked.

The assistant jumped in astonishment.

"It's-it's Ya-yin, little mistress," he said shyly.

Iki got up.

"Will you help me, Mr. Ya-yin?"

"If I can, little mistress."

"I want to send a telewave."

The assistant's polyps danced about in quiet excitement.

"Yes, little mistress!"

Fod was implacable.

"Permission for you to see Master Mikk has been rescinded."

"What?!" Martin cried. "Since when? On whose authority?"

"The Council's."

"*Pairip* is running the tribunal!"

"Doesn't matter. You cannot see Master Mikk."

"There must be some mistake. Where's Raf?"

"He's been reassigned."

Martin smelled conspiracy and his face purpled. "But I must see Mikk!" He tried to push aside the huge Kekoi. "He doesn't understand what Thissizz did!"

"I have my orders." Fod caught Martin in his broad furry hands and easily lifted and set him down outside the jail in the main corridor. "Besides, if I were you I wouldn't want to see the master in his current mood. It wouldn't be safe. Now, be a good Terran and run along home."

"What is the matter with you people?" Martin howled. "Mikk! I know you can hear me! Mikk!"

Fod pressed his palm over Martin's face, silencing him, then tucked the flailing agent under his arm and carried him from the courthouse.

"It's always the little ones, isn't it?" he sighed.

Martin may have lost access to Mikk, but someone new came by that evening who not only had authorization, he had given it to himself. Oplup's immense body eclipsed the portly Korl's outside the energy gate.

"At last!" He smiled at Mikk with deep satisfaction. "You have arrived where you were bound from the beginning."

Mikk, who reclined on the pallet and danced a couple of miniature bolba balls from his surprise tunic over his fingertips, did not even look up.

"I am sure there is much you want to say to me," Oplup said. "Please. Indulge yourself. It doesn't matter anymore. Your career is finished."

Mikk continued to toy with the gold balls and ignore the Councilor.

"I see." Oplup rested his pie-shaped hands on his stomach. He couldn't clasp them; he'd grown too fat for that. "You want to deny me my gloating privileges. Still, while you're meditating, you should ponder this. I can get you out of this cell quite easily. All you have to do is recant and withdraw your challenge. You will be heavily fined, of course, and should you perform against our wishes again you will forfeit everything, even a hearing, and earn a price on your head your own father couldn't resist. But if you behave yourself, you can still be an actor."

Mikk remained silent.

"You have nothing to say to me?"

Mikk kept juggling.

"Fine. You will die, and, frankly, I couldn't care less. I should have known better than to expect generosity of spirit from such a stringy piece of gristle."

Oplup listed about with the drifting, rocking ungainliness of an overladen boat pulling out of a dock, bobbed pneumatically down the line of cells, and was gone.

"Whew!" Korl muttered. "Outworlders stink, don't they?"

"I'm an outworlder, too," Mikk said.

"Oh. Sorry. I forgot."

Korl stroked his chin fur thoughtfully, returned to his post, and sank comfortably on his soft hams. He had another hour or two before Bipti arrived and began to use the time as he always did: he fell asleep.

Mikk dropped one of the bolba balls. He watched it bobble irregularly and roll under the washbasin, then he looked at his hands . . . and their subtle, ominous tremor. His mouth was dry.

Deep in the darkness of the unused cells, something scratched its tiny claws on the stone floor.

Entr'acte: The Final Argument

The response to Thissizz's description of Mikk's surprise tunic as a "creation of dubious merit" vastly exceeded the Droos' hopes. Within hours of the close of the session, children all over the galaxy were telewaving their protests to the court by the thousands. Thissizz had expected this. What he had not expected were the responses from parents, many of whom, shorter-lived than Mikk, had fond memories of begging the performance master for surprises themselves. He also hadn't expected the letters from celebrities, community leaders, and heads of state. The Prime Minister of England on Terra and the Ti-tokan Sultana sent especially moving epistles.

By an unusual stroke of mass cleverness, virtually all of the letters were addressed to Thissizz or Pairip rather than to Mikk, and, since they were tribunes, their mail had to be delivered to them. Pairip roared and stomped all over the floor of diplomatic suites above the courthouse as he tried to escape the Kekoi postmen. Thissizz threw his own letters out the window to the eager media hounds below.

By the time the tribunal reconvened, the court was full of people who had brought their surprises with them, some carefully preserved for decades.

"Free Master Mikk! Free Master Mikk!" they chanted and refused to be silenced by Pairip's all but shaking the clapper out of his bell. When Mikk appeared, the chanting became cheers, and people waved their surprises in the air or tossed their hovering circles. Dozens of them spun in the courtroom and jingled their little melodies.

Mikk was caught completely off guard and, nearly drained of emotional reserves, burst into tears. Thissizz, all of his supposed indifference cast aside like a poorly designed costume, gazed lovingly at the performance master, and Mikk's weeping became laughter. In spite of the chaos, his joy cut through the din, ringing and powerful. The unique silver fire Martin had seen in the still shot flared in Thissizz's eyes and the tip of his coils curled and uncurled with unmistakably erotic excitement.

Heart twins, Martin thought as he saw the same silver ignite Mikk's mercurial irises. I think I understand . . .

The tumult in the courtroom didn't die down until Mikk was in the defendant's circle—and unshackled.

"This is the final session of the Council tribunal regarding Master Mikk and the personal ban on Somalite songdance," Pairip said. "Afterward, the tribunes will be sequestered to meditate on what they have heard and vote either for vindication or condemnation. They will have one day. Now, don't interrupt me! The Council forms clearly specify one day and one day only, regardless of the world on which the tribunal is held. Luckily, a Kekoi day is not unduly abbreviated." He tilted his bulk forward and peered down the line of tribunes.

"You may proceed," he said.

The last tribune, the Spairan, rose to her feet to speak. Compact and elegant with a face as smooth as the inside of a china teacup, Counsel 6 was logical and to the point.

"Mikk of Vyzania, I have watched these proceedings closely and have found the conduct of my fellow tribunes, the people in the galleries, and yourself quite incomprehensible. Perhaps, as a Spairan, I am poorly suited for this kind of trial. However, since I have been appointed a tribune, I will perform my duties to the best of my ability, and, since you have pled guilty, the issue before us is not one of culpability but one of justice, or, as you've suggested, fairness."

Cold, clear, and heartless, Martin concluded. A lawyer's lawyer.

"As is your right, you have invoked Section 1014 of the Council Rules and Regulations Governing Galactic Performance in order to question the validity of the individual ban forbidding you to perform Somalite material. Section 1014, however, provides no protection for someone who has already violated the ban he is questioning. It seems to assume a performer could challenge a ban even while he adheres to it, a not unreasonable assumption. An unjust law needn't be broken to highlight its injustice."

The Spairan crossed her arms stiffly, almost the attitude of a laid-out corpse.

"The Rules is a highly complicated, contradictory body of law," she continued. "It should be recodified and streamlined, but on one point it is clear. The breaking of a Council ban is a high galactic crime. You have admitted committing this high galactic crime, therefore you are subject to the penal statutes of galactic law, which for high crimes are extremely serious. To my eyes, there is no other way to read this situation, and, for that, I am truly sorry."

Are you indeed? Martin wondered. How does a machine register "sorry"?

"I am the only tribune who is not a performer. I was chosen because I am of a class similar to yours—your father is a diplomat and I am government counsel—and because I have expertise in interpreting the law. I may not understand much about your profession, but I do understand that a man who is well regarded in the galaxy may die partly as a result of my work."

The Spairan paused, possibly for breath, but Martin didn't see it. Her arms remained rigidly pinned against her chest.

"Throughout these proceedings, you have trusted in the strength of your beliefs and I have trusted in the strength of mine. You believe that, in spite of breaking the ban, you should be vindicated, and I believe that, in spite of the curiously misbalanced nature of the ban, you should have abided by it until such time as it was deemed invalid. You maintain that this inquiry is about matters of opinion, matters of fairness. Whose opinion? What fairness? Whichever way the ballot goes, the beliefs of one of us will be discredited. Exactly why, Mikk of Vyzania, should you, rather than I, prevail?"

The question hung on the air unanswered, but Martin felt the final argument, the ultimate rebuttal, in the throbbing knot in his throat, the hot, wet sting in his eye. Everything the Spairan had said was true, but it could not account for one undeniable reality: the performance master's very existence. Standing behind the defendant's rail in his surprise tunic, Mikk was his own answer. He and his work could not be explained by law or logic, but his meaning, and the meaning of others like him, was palpable: a recognition of the mystery, beauty, and open boundaries of conscious life. Art had no codifiable "why," but it *was*, all the same.

Would this be enough to save Mikk? How much did a surprise tunic, a dance, or a song weigh against the law?

After Pairip announced it was time for the tribunes' seclusion, Mikk was reshackled and led away.

That night, Martin bought a bottle of powerful Belian brandy, sat on the windowsill to his room, dangled his feet over the square below, and quietly proceeded to double, even triple, the number of stars in the Kekoi sky.

"Get back inside, you stupid Terran!" someone shouted from the street. "You'll kill yourself."

"Fuck you." Martin took another swig. The stars swooped back and forth like indecisive fireflies.

"Hey, Dionysus, where are you?" Martin yawned, then burped. "Don't be a spoilsport just because Vyzanians are immune."

He waved the bottle at the darkness. "Mikk's one of your children!"

"Shut up and go to bed!" came another complaint from the street. Martin ignored it and had some more brandy. It dribbled down his chin and onto his once beautiful coat.

"So many stars, so many worlds . . ."

One of the stars turned out to be a meteor and drew a fine silver line in the darkness over the brooding courthouse.

What can I do? Martin wondered. I'm just a little man. All I do is hover around other people's talent like a moth. Useless. Dionysus probably hates me.

But the god of actors and alcohol, true to his divine capriciousness, took pity on the depressed critic-turned-agent and knocked him out. Martin toppled back off the windowsill into the room. The denning Kekoi never stirred.

Entr'acte: Vision and Whisper

Mikk pumped the lever over the basin in his dark cell until it ripped out of the wall. He beat the spigot with his fists and cursed and wept and begged for the grinding groan of rusty water. Nothing. Not a drop. Another spasm wracked his body and sent an army of invisible fire beetles racing over his skin, burning him with thousands of phantom claws.

"Bipti! For the love of the gods, Bipti!"

At last, the Freen's broad flat feet came slapping along the stone corridor. In one hand Bipti carried a skin jug of water, in the other a small cellulose bag.

"Success, Mikk-sir!" he cried joyfully. "The doctor relented! Look!" He shoved the water under the meal slot and slit open the cellulose bag with his fingernail. "Salt! He even ground it up so you could put it in the water."

The guard set the salt on the floor and Mikk snatched it so quickly through the meal slot that he burned his sleeve on the bottom edge of the energy gate. He wrenched off the skin jug's metal cap, dumped in the salt, and gulped the mixture without taking a breath.

Bipti stepped back from the energy gate, hands pressed against his chest. His inner eyelids blinked slowly, gray curtains over his melancholy eyes.

"Is . . . is that better, sir?"

"Yes." Mikk wiped his forehead with the back of his hand. Why was he sweating? He was still too dehydrated for that. "It will take only a moment or two . . . to . . ."

The basin seemed to jump along the wall and fold back on itself like a wilting flower.

"Mikk-sir?"

The performance master vigorously shook his head but couldn't clear it. A fluid heaviness flooded his limbs, running through his veins like a purified oil that coated and numbed his nerves.

"Mikk-sir? Are you all right?"

"Beast in the pit!" Mikk gasped. "What did they put in the salt?"

The window, the washbasin, the pallet—everything developed rainbow haloes and a delicately undulating animation. The world became soft and pliable, relaxed and twinkling, and his ears filled with static.

"What did they put in the salt!"

"It's just salt, Mikk-sir," Bipti whimpered. He stepped back farther from the gate.

"No! There's some kind of poison in it! I can't . . ."

The shuddering ache of a premonition, magnified many times over, exploded from the small of his back and slammed through his body, nearly dislocating his neck and shoulders.

He laughed. "You poor, miserable little Freen!"

"Sir, you're frightening me . . ."

"What is the meaning of art?"

"Please don't laugh like that!"

"What is the art of meaning?"

Bipti jammed his fingers in his ears, but the laughter still came through.

"*Roochi,* my wretched friend? You'd give me roochi? Ha, ha, ha!"

"Oh, Mikk-sir! Don't go mad on me!" Double streams of tears ran from his eyes.

"Calm yourself, Bipti." Mikk staggered drunkenly up to the

glowing grid. His eyes phosphoresced a lurid acid pink. "How can I hurt you from in here?"

"You're in my head!" the Freen wailed.

"Yes, I think so," Mikk said thoughtfully. "I see everything about you. You sabotaged the heat, you turned off the water, you never did go for salt, did you? You were their spy . . ."

"Be merciful, sir!" Bipti begged. "They have my children!"

Mikk reeled away from the gate and gazed abstractly at the ceiling. It was so close, every imperfection, every bump and pockmark, huge and stark, a landscape of ravines and rocky plateaus stripped clean of life. "Children?" he murmured. "Did you know children are called 'the little gods' because each one reinvents the world?"

Then the world of his cell melted and the performance master collapsed. His limbs beat against the floor for a moment and a line of blood dribbled from his nose. After that, he lay still.

"Gods forgive me!" Bipti sobbed. "I've killed him!"

The Freen covered his face and stumbled into the darkness.

In some time, somewhere, Mikk was poling a canoe on a shallow body of water as still and bright as a lake of mercury. In every direction, mist veiled the horizon. He had no bearings and had nothing to aim for, but he kept poling, inching slowly through the stillness. All he heard was the small drip and ripple as he moved the pole, sought the bottom, pushed ahead, and lifted the pole again. There was no wind, he saw no birds. It had to be the Dormant Season, but this did not feel like his own world. It was a lost place, a dead place.

He stopped the canoe and peered into the fog, but could see nothing. There was nothing to see.

"Master Huud?" he called.

"No," came a whisper from beyond, from every direction. Mikk glanced about nervously.

"Who are you?" he asked.

"You know who I am."

"I cannot see you."

"Of course not. You are inside."

Mikk leaned on the pole to make sure the canoe did not drift.

"You refused," said the whisper. "Why?"

Mikk raked his hand through his hair. He had never expected anyone to ask this question, although he had certainly asked it of himself.

"It is my nature. I distrust completion." He laughed a little. "It's probably my sensory defect. I see in too many directions at once and, what with all I've seen, it just didn't feel right."

"Do you know what does?"

Mikk blushed hotly and lowered his eyes. The voice gentled itself.

"Ah, but you've known that for many years. Why cling to songdance?"

Mikk shrugged.

"Curiosity?"

The whisper chuckled very softly.

"There are many names for ones like you: Keraha, V'z-R'k, Umshoosass, Coyote—you are a troublemaker."

"As long as the trouble has a point," Mikk grinned. "Are you going to keep me or let me go?"

"You are useless here. I will recall you when you are no longer amusing."

"You will have a long wait then."

This time the whisper laughed outright, a low rumble that stirred the flesh of Mikk's sensitive shoulders.

"What an impossible character you are!"

"Characters are my specialty," Mikk said.

"Go back."

Part Five: The Fruit of the Merro Tree

[C.Y.S. XII: 1075]

Chapter Thirty-seven: Escape

The faint scuffling at his ear reached his consciousness first, then the small warm weight on his chest. Mikk opened his eyes. It was not quite dawn but he had no trouble seeing the coney perched on his breastbone staring wall-eyed into his face, its tiny black nose twitching nervously.

Either I've died and the There Beyond is peopled with humbler creatures than I thought, Mikk mused groggily, or I'm still hallucinating. Gods, my head hurts . . .

The coney scratched its ear, squeaked softly—and dissolved. Its body stretched, shifted, grew many times its size, and changed color.

Oh . . . Great Beast . . .

His double, straddling him on all fours, smiled.

"It's you!" Mikk whispered. "From the luxury cruiser."

The shape-shifting entity cocked its head then put its face down very close to Mikk's and licked the blood from the performance master's nose. Its features wrinkled as though what it tasted was bitter.

"I'm not well," Mikk said.

The entity caressed Mikk's face with its cool fingers and its eyebrows puckered in what looked like concern, but before Mikk could determine if that was the case, the entity placed its mouth over his and regurgitated a stream of pure salt water.

The draught was short and violent and shot straight down Mikk's esophagus to his stomach. He didn't even have time to choke, but swallowed the lot and gasped when the entity sat back up. Nevertheless, he felt better almost immediately, much steadier in mind and body.

"Thank you."

His double grinned, hopped to its feet, and strolled around the cell, gently exploring the walls, the stool, and the basin with its fingers, finally touching the energy gate. Since the entity was composed the way Mikk was, it got a nasty burning shock. With a silent scream of pain, it instinctively crammed its fingers into its mouth, only to retrieve them to curiously touch the tears that had issued from its pigment-engorged eyes.

"Now you understand," Mikk said. The entity scowled ferociously at the energy gate. "I'm a captive. Maybe you can transmute and get through, but I can't."

The entity examined the energy gate's frame, particularly the meal slot.

"Oh, that's too small for me. I'm much larger than a coney."

The entity fluttered its hands at Mikk as though swatting his words away, and the performance master sighed and propped himself up on his palm. He was still far from restored and needed all his faculties for the ominous new day, but he was not about to go back to sleep with an earnest, but unpredictable, outworlder in his cell.

The entity studied the frame again and this time gingerly moved its fingers close to the grid much as it had once contemplated the deep, warm pool on the luxury cruiser. Mikk had no idea what it was trying to do and was therefore very surprised when the entity disintegrated out of its Mikk disguise and seeped its mustard yellow cloud into the gate—but not through it. The grid shivered and buckled and changed from blue to green.

It's merged with the gate! Mikk realized, and, as he watched, it drew up in the middle like a curtain, leaving a sizable gap of free space.

Mikk had a wrenching moment of indecision. If he took advantage of the entity's help and got caught, he was a dead man. Where could he go? He would have to run the rest of his life. He could never perform without giving himself away.

On the other hand, it looked as though the tribunal was going to condemn him anyway. At least, if he escaped, he would have his life for a little while longer—and perhaps exposure wasn't such a bad idea. A new plan of action began to take shape in his imagination and a rush of optimistic energy snuffed out the pain in his head and rekindled the strength in his limbs. Maybe it wouldn't last, but that no longer concerned him.

"An actor must act," he whispered.

He eased off the pallet and sneaked through the gap in the gate and into the outer corridor. He stopped to see what the entity intended next.

The entity-infused energy gate unfolded and settled back down over the gap. The green light trembled, turned blue, and the yellow cloud sifted out of the grid into Mikk's cell where it reconfigured into his alternate.

Ah! Mikk nodded: a decoy. You've bought me time, my transubstantial friend.

The entity seemed to know what Mikk was thinking and smiled before lowering itself onto the pallet and duplicating his chin on hand posture, pulling the saddle blanket up over its legs. Mikk gave it a small wave of farewell and crept into the shadows.

He moved quickly through the silent jail for the tunnel leading to the courthouse and found the grate to the plaza. It was stiff, but no match for the performance master's sharp angry tugs. He discarded the empty caviar tins he'd hid in his surprise tunic, scrambled through the hole, and climbed out onto the plaza.

The city was deserted. This was the hour Mikk loved, the hour of his morning dance, but not today. He hugged the walls, keeping to the darkest alleys, and was almost back to his rooms—and Maya—when he heard the crying and piteous ragged whistle common to all suffering canines throughout the galaxy. The sky was red and he was desperate to put his plan into action, but he interrupted his flight to track down the source of this agony.

He followed the sound through the winding maze between two tumbledown tenements and into a forgotten court, dank and smelling of rotten fish. There, behind a rubbish bin, in a wide pool of his own burgundy blood, slumped the living ruin of a Kekoi.

"Aro!"

The Ev-Mobiks had finished their shredding. They'd put out Aro's remaining eye, cut off his hands, feet, and genitals, and left him to die, tongue intact, so he could sing their cruelty.

The jester moaned. "Papa?"

Mikk knelt at his side. "No. It's me." He put his hand on Aro's shoulder. "Gods! What have they done? This is all my fault!"

The mangled Kekoi actually smiled, although it closely resembled the expression of a demonic mask. "Every war has its casualties," he croaked. "You can't take the blame for all of them."

"But why did it have to be you?!" Mikk beat down an urge to gag. "Without your performance, I might never have challenged the Council!"

"I don't believe that, Master Mikk. I think you would have done something eventually. Still," Aro coughed and a clot of blood got caught in his tawny chin fur, "you have eased my conscience. I can die at peace."

"I can't bear to see you this way!" Mikk tightened his fingers on the Kekoi's fur.

"Then help me."

"How?"

"You know how."

Mikk recoiled. "I can't!" he whispered.

"Yes, you can. You've always been strong enough to break me."

"You don't understand! I haven't that kind of will."

"No?" The jester turned his bloody, sightless eyes toward Mikk's voice. "You told the tribunes you were committing murder. Well, I'm already halfway to the There Beyond. All I need is a small push."

"Aro, don't . . ."

"Please, Master Mikk. I trust, and forgive, you. I know you won't hurt me. Be quick."

Mikk wanted to sob, but his throat was a twisted rag. There had been times he'd felt particular individuals were a blight on the galaxy and, in his darkest moments, had even wished them dead, but he'd never truly desired to see his wish fulfilled. Certainly not by his own hand.

And Aro . . . never. Aro of the brave, foolish songdance. The jester who had forced Mikk to confront his own weakness.

"I . . . can't."

"Mikk," Aro said in a soft, loving voice, "you were there when Whees-aru was dying. If you had been able to reach him, what would you have done?"

* * *

When dawn came, a returning night patrol of security dogs came loping through the back alleys on its way to the barracks and bed. Their heavy muscles were slack, their ruffs loose and easy, their side arms locked and holstered. It had been a long, tense night, the night before the tribunes' decision.

Their leader, an older, lighter Kekoi with a bandy-legged gait, a recently reassigned bailiff, stiffened in the morning gray and lifted his busy nose.

"Blood," Raf said. "This way."

He led them through the picked-over garbage, the broken vegetable baskets and piles of old journals, and found the body.

One of the security dogs excused himself to retch.

Raf tapped his boot. In spite of the mutilation and loss of blood, his keen eye quickly determined the true cause of death: a short, powerful yank on the head from above and behind that had snapped the cervical spine. Only once before in his career had he seen a full grown Kekoi's neck broken this way: a professional killing by a paid assassin—a Vyzanian.

In this case, however, Raf recognized a deed of grim, perhaps desperate, compassion, and he was determined to protect its perpetrator.

Sometimes a lie is the greater truth, he told himself.

"Ev-Mobiks. It's their style." He spat to clear the acid taste of death from his mouth. "Not much we can do. They're long gone by now."

Fod was not particularly upset by Bipti's absence.

"Looks like the Freen left early. Good! Something about him makes me want to snap and growl."

With one hand he decoded the energy gate and with the other maneuvered a juicy antelope joint to mouth. He took a large bite and munched and smacked noisily before tucking the meat in his belt.

"Let's just loop up your wrists. I promise I'll take them off when we get to the courtroom. Easy now. There!" He retrieved his breakfast and tore off another mouthful.

"I appreciate this, Master Mikk. I know you were upset the other day, but it wasn't our fault. No hard feelings, eh?"

Korl, cringing submissively at Fod's side, studied their prisoner's placid expression, and his tufted ears flattened.

"Something's wrong, Fod."

"So the master's not talking this morning. I wouldn't have much to say either after all that's happened."

"No! That's not it." Korl lowered his voice. "I don't think this is Master Mikk."

Fod's massive chest rocked with raw, unfriendly laughter. "Korl, sometimes I wonder how you survived past puppyhood! Not Master Mikk? Who is it then? Flia the Clown?"

"I don't know. Some kind of copy."

Fod roared again and nudged his silent charge to get him started down the corridor.

"A copy! My dear gods! You're funny today, Korl!"

When "Mikk" entered the courtroom, Twee took a long hit of methane and removed his mouthpiece.

"Hey, Droos," he stage-whispered down the dais, "what's wrong with your friend?"

Thissizz was not listening. He already saw there was something odd about Mikk. Because of the uproar the previous day, the guards had unshackled the performance master, but he did not move normally. There was a disjointed lightness in his walk and a slack-jawed distraction in the way he looked about the crowded courtroom that were not consistent with the grace or intelligent dignity with which he had comported himself during the entire tribunal. He had to be shown to the defendant's circle and, once there, smiled with such mild emptiness that he seemed stupid.

"If you ask me," Twee said, "someone's been tinkering with his chemistry."

"What are you talking about?" Thissizz asked.

"Nothing." The Borovfian picked up his mouthpiece. "Nothing at all."

Thissizz shifted his coils and frowned unhappily at the red-haired person in the circle. I don't know who you are, he thought, but you are not Mikk.

Pairip opened the session and announced that a decision had been reached.

"The security officials solemnly swear that no one visited the tribunes during their seclusion or tampered with the ballots. Therefore, the count will be recorded as definitive and not subject to appeal."

Pairip now addressed Mikk. "Before I read the verdict, do you have anything more to say on your behalf?"

"Mikk" merely tilted his head stiffly.

"Are you well?"

The defendant grinned.

"Hm, all right." Pairip broke the seal on the folded sheet of cellulose in his hands, smoothed the page over his broad knee, and read silently for a moment. Then he locked his small dark eyes on the pale lavender ones below him.

"Mikk of Vyzania," he intoned, "you have been condemned by a tribunal of your peers, six to five . . ."

The crowd howled. Someone threw a bag of urine at the tribunes, and it splattered apart at Twee's feet. The Borovfian shrieked and tripped back over his seat.

". . . for the galactic crime of violating the personal Council ban forbidding you . . ."

A cluster of women of several races in the back balcony began to trill with the piercing, siren pattern of guests at a Muslim wedding, although it was a darker, grief-stricken sound. An ululation for widows, not brides.

". . . to perform Somalite songdance."

Had Thissizz's attention been more focussed on the proceedings, he might have succumbed to a very un-Droos-like show of violence, but he was intrigued, and baffled, by the cheerfully impassive person in the circle. The guards gently turned the defendant toward the tribunes for sentencing, but there was almost too much noise in the courtroom for Pairip to be heard as he stripped Mikk of galactic citizenship and sentenced him to execution in a manner to be determined at a later date.

"I judge this a less cruel sentence than forcing Master Mikk to endure permanent exile in a distant penal colony for the rest of his very long life. *Furthermore* . . ." Pairip roared against the increasingly shrill cries from the gallery—but he cut himself off voluntarily when the person in the defendant's circle, the one who looked exactly like Mikk, covered his ears as though the sound had become unbearable ... and dissolved. A shimmering, unstable yellow mass floated above the defendant's circle.

"Great Beast in the pit!" Pairip cried.

Several smaller outworlders were trampled as the gallery panicked and rushed for the doors. The guards and security dogs forgot all about crowd control and climbed over the heads of the terrified to get out first.

Thissizz did nothing. He stayed where he was and quietly pondered the entity's shifting contours and transmuting matter, then said, softly, "I know you. Mikk told me about you."

The entity bobbed up to the dais to hover near Thissizz. Out of the band of blue-white light that clung to it, the entity produced five small gold balls that danced in the glow like gnats before dropping into Thissizz's coils. Five bolba juggling balls. Thissizz curled his body around them and smiled at the entity.

"You have done a splendid thing today, my friend. Thank you."

The entity played its energy harmlessly over Thissizz's scaled skin, giving him the impression he was being memorized, inside and out, by a gentle, sentient wall of charged heat. The being did have something ineffable in common with Mikk, a manner of touch.

The entity withdrew. Shifting and warping, cracking small discharges of electricity, it passed through the ceiling of the courtroom and disappeared.

Martin was one of the first out of the courtroom, but he did not run. He crossed the square with a singleness of purpose that carried him completely untouched right through the middle of the scattered mob in spite of a hangover that would have decimated a platoon of Marines. The return of the amorphous entity as a force for good had galvanized the agent; he stomped up to his room in the pensione and snarled at the Kekoi, a male twice his size, who was using the telewave.

"Out!"

The Kekoi opened his mouth, closed it, shrugged, and left. Martin sat down at the telewave and began to enter codes.

Self-reliance and independent action are all very well, he told himself, but sometimes, to get things done, you have to ask for help.

He reached the Interworld Communications Exchange.

It's not a sign of weakness, it's evidence of wisdom.

He had the Belian Cross-Wave Tower.

Pride is a thick, unsavory brew, but you must swallow it.

A pause in the transmission, and he had Terra.

"Hello, Aunt Rose."

"Marty! Dear, maybe you can explain what's happening. Everyone is positively frantic over that scene in court. Consul Ruustan even cancelled our little weekly game. First time in forty-seven years!"

"Easy, Rose, I'll explain in a minute. But first, I need . . . *want* your help."

"Of course, dear. Anything."

"You're still on the Belian A-list, aren't you?"

"Well, yes, but, I don't see . . ."

"You will, Rosie, you will."

After the call, Martin got up from the telewave, went to the window, and opened it. He stood there a long time, imagining the likely outcome of his actions. Then he reached into his pocket, removed his nicotine-free cigarettes, and threw them as far as he could into the square.

Across the way, an upper shutter banged open and a pair of dark tentacles emptied a bowl of its suspicious green contents into the street.

Martin smiled.

The Magna reran the scene on his bedchamber optitube then set it to auto-repeat until it made sense or he went mad, whichever came first. It was a public act of disappearance worthy of the Terran magician who had believed he could escape death as easily as straitjackets. The Magna squirmed in his antigravity tubular VertebraChair and the orthopedic device drifted to the left, softly bumping against its restraining cage.

"What is that thing?" The press had recorded the entity in all its unsettled glory as it floated over the preternaturally calm Droos, sifted through the dome, and vanished.

Where was the real Vyzanian?

"Sir?" The hydra assistant slupped unenthusiastically into the room.

"Is this good news?" the Magna growled.

"That depends on your point of view, sir," the nervous invertebrate said.

"Assume my point of view, just this once."

"Um . . . ah . . ."

"Out with it!"

"B-Belia has cancelled its Council charter," the assistant spluttered. There was a long, tense silence.

"What?"

"Belia has, um, cancelled its charter and recalled all of its mechanical and electronic personnel from Council stations and outposts."

There was another painful pause. The assistant fidgeted, sweated a large blob of mucus that plopped on the floor, and released the rest of his information in a quick burst.

"Some-Terran-woman-Rose-Kirkby-contacted-the-Belian-Lord-Emperor-before-they-cancelled-do-you-want-her-arrested?"

The Magna laughed scornfully and the VertebraChair eased to the right.

"You don't know anything, do you? Arrest a Kirkby? We'd have a Belian war on our hands! Do you honestly think we could defeat the most technologically advanced people in the galaxy?"

"I don't understand, sir. What does this woman . . . ?"

"I want you to leave right now," the Magna said, "before I kill you."

The hydra hesitated, which infuriated his employer.

"Did you hear me?" the Magna cried.

"Yes."

"Well? What are you waiting for?"

The assistant sighed and wobbled away, and the Magna stared back at the endlessly replaying tribunal climax.

"Gods above! The Belians! Now it all starts in earnest."

Chapter Thirty-eight: Outlaw

The authorities recruited Raf to coordinate a search, and he dutifully sent out the security dogs to scour the city although he knew it was a wild coney chase. His knowledge was confirmed that dusk when he leaned on the windowsill of his barracks office to brood on the nearly empty market plaza below—and saw Thissizz slip out of the courthouse into a waiting shuttleport hovervan, the vehicle's hydraulic doors nearly slamming shut on his long green tail.

Not that Raf believed Thissizz knew any more about Mikk's whereabouts than anyone else. He just doubted the Droos would feel able to leave if he sensed the performance master was still on the planet.

Raf turned from the window as Fod entered with a squat elderly Kekoi whose fur was mottled with dirty white spots.

"Put him down, Fod. You're still on probation."

The disgraced rookie, sullen and depressed since the escape, set the wiggling little Kekoi on his feet.

"Now, who is this and why have you brought him here?"

"Auki's the name," the pint-sized Kekoi said, and he licked his claws and smoothed his tufted ears. "I'm a dealer in personal spacecraft."

Raf raised a questioning brow in Fod's direction.

"Sir, he's been boasting all day that he sold one of those new Belian K-bird space yachts to a, well, peculiar outworlder."

"In cash, I might add," said Auki.

"Good for you!" Raf said, smiling.

"Oh, ho, yes! It's been a very good day for me!" The dealer hooked his thumbs in his scarlet vest and thrust out his sharp

411

breastbone. "The K-birds are simply the finest—and fastest—small craft in the galaxy, but they're tough to move. Imports, you know. It takes a highly skilled professional like myself to clinch the deal."

Raf's smile broadened, exposing his broken canine. "I'll bet." He winked at Fod, who didn't seem to appreciate the humor of the situation and crossed his arms sulkily.

"So, tell me, Auki," Raf continued, "what did this outworlder look like?"

"Oh! Pretty funny for a biped."

"How so?"

"He had green skin," the salesman said. "Real green, like a reptile, not a biped."

Raf began to feel positively merry. "Did he? What else?"

"He had yellow eyes. Pure yellow! Very odd with that funny skin. And he had coarse black hair that curled up short in little knots all over his head."

Fod was pouting at the floor. Every bit of him drooped, even his fur.

"*Very* interesting." Raf steepled his fingers. "What did this outworlder sound like?"

"That was the strangest thing of all." Auki shook his head as though he still couldn't believe it. "He had the craziest accent I've ever heard. He whistled his words."

Raf's black eyes twinkled and his nose twitched. This was too good to be true. "Congratulations," he said. "You've just described a Somalite."

"I have? Are they an upright people?"

"They must be!" Raf laughed. "They're extinct!"

Auki's ragged ears stood straight up. "What? But he was right there! A real person!"

"Don't worry," Raf chuckled, "the money was real, wasn't it? You're free to go."

When the dealer was gone, Fod lifted his head. "What do we do now, sir?"

Raf stood up, stretched the toils of the day out of his crooked back, and yawned. "Space is not our jurisdiction, Fod."

* * *

The first performance was on Belia.

"We have had a visitation!" the Lady Minister of Culture broadcast ecstatically over the galactic news. "Instead of the expected ballet at the Grand Imperial Theater yesterday evening, we were treated to an extraordinary performance by a lone outworlder one could swear was Somalite. This mysterious green figure never introduced himself, but opened our hearts to a new version of reality using the best and simplest of tools: song and dance. He gave us music that reached into the ear like a lover's tongue and changed the color of our feelings. He presented movement so exquisite and fluid it coaxed our souls out of our bodies to dance with him, weightless in the perfume of divinity."

Momentarily embarrassed by her purple prose, the Minister tried to recover her composure and, for several seconds of dead air, twiddled her long spidery fingers.

"He was gone as suddenly as he came," she continued. "We do not know where next he will perform but we urge our allies to welcome, and protect him, should he decide to visit their worlds. His mission is blessed and we blue people reiterate the cancellation of our Council charter."

Soon, other worlds reported playing sudden host to the green man who stayed only long enough to perform a ballad for an enraptured audience before jumping back into his K-bird and departing. Not one of the worlds claimed knowledge of his identity, but all of them cancelled their charters after he left. The Bolbans, a shy but highly focussed people, summarily ejected the Council's diplomat, a Lambdan, without giving him time to pack his things. The Mrkusis were more polite but said they "felt compelled to follow the Belian example." They gave their Council diplomat a day and a half.

Eventually, sightings became an almost daily occurrence. The Magna was not pleased. He sat up to his navel in a vat of ice blue brine gel. He'd been there for days. His back was killing him.

"Sir, I have the morning reports," the hydra assistant said as he entered the tiled bath chamber. He moved more quietly and gracefully in this room, wriggling his "foot" comfortably across the glazed flooring.

"From where?" the Magna asked wearily.

"Bar Omega Sept, Alpha Sagittarius 9, Belia . . ."

"Again?"

"He's been zigzagging all over the place, sir. He even performed for the Swinnis of Booluria."

"How the Beast did he do that?" The Magna tried to swivel about in the tub but the gel held him and he strained a tendon in his neck. "The Swinnis are submariner!"

"He performed in a polyglass tank, sir."

The Magna slapped the surface of the brine gel, which heaved ponderously in a single wave then snapped back into a long tight series of aftershocks.

"Where are our ships?" he cried. "Why can't they catch him?"

"The Belians modified his K-bird." The assistant held out the telewave report so the Magna could see. "They put in some kind of experimental wave drive to double his speed. They call it 'payment.' " The assistant rolled up the cellulose.

"And we can barely get any supplies or services at all!" The Magna's wizened features darkened to ochre. "Wherever they cancel a charter they won't accept our scrip! Do you realize what this is starting to cost us in *real* money?" He tried again to wiggle out of the gel and panted and gasped with his assistant scooting back and forth at his side.

"Oh, forget it! Get the scoop, fool!"

The hydra skated out of the bath chamber, none too quickly in the Magna's exasperated opinion. He stared at his spindly limbs shining ghostly green from the depths of the gel.

Mikk gets help wherever he goes, he thought, but he can't last forever. No one can survive the pace he's keeping.

The Magna sang quietly to himself. Off-key. On purpose.

Chapter Thirty-nine: The Queen's Payment

Mikk was tired. More than tired. After cold incarceration, the emotional strain of the tribunal, and prolonged world-hopping without rest, the performance master was near collapse. When the gold web closed on the excited buzz and hum of beating wings—the applause of the insectoid H'n N'kae—Mikk stumbled but snapped to attention when he realized he'd nearly fallen against a tall, austere H'n N'kae female with a gold hexagon painted on the slick, tough black shell of her thorax.

"Gods forgive me! A Queen's vestal priestess!"

"Please remove your dance vestments and cleanse yourself as quickly as possible," the priestess hummed sternly, "and use this scent in your bath." She handed Mikk a fluted dark green bottle. "We have very little time."

"Scent? Forgive me, but don't you wear scent only when . . . ?"

"I tell you again: *Time is fleeting*." The priestess crossed her long hard-shelled front legs and dipped her antennae forward—threateningly.

Mikk dashed backstage.

Bathed and scented, dressed in the finest silks the Vonchoi had stolen for him, Mikk trotted behind the scurrying vestal priestess. No unneutered males except mates had ever been allowed in the presence of the Queen and no outworlders whatsoever had seen her. Nevertheless, the worn-out performance master had been summoned to appear before the H'n N'kae Divine Mother. The Queen was considered a goddess.

Apprehensive, Mikk asked the priestess what he could expect.

"She is greatest," was all she said as she rushed him down the hexagonal tunnel to the inner palace chambers. The walls of the tunnel, like all the walls of H'n N'kae complexes, were made of a thick creamy yellow wax hardened to a tough marblelike sheen, remarkably luminous and refractive. A single taper could fill a large meeting hall constructed of this wax with enough light to read by and a dozen worlds' scientists hoped to duplicate it, but they did not conduct their experiments in the inner palace. Mikk was in a part of H'n N'k no outworlder had set eyes on.

At every turn, a huge H'n N'kae soldier crouched, permanently in the strike position. Mikk had a Gold Wing in these people's fighting skills, but he was no H'n N'kae soldier. These fearsome guards had been bred specifically for war, and they followed Mikk's progress through the tunnel with a steely glare that could frighten more fragile races into seizures. As an experiment, Mikk stopped and stared back at one of them. The soldier did not move, but his complex insect eyes brightened with subtle, coppery interest. Mikk rolled his shoulders forward and dropped his head to let the H'n N'kae know he was aware of his superiority, then hurried on.

"You must not speak unless she requests it," the vestal priestess said, "and you must tell the absolute truth. Any falsehood is a great sin against the goddess."

"Very well, but why does she want to see me?"

"I do not know. I do not need to know."

"How reassuring," Mikk muttered.

The priestess stopped outside a vast ivory white disc set in the wall of the tunnel. Mikk guessed it was a door or gate, although it was at least ten times larger than any ordinary H'n N'kae door. The priestess unfolded her wings and with a steady drone rose to the top of the disc, where a command panel was located. She entered four separate codes, and a spoon-shaped sensor extended from the panel. She quickly rubbed her abdomen on it, smearing it with pheromones. The sensor withdrew.

No wonder few have seen the Queen, Mikk thought. That's a damned effective security system. But—I wonder if it also makes the Queen a prisoner? A strange idea . . .

The enormous disc rolled thunderously aside to expose an inner chamber fully three times larger than the Great Cavern on Droos and lined with millions of glowing hexagonal nursery chambers resembling panelled coffers. They seemed to extend into infinity.

In the center crouched the Queen.

The stare state froze Mikk at rigid attention. The Queen was gigantic. Most H'n N'kae had four wings; the Queen had eight. H'n N'kae had six legs; the Queen had ten. Adult H'n N'kae stood roughly two heads taller than Mikk and weighed six or seven times as much. The Queen towered over her priestess, twenty times over, blue-black and shining, her wings as iridescent as panes of rock crystal. Her tremendous dark orange eyes duplicated Mikk's image thousands of times as she moved her huge head to one side and twitched her unusual multibranched antennae.

Mikk dropped to the floor.

"I am a maggot," he said in ritual greeting. "Crush me."

"Please get up, Master Mikk," the Queen responded. "I want to look at you."

Mikk could not believe his ears. He had expected a mighty roar of sound to bear down on him like the waters from a collapsed dam, but not only did the Queen speak in easy Vyzanian, her voice was delightfully sweet and girlish.

Ah, Mikk thought, I'm in the presence of real power. She doesn't need to parade her authority.

He got up.

"At last I meet you."

"I'm very honored, Your Majesty."

"I've enjoyed your work for years but have never seen you live. Isn't that terrible?"

"If you say so." Mikk giggled self-consciously and felt his skin heat up into a blush. This was the first time he'd met a fan who could crush his house.

"This little unauthorized tour of yours interests me very much," said the Queen. "What do you think will happen?"

"I'm not sure, Your Majesty. Worlds are cancelling their charters and negotiating with artists directly. Either this will destroy the Council or the Council will go to war."

"Do they have that capability?"

"It depends on whether they can get supplies and hold on to allies. I'm afraid I can't say. I have to assume they can and keep running."

"That is certainly the best tactic. But you," the Queen lurched her colossal thorax forward, "do *you* need anything? Supplies? Fuel?"

"Not at present, Your Majesty. The Vonchoi got a perverse pleasure out of stocking my ship with all manner of ill-gotten goods." He grinned. "Their Captain even designated me an 'Honorary First Mate,' so it seems I've become a kind of pirate."

"Pirates and queens often get along very well." The Queen lowered an enormous claw to stroke Mikk's hair. He held absolutely still to accommodate her and protect himself, but the Queen was surprisingly gentle as she ran the broad hard tip through his soft locks. "What would make your journey easier? What would give you pleasure?"

"Sleep, madam! I'm running on nervous energy alone. It's catching up with me."

"Yes," she said thoughtfully, "your light is very low."

"I will manage, Majesty."

"Will you indeed? At least, in the basket, you could slip into coma when the pain overwhelmed you. You cannot afford that now."

Mikk was shocked. "Majesty! Few people in the galaxy know about the basket. How do you—?"

"Nightfolk brought me the message from the There Beyond."

"Nightfolk? Majesty, I don't believe—"

"They also told me that at your master's cremation you bent over his body to kiss him and secretly stole his earring."

Unlike the basket, Mikk had not shared this incident with anyone, not even Thissizz. His distress must have looked unique; the Queen giggled. "He forgives you, but he would like you to give the earring to the first of your apprentices to become a master."

"I am so ashamed!" Mikk shielded his throbbing eyes. "Yes, of course. I promise."

"Now, listen well, Master Mikk—look at me, my child, your eyes do not offend me—I intend to help you whether you desire it or not."

She sat back, as though a black mountain shifted its mass over a different ridge to get comfortable, and gestured to the priestess, who, at first, waggled her prehensile lips and refused. However, when the Queen angrily vibrated her antennae at her, she took off for a far corner of the chamber and returned with a small jar made of the same wax as the walls. She handed it to Mikk.

"Open it," the Queen said.

Mikk unscrewed the lid. Inside was a thick, sticky, light gold jelly that smelled both intensely sweet and intensely sour. Mikk looked up at the Queen and his eyes blackened again.

"Oh, no, Your Majesty! I can't take this. This is for your children."

"I will make plenty more. This jar is nothing, but, for you, it should last several weeks. Be careful with it. The jelly is too potent to be used cavalierly. One drop a day, no more, or it will kill you."

"It could kill me at *that* dosage, Majesty!"

"No." The Queen touched his hair again. "This is something only I know. Trust my knowledge. I am making you this gift that you may continue, restored." Her elaborate antennae curled and uncurled, and Mikk remembered a similar beloved gesture used by another being far away.

"Take care, my little pirate priest. Stay the night on my world. There are no Council ships here."

Darkness had fallen and the clear purple sky was full of the revered nightfolk, tiny glowing flies H'n N'kae considered brethren and guardians of the souls of the dead, when the priestess hugged Mikk around the waist with her claws and escorted him aerially to what he thought was an empty hive flat in the worker district. However, when he entered, he came face to face with the last person he expected.

"Ahva! What are you doing here?"

"I live here now," the Belian actress said meekly. She was rubbing her long spindly hands together, and her beautiful multi-faceted eyes were fixed on the floor, as if in shame.

"But why? When did you . . . ?"

Ahva began to weep and her hands rubbed faster. "I'm sorry, Mikk! B-but I had to t-tell them. I was s-so frightened!"

Mikk moved softly across the palely illuminated hexagonal flat and rested his hands on her shoulders. In the years since he'd seen her, Ahva had aged. Her flesh had wasted to her bones as though a perpetual sadness had eaten its way out from her soul. However, her skin was still lovely. Mikk caressed it.

"Did you move here to escape Oplup?"

She nodded.

"Very clever," he said. "Oplup would never come here in a million years."

Ahva wiped her eyes and smiled shyly. "The H'n N'kae are the clever ones. They didn't tell me they were bringing you here, but when I saw you out my window, wiggling in the priestess's arms . . ." She giggled and Mikk kissed her forehead.

"That's the Ahva I remember."

Embarrassed by the kiss, the actress pulled away and began to rub her hands again. "What is she like, Mikk? The Queen?"

"She's magnificent, Ahva! A marvel of the galaxy, and yet she willingly submits to confinement. It doesn't frighten her!" He became thoughtful. "She wields her power gently," he said, almost to himself. "Her children love her. Look! My hands are shaking."

"Your hands are very thin. The light goes through them."

"It does?" Mikk studied his fingers.

"You need rest."

"That's what the Queen said." Mikk pulled something small from the sleeve of his tunic. "She sees a lot with those huge eyes of hers."

"What's that?"

"A jar of the Queen's jelly. She gave it to me as a gift."

"It can't be! That's the strongest nutrient in the galaxy!" Ahva came over to get a better look.

"And fatal if you take too much." Mikk turned the jar in the glow of the flat's wall sconces. "This little portion could fell a Lodrian land whale."

"I can't believe she'd want to poison you."

"I can't either, but I feel . . . uncomfortable holding this."

Ahva slipped her arm around his narrow waist. Mikk did not appear to notice.

"Maybe you should try it," she said and, now that she was close again, touched the tip of her nose to his sleeve to take in more of his salty, spicy scent.

"You think I should? The last time I ingested an unknown substance, I nearly lost my sanity."

"If you get into trouble, I can have ten of her children here in seconds. Most of these flats belong to military." She removed her arm. "I . . . I'd like to see what it does."

Mikk unscrewed the jar. "Curious as always, I see." He eyed her sideways. "Do you want some?"

"Oh, no! It's for you. It wouldn't be right for me to touch it. I mean, the jelly is a piece of the Divine One's body."

"You're making me nervous." Mikk dipped the tip of his finger in the gold syrup, set down the jar, replaced the lid, and put his finger in his mouth.

"What does it taste like?"

The performance master shrugged. "Sour fruit? It burns a little. I don't think you'd want to spread it on . . . zheraaksha!" Mikk's skin brightened three shades.

"Mikk?"

"No, no!" he grinned. "It's all right. It's . . . Beast!"

"You're trembling."

"Am I? Yes! I suppose I am." Mikk closed his eyes. "Ah, Gods! It's an instant stimulant. I've never felt . . ." He yelped and clenched his fists.

"Mikk, are you sure you're all right?" Ahva edged closer to the hexagonal window in case she needed to yell.

"It's marvelous!" he cried and suddenly began to dance around her flat, catching her as he passed. She screamed when he spun her about.

"It's true! All of it! I feel fantastic!" He kissed the stunned actress, who had the presence of mind to throw her arms around him. The muscles of his back quivered like a skittish thoroughbred's and his temperature rose alarmingly.

"You're feverish!" she said.

He kissed her again, roughly, this time under her ear, and his milky skin flushed deep pink as his blood raced to the surface to cool itself.

"Mikk! Mikk, you mustn't . . ."

He abruptly broke their embrace and backed away toward the window, hugging himself as though his tremor was from cold rather than nervous heat.

"I'm sorry," he said huskily. "I just wish . . ."

A couple of nightfolk, attracted by its burning wine red, came through the window and alighted on his hair. Ahva approached him, held up her forefinger to the flies, and they wandered onto her hand, where they shone like miniature diamonds.

"So do I," she said. She carefully flicked the sacred insects out into the night.

"I may have overdosed, Ahva, just a little."

She smoothed his hot face with her nervous fingers. "Do you think it would help you? In spite of the pain?"

Droplets of sweat slid down Mikk's face from beneath his hair.

"To the Beast with pain!" he whispered.

With the Queen's jelly, Mikk was able to forego food, sleep, and salt, double the number of his songdance performances, and remain astonishingly healthy. However, the side effects curbed his desire to indulge in the jelly's buzz more than once a day, an indulgence he knew, without question, would be "death lily." His hair, already in need of Maya's expertise, began to grow at an unnatural rate. At the end of three weeks, it curled over his shoulders; at five, it reached to his waist, and he tied it back in a long tail to keep it out of his way—and out of sight. Reds and yellows had become much brighter to his sensitive eyes, and looking at his own hair hurt them.

The young women of Ti-tok laughed at his out-of-control locks and double-braided them in the style of an adolescent girl before challenging him to race up the ropes to the Sultana's summer palace on top of the Tower, the steep volcanic core that rose from the middle of the steppes. It was their standard challenge, and Mikk, as usual, accepted, but he swung onto the ropes and scaled the Tower with an ease he did not recognize, and, when he hoisted himself over the lip of the cliff, he realized he had beaten the women for the first time. Unfortunately, somewhere along the way he had sliced open his foot and was bleeding badly. He had not felt it and didn't feel it now.

"Beast! I can't perform songdance with a maimed paw."

He thought he would have to compose an elaborate excuse to the Sultana, but, within a couple hours, the wound had healed without the shadow of a scar.

Maybe she is a goddess, Mikk mused as he dipped the K-bird in and out of the Werevan Asteroid Belt. Seven billion H'n N'kae can't be wrong.

He thought of Ahva, looking happier and braver as she waved good-bye at dawn from the doorway of her flat. What a rollicking night of play they had shared! They hadn't stopped wrestling until the nightfolk withdrew and went to sleep under the sticky leaves of the floss wing trees. Amazingly, Mikk never did suffer the expected burning aftereffects.

He held the tiny jar of Queen's jelly up to the stars in a salute to the female principle. "Sometimes, our true mothers reveal themselves in unexpected forms." He stowed the jar away and increased his velocity until the stars became thin prismatic lines— streak flashes. A Council ship had appeared on the image screen.

Chapter Forty: The End of the Run

The Council ship blipped onto a Terran Galactic Border Authority officer's screen not long after Mikk's K-bird slipped through the clouds of North America. The officer's smile peeled back from her teeth in wicked rapture. In her desk was a fifteen-year-old scent fan that still greeted her with woodsy perfume every time she opened a drawer. She calmly maneuvered the impatient outworld captain through the preliminary identification procedures without incident—then pounced.

". . . 693.75," she said in her specially trained nasal whine.

"693.79!" the Borovfian cried.

"Well, I'm sorry, sir," the Terran officer said, "but you weren't clear the first time and the wrong code is in the machine. I'll have to void everything out and start over."

"We haven't got time for that, you incompetent female!"

"Sir, if you're going to be rude, I'll have to call my supervisor. There are ten ships behind you requesting clearance. Let's take it from the top. Name and purpose on Terra?"

"You people are harboring a fugitive!"

"That's not my department, sir. If you want Interpol, I can transfer you."

"This is ridiculous! We want—"

"Please hold."

"Wait! Oh, Beast in a—"

"Terran Interworld Police, Staff Sergeant Yevgeny Shchedrin speaking."

"We need clearance to—"

"I'm sorry, you'll have to speak to the Galactic Border Authority first," the Russian sergeant interrupted. "I'll give you back to the operator."

"No! Don't!"

"Guten Tag, good day! Your telewave destination, please."

Meanwhile, in a private chamber of a Belian shuttle, Maya looked up and saw something amazing on the optitube.

"Ee-gaa!"

"Oh, don't stop now, sweetheart!" Martin said from his prone position on the shuttle's cold pink floor. "This is the best massage I've ever had. I actually feel taller!"

"Hush, you!" Maya waved a tentacle at the small screen. "Mikk in New York."

Martin lifted his head. Sure enough, there was the performance master, interrupting a concert at New Lincoln Center to perform a songdance ballad in his wide Somalite trousers and green Somalite body paint.

"Well, I'll be damned . . ."

The Terran agent and the cephalopod costumer watched in silence. Maya's sensitive feel felt Martin's pale and, in her opinion, pleasantly yielding flab roughen with gooseflesh.

"Martin cold?"

"No. Martin moved." He grasped a tentacle and gently squeezed it.

"That's all, sir," the border officer said at last.

"Bless the gods! We have clearance!"

"I'm afraid not, sir."

"But I've answered everything! What more do you want?"

"Nothing, sir," the officer said with slow, cool pleasure. "We received word half an hour ago that Terra has cancelled its Council charter. I'm no longer authorized to give you clearance."

"Why didn't you tell me?" the Borovfian captain wailed. "Mikk could be anywhere by now!"

"That's not my fault, sir. Next time, have all of your identification ready and with you so you don't waste my time. Good-bye."

The officer severed the connection.

"What do we do now?" the Borovfian first mate asked. "I've never seen anyone pilot a K-bird the way Mikk does. He flies like a madman." He pushed his rubbery face up under the captain's arm and grinned hopefully. "Can we go home now?"

"Nonsense! We must avenge our kinsman Twee!" the captain said imperiously, and the mate slumped back into his pod. "Mikk's got to run to ground sometime. I wonder where?"

"Vyzania?" the mate ventured.

"Wrong direction." The captain drummed all six fingers on the com. "Where could Mikk hide for as long as he wanted, no questions asked?" His eyes lit up. "Droos!"

"That's twenty-four kymars from here."

"Never mind. If I'm right, it'll be worth the fuel." The yellow spots around his mouth pulled into tight ellipses. "I wonder what price the Council has on his head?"

"Assuming the Council has any money left," the mate grumbled.

"What was that?"

"Nothing, sir. Droos it is."

When the green and black beetle-bodied ship reached Droos, the Borovfians called in a sister vessel to watch the day side while they staked out the night side of the large world.

"What if he doesn't show?" the mate asked.

"I think he will," the captain replied. "He's got a thing for serpents."

"Maybe we should bring in more reinforcements."

"No. That's where we made the mistake before. More than a ship or two—it scares him off. This way, if he does see us, it looks like we're not prepared."

"Are we?"

"What?"

"Just clearing my throat, sir."

"Anyway, we can easily ambush him if we pay attention."

So the Borovfians waited and watched their supplies dwindle. They orbited just outside Droosian space to avoid any protest from the surface. Nevertheless, the mate was uncomfortable.

"I don't know, sir. It's been days now. Maybe he did go back to Vyzania."

The captain, reduced to one helping at dinner, down from his usual three, and intensely cranky, poked the mate in the brisket with a sharp elbow.

"I'm tired of your bellyaching! We'll get this terrorist performer if it's the last thing I do! Watch the horizon. He's likely to head for the shadow side, right into our clutches."

"Maybe he knows that we know that he . . ."

"Shut up! Do you think I became captain by confusing myself?"

"But sir! He's a performance master! He's not like other people."

"Performance master nothing! I'm the master around here, and if you think I'm going to let you question my every decision you've got another thing coming! Why, when I was a junior officer, I never . . ."

During their argument, the captain forgot to secure the helm. The ship drifted into the edge of Droos' shadow and dawn exploded over the bow with a blinding flash. While they scrambled for shield specs, a tiny silver object zipped out of the heart of the glare and dropped precipitously into the Droosian atmosphere.

"There he is!" the captain cried. "Fire!"

"What?!"

"Beast! We lost him!"

"Sir! You said we were going to take him alive!"

"How, idiot?" The captain boxed the mate's prominent tympanic membranes until they warped and wobbled. "If you hadn't distracted me with your ridiculous complaints we could have—"

"Sir!" the communications officer interrupted. "Droos on the com."

It was Oosmoosis. Now in the sun-sensitive pearly scales of very advanced years, Thissizz's father telewaved from the dark, safe bowels of his burrow that Mikk the Vyzanian performance master had been granted political asylum and Droos considered the invasion of its space by a Council vessel "high hostile illegality." The captain banged his fist on the com and broke a finger. Sucking on the damaged digit, he pulled the mate aside.

"How are our supplies holding out?"

"Not good, sir." The mate was still shaking his head to get the rattle out of his ears. "All Mikk has to do is sit tight and we'll be picked clean and dead in the orbit within days."

"Then let's go after him. Droos has lousy defenses."

"I'd advise against that, gentlemen," said a silky, unhurried voice. The captain had no idea where it had come from and glanced anxiously around the bridge as though it had issued from the methane-impregnated air itself. Then he saw the green light on the ship-to-ship voice com.

"Who left that frequency open?" he cried.

"Vyzanian border patrol vessel off our port side," the communications officer announced.

"Can't be!" The captain pushed the officer out of his pod and sat there himself. "We're nowhere near Vyzanian space!"

"That is true," the same languid, disembodied voice said, "but the Droos are our allies and since both of our worlds have cancelled their respective charters, neither of us recognizes the Council as a legitimate governmental body. So, again, I strongly suggest you reconsider before further penetrating Droosian space. We will regard any aggression on your part as an act of war."

"Act of war? You Vyzanians haven't made war in millennia!"

"I can assure you we still know how," came the placid response from the sleek triangular ship. "We have very long memories."

The captain collared his mate again. "Are they armed?" he whispered.

"To the teeth, sir. See those ranks of projections along her prow? The ones pointing at us?"

"You mean the things that look like giant ice saws?"

"Molecular uncouplers, sir. Vyzanian patent. We take another step toward Droos and we're dust."

"Beast on a burner!" the captain snarled. Then he said into the com, "Who are you anyway, Vyzanian?"

"Consul Ruustin Vey on behalf of the Crown," the voice purred. "I'm Master Mikk's father."

The Council vessel "weighed anchor" and departed.

In coming down in front of the dawn, Mikk had arrived on the far side of Droos, opposite Thissizz's burrow city, so he raced through the dreaming nightside of the enormous world, skimming over the frozen clouds with the deep indigo sky above him, and let exhaustion overtake him. He'd used up the H'n N'kae Queen's jelly ten days before, and its healing properties had worn off. Through an act of pure will, Mikk had kept awake the entire ten days and his overtaxed muscles felt ready to drop from his bones. Still, the jelly had left an obscure permanent mark on his body's ability to endure. At every performance, the songdance ballads fit him better, like psychic skins, although the transcendent emptiness of Kekoi Kaery had not returned.

Unfortunately, the jelly had not relieved his painful desire to see his friend. If anything, it had made it worse. All of his free thoughts, when he had them, and all of his premonitions were about Thissizz.

It was dusk when he reached the torchlit clearing outside the Great Cavern. He settled the K-bird into the cooling grasses, climbed out of the cockpit, and hopped down. The chill whispered quickly over the ground, and the heavy flowers made a creaking sigh as they drew their damp petals in out of the cold. Even the grasses gasped softly as they puckered and shrank and roughened their blades for the long frozen night. The silence of Droos' dusk was full of voices.

Mikk shivered but did not hurry inside. He knew Thissizz was coming as if he were with him—within him. Their bond was stronger than ever, their rhythms—heart, breath, soul—moved together in easy balance.

Is this clairvoyance? he wondered. Has love breached my defenses against second sight?

The stars winked in the gathering darkness, millions of them, a gift for his exceptional senses.

I don't know and I don't care, he thought. I can bear everything with Thissizz at my side.

He rested his gaze on the elegant concentric circles of the Cavern and felt very small, alone, and fragile.

Please hurry, serassi. I need to be rescued—and forgiven!—by a superior creature.

Thissizz did not disappoint him. After this silent invocation, the Droos issued out of the darkness into the torchlight where his emerald scales glistened and flashed in fiery splendor. He ripped gently across the clearing and curled the tip of his supple body around the performance master's ankle. Mikk buried his face in the Droos' long neck.

"My beautiful friend," Thissizz hissed, and Mikk clung to him, shaking with the extremity of his joy and grief.

"Ah, Mikk . . ." Thissizz swung a coil around the performance master and lifted him. Sobbing, Mikk pressed in tightly like a juvenile Droos nuzzling its mother, and Thissizz stroked his over-grown hair with his tongue.

"Hush," he said as he carried his friend into the burrows. "Rest with me awhile."

Soon after Mikk, sated and slick with sweat, fell asleep on Thissizz's coils, a couple of the Droos' small children, unable to curb their excitement, came in to see the performance master. Thissizz hissed slightly as a warning that they should be very quiet, and the pups craned themselves over Mikk to get a good look at him.

"Is Master Mikk asleep, daddy?" the boy whispered.

"Yes."

"I've never seen him without his surprise tunic," the girl said. "Does it hurt him when you ribble?"

"No. He's very strong for his size."

The young ones pondered this with serious expressions and inspected the performance master with new interest. The boy gently touched Mikk's naked shoulder with his nose.

"He's getting chilled, daddy. He'll wake up." So the small Droos draped their bodies on top of Mikk to warm him.

"How funny," the girl said. "No scales."

Chapter Forty-one: Release

The Magna watched the stars slowly rotate outside the window of the deserted station outpost. He did not even turn around when his assistant hop-sucked up behind him.

"Sir?"

"Don't bother. I already know. One world, five, a dozen—it doesn't matter." He rested his shriveled hands on the polyglass. "We cannot function this way. Even Ev-Mobix 'Gar has cancelled its charter and absolved that Vyzanian bastard. My own granddaughter won't speak to me unless I pardon the Pocket Man. Pardon! I have no idea how Iki found out I could do that."

The assistant moved around to his side. "I do, sir." He proudly lifted his polyps. "I told her."

The Magna slowly turned his eyes on his assistant, but the hydra did not flinch. The Magna nodded glumly and looked back out at the gracefully swirling galaxy.

"Then you'll be pleased to know I've decided to withdraw Master Mikk's condemnation."

"With-withdraw, s-sir?" Now the assistant trembled, but not with fear.

"Yes. A pardon is not enough. We have to wipe the slate clean and declare that no crime was ever committed."

The assistant's inner organs jiggled and danced with excitement. "Oh, sir! Do you mean that? No crime at all?"

"I don't know," the Magna shrugged. "I thought it was very

clear, just as the Spairan laid out, but everything is upside-down now. I was lying awake last night . . ."

"Your back again, sir?"

"Yes. While I was staring at the ceiling, it occurred to me that maybe the arts are as much about giving people questions as answers. Maybe they don't just provide a diversion from our mundane lives or reaffirm what we already know or attempt to solve what we don't. Maybe, sometimes, they are supposed to throw the wheel out, push us into the wilderness. If that's true," the Magna sighed, "then the Council has no reason to exist."

"That's very profound, sir."

"Not particularly," the Magna smiled, "but my back stopped hurting." He tapped the polyglass and a wistful, nostalgic expression softened the wrinkles of his face. "Ask the cook to make up some gen-karg for Iki and me for supper. I haven't had that in years."

"Yes, sir."

"Oh, and Ya-yin?"

The assistant nearly fainted from surprise at the sound of his name. "Y-yes, s-s-sir?"

"Let the Freen's children go."

The cephalopod's half-dozen fish eyes caught the light of the phosphor lamps and gleamed a dull gold in the predawn gloom and silence of the burrows.

"Hush, you!" she whispered to her companions. "Maya work first."

Raising her double-bladed weapon, she advanced "tip-tentacle" toward her prey and with a single, sure stroke . . .

Snip!

Mikk opened his eyes. "Maya! My dear, can't you at least wait until I've bathed and had something to eat?"

"Up you!" the cephalopod commanded, brandishing her long red prize in his face. "Maya not done."

The Droos pups woke up.

"Look! Mikk's awake! Daddy, daddy, get up!" They began to bounce energetically on the entangled friends.

"Oof! Careful!" Mikk said. "That's a tender spot."

Then he saw his other visitors clustered quietly around the entrance to the burrow. Each held a piece of glowing phosphor resin that lit up his or her or ets smiling face.

Mikk's nine-valve heart beat triple time. He sensed others outside in the tunnel and closed his eyes, the better to hear their breathing.

He opened his eyes and grinned. The sound was complete, not a tone missing. Every member of his troupe, from the Mrkusi acrobats and Belian dancers to the Kekoi jesters and Vyzanian singers, was there.

Martin, too! He was trying to look put out and miserable but was smiling too much to succeed.

"Maya and I had a devil of a time tracking everyone down," he grumped merrily. "We had no idea when you'd show up, and sneaking your troupe onto Droos without the Council getting suspicious required some pretty elaborate diplomatic doublespeak." He poked his cheek out with his tongue.

"Funny what happens when you open the lines of communication," he said. "Turns out my Aunt Rose has been playing telewave Belian chess with Consul Ruustan for years. She had no idea he was your father."

"He is when he needs to be," Mikk murmured. He glanced down at his Droos-draped nakedness. One of the babies was shyly curled up in a hot little wad right on top of his genitals. "I'm not exactly dressed for a cast party."

"Stay where you are!" Martin laughed. "Hegron has a gift for you."

"A gift?"

The dark actress with the medusa braids came out of the shadows and knelt at Mikk's side. She cleared her throat and, with concentration puckering her slim, arched eyebrows, began to speak in slow, recently memorized Vyzanian.

"Good noos, Masser Mikk. The Coocil . . . Concil has withdrawed yir condem-anation . . ."

"What . . . ?"

Mikk sat up and the baby Droos skidded off his groin and plopped gently on the floor.

". . . and they have disban—. . . dis . . ." Hegron slapped her knee and growled. "Dis—band—ded!"

Mikk stared at her, paralyzed. She placed her hand on his cheek and said the one phrase she obviously relished and knew perfectly.

"We are free!"

Mikk gently took Hegron's hand from his cheek, turned it up, and kissed her palm.

"Freer," he whispered. "It's enough for now."

Thissizz rested his chin on Mikk's shoulder.

"Welcome home, my beautiful friend."

Chapter Forty-two: Forgiveness

When Mikk and Thissizz arrived at the waterside shuttle station in Wynt that early evening in the Blossom Season, they were greeted by Briin and several dozen fans bearing wreaths of leaves and flowers, baskets of fruit, and strings of roast red fowl.

"I know you didn't want me to tell anyone," the house manager said as he pushed down the English boater more securely on his overabundant brown curls, "but the word slipped out somehow. I'm very sorry, Master Mikk."

"Just do something about this food before it spoils!" Mikk laughed, handing Briin the strings of red fowl. He stepped back to admire his employee—boater, red fowl, pink and orange dotted tunic, and all—and laughed again.

"Gods love you, Briin! It's good to be back."

After some still shots and autographs, Mikk and Thissizz were free to enjoy the cool perfume of the passing day and decided to stroll down to the Grand West Lagoon.

Parasol leaf trees lined the white pebbled street with an explosion of bright yellow blossoms, and the petals showered onto the two friends. Thissizz whisked them off Mikk's shoulders with his tongue and ate them.

"Be careful," Mikk said. "Those haven't been de-alcolated."

"I'm on holiday," Thissizz replied.

Mikk smiled and picked a wayward petal from the Droos' nose. "You know, Thissizz," he said hesitantly, "back on Kekoi Kaery when I broke the ban? In the middle of the ballad, I may have, for a moment, achieved the Somalite Peace."

The Droos' eyes became great black saucers. "You did? What was it like?"

"It wasn't like anything. It wasn't a thing at all. It was nothing."

"That sounds like death."

"No—I was aware of the world around me, but I wasn't there. Everything was so clear, so . . ." Mikk danced his fingers in the air as he often did after magically making something disappear. "It wasn't enough, somehow. Isn't that strange? I was offered the ultimate calm and I balked. I opted for chaos." He smiled. "Actually, I'm pleased with my choice."

"That may be the true peace. It'd be just like the Somalites to create a mystery whose solution leads back to the point you started from."

"It's worth it, though. I think that decision was the only thing that kept me from giving up. That," he stroked the Droos' coils, "and my desire to see you again. I'd like to teach songdance. Give others the chance to explore the unexplorable."

The golden light shifted, gliding a cluster of small pools leading to the lagoon, and the breeze off the water carried the sweetness of evening sugar roses and night mallows, the spiciness of meals being cooked in the water people's floating houses, and the faint, ever present breath of alcohol. Mikk picked up a stone and threw it so it skipped once off the surface of each pool before disappearing into the lagoon. Some naked boys wading in the shallows whistled and Mikk bowed.

"Pairip came to me after your escape," Thissizz said. "Before I left for Droos."

"Whatever for?"

"He admitted he'd voted for vindication."

"I don't believe it!"

"He also told me he did not question you because Garplen family ties are very strong and Oplup was his brother-in-law."

"Was?"

Thissizz took a deep breath, withholding his reply for greater dramatic effect. It was, as far as Mikk was concerned, very dramatic indeed.

"He exploded that morning."

"No! He finally achieved paradise?"

"If you can call it that."

"Don't laugh! I'm a little sorry he's gone. He was the best tool for reminding myself I should be grateful for any good qualities I might have."

"I won't miss him at all," the Droos sniffed. "I like my meat lean." His long blue tongue quickly darted down the front of Mikk's tunic.

"Thissizz! We're in public!"

"You don't care."

Mikk laughed and put his arm around his friend. "You know me too well."

They turned into the park that ran along the embankment of the Grand West Lagoon. Few people were out, mostly lagging children and amorous couples. The trees bent over the lagoon and dipped their branches into the water like long green hair. It was dark and chilly in the shadows, but the sun remained bright, and Mikk remembered the quiet woman who had washed her muddy children under similar trees years ago.

"Do you think the Somalites would forgive me if they could?"

"All this may have happened exactly as they intended."

"Do you believe that?"

"I don't know, but I think they see us and understand." The Droos stretched his hood. "They may forgive you in a way we cannot foresee."

Mikk felt a short tug on the corner of his tunic.

"Pocket?"

Mikk had been too preoccupied to notice her approach: a small barefoot girl in a ragged shift—a street child.

"You can join me later," Thissizz said, discreetly excusing himself. He swayed off down the path. Mikk watched him go and felt a rich, warm thrill at the sight of the coils curling and shifting along the pebbles.

If my peace is anywhere, he thought, it is in those coils.

"Hello, little one," he said to the girl.

"Hello," she replied, coyly poking out her tongue as she gazed up at the famous performance master.

"Would you like to choose your own pocket?"

The girl immediately rummaged through the tunic with her grubby fingers and retrieved a puzzle box.

"It's pretty!" she cried, and squatted in the dirt to play with it.

Mikk studied the girl as she tried the drawers and hinges of the box, his heart saddened by her poverty and malnourishment. It was remarkable she had asked for a pocket at all. Street "rats" were usually much more suspicious and inclined to steal without preamble.

However, as he continued to watch her play, Mikk noticed something odd about the girl's appearance. She was so filthy, he'd assumed the olive tinge to her creamy skin was mud slime, but now he realized it was her true color and natural, not the byproduct of disease. Also her eyes, which certainly were not blind, nevertheless were not any shade of Vyzanian purple. They were a luminous golden amber. He crouched beside her.

"Where are your parents?" he asked.

"I don't have any."

"Do you remember them?"

"Mommy wore a blue shift with gold spots on it."

A Vyzanian doctor. Possibly a doctor on a galactic trader.

"And your daddy?"

She shook her head.

"Mommy said he wasn't from here."

Mikk touched the girl's coarse black hair and the premonitory chill raced joyously up the muscles of his back. Could it be? He would not have thought it possible.

"Did mommy ever say what daddy's name was?"

"Yes, but I can't say it. It had whistles in it."

Gods above, it had to be true! How long had she been hiding in the streets? Mikk stroked her cheek. She did not pull away.

"Would you like to come with me?" His voice quavered. "Travel the stars making people happy?"

When the girl smiled, Mikk saw the embers of a lost, but not forgotten, people burning in her eyes. He stood up.

"Come," he said tenderly. "I have so much to teach you."

The little girl raised her arms, and Mikk lifted her onto his tingling shoulders—which recognized the weight as though he'd carried her for years.

"Thank you, Celestial Ones. I will remember everything."

The 1995 Del Rey Discovery of the Year

GENELLAN: PLANETFALL
Book One of Genellan
by Scott G. Gier

Genellan—a beautiful, Earth-like world where intelligent cliff-dwellers wait in fear for the day the violent bear people will return . . .

Genellan—the only refuge for a ship's crew and a detachment of spacer marines, abandoned by a fleet fleeing from alien attackers . . .

Genellan—where Lt. Shari Buccari tries desperately to hold on to the threads of command over both the civilians and the marines in a furious attempt to keep her people together . . .

At stake: the secret of hyperlight drive, the key to interstellar flight . . .

And don't miss the continuing story of GENELLAN by Scott G. Gier!

GENELLAN: IN THE SHADOW OF THE MOON
Book Two of Genellan

GENELLAN: FIRST VICTORY
Book Three of Genellan

Published by Del Rey Books.
Available in a bookstore near you.

COMMENCEMENT

Gifted with a rare and amazing power over human minds, Class A talent Ronica McBride is ready to assume her lofty position in the Com's interstellar empire. Then a horrific incident leaves her stranded on a primitive planet, without her memory. But once she remembers her past, Ronica discovers a shocking truth: Everything she has been taught by the Com is a lie . . .

COMMITMENT

Returning to the Com, Ronica vows to confront the powers who have deceived her and an entire civilization. She will have to take her astounding skills to the next level to protect those she loves—and destroy the corruption that is tearing the Com apart.

It is a mission she is willing to die for . . .

Once in every generation, there comes a story so resonant, a tale so remarkable, that it breaks new ground and opens new vistas of imagination. Welcome to an astonishing new world of myth and magic.

THE WATERBORN
by J. Gregory Keyes

The River God holds dominion over all the lands, and in Nhol—the fabled city at the heart of the world—Hezhi, an imperial princess, carries the seeds of the River's power in her very blood. As the magic within her begins to grow, she faces a desperate fight for her own life.

"A new myth maker, a new star of the fantasy genre has arrived."
—R. A. Salvatore
New York Times bestselling author of
Passage to Dawn

And you won't want to miss the sequel . . .

THE BLACKGOD
by J. Gregory Keyes

The myth and the adventure continues . . . Hezhi has escaped from the River God, but she cannot escape her legacy of magic. Pursued into the Mang wastes by the living, the dead, and strange forces between, she must learn to control the powers she never wanted or be doomed to return again to the River God—to serve him, or to kill him.

Published by Del Rey Books.
Available in bookstores everywhere.

✎ FREE DRINKS ✎

Take the Del Rey® survey and get a free newsletter! Answer the questions below and we will send you complimentary copies of the DRINK (Del Rey® Ink) newsletter free for one year. Here's where you will find out all about upcoming books, read articles by top authors, artists, and editors, and get the inside scoop on your favorite books.

Age _____ Sex ❑ M ❑ F

Highest education level: ❑ high school ❑ college ❑ graduate degree

Annual income: ❑ $0-30,000 ❑ $30,001-60,000 ❑ over $60,000

Number of books you read per month: ❑ 0-2 ❑ 3-5 ❑ 6 or more

Preference: ❑ fantasy ❑ science fiction ❑ horror ❑ other fiction ❑ nonfiction

I buy books in hardcover: ❑ frequently ❑ sometimes ❑ rarely

I buy books at: ❑ superstores ❑ mall bookstores ❑ independent bookstores
❑ mail order

I read books by new authors: ❑ frequently ❑ sometimes ❑ rarely

I read comic books: ❑ frequently ❑ sometimes ❑ rarely

I watch the Sci-Fi cable TV channel: ❑ frequently ❑ sometimes ❑ rarely

I am interested in collector editions (signed by the author or illustrated):
❑ yes ❑ no ❑ maybe

I read Star Wars novels: ❑ frequently ❑ sometimes ❑ rarely

I read Star Trek novels: ❑ frequently ❑ sometimes ❑ rarely

I read the following newspapers and magazines:

❑ *Analog*	❑ *Locus*	❑ *Popular Science*
❑ *Asimov*	❑ *Wired*	❑ *USA Today*
❑ *SF Universe*	❑ *Realms of Fantasy*	❑ *The New York Times*

Check the box if you do not want your name and address shared with qualified vendors ❑

Name _____
Address _____
City/State/Zip _____
E-mail _____

waitman

PLEASE SEND TO: DEL REY /The DRINK
201 EAST 50TH STREET NEW YORK NY 10022

DEL REY® ONLINE!

The Del Rey Internet Newsletter...

A monthly electronic publication, posted on the Internet, GEnie, CompuServe, BIX, various BBSs, and the Panix gopher (gopher.panix.com). It features hype-free descriptions of books that are new in the stores, a list of our upcoming books, special announcements, a signing/reading/convention-attendance schedule for Del Rey authors, "In Depth" essays in which professionals in the field (authors, artists, designers, salespeople, etc.) talk about their jobs in science fiction, a question-and-answer section, behind-the-scenes looks at sf publishing, and more!

Internet information source!

A lot of Del Rey material is available to the Internet on our Web site and on a gopher server: all back issues and the current issue of the Del Rey Internet Newsletter, sample chapters of upcoming or current books (readable or downloadable for free), submission requirements, mail-order information, and much more. We will be adding more items of all sorts (mostly new DRINs and sample chapters) regularly. The Web site is http://www.randomhouse.com/delrey/ and the address of the gopher is gopher.panix.com

Why? We at Del Rey realize that the networks are the medium of the future. That's where you'll find us promoting our books, socializing with others in the sf field, and—most important—making contact and sharing information with sf readers.

Online editorial presence: Many of the Del Rey editors are online, on the Internet, GEnie, CompuServe, America Online, and Delphi. There is a Del Rey topic on GEnie and a Del Rey folder on America Online.

Our official e-mail address for Del Rey Books is delrey@randomhouse.com (though it sometimes takes us a while to answer).